"WHAT WAS IT YOU WERE SAYING, AGAIN? SOMETHING ABOUT MY MAKING YOUR KNEES TREMBLE?"

"Shake, Cutter. I said shake. Not tremble."

"Shake—tremble—quiver . . ." He shrugged. "Much the same thing, isn't it?"

Maggie swallowed past the lump in her throat. She forced herself to look up, and stared directly into his too-blue eyes. It was a mistake.

In those lake-blue depths, along with the sprinkle of amusement, there was something else.

Something dangerous.

Something wicked.

Something she'd waited nearly a year to see again.

Desire.

"Maggie," he said, and all traces of his earlier teasing was gone. "We have to settle what's between us."

"I thought you said there was nothing to settle," she said.

"I was wrong."

Other AVON ROMANCES

DARK EYES *by Colleen Corbet*
LONEWOLF'S WOMAN *by Deborah Camp*
MIDNIGHT BRIDE *by Marlene Suson*
SPLENDID *by Julia Quinn*
TEMPT ME NOT *by Eve Byron*
THE WARRIOR *by Nicole Jordan*
WILDFIRE *by Donna Stephens*

Coming Soon

AWAKEN, MY LOVE *by Robin Schone*
CAPTURED *by Victoria Lynne*

And Don't Miss These
ROMANTIC TREASURES
from Avon Books

COMANCHE RAIN *by Genell Dellin*
PROMISE ME *by Kathleen Harrington*
SHAWNEE MOON *by Judith E. French*

Maggie and the Gambler

Ann Carberry

AVON BOOKS  NEW YORK

MAGGIE AND THE GAMBLER is an original publication of Avon
Books. This work has never before appeared in book form. This work
is a novel. Any similarity to actual persons or events is purely coin-
cidental.

AVON BOOKS
A division of
The Hearst Corporation
1350 Avenue of the Americas
New York, New York 10019

Copyright © 1995 by Maureen Child
Inside cover author photo by Mark Child
Published by arrangement with the author
Library of Congress Catalog Card Number: 94–96558
ISBN: 0–380–77880–7

First Avon Books Printing: June 1995

AVON TRADEMARK REG. U.S. PAT. OFF. AND IN OTHER COUNTRIES, MARCA
REGISTRADA, HECHO EN U.S.A.

Printed in the U.S.A.

RA 10 9 8 7 6 5 4 3 2 1

Prologue

San Francisco,
The Barbary Coast, 1873

"**I**'m going to kill our father," Maggie said, and looked at each of her three sisters in turn, "and I thought you all should know."

Mary Frances sighed.

Mary Alice laughed out loud.

Teresa still wasn't speaking to any of them.

"Mary Margaret Donnelly!" Rose Ryan snapped, and set the coffee tray down on the dining table with a clatter. "You keep a civil tongue in your head when you speak of your father!"

"It'd be much easier not to speak of him at all, Rosie," the tall redhead shot back as she dropped into her chair at the head of the table.

"That'll do, miss."

Maggie deliberately ignored their house-keeper until the woman left the room in a huff. Rose Ryan was always taking Kevin Donnelly's side in everything. This would be no different.

Sunlight spilled through the open window and danced on the gleaming walnut tabletop. At ten in the morning, the Coast was quiet, and Maggie appreciated it. Lord knew, she and her sisters would need all their wits about them to take care of their father's latest scheme.

Her sisters. Thank God they had each other,

at least. Four Donnelly daughters. Or, as their father had called them, his Four Roses. Despite her anger, she had to smile at the old nickname. Kevin had been so proud of his four daughters that he'd named each of his businesses after them. And, just like the Donnelly girls, those businesses had thrived.

Maggie took a long moment to study the three women seated in their usual places at the dining-room table.

On her right, Mary Frances. Two years younger than Maggie, Frankie had been born an old woman. Stiff and starchy, she'd somehow escaped the wild blood that Kevin Donnelly had passed down to the rest of his daughters. Even the red in Frankie's hair was subdued into a pale, strawberry blond. And as the shortest of the sisters, as well as the most quiet, Frankie might have been overlooked when it came to business decisions. But her shy nature and small stature disguised a sharp, quick mind. And as manager of the quiet, refined Four Roses Hotel, Frankie was perfect.

Besides, Maggie had often thought she'd caught a glimpse of a simmering temper hiding behind Frankie's placid exterior.

Then there was Mary Alice. The third sister, Al was the son her father'd always wanted. Maggie shook her head as she watched her sister prop her booted feet up on the edge of the table. Preferring to dress in Levi's, buckskins, and boots, Al managed the Four Roses Gold Mine better than any man could have. She wasn't afraid to go deep into the bowels of the mine right along with her employees, and the men respected her for it. She wore her dark red hair pulled into a single long braid that hung down to the gun and holster she wore on her hip. Kevin had seen to it that his girls could shoot as well as any man. Since they lived with elements of society that most women never saw, their father wanted to know that the Donnelly girls could look out for themselves.

At the end of the table, her arms crossed rebelliously across her chest, sat Teresa, the baby of the family. Maggie shook her head. But for the unholy Donnelly temper, the girl might have been a changeling. Named for their mother, who'd died giving birth to her, Teresa also carried her late mother's shining black hair and lake-blue eyes. Black Irish.

But her impatience about being "stuck" on the family ranch, also called Four Roses, Teresa inherited straight from himself, Kevin Donnelly. As the youngest, she'd spent most of her life chasing after her three older sisters, continually trying to prove herself.

Maggie drew in a deep breath and forced her gaze away from Teresa's perpetual scowl. She had no time to listen to her youngest sister's demands on this day.

"What's Da done now, then?" Mary Alice finally asked, once her laughter had dwindled down into a deep-throated chuckle.

"It's fine for you to laugh, Al." Maggie glared at her younger sister. "It's not you he's betrayed!" As an afterthought, she added, "And take your dirty boots off the table."

"Betrayal may be too harsh a term, Maggie."

Maggie turned her head toward the speaker. "Too harsh, is it?" She tossed a folded piece of paper at Mary Frances. "Read it yourself, Frankie. *Then* tell me I'm bein' too harsh."

Mary Frances unfolded the scrap of paper, scanned it quickly, then read it again. Finally, she looked up at Maggie. "I can't believe it," she whispered.

"Here, Frankie." Mary Alice held out one hand for the paper. "Let's see it."

"Now you understand"—Maggie smiled grimly at Frankie—"what the old devil's done!"

"How the hell did he do this?" Al asked, and her feet dropped to the floor with a thud. "I thought he was halfway to New York by now."

"Oh, he is." Maggie nodded grimly. "But he found time to stop off in St. Louis—just long enough to cause trouble!"

"Do I get to see the wire?" Teresa queried complainingly, "or am I not included in the family meetings now?"

Mary Alice frowned at her and slid the telegram across the table. "Stop whining, Terry Ann. Of course you're included. You're here, aren't ya?"

"Don't call me Terry Ann!"

"We're getting away from the problem here," Maggie said quietly, and the other three looked at her. "What are we going to do about Da and this mess?"

"Nothin' much we *can* do, is there?" Al asked.

"If there is," Frankie chimed in, "I, for one, can't see it."

"Me neither," Teresa said, and crumpled the wire in one fist.

"Give that to me," Maggie told her, and when the paper was once again in her hands, she smoothed out the telegram and read the message one more time.

MAGGIE DARLING STOP HAVE SOLD MY INTEREST IN FOUR ROSES STOP YOUR NEW PARTNER ON THE WAY STOP LOVE DA STOP

New partner, indeed, she thought, and wished that she had her father in front of her for just five minutes. How dare the man sell out his half of her saloon! And not even to mention it to her until the blasted new partner was on his way!

"Well, Maggie?" Al asked. "What do we do?"

Maggie frowned. She'd been asking herself that same question since late the night before, when the wire had arrived. As far as she could see, there was only one thing to do.

Mary Margaret Donnelly stood up, laid her palms flat on the polished surface of the table, and said, "We buy him out."

"We don't even know who he is," Teresa pointed out.

"We'll know that soon enough, I'm sure," Maggie shot back.

"What if he won't be bought off?" Frankie asked.

"If he's coming all the way from St. Louis, it's not likely he'll want to turn around and go back," Al pointed out.

"It doesn't matter what he wants," Maggie said sharply. "I don't want or need a new partner."

"What I can't figure out," Al said thoughtfully, "is how the hell Da managed to sell off his share of the saloon so far from home. And why did he? And to who?"

"Who knows why Da does anything?" Maggie straightened up and set her hands on her hips. "And as for who this stranger is . . . Knowing our Da, it could very well be the devil himself!"

Chapter 1

One week later

The mingled scents of money, perfume, and expensive liquor welcomed him home.

He paused just inside the door and let his tired gaze sweep over the familiar room. A thick cloud of smoke hovered a few feet above the gaming tables, where men and women from all over San Francisco jostled for room.

Dice rolled and clacked against the ends of the curved tables. Wheels of fortune spun with dizzying speed, the colors and numbers blurring together into an unbroken swirl of hope. Crystal glasses clinked against the polished bar top, and a lone pianist struggled to be heard over the shouting crowd.

The gambler known only as Cutter took a few more steps deeper into the bustle of people and let their excitement pour into him like fine wine. Swiveling his head slightly, he glanced to his right and caught sight of himself in the mirror hanging behind the bar.

Dark blond hair, deep blue eyes ringed with the shadows of too little sleep, and his usually impeccable suit creased with the wear of travel. He looked like hell. And yet a small smile tugged at the corners of his mouth. There was a definite stamp of triumph on his features. He wondered absently if anyone else would notice.

"Cutter, honey!"

He hardly had time to register the voice before a woman was pressed close against him, her arms around his neck. It only took a moment for his brain to kick in and recognition to flood him. More out of long habit than desire, Cutter's arms closed around her.

"Hello, Lilah," he said, and she nuzzled into his neck. The scent of her cloying perfume was overwhelming, and even in the crowded saloon, suddenly it was all he could smell. Deliberately he reached up, plucked her arms free, and set her back from him.

Her lips pursed into what he was sure she considered an attractive pout.

"What's the matter, honey?" she asked. "Didn't ya miss me?"

"Sure I did, darling." Cutter responded as he knew she wanted him to. He was simply too tired to do anything else.

"That's what I figured," she returned, and moved in close again. Running one blood-red fingernail down the front of his shirt, she licked her lips and continued, "I missed you, too, honey." She lowered her head and looked up at him through spiky black lashes. "I've been so lonely. . . ."

He smiled. Lilah? Lonely? He doubted that very much. His quick gaze swept over her luscious body, encased in a too-tight lavender silk gown that clung to her every curve like a thirsty man's grip on a mug of beer. Her breasts looked to be within a hair of popping out of the dangerously low neckline of her gown, and every short breath she took only enhanced that image.

Ah, Lilah. Somehow, Cutter told himself, it was comforting to know that some things never changed. Desire shimmered in the depths of her dark brown eyes, but Cutter knew it wasn't because of any feeling she had for him in particular. From the top of her beautifully coiffed black head to the tip of her dainty black shoes, Lilah was sex. Pure and simple.

Unfortunately, he wasn't in the mood. Hadn't been for months, if he were to admit the truth. At least, he thought, not for the kind of sex she offered. Hot, undemanding . . . *unfeeling* sex. Cutter snorted a half laugh at himself. Most of the men in the crowded saloon would have called him a fool for even entertaining such a notion. Why, some of them would have given their last breath for a night in Lilah's practiced arms.

Hell, there was a time when he'd felt the same way. But not anymore. The older he got, the more he found himself wishing for other, better things. Like . . . No, he thought firmly. No sense riding down that trail again.

"Cutter, baby"—Lilah leaned in close and whispered right next to his ear—"how about you and me go on upstairs and get reacquainted?"

"Not tonight, darling" he said, and forced a regretful tone into his voice. "I'm just too damn tired to do you justice. Besides," he asked, as he remembered the approximate time of night it was, "don't you have another song to do?"

"Why don't you let me worry about that?"

She slipped her index finger beneath the fabric of his shirt.

Cutter sucked in a gulp of air and shook his head. Setting her back from him again, he said, more firmly this time, "No, thanks, Lilah. I need some sleep."

"You've been doin' an awful lot of 'sleeping' these last few months, Cutter."

He gave her a half smile. "It's hell getting old."

He was sure she wasn't fooled by his evasive measures. Something in her eyes sparked dangerously.

"I guess I know when I'm not wanted," Lilah snapped. Reaching out, she grabbed the arm of the first man to walk past them. The startled, yet pleased, cowboy grinned down at her as if she'd just dropped from Heaven. Her gaze locked on Cutter, Lilah pressed close to the young man and rubbed her breasts gently against his upper arm.

Beads of sweat popped out on the cowhand's forehead, and he almost dropped his drink.

"Hello, handsome," she cooed at him, one eye still on Cutter. "Why don't you come along with Lilah?"

"Yes, *ma'am!*"

Cutter watched the pair cross the room and climb the wide stairway leading to the "ladies" rooms. One sandy blond eyebrow lifted as he noticed the deliberate sway in Lilah's hips.

Instead of the regret he knew Lilah was hoping he'd feel, Cutter felt only relief. At least, he told himself, the cowhand would go home happy that night. If he lived through it.

"Hey, boss."

Cutter's head swiveled, and he grinned at his bar manager.

Ike Shore walked through the crowd and didn't seem to notice the people melting out of his way. Or maybe, Cutter thought, Ike was just used to it. Standing nearly six foot five, the man was a mountain of muscle. He wore a beautifully tailored white suit and moved with a quiet confidence. His dark, coffee-colored features split in a welcoming smile as he stuck out his right hand toward Cutter.

"Glad you're back, boss. Been awhile."

"Too long, Ike, and I'm beat down to the bone."

"Yeah." The big man chuckled. "You look it."

Cutter's mouth quirked. "How's business been?"

"Too damned good to complain . . ."

"But you're going to," Cutter said flatly.

"Nah." Ike shook his head and grinned even more widely. "Not when you're too tuckered to fight back. It'll wait till tomorrow." The big man snorted. "It ain't like it's anything new."

"Digger?"

"Who else?"

Digger Wicks. Hell, the couple of months he'd been away, Cutter hadn't had to spend a single moment thinking about the man. And he hadn't realized until that moment just how pleasant it had been. But even as he thought about his old enemy, Cutter told himself that Ike was right. Digger could wait. "Thanks," he said.

"Where're your bags, Cutter?"

"Down at the station. Will you send one of the boys after them?"

"Sure thing." Ike gave the other man a friendly slap on the back, and, as tired as he was, Cutter staggered.

"I'm going up," Cutter said. "Try to keep the noise down, huh?"

"Yeah." Ike nodded at the old joke. "I'll do that."

Fighting his way through the crowd, Cutter walked to the staircase opposite the one Lilah had taken. Feeling the fatigue of his trip setting into his bones, Cutter had to drag one foot after another up the steps to the landing. There he paused and looked back down at the business he'd taken over only a year before.

From the gaming tables to the waiters, to the liquor at the bar to the show girls who would be performing soon, the Golden Garter was a good saloon. But now, he thought, as he patted the papers in his coat pocket, it would finally be a great saloon.

He rubbed his eyes and yawned. Starting the following day. He could wait one more day.

"If you're going to be staying in town until the new partner arrives," Maggie snapped, "the least you could do is lend a hand around here."

Al looked up briefly from her poker hand and shook her head. "Not a chance, Maggie. I'm on a holiday."

Mary Margaret lifted her chin and set her hands on her hips. She smoothed her fingertips against the cool yellow silk of her gown and sent up a silent prayer for patience. But it was no use, and she knew it.

Patience was a hard-won virtue under the best of circumstances. Especially coming from the long line of tempers that she did. But now it would be impossible. She'd lived the last week as if she were standing on a gallows, waiting for the trapdoor to spring. Every time the batwing doors slapped open, admitting yet another customer into the Four Roses, Maggie held her breath expectantly. Every strange face was met by a questioning glance. Was he the one? Or he?

A new partner.

She gritted her teeth, and her green eyes narrowed into dangerous slits. For all she knew, this mysterious partner could be in the room at that moment. Studying her. Watching her.

Maggie's gaze drifted around the smoke-filled, noisy room. All around her, men and women were gambling at the tables or nestled together in some quiet nook, drinking champagne.

Her gaze stopped on a too-familiar face, and Maggie cursed softly under her breath. David Harper, drunk again. His father, the judge, wouldn't be happy about that. Making a mental note to alert Jake, the head barman, Maggie looked away from the drunken young man. There was nothing to be done about him now, anyway.

In the far corner of the room, a fight was brewing over a card game, but even as she noticed it, Maggie saw O'Reilly, her "man at arms," heading toward the disturbance. She smiled and looked away. There was no need for her to keep an eye on the situation. She knew from long experience that O'Reilly would have everything in hand in a matter of minutes.

Instead she allowed herself another sweeping glance around her place of business. For the last eight years, she'd slaved over the saloon. Maggie was proud of the elegant furnishings and the fine liquors served at the Four Roses. Her show girls were the best on the Coast, and they were paid enough so that they weren't forced to "entertain" men on their own time.

Music played all night, and with four bartenders on duty all night, every night, no one had to wait for service. Actually, five bartenders, if you counted Jake. But he was no mere bartender. Smugly she reminded herself that Jake was the finest mixologist in the West. There were people who came to the Roses simply to watch Jake work!

She inhaled sharply and enjoyed a small burst of pride. Maggie had taken a fairly successful tavern and turned it into the most elegant saloon in San Francisco.

And now, she thought, an angry frown briefly crossing her features, there would be a stranger coming in, trying to tell her what to do.

Well, she wouldn't have it, no matter *what* Kevin Donnelly had done with his share of the business!

Glancing down at her sister again, Maggie scowled at the woman. Sprawled in an oversized captain's chair, Al looked as though she had no intention of moving any time soon. But with Terry back on the ranch and Frankie tucked away in her quiet little hotel, Maggie could have used some help. And Al was just the one to give it to her.

Holiday indeed!

Mary Alice looked at each of the three men seated around the poker table before tossing a stack of chips into the center pile. "I raise you fifty dollars."

"This is no time for a holiday, Al." Maggie stepped closer to the table.

"I fold," one of the men muttered.

"Me too," another said, then added, "She's on a holiday and I'm dyin' here."

"Maggie." Al didn't even look up. "I'm out of the mine for a few days, and I want to enjoy it."

"Oh, and never mind what Da is up to?"

"Da's not here."

"Mary Alice Donnelly," Maggie started, but her sister cut her off with one upraised hand.

The last man at the table counted out a matching stack of chips and hesitated only a moment before throwing them into the pot. He ran one hand over his whisker-stubbled jaw, and Maggie noticed his hand shake. He had only two chips left in front of him. "I'm in," he grumbled. "Let's see what you got, honey."

One dark red eyebrow lifted, and Al smiled at her opponent. Slowly she laid her cards down, face up on the shining oak tabletop. "Full house, king high."

The man's nervous expression dropped into a scowl of disgust. He tossed his two pairs down, pushed himself to his feet, and shouted, "You cheated me!"

Mary Alice had reached for her winnings, but stopped dead at the words.

Maggie stared at the man. She didn't dare look at her younger sister. She knew only too well what she'd see on Al's face. Fury.

That was just what she needed! Al's temper was nearly legendary in San Francisco. And if Maggie didn't act quickly, the unlucky gambler would discover why.

"No one cheated you, mister," Maggie said quietly, all too aware that the man had had far too much to drink.

"The hell she didn't!" His round face was flushed with anger, and beads of sweat dotted his furrowed brow.

"I didn't have to cheat," Al whispered, her eyes narrowed dangerously. "You played like a fool."

Heads were beginning to turn in their direction. Maggie frowned. In the crowded room, if one fight started, the whole place would erupt in brawls.

" 'Fool,' is it?" The disgruntled loser reached for Al, but Maggie was too quick for him. Lifting her right foot, she kicked a chair into his legs. Astonished, his eyes widened, and he swung both arms in an exaggerated arc, before sprawling onto the table behind him.

Stacked chips flew, and liquor spilled out of toppled glasses. The outraged gamblers seated at the upset table promptly tossed him to the floor.

Maggie stepped up to the fallen man and

waved Al back to her chair without even glancing at her.

"Hold your tongue, Al." Then she said clearly,
"I don't allow cheats in my place, mister," adding, as he laboriously pushed himself to his feet,
"no more than I allow whining from people
who shouldn't bet what they can't afford to
lose."

" 'Whining'?" He shook his head violently in
an obvious effort to clear away the liquor-
induced haze. Blinking, he took a half step toward her, apparently hoping to intimidate the
tall redhead.

But Maggie had been handling men since she
was a child. Being raised in a saloon tended to
open one's eyes early to the types of people in
the world. And the secret to handling any man,
drunk or sober, she'd discovered, was to keep
him off his guard.

As she walked toward him, he instinctively
backed up, until they'd circled the table. She
kept him moving, giving him no time to think.
Without even realizing it, the disgruntled loser
was being herded toward the front door.

" 'Whining' is what I said and just what
you're doing" she told him, and impatiently
kicked her skirt out of her way. Hands still at
her hips, she kept walking, increasing her pace
a bit as they neared her objective. "If you can't
afford to lose your money, then stay the hell out
of gambling establishments."

"You can't tell me what to do," he countered,
and looked nervously around him for support
as he was backed through the table- and chair-
littered room. But no one in the crowd made a
move to help him.

"Apparently someone has to!" she snapped, and ignored the delighted smiles of her other customers. Clearly, everyone was enjoying the show. Everyone, that is, but the man facing her. "If you can't behave like a man, I'll thank you not to come back to the Four Roses."

A few chuckles drifted through the crowd, and when he heard them, Maggie saw him stiffen. His pride was about to force him to do something he had no real wish to do. Lord knew, she'd seen it before. When all a man had left was his pride, it was amazing what he would do to hold on to it.

Quickly she shot one glance at the front door. No more than ten feet away. She'd nearly had him there without incident.

He stopped suddenly, swallowed, then said, "You want me to show you how much of a man I really am, honey?"

The slur stabbed at her. It didn't matter how many times she'd heard that same insinuation. It didn't matter that his assumption about her was wrong. It didn't even matter that he was only talking tough in a futile attempt to seem less of a fool. The words still carried a sting.

From the corner of her eye, Maggie saw Jake start to climb over the bar. He looked as though he was eager to do battle. She gave him a shake of her head. She would handle this herself—as she always had. As she always would.

Behind her Maggie heard the band strike up again, and silently blessed whoever'd given that order. Maybe most of her customers would forget about this little scene now and get on with their business.

"There's nothing the likes of you can show

me," she said quietly, her gaze boring into the drunk's. Slowly she reached up with one hand, as if to pat her hair into place.

"Maybe not," the man countered. He licked his lips and sucked in a gulp of whiskey-scented air. "Workin' in a place like this, you've likely spread your legs for half the men in this bedeviled city."

What was left of her patience snapped. Scene or no scene, she wouldn't be standing still to be insulted by the likes of *him*! Maggie pulled a long, diamond-topped hatpin from the mass of curls on top of her head and held it like a sword.

He stared at the needle-sharp length of steel, then shifted his gaze back to hers. What he saw in her green eyes must have given him pause, because he took another step back.

Maggie followed him. It wasn't the first time she'd relied on her hatpin in a sticky situation. And no doubt it wouldn't be the last. He backed up into the swinging double doors, and Maggie stopped beside Seamus Dunn, another of her guards, and held out one hand. "Give me twenty dollars, Seamus," she said, never taking her gaze from the man in front of her.

Instantly the big Irishman laid a twenty-dollar gold piece in the center of her palm. Maggie jerked her head toward the doors and jabbed the pin into the air again. "Get going," she told the hapless drunk.

He backed through the doors, and Maggie caught them before they could swing shut behind him. Stepping out onto the boardwalk, she kept him moving until he stumbled backward off the porch.

The noise outside was every bit as lively as in the saloon. From the adjacent buildings came an uneven blend of music. A tinny, out-of-tune piano; a band with more horns than talent; and, from the panhandler on the corner, an expertly played banjo. Crowds of people, jostling for space on the boardwalk, came to a stop to watch Maggie Donnelly take care of the drunk.

She ignored them all. Dappled spots of muted light from the watery streetlamps fell on her adversary's face. A horse at the hitching rail shifted position, and the man jumped clumsily out of the way. Maggie's gaze locked on him until finally his bravado failed him and he dipped his head to stare at his dusty boots.

Silently Maggie tossed the gold piece, and it landed at his feet. "No man leaves the Four Roses flat broke." She lifted her chin a bit and frowned at him before adding, "Not even you." He looked up, and she continued. "But, mister, I don't expect ever to see your face in my saloon again." She waved the hatpin menacingly and waited a long moment to make sure she had his complete attention. "Because if I do, you'll find I'm not quite so polite a second time. Do you understand me?"

He wanted to argue. She could see it in his face. But even if he'd been armed, which he wasn't, he couldn't very well draw a gun on a woman. And also, he wasn't about to take on a saloon full of her supporters. Finally, Maggie saw acceptance and defeat crowd out the other emotions on his features. When at last he bent double to pick up the coin from the dirt, she deliberately turned her back on him to return to work.

A voice stopped her.

A voice she hadn't heard in nearly a year.

"I see you still hide nasty weapons in your hair."

Maggie frowned, and her fingers curled around the cold steel hatpin.

Cutter.

He'd come back.

Chapter 2

"What are you doing here?" Maggie asked in a breathless voice. Stopped dead, her fingers were still curled over the tops of the doors. The deadly hatpin stuck straight up from her hand, like a warning flag.

Cutter couldn't take his eyes off her. The swarm of people on the boardwalk had started moving again, now that the show was over, and they brushed past him in their eagerness to get on with the evening. Bits of conversations rose up in the air, settled around him, and fell away. A cold sea breeze whipped up from the bay and tugged at his hat brim. But he only noticed her hair and how the curls seemed to dance in the wind.

He wanted to reach out and push his fingers through her hair—to see if it was really as soft and silky as he remembered. But he couldn't. It had been too long.

Several silent moments passed as he watched her, wondering how to begin, what to say. Finally he fell back into the comfortable, teasing tone he'd used on her since she was a young girl.

"Thank you for such a warm welcome," he

said, and stepped into the patch of light thrown from inside the saloon.

"You want warm?" Maggie asked. She half turned toward him, her lips curled into a mockery of a smile. "Then I suggest you take yourself back to hell, Cutter."

He winced and shook his head. "I've missed you, too." Damn, he silently admitted, he'd even missed that razor-sharp tongue of hers.

God, she was beautiful, he thought, and immediately told himself to stop noticing. But Lord, how could a man *not* have noticed? It would have been like standing in broad daylight and not noticing the sun.

With more hunger than he wanted to admit, Cutter's gaze swept over her. Yellow was a good color for her, he decided, as he noted how her ivory skin seemed to glow in the lamplight. The fine silk of her gown caressed her figure and outlined every curve. The deeply cut, lace-edged neckline of her dress just managed to cover the swell of her breasts, and the string of pearls she wore drew his eye to the valley between those breasts. A long strand of small, ivory-colored beads dipped into her cleavage, and he had to curl his hands into fists to keep from touching the soft flesh holding them captive.

Cutter's gaze flicked back up to hers, and he found her deliberately staring away from him. She held herself regally. Chin lifted, back arrow-straight, the only thing she lacked was a crown. When she snapped her head around to glare at him out of now-icy green eyes, a cluster of copper curls fell forward over her shoulder.

Maggie watched him, and he wasn't so dazzled by her beauty that he missed the unmistakable flash of anger she directed at him. But he'd become used to that.

Ever since that night nearly a year ago, he told himself. One night, and everything between them had changed. Hell. For him, that night had changed more than just his relationship with Maggie.

It had threatened everything he'd worked toward for most of his life.

And yet, he told himself, he couldn't regret it. Even the nightly torture of remembering her in his arms wasn't enough to make him regret a moment of it. Memories. Hell, he'd become a man whose whole *life* was a series of memories—good and bad.

"You're beautiful tonight, Maggie." The words flew from his mouth before he could call them back.

She inhaled sharply and crossed her arms in front of her. "Don't."

Cutter's jaw tightened. Chiding himself, he quickly switched back to the teasing, sarcastic note that was so much safer in dealing with Maggie.

"Now," he said, a soft drawl caressing his words, "when a woman fixes herself up as nicely as you have . . . a man *ought* to remark on it."

"I didn't do it for you, Cutter," she snapped.

True, he thought. How could she have? She hadn't even known he was back in town. Besides, they'd been avoiding each other for months! Still, her lightning-fast remark indicated that she *might* have been primping for someone else. Some other man.

A swell of irritation crested in him, goading his tongue into saying something he'd never intended to say.

"Good." He took one step closer to her and inhaled the soft, sweet, flowery scent that belonged only to her. "It would have been a waste of your time. I'd just as soon see you out of that dress as in it."

She slapped him, and the sharp smack seemed to echo around them.

Lifting one hand, Cutter rubbed his jaw and grinned at her. "You hit every bit as hard as I remember, Mag."

"And you're every bit as irksome as *I* remember, Cutter."

A drunk wandering along the crowded boardwalk stumbled into Cutter, who fell against Maggie. He grabbed her waist to steady her, and with his first touch, warmth exploded between them.

He felt her breath catch as his hands spanned her narrow waist. His thumbs smoothed across her silk-clad flesh, and she trembled slightly.

Abruptly he stepped back. Cutter watched her take a deep, steadying breath and envied her. As for himself, his chest felt as though an iron band was wrapped around it. Shoving his hands in his pockets, he jerked a nod at the hatpin she was still clutching at the ready. "I'd feel a lot better if you'd put that thing away."

"I feel better holding it," she countered.

"Look, Maggie." Cutter sighed heavily. "I'm sorry."

"For what?" she asked, lifting her chin even higher. "For talking to me as if I were a whore?

Or for . . ." Her voiced faded away, and she let her gaze slide from his.

"For what I said." He yanked one hand free and reached up to tug his hat off. Crushing the brim in one strong fist, Cutter went on. "I shouldn't have said that, and I'm sorry."

She nodded grudgingly.

"But you should know something else as well," he added. "I'm not sorry about—"

Her eyes narrowed, and her fingers tightened around the hatpin.

Clearly, she didn't want him reminding her about their night together. Fine, he told himself. He didn't have to say anything at all. The memories *must* have been as clear for her as they were for him.

"Not sorry for what, Cutter?" she challenged.

"You know for what."

Maggie relaxed a bit then, and answered stiffly, "It doesn't matter anymore. I'm sorry enough for both of us."

Cutter sucked in a breath and felt the cold sea air go deep into his lungs. He'd had no right to expect anything different, but somehow, hearing her say she regretted having been with him had hit him harder than her slap.

"Good night, Cutter." She half turned for the door again. "I have work to do."

But when it came right down to it, the past didn't matter. At least, not now. He had something to say to her, and she had to listen.

"We have to talk." He grabbed her arm.

"Talk?" A harsh snort of laughter shot out from her, and she shook him off. "After nearly a year, you decide we have to talk, and I'm supposed to jump?"

"Maggie, I stayed away for your sake as much as for mine."

"Well"—her lips curved into a smile that never reached her eyes—"that's very comforting, Cutter. But I'd say it was more for you than for anything."

"Maggie—"

"Our saloons stand right next to each other, Cutter." She waved one hand at him, and he was sure she didn't realize the hatpin was still clutched in her fingers. "We even share a common wall, for God's sake! Yet somehow, but for the occasional 'Good morning,' you managed to avoid speaking to me for almost a year." Her hands dropped to her hips, and she lifted her chin even higher. Looking at him through angry eyes, she finished, "That kind of thing takes a lot of effort, Cutter."

"It had to be that way, Maggie."

"Go away, Cutter," she muttered, and slowly reached up to tuck the hatpin back into its hiding place.

"Maggie, we have to talk. Now. It's important." And, he told himself, he sure as hell didn't want to discuss it out there in the street. Knowing Maggie, their little conversation was bound to be a loud one.

"I don't care, Cutter." Her gaze snapped briefly up to his, then turned away again. "There was a time when I would have listened to anything you had to say. But that time's long past. Go back to the Golden Garter. There's nothing for you here anymore."

Before he could say anything further, Maggie slipped back into the saloon and was swallowed up by the crowd.

Over the top of the doors, Cutter watched her. Even in the crush of people, she was easy to spot. That splash of red hair stood out like a fire on a dark night. She hurried down the length of the bar, ignoring the questions Jake hurled at her. She didn't even pause as she passed her sister. At the foot of the stairs, she lifted the hem of her gown and nearly flew up the steps.

Cutter watched Maggie's progress and didn't look away until the tall redhead had disappeared inside the second-story office. Then he pushed through the swinging doors and stepped into the noisy crowd.

When he reached the shining mahogany bar, Cutter set one boot on the brass railing.

"Evenin', Cutter," the barman said. "What'll it be?"

"A shot of your best whiskey, Jake," he answered, and slapped a coin down on the bar. He was going to need it.

The dark-haired man poured the drink, set it in front of Cutter, and picked up the coin. Jake flicked a quick glance upstairs at the now-closed office door. Then, leaning over the bar top, he confided, "This ain't the best time to be talkin' to Maggie, y'know."

"That right?"

"Yeah, she's all worked up over somethin' Kevin went and done."

"Worked up" probably didn't say it by half, he thought. Kevin. Cutter snorted. If he was a man who believed in such things, he would be tempted to swear that Kevin Donnelly wasn't a man at all, but a mischievous leprechaun. "What's the ol' bastard up to now?" Cutter asked, just to be polite.

"He's sold the place out from under her." Mary Alice broke into the conversation as she stepped up beside Cutter. "Give me a beer, will ya, Jake?"

The barman frowned, but drew a beer and set the foaming mug in front of her. Al ignored him.

"Ladies don't drink beer, Mary Alice."

"And most gamblers don't give lessons in manners, Cutter," she shot back. After taking a healthy drink of the cold beer, she narrowed her gaze and asked pointedly, "What do you want, anyway?"

"I'm here to see Maggie."

"After a year."

He frowned, wondering just how much Maggie had told her younger sister. "I was away, Al."

"Sure," she admitted, "the last three months. What about the rest of the year?"

"That's between Maggie and me," he said shortly.

"Maybe"—Al leaned in close to him—"and maybe it'll be between you and Maggie's family." She set the beer down, turned her back on the bar, and braced both elbows on its shining top.

"All right, Al," he said stiffly, "out with it. What is it you're trying so hard not to say?"

"Nothin'." Mary Alice Donnelly's eyes narrowed, and Cutter saw the warning glittering in her dark, forest-green gaze. "For now," she added pointedly.

Tossing the Irish whiskey down his throat, he set the empty glass down and straightened away from the bar.

"Cutter," Al said quickly, softly. "Why don't you leave her alone?"

He looked at the pretty woman and could hardly credit how she'd changed over the years. For a moment, he wondered why he hadn't noticed before. Did a man have to leave for a few months to be able to see the people around him clearly? When had Al grown up? Even in the buckskins she still insisted on wearing, Mary Alice Donnelly was definitely a woman grown.

Time. Too much of it was passing too quickly. He wouldn't have many years left to complete what he'd set out to do so long ago. A cold, hard stone of determination settled in his chest.

"Can't do that, Al." He shook his head and started walking.

"She won't let you in," Al warned.

"Yes, she will," he said, and told himself that he *would* talk to Maggie, even if he had to break down her door.

Perfect!

Maggie opened the small square of wallpapered paneling and stared down at the saloon floor. She couldn't see him, but that didn't mean a thing. Cutter was, she thought, a lot like an Apache. You didn't have to see him to know he was around, waiting to ambush the unwary.

Suddenly furious, Maggie closed the little door again, then ran her fingers across what looked to be a seamless piece of wallpaper. Turning around, her back to the wall, she looked at the office. Her office.

And for the first time, she took no comfort in the casually elegant furnishings. In fact, she didn't *see* anything in the room except the long blue velvet sofa set beneath the tall, narrow windows on the far wall.

She noted the intricately carved walnut arms and the array of dark blue tassels along the sofa's base. Maggie swallowed heavily and thanked heaven she'd had the piece reupholstered almost a year before. It was different now. She was different now.

On the side wall of the office, its latch, too, cleverly disguised by the wallpaper, was a narrow door that opened onto a staircase. From there, Maggie could go either down the steps to the cellar or up to the roof, unseen.

A small smile crossed her face at the thought. How many times had she used that little passage to escape her sisters or the constant demands of work? She stared at the doorway and told herself that perhaps what she needed just then was some time alone. Up on the roof, where she could stare blankly out to sea. Where she could forget, even if for too short a time, that her life was in upheaval.

At the very least, she told herself firmly, it would put her further out of Cutter's reach.

Cutter. Why the devil had he come back early? Ike had assured her only a few days ago that Cutter was in no hurry to return and would probably be gone for several more weeks. The last few months had been an absolute pleasure with him gone. She hadn't had to think about him every day. She hadn't had to remember the hours they'd spent together on that couch in her office. She hadn't had to relive the hurt and humiliation that had followed. And most importantly, she hadn't had to live with the knowledge that he was deliberately avoiding her.

Now, though, he was back. And, damn his eyes, he looked even better than she remembered.

A knock on the door brought her up short, and she jumped. Turning toward the sound, she stared at the heavy oak panel as though she could see right through it. And in a way, she could. Because somewhere deep in the heart of her she knew that Cutter was on the other side of that door.

He knocked again, louder this time.

Maggie bit down on her bottom lip and clenched her hands tightly together. She wouldn't answer.

"Maggie?" he called, and his voice, though muffled by the door, still had the power to send a chill up her spine.

Maggie shook herself and frowned at her body's reaction to the man.

"Dammit, Maggie," he said slowly, his soft southern accent making his words feel like a caress. "I know you're in there! I saw you at the peephole door!"

Blast! Maggie glared at the offending square of wallpaper as though it were the door's fault she'd been caught.

"We have to talk," he insisted.

"*We* don't have anything more to say to each other, Cutter." Her hands moved to grip her forearms. Her skin felt cold. "You have to leave. Now. Before I call for O'Reilly to throw you out."

"Go ahead," he challenged. "Call O'Reilly. You'll have to open this damned door to do it."

A frustrated sigh shook her. He was right about that. She was well and truly trapped in her own office. Unless . . . She turned to glance at the hidden door in the corner.

"I'm not leaving until I talk to you, Maggie."

"You already did, Cutter. You apologized: let's leave it at that." A small, triumphant smile curled around her lips as she began to walk quietly toward her escape route. "Go back to your own place and leave me and mine alone."

"I can't do that."

Of course not, she fumed silently. Cutter could never bring himself to do anything other than exactly what he wanted. Well, this time would be different. This time she wasn't blinded by what she thought was love.

"You'll just have to, Cutter. Now, go away, there's nothing for you here."

Several long moments of silence passed. Surprised at his too-easy surrender, she stopped just as she opened the paneled door. Cocking her head, she listened for sounds of his retreat. She held her breath, straining to hear him leaving.

But there was nothing. He was still there. She knew it. She could feel it. Cutter always *had* been as hardheaded as he was good-looking. Maggie shook her head and stepped into the passageway. She stopped when he spoke again—louder, this time.

"Kevin's little door to the roof won't work with me either, Maggie."

She cursed under her breath at her own foolishness and ground her teeth together. How stupid of her. Of course he would remember Kevin's little escapeway. Cutter knew his way around the Four Roses every bit as well as the Donnelly girls did.

"I'll just climb up from outside," he promised. "And if you go to the cellar instead, I'll break a window to get in, if I have to."

He'd do it, too, she told herself, and slipped back into the office. Maggie closed her eyes briefly, then slammed the hidden door shut. She leaned against it for a long moment and tried to steady herself. Finally, as calm as she was likely to be, she walked across the room and wrenched open the heavy oak door.

Cutter was leaning forward, with one hand on either side of the doorjamb. "Dammit Maggie," he said, his voice quieter now, "this doesn't have to be so hard."

"Everything is hard with you, Cutter," she replied, and turned her back on him as she walked to her desk.

"Mag," he said, and she heard him close the door behind him, "it's about Kevin."

Her father. The one other man in this wide world she didn't want to think about just then.

"I'm in no mood to be discussing Da, Cutter." She pulled in a deep breath and once more ordered herself to be calm.

It wasn't working.

"I saw him in St. Louis."

That figured, she thought, and shook her head. Somehow, Maggie wasn't surprised that the two of them had run into each other. Cutter and Kevin Donnelly had always been too close by half.

"That's grand, Cutter," she said, and heard the sarcasm in her voice. "I feel so much better now, knowing the two of you had a lovely time together."

"Dammit, Maggie," he snapped, and crossed

the room to her side in a few quick steps. One hand on her elbow, he turned her around to face him. Maggie immediately pulled out of his grasp. "Will you just listen for a damn minute?"

"I will not. And don't be cursin' at me in my place!" Hands at her waist, she kicked her skirt out of her way and started pacing angrily. "I'll thank you to keep a civil tongue in your head."

"If you want me to be civil," he ground out, "then stand still and talk to me!"

"This is my place and my bloody office, and if I want to pace all night, I will!"

"That's what I have to talk to you about, and I don't want to have to chase you around the room to do it!"

She smiled grimly. If Cutter didn't want it, then she damn well did. "Too bad, Cutter. If you're bound and determined to talk to me, you'll do it while I pace or dance or whatever else may come into my head—or you won't do it at all."

"Fine, then!" He turned in a slow circle, following her progress around the room. "Al tells me that Kevin sold his share of the saloon."

"So?" She surely didn't want to discuss her father with Cutter, of all people. She deliberately kept her back to him and began to adjust the flowers in the vase beneath the window.

"So," Cutter went on determinedly, "did he say nothing about your new partner?"

"Nothing!" She spun about, and one of the tall stalks of larkspur fell to the tabletop, sprinkling water across the shining surface. "Da's like you that way, Cutter. He talks only when it suits *him*. All I know is that this 'partner' will be arriving soon."

"He has."

"What?"

"I said, he has."

Maggie took a hesitant step toward him. Her legs felt like lead, and she had to force them to move. Her gait unsteady, she kept moving across the room until she was within an arm's reach of him. Eyes wary, she stared up at Cutter and tried not to notice the blue of his eyes. Concentrating on the most important thing just then, she heard herself ask in a harsh whisper, "How do ya know? You've met him?"

"You could say that," he answered, hedging, and Maggie didn't like the flash of amusement she read in his gaze.

"What're you tryin' to tell me, Cutter?" she forced herself to ask. God help her, she had a fairly good idea of what his answer was going to be. And if she was right, Kevin Donnelly had better wait years before coming home.

"It's very simple, Maggie," Cutter said, and leaned one shoulder against the doorjamb. "I'm your new partner."

"At least she finally let him in," Mary Alice said, and took another drink of her beer.

"Yeah, but did ya see the look on her face when she did?" The bartender shook his shaggy head and continued drying the crystal bar glasses. "There's trouble brewin', Al. I can smell it."

Al swiveled her head to look at the now-shut office door. Cutter and Maggie in a closed room? Together? She half snorted. It would be a miracle if they both survived.

Why, during the past year, the two of them had barely spoken.

Then the half smile on Al's face faded away. Why had Cutter suddenly been so set on talking to Maggie? What could he possibly have had to say that couldn't have waited?

And what was so important that Maggie had allowed the man into her office?

The longer she thought about it, the more Al began to think that Jake was right. There *was* trouble brewing. Nodding to herself, she drained her glass, set it down, and started for the door.

"Where you off to in such a rush?" Jake called out after her.

"To get my sisters."

"Partner?"

"I have the papers right here." Cutter patted his coat pocket.

"Let me see them," she demanded, and held out one hand.

Cutter looked at her thoughtfully as he slowly drew out the contracts. He knew Maggie wouldn't be above ripping the papers in half the moment she got her hands on them. Carefully he laid the packet across her palm, and before she'd even begun to unfold it, he told her, "There's another copy at the bank, Maggie."

She threw him a quick frown but didn't say anything as she opened the papers and started reading.

Cutter watched her thumb through the legal briefs, her gaze darting from paragraph to paragraph, no doubt looking for a way out of the deal. But he already knew there was no way out. He'd made sure of it.

Hell, he'd wanted the Four Roses for years. It was no secret. Yet Kevin had always made it plain that he had no intention of selling out. The older man had insisted for years that the saloon was a family business.

In his mind, Cutter could still hear Kevin's voice, thick with an Irish brogue he'd never bothered to lose.

"Nay, lad." The cheery-looking man with the red cheeks and even redder hair had told him. "The Four Roses is not for sale at any price. 'Tis family, Cutter. And family is more than a buildin', or a fancy price, or even profit." Cutter remembered how Kevin had slapped his shoulder with fatherly vigor and added, "The Donnellys will always stand together. Sink or swim. The bunch of us will either make it or we won't. But whatever the good Lord decides, he'll have to take us all."

Family. It always came back to that. And always, it was enough to make Cutter feel the outsider he knew he was.

Shaking his head, he asked himself again what had changed the old man's mind. But he'd been asking himself that question since he'd left St. Louis, and he was no closer to an answer than he'd been then. For whatever reasons, Kevin Donnelly had sold out to Cutter, and by God, Maggie would just have to find a way to deal with that.

"I can't believe he did this," Maggie muttered, and dropped into the chair behind her desk.

Watching Maggie's face, Cutter was almost

sorry he'd finally managed to wear her father down. Almost.

Then other memories crowded into his brain. Memories of a different time, a different place, a different family.

Echoes of long-silent voices rose up inside him, and it was all Cutter could do to keep from wincing at the remembered pain. Shadowy images danced in front of his shuttered eyes, and in his mind, he caught the faint scent of magnolias, drifting on a warm summer wind.

"We'll buy you out."

He gave himself a mental shake and looked down into Maggie's eyes. "What?"

"I said, 'We'll buy you out.' My sisters and I."

"No."

She inhaled sharply and kept talking as if he hadn't already refused her. "We'll pay more than you gave Da. You'll see a handsome profit, I promise you."

"I said, 'No.'"

Maggie stood up and began to pace once more. The swish of her skirt was the only sound other than her frantic mutterings.

"It shouldn't take more than a day or two to come up with the money, Cutter."

"You're not listening to me."

She stopped suddenly and looked up at him. Silent, still, she waited.

"I won't be bought off. And I won't go away." He pulled his hat from his head and tossed it to the desk top. "We're partners, Maggie, and that's just how it's going to be."

Her breathing came fast and furious. He had no doubt that if the room were thrown into darkness, he would be able to see sparks shooting from her eyes. From the tilt of her chin to the rigidity of her shoulders, every line of Maggie's body screamed with anger.

When she finally gave that rage of hers free rein, it would, as he knew from long experience, be a sight to behold. The Donnellys were well known along the Coast for the Irish temper that seemed to plague all of them but Mary Frances. And though Maggie had always had a bit more control than the others, once she let loose, she more than made up for it.

He braced himself for the blast of fury he knew would come.

Minutes passed.

Nothing happened.

Maggie simply glared at him.

Cutter began to worry.

Chapter 3

Maggie tugged her bonnet ribbons free, and as she walked into the Four Roses, she tossed the tiny rose-velvet hat onto the bar top.

Right behind her Al, Frankie, and Teresa were still talking.

She stifled a groan and circled the edge of the bar. As she walked to the small stove at the far end, Maggie wished again that all her sisters were where they were supposed to be rather than in town with her. Oh, no doubt Al had thought she was doing the right thing by gathering all the Donnelly girls together. But Maggie would have been much happier dealing with this problem on her own.

Heaven knew she was fast approaching the end of her patience with Frankie's interminably rational, logical mind. Al's impatience merely fed her own, and apparently Teresa had never outgrown her childhood admiration for Cutter.

Naturally, all three sisters felt compelled to give Maggie advice, and naturally ... none of the three could agree on a blessed thing!

Grumbling under her breath, Maggie grabbed a heavy ceramic cup and saucer and poured herself a cup of coffee. Then slowly, reluctantly, she strolled back to join her sisters.

41

The three of them were so busy talking to each other, though, that they hardly noticed her. Grateful for the reprieve, Maggie stifled a sigh and glanced about the Four Roses.

Except for the cleaning women, the saloon was empty. Her employees all had rooms at different boardinghouses in the city, and at that moment, the performers, bartenders, and waiters were no doubt sound asleep. If it hadn't been for the early-morning meeting with the lawyer, Maggie herself wouldn't have *thought* about waking up before noon.

She shook her head and yawned. Like herself, a saloon wasn't at its best in the morning. Chairs sat upended on the tables, the emerald-green curtain was pulled shut across the deserted stage, and plain white linen covers were draped over the roulette and faro tables.

Tiny sparkles of dust drifted in the sunshine pouring in through the wide front windows. In the harsh light of day, she thought, a saloon was a lonely, empty place. Its furnishings, so elegant by lamp- and candlelight, looked loud and garish in the less-forgiving morning sun.

It was a room designed for the night. The Four Roses needed darkness and people. Without the sounds of poker chips clacking against one another, the wheel of fortune spinning, and the roll of dice, the magic was gone.

Even the sumptuous marble entry, the inlaid wood panels on the walls, and the crystal chandeliers overhead looked . . . tawdry.

At this early hour, the saloon—her saloon—was missing something.

Another yawn crept up on her, and she hid it behind one hand. In fact, Maggie thought, she was much like the Four Roses. She needed the night—without it, she was only half alive.

Like the saloon, in the harsh glare of the sun, she was less than what she was meant to be.

"You might just as well get used to the notion, Mary Margaret," Frankie said, and her voice shook Maggie from her thoughts. "From what the lawyer says, there's nothing we can do."

Maggie took a sip of coffee and shuddered at the slightly bitter brew. But better to choke on terrible coffee than to get into another argument with Mary Frances that early in the day.

Frankie continued to talk in the calm, logical tone that infuriated her sisters, but Maggie wasn't listening anymore. Instead she stared down into the inky liquid in her cup and remembered the scene with their lawyer.

She should have known by the closed look on the man's face that the war was over without her having fired a shot.

"Everything is in order, Mary Margaret," he'd said. "Your father took care of everything on this end before he left town."

"Well, why the devil didn't you tell me sooner?" Maggie had leaped to her feet, laid her palms flat on the desk, and glared at the little man.

The lawyer, Mr. Dunworthy, hadn't even twitched. He was accustomed to dealing with the volatile Donnellys. Adjusting his wire-framed spectacles, he'd pursed his lips distastefully.

"It would have been unethical to divulge my client's intentions."

Maggie's fingers had curled around the edge of the desk and squeezed. Behind her, she'd vaguely heard Frankie making clucking noises with her tongue, but she'd ignored the implied warning. Making every effort to keep from screaming in frustration, Maggie had reminded him, "I am your client, too."

"Very true," he had acknowledged. "And I must admit to a bit of hesitancy in this matter, but Kevin . . . your father assured me that his arrangements were for the best."

"The best?" she'd echoed. "The best for who?"

"All concerned, I presume," he'd answered matter-of-factly. Then he'd glanced at the grandfather clock in the corner of his austere office. "And now, if you'll excuse me, I have another appointment shortly that I must prepare for."

Maggie would have stayed and argued with the man all day—hang his other appointments! But her sisters had dragged her from the room before she'd had the chance to say another word.

The mental image faded, leaving only a lingering sense of helplessness. Quietly fuming, Maggie thought that her sisters were taking their father's betrayal much more lightly than she was. But then, she amended silently, they weren't directly affected. *Their* businesses were being left alone. Kevin Donnelly had taken it into his head to ruin only his oldest daughter's life!

She was willing to wager, though, that if the Donnelly girls had any idea of what had passed between Maggie and Cutter nearly a year before, they'd be reacting differently.

She glanced up guiltily and looked at first one, then another, of her sisters, as if expecting to see some reaction to her thoughts. For heaven's sake—they couldn't read her mind! Her secret was safe.

So far.

"Maggie," Frankie said with exaggerated politeness, "you're not listening to a word I'm saying."

"Hmmm?" Deliberately she pushed all thoughts of Cutter out of her head and tried to concentrate on Frankie. "What?"

Mary Frances Donnelly sighed heavily, lifted a chair from a nearby table, and, when it was uprighted, seated herself gingerly. "I said, you're simply going to have to adjust to this new situation, Maggie."

"Adjust?"

Adjust? she repeated silently. Adjust to being with a man who'd taken her virtue without a second thought and then tossed her aside with even less consideration?

"Certainly." Frankie tugged gently at the wrists of her gloves, then smiled patiently at her older sister. "After all, it isn't as though you'll be having to work with a complete stranger, for goodness' sake."

If she only knew how right she was, Maggie told herself. She couldn't help wondering whether Frankie would have a different opinion if she knew exactly how far from a stranger Cutter really was.

Unbidden, memories of that one, long night with him rose up in her brain. But before the images were clear enough to torment her, Maggie buried them.

"What's really botherin' you, Maggie?"

Her gaze snapped to Mary Alice. "What do you mean?"

Al picked up another chair, set it on the floor, and straddled it, resting her crossed arms on top of the chair back.

Her eyes narrowed thoughtfully. "I mean, I'm beginnin' to wonder if you're more upset that Cutter's your partner than you are about the notion of Da's selling out."

"That's not so," she argued, but privately she wondered if there wasn't a grain of truth in what Al had said. Would she have been just as angry if the partner had turned out to be a stranger?

A moment later, the answer came hurtling through her mind.

Yes.

The fact that her new partner was the man she'd believed herself in love with made the situation a bit more humiliating than it might have been. But her father's betrayal would have cut as deeply, had it been someone other than Cutter.

"I just don't see what's so terrible about all of this anyway," Teresa threw in.

Maggie was so grateful for the change in subject, she could've kissed her youngest sister.

"What do you mean?" Frankie asked.

"Well," Teresa said, and took a chair for herself before continuing, "the new partner could've been anyone. But this is Cutter. He's almost family anyhow!"

Family, indeed, Maggie thought grimly. But for the grace of God, she and Cutter might have started their own branch of the family that night. She sighed, lifted one hand and rubbed her temple gently. The pounding behind her eyes had settled into a low, throbbing ache.

How in heaven was she going to be able to stand being near him every day? Seeing him, hearing him, was going to be harder than the last few months of not seeing him at all!

Oh, she wasn't concerned about any old feelings blossoming back into life. No. She'd spent the last several months doing everything she could to stamp out even the smallest flicker of surviving emotion.

And even if, for some bizarre reason, her love for him did worm its way back into her heart, the memory of his rejection was still so painful, she'd never risk experiencing it again.

But dammit, she thought. How could she be expected to conduct business with a man who'd seen her naked? Who'd held her in his arms and kissed her until she'd nearly cried with wanting him?

A curl of desire snaked through her body, and her knees trembled. The memories were clear and strong. Time and pain hadn't dimmed them a bit. Her heartbeat sped up, and the palms of her hands were damp.

Maggie groaned quietly.

This would never work.

"Well," Teresa went on when no one said anything, "I think it's wonderful!"

"You do, huh?" Al asked quietly. "Tell me somethin', Terry Ann, would you think it was wonderful if Da sent some man to the ranch to tell you what to do?"

The youngest Donnelly girl bristled at the dreaded nickname. "Don't call me that. And what do I care if somebody else runs that ranch?

I don't even want to be there!" She jumped to her feet and glared at each of her sisters. "I keep telling you all that I want to be in the city!"

"We know, Teresa." Frankie sighed. "We know."

Maggie had to bite the inside of her cheek to keep herself from shouting. They were supposed to be dealing with the new problem! Instead they'd gone back to the same old argument. Teresa wanted off the ranch. For the life of her, though, Maggie couldn't understand why.

At that moment, the peace and quiet of Four Roses Ranch sounded delightful to her. Just two hours outside of town, the ranch was like another world.

Instantly her mind conjured up the image of the one-story, Spanish-style ranch house. Giant cottonwood trees surrounded the place, dappling the wide front porch with shade all afternoon. In her mind, she heard the soft rustle of leaves as they brushed together in the wind and the gentle rush of water over stones in the nearby creek. She was sorely tempted to pack up and go to the ranch herself for a few days, just to have some time to think. But even as the idea presented itself, Maggie sighed. With Terry Ann moping about, there probably wouldn't be much peace there anyway.

Besides, she told herself firmly, running away wasn't the answer. Cutter wasn't going anywhere. He'd be right there, waiting for her, when she came back. And if she left town now, he'd only get a stronger foothold on the saloon.

The only thing to do was to beard the lion in his den. She straightened up and nodded determinedly. Face down the dragon, she thought. Beat the handsome troll at his own game.

Slapping her palms onto the bar top, Maggie shouted to be heard over Teresa and Al.

"All right, it's finished!"

The others gaped at her.

At the far end of the saloon, even the cleaning women paused in their sweeping. Maggie sent them a halfhearted smile and waved them back to work.

"What's finished?" Al asked.

"This . . . meeting of the Donnelly sisters. It's over." Maggie quickly stepped out from behind the bar and stopped in front of the three women. "Thanks for your help, but I'll take care of this mess myself."

"How?"

She glanced at Frankie. "I'm not sure yet, but whatever I do, it's between Cutter and me. The rest of you can go on home."

"I'm not ready to go back yet," Teresa said flatly.

Maggie sighed with impatience. "Isn't there a shipment of cattle arriving this week?"

Teresa shrugged. "Just a few head. Jackson can take care of it."

"It's the Donnelly ranch, Teresa." Maggie's eyebrows arched pointedly. "Jackson Quinn's a good man, but he's the foreman, not the owner."

A long moment passed while the two women stared at each other, neither willing to give an inch.

In the strained silence, Al's voice sounded loud as she said, "Y'know, Teresa, you're always talkin' about how you want your turn at runnin' things. Well, that ranch is one of the businesses too."

Teresa's gaze shifted to her.

"You might think of provin' yourself on the ranch."

"Al's right," Frankie said softly. "Stop treating the ranch as if it were a prison sentence."

"Show us what you can do with the place, Teresa Ann," Maggie added.

The four of them stood in a haphazard circle, the three oldest sisters staring at the youngest. Finally Teresa nodded.

"All right," she said grudgingly. "I'll do it. But when I've proven myself to all of you . . . I'll want an equal say in what we do from now on."

"If you've earned it." Mary Alice sounded unconvinced.

"I will," Teresa countered, and lifted her chin defiantly.

"Al"—Maggie spoke up, continuing what she'd started to say earlier—"I know you should be back at the mine by now."

"True," her sister agreed, "but are you sure you don't want my help with Cutter?"

Honestly! Teresa still hero-worshiped Cutter, and apparently Al's distrust of the man was as strong as ever.

"To do what?" Maggie snorted a laugh. "Hogtie him until he agrees to sell out?"

Al smiled as though enjoying that mental image.

"No, but thanks." Maggie shook her head. "If I need something, I'll talk to Frankie. She's right here in town."

Frankie looked horrified at the idea.

"Good idea." Al laughed. "She can talk him to sleep, and we can have him shanghaied."

Maggie ignored Al's retort and walked to the front doors.

"Where are you going?" Teresa called out.

"To talk to my new partner," Maggie answered, and pushed through the swinging doors.

"You sure about this? Not telling anybody, I mean?" Cutter asked as he studied his friend's features.

Ike held a coffee cup between his two huge hands and idly turned it in circles. After a long moment, he answered, "Yeah. I'se . . . I'm sure."

Cutter nodded, ignoring the man's habit of correcting his own speech when he talked. Ike had been doing it for so long, in an effort to lose all traces of what he called his "slave talk," that the corrections were a part of him.

Still, Cutter wished Ike would change his mind about keeping their partnership a secret. Hell, Cutter didn't give a good damn *who* knew or what anyone thought about it. But obviously Ike did. "All right, then," Cutter reluctantly agreed, "we'll do it your way. For now."

"How 'bout that?" Ike released his hold on the ceramic cup and leaned back in his chair. Glancing around at the silent Golden Garter saloon, he grinned and said aloud, "Who'd 'a' figured that a black man from Alabama would end up partners in a saloon with a white man in San Francisco?"

"Not me." Cutter laughed too. "Hell, I figured to spend my whole damn life in Georgia!"

Ike shook his head slightly and smiled disbelievingly. "A *southern* white man, to boot!"

Strange, Cutter thought. He didn't *feel* southern anymore. Except for the slow drawl in his speech, which he had to admit he exaggerated sometimes, he didn't think there was anything left of that Georgia boy in him.

He knew for a fact that the folks he'd known back there never would have been sitting down with a black man, let alone making him a partner of any sort. Covertly, he watched the man across from him.

From the moment they'd met, Ike Shore had been more of a friend to Cutter than anyone he'd ever known. Cutter chuckled to himself as the memory of their first meeting rolled through his mind.

At twenty, he'd left San Francisco behind him to seek his fortune. It was in Sacramento that he'd made his first mistake.

Young and stupid, he'd assumed that all men took their poker losses like gentlemen. After a very successful night at the tables, Cutter had pocketed his winnings and walked out into the darkness.

The summer night was warm, and the scent of jasmine drifted on the air. It was late, most of the saloons were closed, and the only sounds he'd heard were his own boot steps on the wooden boardwalk. Maybe if he'd been less preoccupied with his own thoughts and plans, he would have heard his attackers approach.

As it was, though, he didn't hear a thing until it was much too late.

As he stepped off the boardwalk, someone in the dark alley grabbed him and dragged him into the narrow corridor. He spun around blindly, instinctively, throwing his fist in what he hoped was the right direction.

The solid smack of fist meeting jaw told him he'd hit his target, but that was the last blow he delivered. More faceless men came out of the shadows, and they carried him to the ground.

He groaned aloud when the first blow came, but after that, there were too many to distinguish. Fists and boots pummeled his body. Cutter felt a rib break, and pain sliced through him like a hot bolt of lightning. He curled into himself, trying to make as small a target as possible, but still his attackers went on. They paused only long enough for one of them to rifle his pockets and steal back all the money Cutter had won at the poker table.

A wicked swipe from a hamlike fist slammed his face into the dirt. The scent of jasmine was gone, replaced by the stench of rotting garbage and the unmistakable smell of whiskey on his attackers' breath. Then the beating continued.

Somewhere amidst the red haze of agony swamping his body, Cutter accepted the fact that he was going to die. His corpse would be found, but no one would know him. He would be buried in some pauper's grave, without even a stone to mark his passage.

In those last few moments of clarity, he remembered everything. Visions of Georgia raced across his mind. The image of his late father rose up, frowned sadly, and faded away. And then more recent images crowded into his brain.

San Francisco. The "family" he'd had for such a short time—Kevin Donnelly and his daughters. As the pain rolled over him like a strong river current, he only had a moment to wish he'd listened to Kevin and stayed on the Barbary Coast.

Then Cutter surrendered to the dark, and though the blows continued to rain down on him, the pain was muffled, almost as if it were happening to someone else. As he slipped further away from the agony, drawing back into the deepest corner of his mind, he heard something.

A full-throated shout of fury.

There was a scrambling of feet as his attackers tried to run.

Though he couldn't really see anything clearly, Cutter heard the distinctive sound of punches being thrown. Only, this time, they weren't directed at him.

He tried to raise his head to look around. But he couldn't move. Every breath sent a new slash of pain shooting through him.

It was a long while before he noticed that an eerie silence had dropped over the alleyway.

Too numb to move, he had no idea how long he lay there. Later, he wasn't sure how he'd been taken from the alley. He only knew that when he woke up, he was lying beneath a tree, with the sound of a river nearby. Every square inch of his body throbbed with a misery so intense, it was almost blinding.

Yet he was alive. Turning his head slightly, he saw his rescuer, who introduced himself as Ike Shore, bending over a small fire and smiling.

"Why?" Cutter managed to ask, and was pleased with himself for mastering the simple word.

The huge black man's grin faded. His incredibly wide, muscled shoulders lifted and fell in a shrug, and he said simply, "I seen too many men clubbed to death for nothin'. Won't watch it again."

Barely able to manage a nod, Cutter tried to smile nonetheless. "Thanks," he whispered through swollen lips.

"You gonna be all right, mister," Ike told him. "Jus' lie easy, now."

Cutter blinked suddenly and let the memories slide into the back of his mind. A soft smile curved his lips. So long ago.

"What're you smilin' at, partner?" Ike asked.

"Nothing, partner," Cutter answered with a grin.

"Partner, is it?" a feminine voice interrupted. "You've hardly been back a day, and now you have *two* partners?"

Cutter swiveled his head toward the front door. "Morning, Maggie."

"Maggie," Ike said, and nodded to her.

"Good morning, Ike," Maggie said, then turned to Cutter again. "You mean to say you've kept your share of the Garter? One saloon isn't good enough for you, then? How many will it take, Cutter? Two? Five? Ten?"

He stood up and walked partway to meet her.

"Oh, I think two should do it, Maggie." Lord, he thought, he'd forgotten that she managed to look good even in the morning.

Maggie frowned at him. "We need to talk about this, Cutter. It isn't going to work."

"What isn't?"

"I believe"—Ike cut in and stood up—"I'll head on back and start countin' somethin'."

Neither of the other two even glanced at him.

"We can't work together, Cutter."

"Sure, we can."

"No." Maggie shook her head and stared up at him.

Despite all his talk about maintaining strictly a business relationship, Cutter wanted nothing more than to pull her into his arms and kiss her until they were both screaming for air. But he wouldn't do it. Couldn't do it. Not until he'd finished what he'd set out to do so long before.

"Everything will work out, Maggie," he said, and his voice sounded strained to his own ears.

"Not this time, Cutter." She shook her head. "Things are different now. We can't be ... friends."

Friends? The idea was laughable and at the same time sad. They'd started out as friends, for one incredible night they'd been lovers—and now ... What was left for them? Certainly not friendship. That road had ended forever, the night he'd held her in his arms.

Hiding his own doubts behind the comfortable shield of light, teasing conversation, he said, "You're right. Things *are* different now. I'm your partner, Mag." She opened her mouth to speak, but he cut her off by saying something guaranteed to make her furious. "If you can't think of me as your friend, think of me as your boss."

"Boss!"

He winked at her burst of outrage. He preferred to have her shout at him—it was easier on both of them. Besides, he'd always enjoyed Maggie's temper. In a red haze of fury, she was magnificent! Prodding her even further, he added, "No? Then, Maggie, you go ahead and think of me any way you want. But however you think of me, we *will* work together on this."

"That's impossible!" she snapped.

"Oh,"—he lifted her chin with his index finger—"nothing is impossible."

"We are!"

"Now, Maggie, if I remember right"—he smiled, already anticipating her reaction to what he was about to say—"we already proved that we can 'work' together very well indeed."

Chapter 4

~~~~~~~

She wanted to slap him.

The glint in his blue eyes told her exactly what he was thinking—and she knew damn well it had nothing to do with *work*. Fine lines around his eyes deepened as a half smile tugged at one corner of his mouth.

He looked so . . . confident. So sure of himself. So sure of *her*. *And why shouldn't he have been?* she thought. Hadn't she already given herself to him once?

For a heart-stopping moment, Maggie remembered lying beside him in the dark. She recalled running the tip of her index finger over the curve of his lips, and she could almost feel the touch of his tongue as he drew her finger into his mouth.

She swallowed, sucked in a gulp of air, and forced herself to remember how that night had ended. And still it was hard to ignore the flutter of unwanted desire stirring in the pit of her stomach.

"So, Maggie," he said softly, "are you willing to talk now?"

She stepped back from his outstretched hand and dropped onto the chair Ike had recently vacated. Flicking a quick glance at him, Maggie nodded. "All right, Cutter. Talk."

He hesitated a long moment, then let his hand fall to his side. Slowly he took his seat again and leaned his forearms on the table.

"This doesn't have to be so damned difficult," he began.

"That's the *only* thing it can be."

"Maggie, we've known each other more than ten years—too long to be enemies."

"And far too well," she shot back, "to be friends."

Cutter reached up and rubbed the back of his neck. "Jesus, you've got a hard head."

"And a good memory, but that shouldn't be a surprise," she countered quickly, and folded her hands together on the tabletop. "God knows you spent enough time around us Donnellys to know that much, at least."

He snorted a laugh. "Yeah, but I guess I'd forgotten what it was like to do business with one of you."

"Next time, maybe you'll be more careful about picking a partner."

"There won't be a next time."

"How do I know that, Cutter?" Maggie laid both palms flat on the table as if to steady herself. "How do I know that you won't sell out your share of the Roses to two or three other fellows, then take off down the road?"

Even as she asked the question, Maggie knew the answer. Now that he'd finally succeeded in getting a piece of the Roses, Cutter would never part with it—despite the fact that it meant he would have to face her every day.

As if he were reading her mind, Cutter said, "I wouldn't do that to you, Maggie."

He shifted slightly, stretched out his right hand, and covered hers.

Maggie jerked her hand free and laid it in her lap. Glaring at the man opposite her, she said, "Don't pretend to be doing any of this for *me*, Cutter."

"I didn't say I was."

"You just said that very thing!"

"I didn't," he argued, his own temper climbing at last. "What I said was, I wouldn't do anything to deliberately hurt you."

Maggie froze. Her lip curled slightly as she stared at him stonily. "It's a bit late for a promise like *that*, don't ya think?"

"Jesus!" Cutter pushed both hands through his hair, gave his head a hard rub, then dropped both hands to the table. Leaning forward, he said thickly, "Let it go, Maggie. What happened, happened." He ducked his head, and his voice lowered until it was a husky whisper. "It was a mistake."

She flinched.

He pulled in a deep breath, met her eyes briefly before looking away again, and said in a rush, "I apologized, didn't I? Can't you just let it die?"

Let it die? If only it were that easy. She'd discovered in the past few months that dreams didn't die easily ... especially dreams that had been fostered and nurtured for years. The moment was difficult, but Maggie fought for control and won. Inside, her stomach was churning, twisting into knots, and a hard, aching lump formed in her throat, threatening to choke off her air.

He'd apologized.

Oh, yes, she told herself in a whirl of emotion, she remembered his apology very well indeed. The memory swam before her eyes, and she couldn't—wouldn't—try to stop it.

The office at the Four Roses was flooded with moonlight. A soft summer wind, scented with a hint of the sea, slipped into the room through the open window and caressed the two people lying together in the shadows.

Cutter moved, shifted himself off of her, and turned to sit on the edge of the couch. Elbows on his knees, his head cupped in his hands, he tried to steady his rapid breathing.

Her body was still throbbing from their lovemaking. Her hair fell loose around her naked shoulders, and she could feel the coarse fabric of the office sofa beneath her. Maggie looked at the man who had just introduced her to the incredible sensation of being physically loved and wanted to tell him how glorious she felt. But a wonderful languor had claimed her, and she reached out one hand and let her fingertips slide down Cutter's naked back.

His body jerked at her touch as if she'd burned him.

Surprised and hurt, Maggie let her hand drop.

Cutter glanced at her, sighed, and pushed himself to his feet. His naked flesh bathed in moonlight, he walked slowly across the room and stopped in front of the wide window.

From the street below came the usual raucous noises of crowds of people trying to outshout one another. Underlying the voices was an incredible mix-

ture of tunes from the pianos, hand organs, music boxes, and guitars being played on the street corners.

But Maggie paid them no mind. She was used to the discord, and was, in fact, more bothered by silence. Especially the uneasy silence that had fallen between her and the man she loved. She stared at the tall, quiet man, and when he turned his head to look at her, she held her breath.

Even from across the room, she saw the regret in his eyes. In an instant, she knew that her lovely little world was about to dissolve. Briefly she squeezed her own eyes shut, then opened them again and braced herself for what was to come.

"Jesus, Maggie" he said softly, and she had to strain to hear him. "I'm—"

"Please don't say you're sorry," Maggie interrupted.

"That's all I can say."

"No." She licked suddenly dry lips. Desperate to hang on to the quickly receding afterglow of loving him, she said, "You could tell me you love me."

"No," he answered with a slow shake of his head. "I can't."

"I see." The last, lingering spark in her body flickered out, and she felt suddenly cold.

"I don't think you do."

She laughed—a short, harsh laugh that scraped against her throat. Jerkily Maggie reached down for the dress she'd so willingly pulled off only moments before. With a trembling hand, she grabbed the night-blue silk and clasped it against her chest in a belated attempt to shield her nudity.

On a shaky breath, she said, "I see more than enough, Cutter."

In fact, she saw very clearly that she had just become one of those sad women with an "unsavory"

*past. Her lips twisted in an effort to hold in the tears.
She hadn't believed it would happen to her. She had
waited so long—been so sure . . .*

*"Maggie." He took a step toward her, but she held
up one hand to stop him.*

*"Don't say anything else. Please." Pushing her
hair out of her face with one hand, she added softly,
"Leave, Cutter. Just leave. Now."*

*He looked as if he wanted to say more. But Maggie
couldn't listen to him. She'd already heard more than
she wished to. It was bad enough, knowing that she'd
just given herself to a man who had admitted he
didn't love her. Lord alone knew what else he might
say if given the chance.*

*She listened to his footsteps as he crossed the floor.
From the corner of her eye, she watched him pull on
his trousers and boots, then shove his arms through
the sleeves of his shirt. At least, her mind whispered
sympathetically, no one else would know what had
happened. And if she tried very hard . . . maybe she
could forget.*

*When he quickly slipped from the room and closed
the door behind him, Maggie finally allowed the tears
to come.*

"Maggie?"

Cutter's voice—sharp, insistent—sliced through
the pattern of her memories and drew Maggie
back to the present with a jerk.

"Dammit, Maggie," he said in a strangled
tone. "How many times do I have to apologize
for that night?"

"You've already done more than enough of
that, Cutter." She inhaled deeply, willing her
memories into the farthest corner of her brain.
Staring straight into his too-blue eyes, she said,

"Maybe it's you, not me, who won't let the past die."

Cutter saw her eyes harden and didn't much care for knowing that he was the cause. Hell, maybe she was right. Maybe it *was* him. Maybe he'd known all along that by avoiding her for the past several months, he'd kept that night alive. If he'd forced his way into her office and demanded that she listen to him, they could have resolved all of this long before.

But what could he have told her?

Not the truth. Hell, she probably wouldn't have believed him anyway. And even if she had, she wouldn't have understood. How could she?

How could she possibly understand what it was like to know that you're just not good enough, for anything or anybody?

Cutter grumbled under his breath. It was a waste of time thinking about that, he told himself. It was too late now anyway. She'd been hurt too much and had too much time to dwell on it. Whatever might have been between them was lost forever, and he knew he might as well make up his mind to face it.

She had.

"All right," Cutter finally said. "Maybe I'm as much to blame as you." She opened her mouth to argue, and he quickly added, "Maybe more. But that's done and gone now. You and I have got to find a way to work together on this, Maggie, because I'm not going away."

"That's why I'm here," she answered. Her chin lifted slightly. "Talk, Cutter. Tell me what you've got planned for the Four Roses, and I'll tell you why it won't work."

A reluctant smile curved one side of his mouth. Trust Maggie to find a way to offer a compromise and snatch it back, all in the same breath.

One sharp stab of regret for chances missed sliced through him. If he hadn't been an ass ... If he hadn't betrayed her—and her father ... If he hadn't hurt her ...

Too many ifs. Too many regrets. And too damn late to do anything about them now.

"Cutter?"

He took a breath and pushed the past away. Better to concentrate on the here and now. There was no easy way to tell her his idea, so Cutter simply blurted it out.

"I want to combine the Roses and the Garter."

"What?" She stared at him as if he'd just sprouted another head. "You can't be serious!"

"Dead serious."

"Combine the saloons?"

"You heard me." He waved at the common wall between the two saloons. "We'll knock that wall out, redecorate both places, and have us the best damn saloon on the Coast in no time."

She crossed her arms in front of her chest, leaned back in the chair, and pointed out, "You forget, Cutter. I already have the best saloon on the Coast."

He shook his head. "*We* have."

"Fine," she said through gritted teeth. "We."

Cutter nodded, acknowledging her concession, then said firmly, "It can be better."

"Why should it be?"

"You're against a bigger profit?" Cutter clucked his tongue at her. "What would Kevin say?"

"Blast Da!" Maggie said, unfolding her arms and leaning toward him. "And blast you, too, while we're at it. You know damn well that the Roses is the most profitable place around here. That's why you've been after it ever since you were eighteen years old."

"Not the only reason."

"The *only* reason."

Cutter's jaw clenched. Fine. If that was what she wanted to believe, then so be it. But the truth of the matter was that ever since the day Kevin Donnelly had found him by the docks and brought him home for supper, Cutter had wanted it all. The saloon, the family ... the *belonging*.

And there he was, more than ten years later, no closer to his dream than he'd been on that long-ago day. No, he reminded himself silently, that wasn't quite so. At least he'd finally reached one of his goals. He had a share in the Four Roses.

Of course, claiming a share in the saloon meant severing any chances he might have had to find his way back to Maggie. But maybe he simply wasn't destined to have a woman and a home of his own. Maybe he'd just have to settle for justice.

He hoped there would be some kind of peace in that.

"Forget my reasons, then," he said and tipped his chair back onto its rear legs. Rocking slowly, Cutter went on, "The point is, we're partners, and I have big plans for the place."

"Partners have to agree on changes."

"Not necessarily."

"Then," Maggie argued, "how do we decide which of us gets his—or *her*—way?"

"Hmm ..." Cutter rubbed his jaw with one hand and tried to think of something.

Maggie tilted her head to one side and looked at him through narrowed eyes. "I've seen that look before, Cutter."

"What look?"

"That one." She drummed her fingertips on the tabletop. "That's the same look you were wearing the day you told Da we should wall off a section of the saloon so ladies would feel free to come in and gamble."

"It was a good idea," he said in a feeble attempt to defend himself.

"Except that we lost money when not one 'lady' showed up to take advantage of the idea."

"At least your father was willing to try."

Her fingers stilled. "I've never been afraid to try something, Cutter. *You* should know that, better than anyone."

The wistful expression on her face dug at him. He did know that. Whatever else had gone on between them, Maggie Donnelly had always been the one to encourage his plans and schemes. She'd urged him on in his wild notions and had helped make some of them work. More than once over the years, she'd gone to Kevin herself to plead Cutter's case, and Maggie almost never took no for an answer.

Lord, how he'd missed her these last few months.

"That was one idea that will never work, Cutter."

He blinked away his idle thoughts and joined

in the argument. At least she was talking to him. "I still say that ladies will one day be gambling alongside their men."

Maggie shook her head, and her diamond earrings winked at him in the light. "Women don't like gambling. They don't have the patience or the head for it."

His eyebrows shot straight up into his hairline. "You like it fine. And as far as ladies having 'the head' for the game, the only gambler I know who can best you in a card game is me."

"I was born and raised to it, Cutter. That's different." She smiled and added, "And as for the other, I'll remind you, I've beat you as many times as I've lost to you."

It was the first genuine smile he'd had from her in months, and Cutter paused a moment to enjoy the warmth of her. He felt as though he'd been living in darkness and had finally stumbled out of his cave into the sunlight.

That he'd been shut inside that cave by his own hand had nothing to do with anything.

"So," Maggie went on, "if you think that I'll just step aside quietly and let you take over . . . you're sadly mistaken."

"I've never known you to do a damn thing quietly, Maggie." Pride echoed in his voice. He couldn't disguise it, and didn't try.

The curve of her lips straightened into a thin line. Obviously, she wasn't interested in receiving compliments from him.

"So how do we come to a decision, then, *Mr.* Cutter?"

He thought for another moment, then smiled as the answer came to him. It was so simple, he couldn't imagine why it hadn't occurred to him before.

"What?" she asked warily, a gleam of suspicion in her eyes.

Cutter ignored her, straightened his chair, then stood and walked to the bar. The Golden Garter wasn't as fancy as the Roses. But compared to the rest of the Coast, it was downright elegant.

Wagon-wheel chandeliers, with an oil lamp fastened at the end of each spoke, hung from the ceiling. Several paintings of reclining nude women decorated the walls, and shining brass spittoons seemed to be everywhere. The floor was pine, but it was clean and polished. The long, hand-carved cherry-wood bar was old and carried more than its share of cigar burns and spur nicks. And hanging behind the bar was a silvered mirror that had long since passed its glory days.

Nevertheless, the Garter was comfortable and made a good profit from trail hands in town on business or the sailors from ships in port. At the Garter, customers could drink themselves into a stupor and not worry about waking up aboard a China-bound vessel.

Cutter walked around behind the bar and ducked down to yank open a bottom drawer.

"What're you up to, Cutter?"

"Have you ever noticed, Mary Margaret Donnelly," he said as he straightened up slightly to toss her a quick glance, "that your Irish brogue thickens whenever you're upset or bothered . . . or worried?"

She frowned. "It doesn't."

"Aye," he mimicked gently, "it does."

"You're avoiding my question, Cutter."

"Not at all." His southern drawl colored his interpretation of her Irish-tinged speech.

She crossed her arms over her chest and waited. Silently.

"I'm only looking for the easy solution, Maggie." Slowly rising, he held up a new deck of cards. "We'll cut for it."

"Cut for it?"

"Yeah," he said as he walked back to the table. "What better way for two gamblers to decide something?" He plopped down into the chair and handed her the unopened deck. "Look them over. The seal hasn't been broken."

She turned the deck in her hand. "All right."

"Good. Then you can't claim later that I cheated."

"Cheated?" Maggie batted her eyelashes. "You?"

His lips quirked slightly. "I say we draw cards to decide. High card wins." Cutter reached for the cards, broke the seal, and slipped the deck into his practiced hands. Deftly he removed the two jokers and set them aside. As he shuffled expertly, he felt himself relax. Keeping his eyes on the rapidly moving cards, he kept talking. "If I win, we knock out that wall and make the changes I want."

"When *I* win," Maggie said firmly, "things stay as they are."

"If."

Two pale copper eyebrows lifted, and a hesitant smile hovered around her lips. "If."

A familiar curl of expectation began to spiral through Cutter. This feeling he was comfortable with. This he *knew*. Staking everything on a chance. Gambling that your luck would hold longer than your opponent's. He flicked a quick glance at Maggie and saw the same sense of eagerness on her features.

Eyes gleaming, she sat up straighter in her chair and gave all her attention to the deck in his hands. Her breathing was a bit more rapid now, and Cutter's gaze slipped to the bodice of her high-necked gown. His eyes narrowed slightly as he let himself recall the image of her breasts in his hands. He remembered the satisfying feel of cupping her flesh in his palms and drawing, first one erect nipple, and then the other, into his mouth. He remembered clearly how she had arched into him and moaned softly from the back of her throat.

Cutter's own throat closed, and the muscles in his abdomen clenched painfully as he let himself remember the incredible rightness he'd experienced when he'd slid his body into hers.

It had been the first time in years that he'd truly felt as though he'd come home.

Abruptly his concentration slipped, and several of the cards fell from his grasp onto the tabletop.

"Nervous, Cutter?" she asked, leaning her elbows on the table.

"Anxious, Maggie," he answered, and was surprised to find that his voice worked. Quickly he recovered the fallen cards and shuffled them back into the deck.

He lowered his gaze to the task at hand and told himself to forget those hours spent with Maggie.

In seconds the deck was thoroughly shuffled and Cutter set the cards facedown on the table.

Looking up at Maggie, he asked, "Shall we cut them or spread 'em out?"

"Fan them," she said, and leaned in even closer, her gaze locked on the cards and his hands.

"Fair enough." One swift, sure motion, and Cutter had the deck swirled out in a half circle, a corner of each card showing. He glanced up at her and challenged, "You first."

Her teeth bit into her bottom lip as she studied the cards. As if she could see through the flag-decorated backs to the pips on the other side, Maggie looked at each individual card. Slowly she reached out and moved her hand over the semicircle, just inches above the playing cards.

Cutter swallowed a smile. Maggie wasn't one to hurry a decision.

He understood that. This was yet another thing they shared. The love of the game. Matching wits against other players. Tempting fate. Trusting luck.

Slowly she lowered her index finger, and with the tip of her nail dragged one card free of its companions and slid it, facedown, to her side of the table.

"Aren't you going to look?" he asked.

"We'll turn them together."

"Ah." Cutter grinned. "You seem to be getting the feel for this partnership thing, Maggie."

"Just draw, Cutter."

"Anything you say, madam." Without hesitating an instant, Cutter closed his eyes, stretched out one hand and dropped it onto the circle of cards. Blindly, his fingers separated one from the deck and dragged it back to him. Then he opened his eyes and looked at the woman opposite him.

Her green eyes were lit with excitement. "Go ahead."

Cutter nodded, picked up his cards, and turned it over. "Ten of diamonds."

Maggie's teeth began to worry her bottom lip again. He knew what she was thinking. A ten was right in the middle. There was a better-than-even chance that she'd picked a lower card. Her finger tapped the back of her card for a moment: then she turned it quickly.

Three of clubs.

He smiled. "I can have the workmen start tomorrow," Cutter told her as he gathered up the deck.

Maggie inhaled deeply, held it, then blew it out again. Standing, she looked down at her partner and said, "All right, Cutter, you win this one. We join the saloons. But I warn you . . ."

He looked up at her and only just managed to keep himself from openly admiring her.

"I'll not give you an inch more than you've won here today."

"Maggie," he said as he stood up, "I look forward to the challenge." Then, acting on impulse, Cutter snatched her right hand and brought it to his lips. He only had time to give her flesh the lightest of kisses before she pulled it back as if she'd been burned.

"We open at three," she told him unnecessarily.

"I'll be there."

Maggie nodded, turned around, and left him alone.

* * *

"Where are you going?"

David Harper stopped, looked over his shoulder at his gray-haired father standing at the foot of the stairs, and shrugged. "Out."

"Back to that den of sin?"

The younger man reached out, snatched his overcoat off the hall tree, and pushed his arms through the sleeves. "Just as fast as I can," he agreed pleasantly.

His father sneered. "You're already drunk."

"Almost. Not quite." David gave him a half smile and added, "As some famous fellow once said, 'I have just begun to drink.' " He frowned, shook his head, and mumbled, "Or was that 'fight'? No matter."

"You disgust me."

"So you keep telling me."

Judge Samuel Harper crossed the marble-tiled foyer in a few quick strides, his bedroom slippers slapping with each step. "I forbid you to go back to that . . . place."

Amazing. David almost laughed aloud. The old man was damned amazing. "It's long past the time when you can forbid me anything, Father."

"A bit late to go searching for a backbone, don't you think?"

David flushed. "Better late than never."

"You're still my son," the old man reminded him.

"And as such, I should feel perfectly at home at the Four Roses." David watched his barb hit its mark. His sire's face froze over. Two black eyes, shining like pieces of wet coal, were the only signs of life.

"I do not consort with the dregs of society!"

"No," David said, and silently congratulated himself on keeping his voice remarkably calm, "the thieves and whores you call friends reside in a much finer neighborhood. I'll grant you."

Color flooded Judge Harper's features.

Idly David noticed the pulse beat in the old man's temple. One of these days, he thought, the judge is going to show one temper too many and keel over right in the middle of his precious mansion.

"How dare you sit in judgment on me?" The old man leaned in close and tipped his head back to stare up into the reddened eyes of his only son. "You, with your drinking and whoring!"

At that moment David was grateful he'd taken the trouble to have a double brandy before leaving his room. If it were not for the warm, comfortable glow drifting through him, he might have been tempted to shout the old bastard down. As it was, all he could think of was to escape to his regular table at the Roses.

Amid the noise and distractions, with the aid of a never-ceasing flow of liquor, he could forget for a while what a miserable disappointment he was as a son. Of course, in his saner moments, he liked to think that as a father, the old bastard standing next to him hadn't done so well, either.

"As you say, Father." David bowed unsteadily and curved his lips into a smile that never touched his eyes. "I'm a busy man. My companions await me, and I should hate to be tardy."

David shrugged more deeply into his coat, grabbed the doorknob, and turned it. The cold night air swept in, ruffling the judge's hair into an ill-fitting halo.

"I'll disown you," the judge warned. "I'll throw you out on your useless ass and let you starve."

David clucked his tongue at the man. "Such language. And from a judge, no less!"

The old man inhaled sharply. Before he could say anything else, though, David went on.

"You won't throw me out, *Father*, and you know it. What would your fine friends think if they saw the son of the illustrious Judge Harper living penniless on the streets outside this magnificent house?"

The judge ground his teeth together.

"We can't have anyone else seeing the family's dirty laundry, now, can we?"

Really, it was astonishing just how purple a person's face could become. David stared at the man who'd made his life a miserable, futile quest for perfection, and felt nothing. Not even satisfaction for a well-aimed thrust and parry.

When had he stopped caring? At ten? Fifteen? Surely by the age of twenty? He shook his head slightly. What did it matter, anyway? The point was, he'd long ago resigned himself to his life's work. Living up to the low expectations his father had of him.

It was surprising how easy that had become.

"Nothing more to say, Father?"

The old man remained furiously silent.

"No?" David pulled up the collar of his coat around his neck and gave his father another wink and a smile. "Then I'll be off. Don't want my friends to worry, do we?"

He was halfway down the steps, headed for the waiting carriage, when his father slammed the front door shut, slicing off the wedge of lamplight that had pointed the way to freedom. David stopped suddenly. His head dropped back on his neck, and he stared up at the star-sprinkled sky. Unexpectedly, he felt a burning sensation in his eyes.

A muffled snort escaped him at his own foolishness. Tears? At this late date?

He blinked the unwelcome moisture away and glanced at his driver, standing beside an open door. After a moment, shoulders drooping just a bit, he continued down the steps, climbed into the carriage, and slumped back against the leather seat. Deliberately he closed his eyes.

He didn't open them again until the horses had stopped at the Four Roses.

Chapter 5

If he touched that female one more time, Maggie would scream.

From across the crowded saloon, almost as if he had heard her thoughts, Cutter turned away from the elegantly dressed woman with whom he'd been speaking and leaned across the bar top to talk to Jake. The society woman Cutter had just dismissed began to thread her way through the crowd to a table near the stage, her escort's hand on the small of her back.

Maggie relaxed and slowly uncurled her fingers from the tight fists she'd been hiding in the folds of her skirt for the past several minutes. Being around Cutter was harder than she'd ever thought it would be.

Just watching him flirt with and smile at that woman had been torturous. Every time he leaned in close, or smiled, or laid a hand on the woman's forearm, Maggie fumed.

It didn't matter that the saloon was packed with people. It didn't matter that Cutter was no doubt using his charm to ensure them of yet another steady customer. All that mattered was that Maggie wasn't the woman he was charming.

In fact, Maggie was the woman he was ignoring. He hadn't even spoken to her since that morning, when they'd played their short but decisive game of cards.

That should have pleased her. Oddly enough, it didn't. Actually, his silence rankled her. It made her feel as though she were locked in a room with a wildcat. The animal might ignore her for a while ... but sooner or later, she would be dinner.

It wasn't as if Cutter were unaware of her. She'd felt his gaze on her several times in the past few hours. But each time she had turned to meet his stare, he had looked away. His features were unreadable. Even to her. And she used to pride herself on knowing what he was thinking.

Maggie had always thought of them as the perfect match. From the first night her father had brought home an underfed, wary young man known only as Cutter, Maggie had been entranced.

Of course, she'd only been ten years old to Cutter's eighteen. And she seemed to recall thinking at the time that Cutter vaguely resembled the storybook prince she'd been reading about.

Kevin had taken the young man under his wing and taught him the business of running a successful saloon. Cutter had lapped up the information and the attention like a starving kitten being offered a saucer of warm milk. The young man had become confident, self-assured.

And with each passing day, Maggie had loved him more.

Cutter had greedily accepted her love, and he'd returned it as an indulgent older brother would. He became one of them. A Donnelly in all but name, he shared the work and worry of the Four Roses with Kevin and delighted in teasing his "sisters."

But when Maggie was twelve, Cutter took off, determined to make his own way. Kevin's disappointment hadn't dissuaded him. Neither had the tears of a heartbroken little girl. With a hug and a brotherly pat on the head, Cutter had disappeared from Maggie's life, leaving behind only his promise that he would return. Someday.

Maggie had held on to that promise and told herself nightly that when he came back, she would make him stay until she was old enough to marry him.

It was ten long years before he'd returned to San Francisco.

At twenty-two, Maggie had become the beauty her father had always predicted she would be. And despite a few proposals of marriage and a few less-decent proposals, Maggie had waited. For Cutter. She'd delighted in watching the amazement on Cutter's features when he first saw her. Briefly she'd thought that her dreams would all come true, just as she had planned. But her happiness was short-lived.

Somehow she'd expected that when she was fully grown, Cutter would see that they belonged together. Instead he avoided her. Though always polite, he somehow managed never to be alone with her . . . until one night three years later, when her hopes and plans finally came to life, only to die the same night.

"Maggie?"

She shook herself, blinked, and turned to look at Seamus Dunn. "What is it?"

The ruddy-faced Irishman's brow burrowed. "Are you all right?"

"I'm fine, Seamus." Really, sometimes the saloon guard took his responsibilities a bit too seriously. "What is it?"

"I've a message from himself." He jerked his head toward the bar. "Cutter."

Despite her best intentions, Maggie's heart fluttered. Mentally cursing herself for not being smart enough to learn when enough was enough, she asked abruptly, "What's he want, then?"

"He says to keep your eye on Jake and watch the show."

"What?" Her gaze shot to Cutter, standing at the end of the bar. The gambler raised his drink in a salute and grinned.

Her ridiculous heart skittered.

"That's what he said." Seamus shrugged as if to say that he couldn't make heads or tails of it either; but then, no one paid him to think.

"Fine. Thank you." She lifted the hem of her deep-peach-colored gown, intending to walk down the stairs, cross the floor, and ask Cutter just what he was up to. By heaven, he might have won the bet about combining the saloons, but that was *all* he'd won. She wasn't going to stand by and let him take complete control of her business!

But before she could take another step, the band played a loud chord and the conductor called for silence.

Maggie frowned at Cutter, then turned her head slightly to watch the man with the baton.

She had a feeling she wasn't going to like what was about to happen.

"Ladies and gentlemen," the scrawny man in an elegant black suit called out in a surprisingly strong voice, "our waiters are moving among you, lowering the lights."

Maggie noted movement from the corner of her eye and saw that, indeed, several of the waiters were hurrying through the crowd with long-handled brass candlesnuffers. At every crystal chandelier, each of them stopped and put out half the candles.

In a few short minutes, the saloon was only half as bright as it usually was.

What the devil? she asked herself, and squinted into the gloom, searching for Cutter's face. But between the milling throngs, the lowered lights, and the blue haze of cigar smoke, she could hardly make out the features of those customers closest to her.

Something told her, though, that Cutter was still smiling. Fuming silently, she could only wait to see what he was up to.

She heard the questioning voices as people wondered aloud about was going on. The murmur grew and intensified until the band once more was forced to strike a loud note for attention.

The conductor spoke into the sudden stillness.

"If you'll all turn around to face the bar for a moment, we have a treat for you."

The bar? A treat?

"Our world-famous mixologist, Jake." He paused for effect.

The bartender took a bow.

"Ladies and gentlemen," the conductor went on. "This evening Jake will amaze and delight you with the creation of"—he paused, and the drummer gave him a roll of thunder—"the *Blue Blazer!*"

"Dammit!" she muttered, and her soft voice was swallowed by the crowd.

Whispered speculation swept through the crowd as the customers turned to face the bar. A sprinkling of applause came from the few people who recognized the name of the famous concoction about to be poured.

Maggie gritted her teeth. *She* didn't feel like applauding. On the contrary, if she'd thought she had half a chance of reaching the bar before Jake began his little performance, she would have stopped him. But she knew she'd never make it through the mob in time. And she certainly wasn't going to shout her disapproval from across the room.

All she could do was hope that all went well. Once it was over, then she would have a few things to say to Cutter. And Jake. For God's sake, the bartender knew damn well that Maggie didn't want him pouring that drink. They'd talked about it often enough.

Jake considered himself an artist at the craft of mixing drinks. And it was true that the man's flair for showmanship and his abilities drew in quite a number of customers. Other saloon owners were always trying to steal the talented bartender from the Roses. Not too long ago, in fact, Cutter had been the worst offender in that department.

But Jake was happy at the Roses. Mostly. The only complaint he had was the fact that Maggie refused to let him pour his most impressive drink. The Blue Blazer.

Now it seemed that Cutter had taken over there as well as everywhere else.

Anticipation filled the air with its own scent and taste. All around her, people waited in the half darkness, squinting into the dim light. The tang of salt air sweeping through the open doors and windows blended with the distinct odor of eager expectation and made for a heady atmosphere.

In the back of her mind, Maggie heard the band's drummer continue with the low, rolling thunder that seemed to hypnotize everyone in the room. As the rhythmic pounding grew louder, it swept all other sound from its path.

The excitement, the speculation, began to work their magic on Maggie, despite her anger at Jake and Cutter. The room was alive. Eager. Breathless.

Maggie felt the rumble of the drums start at the soles of her feet. In inches, the pounding throb moved up her calves, along her thighs, and settled in her center, where it became a damp, quivering ache. Her heart began to beat in time with the insistent pulsing in her veins.

From across the room, she felt something else. Something she recognized immediately. Cutter's gaze touched her as surely as if he'd reached out a hand and grabbed her.

Instinctively Maggie turned slightly to face the shadowy corner where she'd spied him last. A shudder of sensation coursed through her, and her breathing became staggered. Suddenly grateful for the dim lighting, Maggie knew that if she'd been able to see his eyes, she would have been lost. She would have given herself up gladly, *eagerly*, to the heat swamping her.

Even knowing what that surrender had already cost her.

Her knees trembled, and she quickly grabbed the cool, polished surface of the banister beside her. Curling her fingers around the wood, she drew one agonizing breath after another into her lungs and prayed fervently for the strength to turn away.

How had this happened to her? What had become of her firm resolve? But, most important, how could Cutter turn her insides to fire from across the room?

Seconds crawled by. With a tremendous effort of will, Maggie slowly turned her head until she was staring blankly at the bar. Only then did she feel the connection between her and Cutter end; abruptly, suddenly, as if a cord linking the two of them had been sliced apart.

She swallowed heavily and willed life back into her limbs. Unsteadily she took a step, and then another, until she was at the foot of the staircase.

Behind the bar, she could see Jake's shadowy form. Despite the dimness of the room, the man moved confidently, expertly, as he lined up the various bottles and glasses he would need for his "performance."

The drums were louder now, faster. The people in the room were leaning forward, anxiously waiting.

Jake lifted two sterling-silver mugs, one in each hand, and held them high over his head. The shining silver caught what little light there was in the room and sparkled. After a long moment, the bartender set the mugs on the bar top, splashed liquid into the first cup, then reached behind him for a teakettle.

Maggie held her breath. Her anger could come later. Just then she had to concentrate on hoping everything would go as it should.

She knew what came next. Jake would pour boiling water into the ninety-proof Irish whiskey already in the mug, then set the mixture on fire. As she watched, he did just that, and a small flame flared into life in the darkness.

Biting down on her lip, Maggie clenched her fingers tightly around the newel-post knob and waited for him to finish.

As the people around her sighed in anticipation, Jake lifted the flaming mug high, then tipped it, spilling the contents into the mug he held waiting below.

Appreciative sighs erupted from the crowd as a stream of liquid fire dazzled the darkness. It *was* a wondrous sight, Maggie admitted silently. And a dangerous one. One slip, one miscalculation, and the bartender could have been horribly burned—not to mention the fact that the eager flames could easily have spread and consumed the Four Roses.

Oblivious to Maggie's worries, Jake poured the flame from one mug to the other, over and over, until most of the liquor was burned off. Then he set the mugs down, blew out the last remaining flicker of fire, and bowed to the thunderous applause that followed.

Maggie pulled in a deep breath and muttered a prayer of thanks to whichever saints had been keeping watch.

Instantly the waiters surged through the

crowd, relighting the chandeliers. As the room gradually grew brighter, Maggie turned her head again, deliberately seeking out Cutter. When she spied him, he had the audacity to lift his own glass in salute and nod to her.

She gave him a stiff nod in return, but as she looked across the room, directly into his eyes, she felt a fire quicken in her blood that burned every bit as brightly as the Blue Blazer had done moments before.

Once again her body was humming with a need she remembered all too clearly—a need she could do nothing to fulfill.

As if he could read her mind, Cutter's smile faded, and an undeniable hunger slashed across his features. But it was gone as quickly as the fire in Jake's drink. Immediately Cutter turned from her, picked up a deck of cards, and began to deal a poker hand to the four other men at his table.

Trembling, Maggie looked away and walked toward the bar. As she came closer, Jake had the good grace to look abashed. But instead of speaking with him, she left the man to receive customers' compliments and walked straight through to the kitchen.

She couldn't talk to him just then. Couldn't talk to anyone. Her anger had been devoured by the more pervasive hunger that still held her in its grip. Before she could trust herself to speak to anybody, she *had* to get herself under control.

In the huge kitchen, she marched stiffly past the men and women preparing the food provided free to their customers. She didn't notice the odd looks sent her way; she was much too focused on reaching her goal—solitude. Maggie opened the wide door on the far wall and almost ran down the narrow flight of stairs to the cool, dark cellar.

She didn't stop until she was hidden from sight between the giant casks of beer and wine. Out of habit more than a desire for light, she reached out to a nearby shelf, grabbed one of the candles stored there, and snatched up a stick match. The candle flame was a pitifully small light in the cavernous darkness, but it was all she wanted . . . all she needed.

Standing in the tiny circle of yellow light, Maggie inhaled deeply, drawing the familiar scent of wet wood and beer deep into her lungs. Then she bent her head against the damp side of an oak cask and squeezed her eyes shut.

No tears came. She hadn't expected any. She'd cried herself dry nearly a year ago. All that was left now was the humiliating fact that even though Cutter had thrown her aside immediately after taking her innocence, she still wanted him.

And worse yet . . . she still loved him.

Ike stood in the half-finished archway joining the two saloons and stared across the busy room. Something more was going on than Cutter was willing to talk about. That something was making both Cutter and Maggie miserable.

He watched as Maggie turned and hurried toward the kitchen. Immediately his gaze shifted to Cutter. Ike frowned. The damn fool. Even from across the room, Ike could see the shuttered look on his friend's features.

Ike took a long, thin cigar from his inside pocket and bit off the end. Pulling out a stick match, he moved to strike it on the wall, then stopped himself. Shaking his head, he struck the match instead on the sole of his shoe. This fixing up of the saloons was hard to get used to. But he would manage. He wanted to get ahead as much as, and maybe more than, the next man.

As he lit the cigar, Ike looked through the dancing plume of smoke at Cutter. Now, Cutter, he told himself, was a man who *needed* to win. But maybe it was time somebody told him about what was worth winning.

"I call and raise you fifty."

"Hmm?" Cutter asked, and looked at the young farmer on his right.

"I said," the farmer called Jesse replied a bit too testily for Cutter's taste, "I raise you fifty dollars. Are you in or out?"

Cutter's eyebrows arched dangerously. Really, he was becoming rather tired of having to deal with the obnoxious kid, no matter how heavy the purse he brought to the table. And the longer he played with the younger man, the more Cutter was inclined to believe that this was no farm boy.

The blond, cherubic-looking youth's hands were much too smooth and unscarred to have been digging in the earth for a living. In fact, Cutter was willing to wager that the only dirt that had ever accumulated under the young man's nails had been gathered there by sweeping up ill-gotten winnings from card games.

The boy was a sharp, or Cutter would eat his favorite hat.

That he hadn't noticed until that moment was an embarrassment to his professionalism. Of course, he reminded himself, his mind hadn't been on the game from the start.

He'd expected Maggie to be angry. Hell, he'd been preparing all afternoon just what he'd say to her when she came at him after Jake's performance.

What he hadn't expected was to see that look of open desire on her features.

Just recalling it made his body hard again in response. At the time, he'd had to grab a deck of cards and throw himself into a game, for the simple reason that his body wasn't *decent* enough to allow him to walk across the room and go to her.

He shifted uncomfortably in his chair as his rock-hard flesh taunted him. All dressed up and nowhere to go, he thought with a dismal, silent chuckle. Jesus, was this what his life would be like? Allowed to look at her, remember the feel and taste of her—and not be permitted to touch her?

Yes, a soundless voice whispered in his head. That was exactly what his life had come to. And whose fault was it?

His own.

That fact hardly made the rest more palatable.

"C'mon, mister," Jesse chided. "We're waitin'."

"I do beg your pardon," Cutter said quietly, and folded his cards together. He reached down to his stack of chips, fingered them for a long, thoughtful moment, then tossed his cards facedown on the table. "I fold."

"No stomach for the game, Cutter?" a man on his right asked.

"Not tonight."

"Well," David Harper muttered thickly, "I'm in too deep to back out now. Here's my fifty." He tossed a handful of chips to the center of the table.

Jesse's eyes glittered.

The last man at the table glanced from Cutter to David to the man on Cutter's right to Jesse before laying his cards down. "Too rich for me."

"Me too," the last man said on a sigh.

"Just you and me, boy," David pointed out unneccessarily, and Cutter wondered idly how much young Harper had already drunk.

Jesse smiled innocently, picked up the last of his chips, and set them down carefully on the spilled pile of poker tokens. "Let's just finish this up, then, huh? I bet all I got left. How 'bout you?"

David frowned, and Cutter knew that the man wasn't nearly as drunk as he usually was. At least he had *some* sense left. Maybe this night would be different. Maybe this time the judge's boy wouldn't bet everything he had. Harper studied his hand, glanced at the pile of chips, then turned his thoughtful gaze to Jesse.

Long moments passed. Cutter's gaze shifted from David Harper to Jesse, whom he now knew to be a card sharp. His practiced eyes watched the younger man keenly, looking for some slip, something that he could call him on.

"All right," David finally agreed, and pushed his remaining chips into the pile. "I'm in."

Cutter frowned.

Jesse smiled, dipped his hands slightly, and unknowingly gave Cutter the ammunition he needed. Content now to wait out the end of the farce, Cutter leaned back in his chair.

David laid his hand down and awkwardly spread the cards. "Full house. Jacks over threes."

Jesse gave David an innocent, wide-eyed grin and triumphantly set down his own cards. "Sorry, mister. Guess it's just my lucky night. Four kings."

David grimaced in disgust as the other man began to drag his winnings toward him.

Cutter moved so fast, his chair legs scraped against the floor. Reaching out one hand, he grabbed Jesse's right wrist and held it trapped against the tabletop.

"Hey," Jesse complained uneasily. "What's this?"

"This," Cutter explained with a deadly smile, "as you so elegantly phrased it, is the end of your game at the Roses."

"What d'ya mean?" Jesse shouted, still somehow maintaining his air of innocence.

Cutter shook his head slowly. "You're very good, you know. Oh, not perfect, by any means. And I'd like to think that, had I been concentrating properly, I would have spotted it earlier."

"Spotted what?" the man on Cutter's right asked. "Say, what the devil's goin' on here, Cutter?"

"Only this." Cutter held his captive's wrist firmly down and with his other hand pushed up the man's coat sleeve. A complicated-looking wrist strap encircled Jesse's forearm, and held securely by wires was a two of hearts.

"One of your original cards?" he asked, indicating the red two.

"Hey!"

"A cheat!"

"Damned thief!"

Jesse looked decidedly uncomfortable at that moment, Cutter thought, and found himself enjoying the other man's distress.

"Well?" Cutter demanded. "Is that the real card you were dealt?"

The cheat nodded.

"David," Cutter said easily, as he released the sharp, "the money's yours."

"Now, see here, Cutter," one of the other players objected. "Some of that's mine and Joe's money, too, y'know."

"True." Cutter nodded, his eyes still locked on the sharp. "And a good deal of it is mine. But you, Joe, and I all folded. We gave up the claim to the money before the cheat was discovered. Harper's the only one of us who stayed in."

David gave him a lopsided smile and began to gather his winnings. "Thanks, Cutter."

"And what happens to me?" the cheater asked.

"Ought to horsewhip him," one of the men suggested.

"Tar and feathers suits me," Joe offered.

The cheater swallowed heavily as he glanced from one unfriendly face to the next.

Cutter silenced them all. "I think not."

"You gonna turn me over to the law?"

"No." Cutter stared thoughtfully at the younger man. If he was right, he knew exactly who was behind this clumsy attempt to make the Roses look bad.

Digger.

Digger Wicks had hated Cutter for years. Knowing that Cutter was now a full partner in the biggest, most successful saloon on the Coast was probably driving the man wild. But he must have been truly desperate if he thought his half-baked plan would work.

Not even the most foolish of the Roses' customers would have believed that Cutter would stand for cheating. Why, if word of something like that had gotten around town, he'd have been out of business in a month.

Which, he thought with an inward smile, probably explained why Digger was always on the brink of bankruptcy. He cheated his customers and his saloon was little more than a shack on the waterfront.

"Then what?"

Surprising how quickly the innocence of the boy's expression had faded to reveal his true, crafty nature.

"Why," Cutter explained calmly, "I think I'll just have Seamus escort you back to your boss."

"Huh?"

"Your innocent act is convincing," Cutter shot back, "but we'll do it my way anyway." He nodded briefly at the boy, then glanced over his shoulder. When he caught Seamus Dunn's eye, he signaled the man to come over.

"What're you talkin' about, mister?" Jesse complained loudly, for the benefit of the crowd. "I don't have no boss. You know darn well *you* asked me here tonight."

Cutter frowned. He gave a quick look around him and didn't care for the speculative expressions on some of the faces turned toward him. Too many people were listening. That was all he would take, he told himself. He'd been more than patient with the young pup. Now it was time to end this fiasco.

"That true, Cutter?" the man called Joe asked quietly.

Jesse was smiling.

"Certainly not!" Cutter managed to hold on to his temper, despite his outrage at being thought of as a cheat. Hell, he'd never had to cheat at a game of cards in his life. That had always been a point of honor with him. Besides, he was just too damned good. This, however, he thought as he looked at the stony faces around him, was the time for discretion. Charm. "Joe," he asked the man who was looking suspiciously at him, "you've been a customer at the Garter and the Roses for years, right?"

"Yeah . . ."

"Have you ever been cheated by me or any of the regular dealers?"

"No . . . but—"

"Of course not!" Cutter slapped the older man's arm in a show of comradeship. "Hell, you lose enough money *honestly* to please us!"

A few chuckles were heard along with a couple of murmured agreements.

Cutter waited for Joe's reaction. If he'd convinced *him*, the others would be satisfied.

If he hadn't . . . well, he would think of something.

Joe's heavy features twisted in thought. He rubbed his whisker-stubbled jawline for what seemed forever, before a sheepish grin curved his generous lips. "Reckon that's so, all right."

Cutter released his pent-up breath, nodded at Joe, and turned as the saloon guard walked up. One problem solved. Another about to be.

"What is it, boss?" Seamus asked as he stepped up behind Cutter's chair.

"Ah, Seamus." Cutter looked at Jesse and waited for the kid to realize he knew who had sent him. "I'd like you to take our 'friend,' here, back where he came from."

Seamus snorted. "Where'd that be? Iowa?"

Apparently Seamus was not as observant of what was going on as everyone else.

"No," Cutter replied with a half smile. "I should think Digger's place would be far enough."

The cheat's smile fell from his face, and his eyes shifted from side to side, as if looking for a quick escape.

"Digger, is it?" Seamus growled. "That no good son-of-a—"

"Yes, Seamus. That's the one." Cutter interrupted the other man's colorful description quickly. "I'm sure Digger's wondering how his little helper has fared tonight. You be sure and tell him, won't you?"

"I damned sure will," Seamus agreed as he rounded the table, laid one meaty hand on the cheat's shoulder, and yanked him up from his chair, "an' a few other things as well."

Jesse twisted and turned in Seamus's grip, but the big man hardly budged.

Taking pity on the cheat's puniness, Cutter informed him, "Really, it is a waste of your efforts trying to escape our Seamus, boy. Before he came to America to work for Kevin Donnelly, Seamus, here, was the wrestling champion for all Ireland." He glanced at the huge man. "Isn't that right?"

"It is." Seamus's chest swelled to amazing proportions. "And I could handle *you*, my lad"—he gave the cheat a shake as if he were a puppy in the jaws of its mother—"with two broken arms."

"Of course you could, Seamus," Cutter agreed. From around him came a few muffled laughs, and he found himself feeling almost sorry for what Jesse was bound to go through at Digger's hands.

Almost.

"D'ya want I should tell herself, Maggie, about this before I go?" Seamus asked.

"Hmmm?" Cutter looked up quickly. "No. That won't be necessary. I'll tell her myself." He stood up, adjusted the fit of his jacket, and glanced unobtrusively down at his crotch. Silently he gave momentary thanks that the distraction of dealing with the cheater had allowed his body time to recover from its reaction to Maggie. "Jake!" he called. "A round of drinks for this table. On the house." Cutter glanced at each of the men in turn, nodded, and said, "If you gentlemen will excuse me?"

He turned away then, leaving the others to do as they liked. As for him, he would do something he'd been putting off all afternoon.

Be alone with Maggie.

Chapter 6

~~~~~⁓◯◯◯⁓~~~~~

"**I**'m *not* hiding!" Maggie muttered in a retort to the small voice in the back of her mind.

Then why are you still in the cellar? Why didn't you speak to Jake? And for heaven's sake, why haven't you faced Cutter? Afraid your knees will shake again?

"My knees were *not* shaking," she insisted in a whisper. "And even if they were, that doesn't mean Cutter was responsible."

Even as she said it, she knew it was a lie. As much as she wanted to deny it, she couldn't. Of course, simply because she was willing to admit the obvious to herself didn't necessarily mean that she would ever admit it to Cutter!

"I made your knees tremble?"

Maggie groaned and raised one hand to cover her eyes. When the hell had he come downstairs? Why hadn't she noticed the spill of light when the cellar door opened and then closed again? Why hadn't she heard him approach?

But most important, how much had he heard?

"I, uh . . . didn't hear you come down."

"So I noticed."

Even with one hand over her eyes, she knew when he came closer. She didn't have to hear his slow, sure footsteps on the uneven, knotty-pine floorboards. She felt his presence as surely as she could the damp surrounding her.

"Why are you here, Cutter?" She forced herself to let her hand drop to her side, but wasn't quite able to look at him. She didn't trust herself that much.

"In San Francisco? In the saloon?" he asked. "Or in this cellar in particular?"

Maggie sighed. "In this cellar, if you don't mind."

"Easily enough answered," he replied, the flippant tone still in his voice. "I came to see if you were a secret drinker. Lord knows, you've been down here long enough to drink us dry."

"What?" She glanced at him then and saw a teasing half smile on his face. His attitude should have made things easier on her. But it didn't. She knew damn well what he was doing. He'd done it often enough in the past.

Countless times over the years, Cutter had hidden his real feelings behind the glib wall of amusement. Only once before had he dropped his guard. Let her see the real man. Allowed her a brief glimpse inside his soul and his heart.

But before she'd been able to see all she'd ached to see, he'd shut her out again. This night was no different from that one.

Except for the fact that they were both dressed.

"Frankly, though," he was saying, "I'm far more interested in what *you* were talking about." He took a step closer. "You were talking, weren't you? To yourself?"

"That's right, Cutter. To myself."

"Tsk, tsk, tsk. What would people think, Mary Margaret?"

She inhaled sharply.

"What was it you were saying, again?" he muttered thoughtfully as he took the last step separating them. "Something about my making your knees tremble?"

"Shake, Cutter. I said shake. Not tremble."

"Shake—tremble—quiver . . ." He shrugged. "Much the same thing, isn't it?"

Maggie swallowed past the lump in her throat. She forced herself to look up, and stared directly into his too-blue eyes. It was a mistake.

In those lake-blue depths, along with the sparkle of amusement, there was something else.

Something dangerous.

Something wicked.

Something she'd waited nearly a year to see again.

Desire.

He wanted her as much as she did him.

If she had had the slightest amount of sense, she would have gotten out of the dark, private place . . . fast.

She stayed instead.

"Maggie," he said, and all trace of his earlier teasing was gone. "Maggie, we have to settle what's between us."

Spirals of heat flowed through her veins, and it was all she could do to remember how to breathe. The shaking in her knees began again, and Maggie straightened, locking her limbs tightly, desperate not to let him see how easily he could affect her.

"I thought you said there was nothing to settle," she finally said.

"I was wrong."

"Wrong?" She forced a laugh. "You?" Tearing her gaze from his, she spoke again, and her voice sounded thick, husky. "Don't tell me you're going to apologize again, Cutter."

"Do I have to?"

"No!" She shot him a quick, furious glance. "And you didn't have to the last time, either."

"Maggie ..."

"But you did," she went on, "and you will this time, too. Won't you?"

"Probably."

"Don't." As much as she wanted to look away again, Maggie didn't. Instead she let her gaze move over him ... from his neatly combed dark blond hair to his square, clean-shaven jaw to the perfectly arranged string tie at his throat. From there, her gaze slipped to the width of his shoulders, down to his narrow waist and hips ... and then stopped.

Proof of his desire, his hunger, was there for her to see. His flesh was hard, swollen against the confines of his black trousers. She felt the heat of a blush steal up her cheeks.

She was suddenly and profoundly grateful that she'd only lit the one candle. With the door to the kitchens closed, the cellar was as dark as a cave. But just in case Cutter *could* see her well enough to notice her embarrassment, she kept her head down.

Unfortunately, that meant she was left staring at the cause of her fiery blush.

She licked her dry lips as a damp warmth settled in the juncture of her thighs. Tendrils of excitement, want, reached up from the pit of her abdomen and raced through her body. Maggie sucked in a gulp of air as she felt her nipples harden and strain against the bosom of her peach silk gown. Her fingers curled into fists, and her nails dug into the palms of her hands in a wild attempt to distract herself.

It didn't work.

"Maggie ..." Cutter whispered, and grabbed her forearms in a grip that was at once gentle and fierce.

Reluctantly she dragged her gaze up until she met his eyes, filled with the same torment she knew haunted her own.

"Maggie," he said in a hush, "I swear to you, I didn't come down here for ... this."

"I believe you," she answered, and she meant it. After all he'd done to avoid her over the last year or so, it was hardly likely that he would follow her to a cellar to have his way with her. What was also true was that right at that moment, she didn't care. She only knew that she wanted him to kiss her again. To hold her. To ease the fire he'd first brought to life.

Before she could think better of it, Maggie reached up, laid one hand on his cheek, and guided his head down close. Long, breathless moments passed as he hesitated before finally surrendering to the inevitable and crushing his mouth to hers.

Maggie groaned and leaned into him. Her lips parted eagerly under his, and she was robbed of breath as Cutter's tongue caressed the inside of her mouth. Her right hand moved to cup the back of his head, and her fingers threaded through the soft, thick mass of his hair.

Old hurts, new anger, were forgotten in the first rush of pleasure. It had been so long. She'd missed him so.

She felt his hands roam over her back and behind. His palms cupped her bottom and pressed her firmly against the hard strength of his erection.

Maggie moved her hips from side to side, exploring the delicious feel of his ready body, eager for hers. Her movement brought a groan from Cutter, and he broke their kiss, desperately dragging air into his lungs.

Maggie's breath came in short gasps as he moved his mouth along the line of her throat, his tongue tracing a damp trail across her flesh. His teeth nibbled at her already sensitive skin, and Maggie held him to her more tightly than before.

Cutter's right hand moved from her bottom, up along the curve of her hip, followed the dip of her waist, and stopped only when her breast was cupped in his palm. Maggie stiffened, arching slightly into his touch.

Tenderly he slipped his hand into the low décolletage of her gown and freed her breast. She looked down at him through passion-glazed eyes. In the dancing shadows of the candle flame, she watched as Cutter took her rigid nipple into his mouth.

She gasped at the unbearable gentleness of his caress. He ran his tongue across the hard pink tip, then circled the pale pink skin that surrounded it. His breath brushed her flesh with added warmth, and Maggie let her head fall back on her neck as she luxuriated in him.

Holding his head to her breast, Maggie pressed him tighter, closer, when his mouth closed over her nipple again and he began to suckle her. An incredible feeling washed through her with the force of a tidal wave sweeping away a coastal town. As he tugged and pulled at her nipple, her fingers moved to smooth over his cheek, to touch his mouth as he touched her.

Cutter groaned and leaned her gently back against one of the damp oak beer casks. She felt the cool wood against her bare back as just one more sensation in a sea of overwhelming experiences.

"Maggie," he whispered as he lifted his head only long enough to seek out her other breast. "Maggie, God! I have to touch you. To feel your heat."

"I need you, Cutter," she answered, and wasn't surprised to hear her own voice sounding as shaken as she felt. But she only spoke the truth. Damn the saloon! Damn broken promises! Damn everything but this moment. She needed his touch every bit as much as he needed to give it.

To prove it, she lifted his right hand and placed it on her left breast. His other hand, she laid softly on her abdomen.

Cutter leaned down and kissed her lips briefly, tenderly. His thumb rubbed across the tip of her nipple even as his left hand began to gather up the folds of her gown.

The damp cellar air felt cool against her heated limbs, and despite her hunger for what was to come, Maggie shivered.

"Ah, Maggie," he breathed into her mouth before sliding his tongue across her lips. "My beautiful Maggie."

Her hands tightened on his shoulders in response to the trembling in her legs. And as his hand came into contact with her inner thigh, her body jerked against him. Even through the thin material of her drawers, his flesh felt hot against hers.

"Hush, Maggie," he said on a sigh, and stroked her hardened nipple again, a bit harder, faster.

Too many feelings crowded into her body, her mind. Maggie's head twisted from side to side against the rough wooden barrel, and her hips bucked slightly in anticipation.

Closer, closer, his fingers moved slowly, lingeringly, drawing out the pleasure in this for both of them. Finally, when Maggie thought she couldn't wait another moment, his palm cupped her damp warmth.

"Oh, God." Maggie sighed and wiggled her hips as she straddled his hand. It felt wonderful. So good. So right. And yet, she wanted more.

"Patience, Maggie," Cutter whispered as his hand moved up her stomach to the waistband of her pantaloons. Deftly he untied the ribbon and let the fine lawn fabric drop to the floor.

Cutter's breath caught in his throat. He looked his fill at her smooth, creamy skin and the triangle of deep red curls hiding the very warmth he was seeking. He'd dreamed about this for months. Every night, Maggie came to him in a soft haze, preventing sleep, tormenting him to the brink of madness. And every waking hour had been filled with the knowledge that he could never possess her again, that he'd ruined his last best chance for happiness.

Like a man possessed, he'd gone through the days and nights in a waking sleep, unable to think about anything or anyone but her. And now she was there. With him. Almost reverently, he reached for her and ran the flat of his hand across her abdomen, his fingertips brushing lightly against her curls.

Maggie moaned softly, and it was all he could do not to throw her to the dirty floor, toss off his clothes, and drive himself into her. He wanted ... *needed* ... to feel alive again. To feel the incredible rightness of becoming a part of her.

And even as he thought it, his fingers dipped lower, questing past the patch of auburn and into her heat.

Her fingers dug into his shoulders, and he watched breathlessly as Maggie's head fell back and her mouth dropped open on another sigh. Despite the pain he'd given her, despite the way he'd treated her, she could still trust herself to him. Cutter's heart pounded in his chest. In an instant, his own wants and needs became secondary. For this moment, he would give. He would pleasure her until she couldn't stand.

It was all he had to give. All he could offer her.

For himself ... his unsatisfied need would be a fit punishment indeed for allowing this to happen a second time.

Without another thought, Cutter bent his head to her breast. He took her sweet flesh into his mouth and rolled his tongue over the tiny nub, savoring the taste of her, committing her scent and the feel of her skin to memory. Slowly, tenderly, he began to suck at her, to draw at her breast as if he could pull her warmth inside of him ... make it a part of his soul and bandage the gaping holes in his heart that made it impossible to be what she wanted him to be.

His heart racing, his groin threatening to burst, he slipped his right hand around her waist and held her up slightly, to give him freer access to her breasts. One after the other, he gave them the loving attention they deserved. And all the while the fingers of his left hand moved in and out of her warmth with a steady, hypnotic rhythm.

First one finger, then two, he thrust inside her, wishing only that it was another, larger part of his body to be surrounded by her heat. His thumb moved over the tiny, sensitive piece of flesh that he knew would bring her the most pleasure. Each time she jumped or rocked in his arms, Cutter's satisfaction mounted.

He felt her spread her legs wider in open invitation for him to do as he willed. Inwardly, he smiled and drew his mouth from her breasts.

"Don't stop, Cutter. Dear God, don't stop and leave me like this," she murmured.

"Never, Maggie. I've only just begun with you." He brushed his lips over hers and then slowly dropped down to one knee in front of her. His free hand slipped beneath her gown and moved to caress the smooth flesh of her bare bottom.

Maggie swayed drunkenly, and briefly he held her tight, to steady her. Glancing up, Cutter saw that she was watching him, a question in her passion-glazed eyes.

"Relax, Maggie mine," he said, giving her a half smile, "and let me love you."

His thumb moved over that small piece of flesh again, and her eyes squeezed shut as she arched her hips in response.

Cutter smiled to himself and leaned closer. He

kissed the inside of her thigh and heard her sigh. Carefully he moved his lips up her leg to her abdomen and down to her other thigh.

Maggie's hips moved beneath his hands in a frantic quest for release.

His hand on her rear stilled her movements just as Cutter slid his fingers free of her body.

She moaned in disappointment.

He glanced up at her, noted that she was once again watching him, then covered her warmth with his mouth.

"Oh! God, Cutter!" She twisted desperately now, and he knew it was more from embarrassment than an effort to make him stop what he was doing.

Deliberately he ignored her pleas and smoothed his tongue across the hardened bud of her sex.

"Holy Mother and all the saints," she muttered, and moved into him. "What in heaven are ya doin' to me, man? And for the love of God—don't stop!"

He couldn't have stopped even if he'd wanted to. The more excited she became, the more he loved it—the more he wanted to do to her, for her. His hand smoothed across the flesh of her bottom, and then his fingers found her opening. Gently he impaled her from behind with a touch of his index finger and at the same time slid the fingers of his left hand deep into her welcoming warmth.

"Dear heaven," she muttered, and threaded her fingers through his hair, holding him to her.

His mouth worked her body into a frenzy even as his hands invaded it. She tasted of love and promise and need, and he greedily drank her in and *still* craved move.

When the first tremors began to claim her, Cutter redoubled his efforts and was rewarded by her breathless groans and the rocking of her hips. As release finally claimed her, he tasted her satisfaction and found it was almost enough to ease his own pain.

Seamus tossed his prisoner through the front door of Digger Wicks's place. Before the younger man had hit the floor, Seamus was inside, glaring at the startled crowd, looking around for the proprietor.

A piano player with more guts than talent was pounding on an upright piano with four bullet holes through its front. A dozen or more men, each one more grubby-looking than the next, sat at the scarred pine tables scattered about the room. Thick, undulating clouds of blue smoke hung heavily in the air, and the odor of unwashed bodies and cheap liquor added its own pall.

Seamus wrinkled his nose in distaste but didn't move from his spot. He wanted nothing more than an excuse to push his fist through Digger's ugly face, and he wasn't going to leave without trying for it.

"What do *you* want, Dunn?" A gravelly voice spoke up, and Seamus turned toward it.

In the far corner, like a rat hiding in shadows, sat Digger Wicks.

Seamus covered the space between them in a few quick strides. "I've brought your trash back."

Digger flicked a glance at the younger man,

only now pushing himself to his feet. "So I see." He looked back at Seamus. "That all?"

"You're not gonna deny sendin' 'im?"

"Why should I?"

Leaning forward into the light, Digger grinned, exposing a missing front tooth and an exceptional yellow sheen on the remaining teeth in his head. His wild gray hair stood out around his pie-shaped face like snakes writhing in a basket. Whiskey-glazed blue eyes stared at Seamus, and it was all the latter could do not to cross himself.

There was an evil stench about Digger Wicks that had nothing to do with the fact that the man seldom took a bath. This evil rose up from the depths of what had used to be his soul.

"I knew when I sent him that he'd fail." Digger laughed, making a sound like a broken bellows.

"Seems a stupid plan to me," Seamus allowed.

"It served a purpose." Digger sat back again, and his features were lost in the shadows.

Nonetheless, Seamus could feel the old bastard's eyes on him, and he tensed for whatever might come.

"It told Cutter that the war's not over yet."

"What war, ya fool?"

A long silence stretched out before Digger answered, in a tone that screamed of barely contained rage.

"The one between him and me. That damned reb's got no business comin' here, openin' up a place, and stealin' my customers."

Seamus laughed. "Your customers?" Waving

one muscled arm around, he added, "No one but you would let this lot inside, Digger."

"And now I hear," the other man went on, as if Seamus hadn't said a word, "that he's made his tame darky a partner."

Seamus stiffened. He had no quarrels with Ike. And there were just as many places and people looking down on the Irish as on the colored man.

"Can't have blacks doin' better than a hardworkin' white man!"

"You wouldn't know hard work if it jumped up and bit ya on your fat ass," Seamus muttered.

"I've nothin' more to say to you, mick. But you tell Cutter what I said, y'hear?"

"I'll tell 'im. And Ike as well."

That laugh again. "You do that, mick. You do that."

Out on the street, Seamus pulled in breath after breath of fresh, salt-tinged air. Rubbing one hand across his jaw, he decided he needed a bath and a drink. Not necessarily in that order.

The trembling seemed to last forever. Just when she thought it had stopped, another wave of throbbing pleasure shook her down to her toes, and Maggie could only hold on desperately to Cutter.

And then it was over. Beneath her hands, Cutter drew his head back from her body with a last, gentle kiss. She stood there, helpless to move, and felt him draw up her pantaloons and tie them into place. Then he smoothed her skirt down and stood up, pulling her into the circle of his arms.

The world seemed to be rocking badly, so Maggie held on to him. Her cheek against his chest, she listened to the frantic pounding of his heart and knew her own was beating in the same rhythm.

Dear God, what was she going to do?

Now that the haze of passion was fading, she was left with the knowledge that she'd once again given herself to a man who had already made it clear that he didn't want her love.

And, God help her, she didn't regret a moment of it.

What kind of a woman did that make her? she wondered. A whore? A woman so interested in the needs of her own body, she didn't care what she had to do to take care of them?

No. Silently she told herself that wasn't true. It wasn't just *any* man she wanted. Only Cutter.

And that didn't make her a slut.

Just a fool.

Reluctantly she pushed away from his broad, strong chest. Smoothing her hands down the front of her gown, she wondered just how she was supposed to look him in the eye after he'd done ... *that* to her.

"Maggie ..."

"If you apologize, Cutter, so help me, I'll find a pistol and shoot you stone dead."

A strangled chuckle shot from his throat, and Maggie looked up. Doing that was easier than she'd thought it would be. Besides, it was a bit late to be playing the part of injured virgin or outraged spinster.

"You would, wouldn't you?"

"Bet on it."

"I won't take that bet."

"You always were a smart gambler."

"Just a stupid man?"

She nodded.

"All right, then," he said, and shoved his hands through his rumpled hair. "If you don't want an apology, what can I say?"

"I told you almost a year ago what I wanted to hear."

His features froze, and Maggie swallowed hard. She hadn't really expected to hear him declare undying love, but dammit! Did he have to look so appalled by the thought of it?

He opened his mouth to speak, but Maggie held up one hand and silenced him.

"Don't bother, Cutter." She shook her head tiredly. "It's an old argument, and I'd rather not go through it all over again."

"If things were different—"

She wanted to shout, "What things?" "Different how?" But she didn't. Lord knew she didn't have *much* pride left, but by the saints, she'd hang on to the few bits and pieces that remained.

"Things aren't different, though. Are they? Things are exactly the same as they were a year ago." She choked on a laugh. After what they'd just done, things were more the same than even she had thought. Inhaling deeply, she lifted her chin and looked him square in the eye. "Why did you come down here, anyway, Cutter?"

"To talk to you about Jake and the Blue Blazer." He answered quickly, as if he were as relieved as she was to brush aside what had happened between them. But of course he was, she told herself. That was what he was best at.

"Jake." Maggie laughed again, and there

wasn't the slightest trace of amusement in her tone. Strangely, she'd been furious at the time, but at the moment ... Jake's performance hardly seemed worth talking about.

Still, it was better than talking about the other.

"Fine," she said. "Talk."

"Maggie, when you've got a bartender like Jake, it's foolish not to let him do what he does best."

"Foolish, am I?"

"I didn't say that."

"You surely did."

"If you're looking for a fight, Maggie—"

"If I were, I'd surely not have to look far, would I, Cutter?"

He pulled air into his lungs, dropped his hands to his hips, and stared at her. "I thought you didn't want to talk about this."

"I thought so too." Hell, she thought, her own emotions were running so wild and free, she didn't know from one moment to the next what she wanted. If anyone had asked her even an hour before, she would have been pleased to say that she had not the slightest intention of talking to Cutter about the night they'd spent together.

Of course, she hadn't had the slightest notion of letting what had just occurred happen either. It would seem, she told herself, that there were some things that she was going to have very little control over. And her reaction to Cutter was apparently one of them.

Fine. She could accept that. After all, she'd loved him more than half her life—as girl and woman. But she knew one thing must change— the way she went about loving him.

For the past year or so, she'd come damned close to apologizing to him for bothering him with her love! Well, no more! By heaven, loving was nothing to be ashamed of. Sure, she wouldn't be bragging about losing her virtue to the man, but why the devil should she pretend she didn't care?

To make things easier for *him?*

Hah!

No. If he was going to turn his back on her, then let him see firsthand what it was he'd be missing. Maggie's chin lifted as her thoughts began to take form and blossom in her mind. She'd show that gambler a thing or two about winning and losing; be damned if she didn't.

Before she could talk herself out of it, she said exactly what was on her mind. "But I don't want to let it go anymore, Cutter." Maggie took a half step closer to him and jabbed him in the middle of his chest with her forefinger before she said simply, "No."

" 'No' what?"

"No, I'll not make it easy on you a second time."

"Easy?" His voice was deep. Almost a growl. "Nothing about you comes easy, Mary Margaret Donnelly!"

"Get used to thinking that, boy-o." Maggie tossed her head and sent what was left of her elegant hairdo flying over her shoulder to lay against her back.

His eyes narrowed, and she watched his features close.

But she wouldn't let him ignore her. Not anymore. Not again. She would *force* him to listen.

"The last time," she started, "we did it your

way. Cutter stayed holed up in the Golden Garter, and Maggie, poor little thing, slunk her way home to lick her wounds."

He flinched.

Good, she thought. At least he was listening.

"You spent *months* avoidin' me, Cutter. Determined to prove that nothing had happened between us. As if pretendin' would make it so."

"Maggie," he said warningly, "I had my reasons."

"But none that you were willin' to share, is that it?"

"You don't understand."

"And I'm through tryin'!" she snapped. Poking his chest a little harder, she told him, "I'm through bein' the one left lookin' like a fool, Cutter. From here on out, the rules are goin' to change."

"Rules?" He cocked his head and glared at her. "What do you mean?"

That Georgia drawl of his caressed her ears, but she closed her mind to the softness of it.

"Just this." Her hands fell to her hips, and she leaned toward him, staring straight into the unreadable blue eyes focused on her. "*This* time there will be no avoidin' me, Cutter. *This* time I'll not waste away in my room, cryin' for you."

His eyes shut briefly, as if he were in pain, but Maggie was beyond caring.

"*This* time you'll have to see me every day. You'll have to deal with me and what's between us. It's just like you said a few days ago, partner. Neither of us is goin' anywhere." She leaned in even closer, until she could feel his breath on her face.

"And *this* time, boy-o, Maggie Donnelly won't be ignored."

When she reached up and dragged the tip of her fingernail down his cheek, it was all Cutter could do to hold himself still.

But she wasn't through talking. Not by a long shot.

"Every time you see me, Cutter," she promised, her voice a husky whisper in the darkness, "I'll make you remember. I'll make you want me so badly, your pants will be on fire."

That wouldn't be difficult, he thought, already groaning silently at the long months stretching ahead of him.

"And when I've worn you down to a frazzle"—Maggie smiled, and in the candlelight, she was breathtaking—"I'll only just be beginning."

His breath escaped him in a rush.

Her finger dropped to his chest again. But this time, instead of prodding and poking at him, she slid her finger along the line of buttons on his shirt. He held his breath, afraid to move. If he did, he knew he *would* throw her to the damn floor, and to hell with the consequences.

"When I'm through with you, Cutter," she swore, "you'll be beggin' me to marry you just so's you'll have some peace."

Damn this whole situation. Damn her for being right. And damn his own bloody hide for not having had the sense to stay away from San Francisco.

In an effort to save his pride, he forced himself to ask, in as light a tone as he could manage, "And then what, Maggie mine? Will you drag me to the church yourself?"

"Then, Cutter, me lad"—she grinned and slipped her finger between the buttons of his shirt to stroke his already heated flesh. Somehow, he managed to swallow a groan—"*then* I'll think about it and let you know if I'm still interested."

He winced when she pulled a single chest hair before stepping back from him. She gave him a saucy wink, turned away, and marched to the staircase. He watched as she climbed the short flight of steps to the kitchen without so much as a backward glance.

Alone in the cellar, with only the throbbing ache of his own body to remind him of what had just happened, Cutter wondered how in the hell he'd lost control of everything.

How had Maggie taken the reins into her own small hands?

And how would he live through what she had in store for him?

Chapter 7

Seven Oaks, Georgia. The painting didn't do it justice. Cutter set the accounts book down on his desk and leaned back in the worn leather chair, his gaze locked on the painting hanging on the far wall.

He'd already added up the same column of figures five times and come up with five different totals. Maybe it was time he admitted that his mind just wasn't on business. Instead, his tired brain kept insisting on dredging up memories of a long-gone past.

Elbow on the arm of his chair, he leaned his chin on his upraised palm and looked at the likeness of his old home.

Well, he amended, not really his home. The house he'd grown up in. He certainly didn't need the painting to remind him of the place. Every stick of furniture, every creaking stair, every spot of flaking paint was embedded in his memory. A part of him.

All he had to do was close his eyes, and he could feel a soft summer wind easing across the veranda, where the family would gather on warm evenings in search of a respite from the heat. He could hear the smooth, easy tones of his father's voice as he told the same stories over and over, still managing to make them seem new, exciting, with each telling.

As he stared at the painting he'd commissioned more than ten years before, Cutter allowed himself to remember other things too.

The night his father died. His brother's and cousin's triumphant shouts when they entered Cutter's room to tell him. The sound of the word *bastard* the first time he'd had it hurled at him. And the slam of the front door when he was given twenty dollars and told to take himself off.

Cutter's right hand curled into a fist and squeezed. The pencil he still held snapped in two.

"You gonna tell me what's got you so stirred up?"

Cutter glanced at Ike, then shook his head. He'd forgotten his friend was in the room. Hell, he'd forgotten everything but the sting of those memories.

"Don't wanna talk, huh?" Ike lay slouched in the oxblood leather tufted chair opposite the desk. Idly his long, thick fingers smoothed over the chair arm. "Then I'll jus' take a guess."

Cutter frowned and looked away from the damned painting.

" 'Bout the only thing I figure could set you off like this is a female."

A muttered curse was Cutter's only response. Since he'd never even told Ike about his family, there was no way the man could have known that Maggie wasn't the only thought occupying him these days. Still, Cutter wasn't interested in talking about Maggie, either, and thought he'd made that fairly clear. Unfortunately, Ike never had been one to take a hint.

"And," the man beside him went on, "since you hardly stuck your nose out the front door since you came back"—Cutter flashed him a quick look—"I'd say that female we's—we're talkin' 'bout is prob'ly Maggie."

Just hearing her name was enough to send Cutter's brain skittering off in five different directions. Of course, that didn't surprise him any. In the three days since their "meeting" in the cellar, he'd entertained all sorts of notions.

Up to and including strangling her.

True to her word, she was driving him around the bend. And it was amazingly easy for her.

Hell, all she had to do was walk across the room, swaying those magnificent hips of hers, and he was lost. But she wasn't satisfied with anything that simple. No, Maggie always had been of a mind that if you were going to do something . . . then, do it right.

She smiled; she flirted with the customers; she wore gowns with so little neckline, it was a wonder she hadn't been arrested. And it seemed that anytime she was near him—which was pretty damned often—she felt the need to sigh dramatically.

Those sighs reminded him (as he was sure she meant them to) of the times they'd been together.

It didn't matter where they were or what was going on, either. Only the night before, he'd held a poker hand that most men spend their lives dreaming about.

Four kings. And to make the situation better,

he was playing against men who'd filled the pot with enough chips, coins, and bills to make a saint think about being a sinner.

But just when he would have made his move, Maggie was beside him. A sudden intake of breath ... then the slow rush of air as it left her body on a sigh and brushed against his cheek. Before he knew what he was doing, Cutter had folded, and a farmer with a pair of nines had walked off with the pot.

Not only was she making him crazy, she'd ruined him for poker.

Never again would he look at a king without feeling her breath against his face.

"So," Ike said again, "you gonna tell me, or you plannin' on bein' this damn quiet the rest of your life?"

"Nothing to tell," Cutter said. As close as Ike was to him, he wasn't about to tell the other man about Maggie. He might have done some low things over the years, but talking about what he did with a woman wasn't one of them.

A long, thoughtful silence passed. Cutter could hear the clock on the far wall. He heard the squeak of leather as Ike shifted position. Hell, he could even hear his own heart beating.

"So," Ike said thoughtfully, "guess you got your reasons for not goin' to the Roses for inventory, like you was supposed to, huh?"

"Maggie can handle it. She's been doing it for years."

"Uh-huh. But you're the new partner. You ought to be havin' a hand in it."

"I've got to get these books finished."

"I'm your partner, ain't I?"

"Yeah."

Ike shrugged. "I'll do 'em."

Cutter said nothing.

"First time I ever seen—saw—you like this, Cutter."

"Like what?"

"Scared."

He shot his friend an evil look and slowly rose to his feet. Damn his eyes, Ike knew that Cutter would never be able to let *that* lie. Especially since it was true.

He *was* scared. Not of Maggie, but of what she made him feel and think and want.

Forcing himself, he crossed the room and opened the door. Glancing back at Ike, he said quietly, "If you need me, I'll be at the Roses, doing inventory."

When the door shut behind his partner, Ike gave his grin full rein, then laid his head back against the chair and closed his eyes for a nap.

"What in the name of heaven are ya thinkin', girl?"

"I'm not thinking anything, Rose," Maggie shot back, and looked down at the list in her hand. "I'm doing the inventory."

"In *that*?"

Maggie glanced at the housekeeper's outraged expression, then smoothed her palm down the front of her gown. Of course, Rose was right. The dress was completely inappropriate for the task at hand. But it was perfect for what Maggie hoped to accomplish.

Emerald-green satin hugged her figure with a loving touch. With each step she took, the three starched petticoats beneath her skirt rustled invitingly. With each breath she took, her breasts threatened to spill over the appallingly low neckline.

Just the idea of that happening caused Maggie to lift her hand and lay her palm over the indecent amount of cleavage she was displaying.

"I should think you *would* be embarrassed, Mary Margaret Donnelly," Rose admonished. "Your mother's probably spinnin' in her grave as we speak. And what himself, your father, would say about this doesn't bear thinkin' on."

"If himself has anything to say about this, I'll have a word or two for *him* as well. This is all his fault, Rose Ryan, and don't you be forgetting that."

Rose brushed the warning aside and stared at Maggie's bosom. "Didn't that dress have a mess of lace, and such, coverin' up the chest?"

Until that very morning it had, Maggie admitted silently. It had taken her nearly two hours to pull out the tiny stitches, remove the lace, and then sew on a tiny yellow rosebud in the center of the neckline.

Just on the off chance that Cutter would be struck blind and not notice her cleavage, she'd hoped the single satin rose would draw his gaze to just the right place. Looking down at herself now, Maggie had to admit that she *was* a little nervous about the dress.

Somehow, it hadn't seemed quite so scandalous when she'd tried it on, alone in her room. But now, it appeared that the green satin was barely managing to cover her nipples. Good Lord, if she bent over in the slightest, more people than Cutter would be getting a good look at the pale flesh of her bosom.

Perhaps she should go upstairs and change. There was time enough yet, she told herself.

A step on the cellar stairs behind her proved her wrong.

Cutter.

Whether she liked it or not—she was out of time. She pulled in a deep breath, then immediately caught herself. None of that, she thought wildly. At least not in that dress.

True, she wanted to drive him mad, but she didn't want to be stark naked when she did it.

"Maggie?" he called. "You down here?"

"Yes," she answered. "I've already started."

"That you have," Rose muttered, "but *what* you've started, I don't think even *you* know."

"Rose—"

"No." the older woman held up one hand for silence and shook her head. "I don't want to know what you're up to. You might have been raised in a saloon, my lass, but you were raised decent."

"I'm not doing anything—"

"I said, I don't want to know." Rose started walking toward the stairs even as Cutter's footsteps signaled that he was on the way down. "I'll leave you to it. But mind"—she crooked one finger at the younger woman—"I'm leavin' the door open. And I expect it to stay that way."

"Yes, ma'am."

Maggie didn't look at Rose when she agreed. If she had, Rose might have realized that it was a bit late to leave the door open. Looking around the cellar now, Maggie herself could hardly believe what had happened there only three short days before.

With a dozen or more candles lit, the shadows

were banished to the farthest corners. There was no dark, sheltering place between beer casks to hide her and Cutter, as there had been then. Unerringly her gaze flew to the very spot where she'd stood helpless under his ministrations. Her knees shook at the memory, and a familiar curl of damp heat blossomed at her center and began to grow. Her mouth dry, Maggie tried to swallow past the tightness in her throat.

She'd had three days and three long nights to relive what he'd done to her there in the cellar. And every minute of every hour of them had been filled with longing and anger.

Longing, because she dared to hope that somehow they might still come together again—and anger, because Cutter was the most thickheaded, stubborn, unreasonable man she'd ever had the misfortune to know.

"Maggie," he said, and it was only then that she noticed he had slipped up right behind her. "I'm here. What do you want me to do first?"

She flicked a quick look at him and saw that he'd stopped a good two feet away from her. Safety in distance? she wondered silently. Then she asked herself what he would think if she told him what she really wanted him to do.

Would he actually go lie down in the middle of the street and let wagons roll over him?

"Maggie?"

She gave herself a mental shake, then turned around to face him. At once, she knew she needn't have bothered to sew on that rosebud. His clear blue gaze flew straight to her bosom . . . just as she'd hoped.

Deliberately, she drew in a deep, dangerous breath.

He paled slightly.

Maggie smiled.

Cutter didn't know how much more of that he could take. As his gaze moved over the swell of her breasts, he watched in awe as the neckline of her gown seemed to dip lower with every breath she took.

One touch of his finger was all that would be required to free her breasts for his caress. One soft, delicious touch, and her bosom would fill his hands. His thumbs could stroke her nipples into small, firm peaks.

She would moan softly and move into him. He would dip his head and take her nipples, each in turn, into his mouth and roll his tongue over the rigid, sensitive flesh.

A low ache settled in his groin, and Cutter shifted uneasily, trying to accommodate the swollen flesh that had become so much a part of his everyday life.

He forced himself to look away from the creamy flesh that tempted him so, and when he did, he looked straight into a pair of knowing green eyes. Cutter clenched his jaw tight. That smile on her face told him that Maggie was very much aware of what she was doing to him—and that she also knew she was succeeding.

And, of course, to be back in the cellar with her—after doing nothing but thinking about it for the past three days . . .

Cutter cursed under his breath and forced his weary mind away from the images it was becoming exceptionally clever at producing.

"You should have waited," he managed to

say. "No need for you to do inventory alone anymore."

A slight frown puckered the space between her brows. *Good.*

"I'm used to it," Maggie said, and slowly turned her back on him to inspect a tower of crates stacked against the cellar wall.

Grateful that she'd turned her delectable bosom away from him, Cutter had barely taken an easy breath when his gaze fell on the naked expanse of her back. Pale and smooth, her fair skin seemed to glow in the candlelight, and the deep green of her gown seemed to emphasize the fragile look of her shoulders.

Cutter caught himself. Fragile? Maggie?

Seductive, yes.

Maddening, yes.

Tempting, *God*, yes.

But never fragile.

He glanced over her head at the line of crates. As he focused on the lettering, he smiled.

Maggie was flipping the pages of her inventory back and forth, as if searching for something.

"Cutter," she finally asked, "do you know anything about these boxes?" She didn't look up at him. Instead she continued to flip through the papers in her hands. "I thought maybe Da had ordered something from St. Louis, but he usually leaves me some kind of note. Something to tell me what he's done. And there's nothing."

Still smiling, Cutter stepped around her, walked up to the tower of crates, and slapped one of the wooden boxes. Glancing at her over his shoulder, he grinned. "I ordered them. It's just surprising that they're here so soon."

"What? What's here?" She crossed her arms over her chest, and Cutter breathed a bit more easily.

"Billiard balls. And cues."

"What?"

"Why do you keep saying that?" he teased. "Have you gone deaf overnight?"

"No, I'm not deaf. Just confused. Why on earth would you order billiard balls?"

"Obviously, so that I would have something to roll across the billiard tables, which I also ordered."

The company must have shipped the tables and equipment even before Cutter had left St. Louis. It was the best news he'd had in days. Now his plans could really start.

"And just where are you planning on putting your new balls?"

He turned his head and looked at her.

It took a moment, but she finally seemed to realize what she'd said. Clearing her throat, she reworded the question.

"I mean, your tables and such. Where do you think you're going to be putting them?"

"I *think* I'm going to be putting them in the Garter."

She relaxed a bit. But, Cutter reminded himself, she hadn't heard everything yet.

Leaning his forearm on the corner of one of the wooden crates, Cutter crossed one booted foot in front of the other and looked her dead in the eye.

"I plan to keep the billiard tables in the Garter and all the card and faro tables in the Roses."

"And had you planned on mentioning any of this to me?"

"Of course." She really was taking all that very well. "I simply thought that I might as well wait until the equipment arrived. No sense in putting the cart before the horse, so to speak."

"Uh-huh." Maggie kicked her skirt out of the way and stepped over a loose floorboard that had jutted up. "But you *were* going to tell me."

"Certainly."

"Just like you were going to tell me about Jake and the Blue Blazer."

"No, that was different—" he began, but Maggie cut him off.

"And what about the card cheat whom Digger Wicks sent here the other night?" Her gaze flashed on him, and Cutter saw the emerald-green fire in her eyes. "Were you going to tell me about that, as well?"

She was getting angry, all right. Cutter didn't know whether that was good or bad. On the one hand, as long as she was mad, she wouldn't try to seduce him. But on the other hand, he'd seen Maggie mad, and hadn't much cared for the experience.

What he was having a devil of a time figuring out was how she could turn from hot to cold so quickly.

Maggie was furious. Oh, she'd heard about Digger and she'd talked to Jake, but now this. Cutter had ordered supplies for her saloon before she'd even known he was her partner. Somehow that knowledge really stung.

And he hadn't even bothered to tell her about it. Was she not important enough in his mind to warrant a discussion? Had she completely misread him?

Lord, she'd thought that at least he respected her talents as a businesswoman. But apparently she was wrong. He was as bad as her father—going off and making decisions that he expected everyone else to put up with silently.

Well, he'd learn different that day. She'd been taking care of herself and the saloon for some time now, and she certainly didn't need a keeper.

"What if I don't agree to your plan about the billiard parlor?" That it was a good idea didn't come into play, she told herself. The important thing was that he'd never even mentioned it.

"I don't know—I assumed you would see it as a good business move."

"As it happens, I do." Maggie took a step closer to him. Tilting her head back, she stared into his eyes and said, "But that's not the point, Cutter. You said you wanted us to be real partners."

"I do."

"Well, boy-o, real partners talk to each other. They talk about the business. They make plans *together*. They sure as sin don't buy up supplies for a new venture and then claim they forgot to mention it."

It felt good, Maggie thought, telling him exactly how she felt. She should have done that years ago, with both Cutter and her da. She might have been able to save them all a lot of trouble.

"You're right."

"What?"

Cutter grinned, and a dimple on his right cheek deepened. "I said, you're right. I should have told you. I will next time."

"No, Cutter," she corrected him. Although she was surprised that he'd agreed with her, she wanted to make sure he understood what it was she wanted from him. "Next time, *ask* me."

Cutter gave her a slow, thoughtful nod before saying, "All right Maggie. I'll ask."

The look in his eyes warmed her to her soul, but she wasn't going to give in to him again. She'd meant what she'd said the other night in that very room. She was going to drive him to the point where he'd have no choice but to marry her or lose his mind.

He'd be getting nothing more from her until he could look her in the eye and swear that he loved her. She had known it for years. She'd felt his love in his every touch and look. She'd heard it in his voice when he spoke to her.

Only, he was too big a fool to realize it.

Yet.

Deciding she'd had enough of the cellar and him for a while, Maggie handed him the inventory sheets and said, "If you don't mind, why don't you finish up in here? I'll just go back up and see to the kitchens."

She hadn't gotten more than a few steps away when his voice stopped her.

"Before you go," he said, his voice a lazy drawl, "there's something else."

Maggie turned her head slowly to look at him. "What is it?"

"As my partner," he explained, "you should know that I've hired a new singer for the Roses."

Maggie's brow furrowed. She hadn't expected him to turn over a new leaf quite so quickly. Then she immediately thought about the man who'd been singing at the Roses for the past several months.

Dennis was a barely-more-than-adequate tenor and heaven knew that talent was harder to find on the Barbary Coast than an honest card game. Whether Cutter knew it or not, his singer was bound to be an improvement, no matter *how* he sounded.

"Thanks for telling me, Cutter." She could afford to be generous. After all, he was trying, and he could hardly have *asked* her, since he'd obviously hired the singer before coming back home. "I suppose we can move Dennis to the Garter." Since there had never been a singer at all at the Garter, no doubt Dennis would be better than nothing. "When will your new singer be arriving?"

"Oh, any day now."

"Ah," Maggie said thoughtfully, "that's grand."

"I'm glad you think so," Cutter went on, "because I've been doing some thinking too."

"About what?"

"About where the new singer will stay."

"I suppose a hotel—"

"I was thinking of something closer."

"Like where?"

He shrugged. "Kevin's room here at the Roses."

"Kevin's room?" Allow a stranger to stay in her father's room? "For heaven's sake, why?"

"Just temporarily," Cutter said. "We're going to make over some of the rooms at the Garter. When they're finished, the new singer can move. Besides, Kevin will likely be gone for months yet, and his room is just standing empty."

True, she thought. Even God didn't know how long her da would take it into his head to be gone. And his room was empty. But that was beside the point, wasn't it? All of the other entertainers found rooms at the boardinghouses and hotels. Maggie saw no reason at all to change all that now.

She shook her head and offered a more reasonable solution. "The new lad can move in with Dennis at his place, until the Garter's ready for him." Really, it was surprising Cutter hadn't thought of that himself.

"I don't think so," he hedged.

"Whyever not?"

"Because the new 'lad's' name is Michelle Fontaine."

Maggie stared at him openmouthed.

"She's French."

Maggie's jaw snapped shut.

David opened his eyes slowly, cautiously, then quickly shut them again.

Damn that maid, he thought. There ought to be a law about a woman sneaking into a man's room and opening the drapes while he sleeps. A man has to be prepared for sunshine. It's not something to be witnessed lightly, for God's sake.

One at a time, he pried his eyelids open again and forced them to stay that way.

Late-morning sunlight poured in through the wide-open, blue-velvet drapes. A chilly, sea breeze shot through the opening at the top of the window and swept away the last remaining cobwebs from his brain.

He stared up at the domed ceiling of his room and tried to tell himself to get up and go to the office. But even as he tried, he realized there wasn't much point in it.

Oh, he was a lawyer, right enough. But the firm had only hired him because of the judge. And, just as the judge did, they kept expecting him to be a younger version of the old man.

Well, he'd learned some time ago that he could never be like his father. He'd spent long enough trying, until he'd discovered that his father wasn't a man he should be attempting to emulate.

Of course, the judge didn't see things that way. To his way of thinking, the money slipped to him by rich defendants or desperate attorneys represented his just dues for working so hard to make society a better place. Judge Harper didn't take bribes. He accepted "tokens of esteem"—with greedy, grasping hands.

The funny part was, David knew that the judge didn't understand why his son was so appalled. After all, the younger man had had a fine education, lived in an elegant home, and associated with all the "best" people. And all of those things were owed to Judge Harper.

A lying, cheating, whoring judge who'd driven his wife to drink herself to death and his son to questioning his own manhood.

A fine, upstanding member of society.

David laughed shortly, winced at the accompanying pain in his head, and sat up. If he could only find his clothes, he'd get himself down to the Roses early—maybe talk Jake into mixing one of his famous hangover cures before he had to stumble off to court.

A woman. A Frenchwoman, no less.

Maggie's mind whirled with the effort to think clearly. She should have known that Cutter would find a female singer. And it was as if he'd come up with this new plan simply to cause more problems. Because, dammit all, he was right.

They couldn't very well send a female stranger off to find rooms of her own in an unfamiliar city. And it was unlikely that one of the other girls would be willing to take her in. The women who worked at the saloon either already shared their rooms with others or made a habit of entertaining "callers," which made a housemate an unwelcome intrusion.

Still, Maggie told herself, there might be yet another answer, one Cutter hadn't thought of. But then again, she thought with an inward smile, maybe it *had* occurred to him and he'd been hoping *she* wouldn't think of it.

Folding her arms over her chest, Maggie looked up at him and smiled slowly.

His eyes narrowed, and he took an instinctive step back.

"What are you thinking?"

"There's another way to do this, Cutter."

He tilted his head to one side and stared at her thoughtfully for a long moment. "What way is that?"

"It's very simple, really." Maggie planted her hands on her hips and gave him a slow smile. "I don't think Da would like the notion of a stranger staying in his room—"

"Oh," Cutter interrupted quickly, "Kevin wouldn't—"

Maggie cut him off. "So the best thing surely, would be for this Michelle to stay in *your* room at the Garter. Temporarily."

His eyebrows shot straight up. "It's thoughtful of you to suggest that, Maggie. But I don't think the lady would agree with you. Besides, my room's a bit small for two people."

"That's not what I meant."

"Of course not."

Maggie cocked her head, and her smile blossomed into a grin. "While Michelle uses your room, *you* can stay in Da's."

"Me?" His features took on the look of a trapped animal.

Wide-eyed, she added, "I'm sure Da wouldn't mind at all if *you* stayed there for a while. And if you'll just think about it for a minute, you'll see it's the best solution."

He was thinking, all right, Maggie told herself. And she knew exactly what thoughts were flying around in his head.

Not only was Kevin's room standing empty; it was also directly across a very narrow hall from her own room.

Chapter 8

Trapped.

Cutter stared down into her brilliant green eyes and couldn't help but see the self-satisfied gleam shining there.

He'd walked right into her plans to drive him insane and given her a few more rounds of ammunition, to boot. It wasn't the slightest bit of consolation to know that she was right.

The only answer that made sense was for him to give his room to Michelle and to move into Kevin's room. But, sweet Jesus, how was he going to stand it?

Being only a step away from Maggie's room might be just the push that would send him over the edge. How was he going to keep himself from crossing that hall and claiming her for his own?

Hell, it was hard enough staying clear of her as it was. This situation was going to be a nightmare.

She was smiling at him, and he would have sworn she could read his mind. No doubt she knew that he was even then trying desperately to find a way out of it, a way to stay as far from her as possible.

But there wasn't one.

And she knew it.

He didn't have a choice, unless he was willing to try to find a hotel room himself. Or move in with Ike.

Cutter snorted. As much as he loved his friend, Cutter wasn't about to start sharing a room with him.

He rubbed the back of his neck and reminded himself that this was all his own fault.

He never should have bought Kevin's half of the Roses. But, dammit, when the older man had crossed his path in St. Louis, it had seemed like fate. When Kevin had told him that he was short of money—that he needed to find a buyer quickly—Cutter's first feeling had been one of relief. It was almost as if Fortune were giving him a chance to redeem himself for betraying Kevin's trust, offering a way for Cutter to assuage the guilt he felt about having seduced the daughter of the man who'd treated him like a son.

He shook his head and told himself he should have known that nothing to do with the Donnellys would be so easy.

"Well, Cutter?" She stepped a bit closer. Her hands still resting on the curve of her shapely hips, her index fingers began to tap—a sure sign of her failing patience. "What's it to be, then?"

She took another step, and Cutter was caught up in the faint, promise-filled scent of rose water that clung to her.

Lord, he was in trouble.

"All right, Maggie." He nodded slowly, and could have sworn he felt the heavy weight of a noose being slipped over his neck. "I'll move my things into Kevin's rooms as soon as Michelle arrives."

One side of her mouth curved in a knowing smile, and she shook her head. "No, Cutter, it'd be best if you moved into Da's room today."

"Today?" God help him. If there was a noose around his neck, he had just felt the trapdoor beneath his feet fall away. Maggie took a breath, and his gaze flew to the would-be neckline of her gown. He was in serious trouble.

"Of course today—no sense wasting time, is there? Once you've got your things cleared out, I'll have Rose fix up your room at the Garter so's it's ready and waiting for Michelle."

"We can do that when she gets here," he protested. Lord, did he sound as desperate to her as he did to himself?

She clucked her tongue at him and shook her head again. A copper curl danced across her shoulder and fell forward to lay against her creamy skin. "Now, that would make her feel as if we weren't prepared and waiting for her, wouldn't it? Why, she might even think that we didn't really want her here at the Roses, mightn't she?"

Maggie smiled again, and this time he *knew* she was laughing at his bumbling, futile escape attempts.

"No," she went on, "it's best if we do this my way. Then this Michelle will arrive to find a room waiting for her, and she'll feel welcome."

Cutter pulled in a gulp of air and cursed himself for a fool as the cool, clean scent of roses swept deep inside him. Dammit. She was right. And if he kept on trying to find an escape from her plan, she'd know that he was scared.

Scared? his brain echoed. Cutter looked down into her shining green eyes and silently corrected himself. Not scared. *Terrified*. For too long, she'd had the ability to slip beyond the barriers he'd erected around his soul so long ago. And twice she'd actually managed to touch something in him he'd thought dead and buried. With her quick temper, tart tongue, and the strength of her loving, she'd smashed his defenses until the only thing left standing between them was his own ever-shrinking determination to save Maggie from wasting herself on a gambler too empty to give her what she deserved.

No. He couldn't let her know the depth of his fear.

Somehow, he managed to nod. They would play this out her way ... even if it killed him.

"It's settled, then," Maggie said, and turned from him. She walked halfway to the stairs before glancing back over her shoulder. "I'll be sending Rose over to the Garter. She'll get started packing up your things."

"Don't go to any trouble, Maggie." *Please*, he added silently. *There's no hurry*.

"Oh, it's no bother a'tall, Cutter." At the foot of the stairs, she lifted the hem of her skirt slightly to give him a peek at her trim ankle as she set her foot down on the first step. "Nothing's too much for my new partner, Cutter. Anything I can do to help."

Nobody could help him then, he thought—least of all her.

"Thanks, Maggie," he said, and watched her grin.

"Not a'tall, Cutter, darling." Turning back

around, she nearly ran up the short flight of stairs to the kitchens and the saloon beyond.

When he was alone, Cutter drew up a nearby beer keg and plopped himself down on the small wooden cask.

How had he lost control of everything?

And so quickly?

Two hours later, he still had no answers.

Cutter moved restlessly about Kevin's room. His gaze swept over the chamber, noting the familiar furnishings. It didn't matter that *his* things were now scattered about the huge bedroom. This was still Kevin Donnelly's domain.

The Irishman's stamp was on everything, from the big, four-poster bed to the emerald-green curtains hanging at the window to the framed, faded map of Ireland hanging on the far wall. Most of Kevin's suits still hung in the wardrobe alongside Cutter's clothes. And the faint odor of fine cigars still lingered in the air. Cutter almost expected to see his old friend come charging through the bedroom door.

On the small, square table beside the bed was the decanter of Irish whiskey that was never far from Kevin's right hand. Beside it, propped on an Irish-lace doily, was a silver-framed daguerreotype of a younger Kevin, his late wife, and three of the four Donnelly girls.

Slowly Cutter walked to the table, lifted the old print, and studied the faces staring at him as if he'd never seen them before. Kevin looked proud, confident. His wife, Teresa, a dark-haired beauty, sat on a chair beside him, holding an infant Mary Alice. Cutter grinned. True to her nature, Alice was in motion, and her tiny foot was a blurred streak of gray. His gaze moved over Frankie, stiff and solemn from her perfect little dress to the precise bow atop her head.

And then there was Maggie. As she leaned against her father, Mary Margaret's small features looked frankly into the camera lens, as if issuing a challenge. A bow on one of her long braids had come undone and straggled over her narrow chest. She had a rip in one of her stockings, and if he looked closely enough, Cutter could see a shadowed darkness under her right eye.

Cutter smoothed his forefinger over the glass-covered image of Maggie. In his mind, he heard Kevin's voice the night he'd first shown Cutter the photograph.

"Ah, Maggie," the older man had said with a sigh. "Ever a fighter, that one. Her mother near wore her little butt out for daring to have a shiner for the family sitting."

Cutter had laughed and leaned over the shorter man's shoulder for a closer look. "A black eye? But she couldn't have been more than six or so, there."

"More like five, I should think." After a long pause, Kevin had nodded thoughtfully. "Aye, Al was near on to one here—so, yeah, Maggie was five."

"Then, she's had a temper all her life?"

"Oh, aye." Kevin had grinned at the eighteen-year-old Cutter beside him. "And a sense of justice that most grown men lack."

Cutter had looked at the man and seen the pride Kevin felt in his oldest daughter. "How'd she get the black eye?"

"Ah, she happened on a couple of boys a few years older than herself"—Kevin had rubbed his thumb across the image of Maggie's face—"and they were

stealin' a beggar's few coins. Poor old fella had a bad leg, so he couldn't give chase." Chuckling softly in memory, Kevin had gone on. *"My Maggie flew into those two young hoodlums like St. Patrick himself was on her shoulder."*

"She started the fight?"

"Oh, aye. And finished it, as well." Kevin's chest had puffed up, and his eyes had grown a bit misty. *"True, she got a shiner for her troubles, but she also got the old man's money back and managed to yell loud enough that she drew help from every saloon on the block."* Glancing up at Cutter, Kevin had finished with a grin, *"Those two boys never knew what hit 'em."*

The man's Irish brogue faded into memory as Cutter looked down at the image of a battle-weary but triumphant Maggie. Strange, he told himself. It had taken more than fifteen years, but he finally understood exactly how those two boys must have felt when Maggie went after them.

When it came to dealing with her and the emotions she stirred in him, Cutter felt as if he, too, didn't know what had hit him.

Carefully he set the frame back in its place and gave it one last glance before turning his back on it and striding across the room to the fireplace. There he laid both hands on the mantle and leaned forward.

She hadn't changed. Oh, she'd matured and grown and become even lovelier than any of them had imagined she would so many years before. But inside—in her heart, her soul—Mary Margaret Donnelly was still the little girl throwing herself into battles she had little hope of winning.

Cutter raised his head, then tilted it back to stare up at the painting of Seven Oaks, hanging in its new home, over Kevin's cold hearth. He'd brought it with him as a reminder, a touchstone that he would see every morning and every night . . . something that would help him remember exactly why he didn't have the right to be what Maggie wanted him to be.

But it also reminded him of how much he'd already lost and how much more was slipping away from him.

Maggie. His brain conjured her image, and he smiled sadly. Now, he told himself, she was doing battle in an effort to win his heart. His soul.

But this battle would not be won. Could not be won.

For a very simple reason.

Cutter didn't have a heart and soul anymore. He'd left them both behind him more than fifteen years ago.

In a place called Seven Oaks.

Two days. Two days, and she'd hardly seen him but for the too-public meetings they had in the saloon each night. Idly Maggie toyed with the handle of her coffee cup. The double front doors were still closed, and dazzling late-morning sunshine filtered through the leaded-glass panes. Blurred patches of light fell across her table and the untouched record books lying before her. Sighing, she propped both elbows on the pages and held her cup in two hands to take another sip of the hot brew.

Maggie wouldn't have thought it possible for a man to live and sleep directly across the hall from her and still maintain his distance. But somehow Cutter was managing it.

Her patience was frayed, and her temper seemed to be always near the boil. But her determination had only gotten stronger. In fact, the harder he tried to ignore her very presence, the more convinced she was of his love for her. No man would work that obstinately to avoid a woman he had no feelings for.

Wouldn't you know, Maggie told herself, that when it came down to love, she would choose a man who was proving to be every bit as stubborn and pigheaded as herself?

"Maggie?"

She turned away from her daydreaming and looked up at Seamus.

"They're back." He jerked his head in the direction of the kitchen. "Waitin' for ya."

For a moment, she wondered who the man was talking about. Why would someone come to the kitchen, and not through the front door? Then, for the first time, she noticed the disgusted expression on Seamus's face and immediately understood.

"Is it two months already?" she asked, amazed at how much time had drifted past without noticing.

"Like a fine timepiece they are," Seamus muttered. "Not that the lot of them could afford one watch between them."

"Seamus . . ."

"Aye, I know." He inhaled and exhaled on a tired but resigned sigh. "They're friends of Kevin's. They're welcome here anytime."

Maggie stood up, and she heard Seamus mutter under his breath, "And don't think they don't count on *that*."

She ignored him and hurried to the kitchen.

Cutter strolled downstairs in time to see Maggie pushing her way through the kitchen door, a wide smile on her face.

"What's going on?" he asked Seamus, noting the big man's features twisted with distaste.

"Nothin'."

"Well, who's she so bloody happy to see?"

"The Raffertys."

"Rafferty?"

"A bunch of no-goods, if ya ask me, but since nobody did, I'm sayin' nothin'."

Cutter's lips quirked at the likelihood of that. "All right, *I'm* asking. Who the hell are the Raffertys?"

Seamus rubbed his jaw, tugged at his suspenders, then snapped them against his huge, barrel chest. "Three of the laziest, most good-for-nothin', lyin' sons of St. Patrick that ever stepped off a boat."

"Interesting."

Snorting, the other man continued. "You want 'interesting'? I'll give ya interesting. The three of them"—he waved one hand at the kitchen—"have been in and out of more jails than the marshal of San Francisco. They've got blisters on their backsides from bein' tossed out of more saloons than we've got in Ireland, and hardly a tooth left in their heads from all the times some right-thinkin' man has put a fist in one of their mouths."

The description could have fit half the men on

the Barbary Coast, but Cutter didn't bother to say so. Instead he asked, "Why are they here?"

"Ah, like a bad penny or a plague, they show up regular here at the Roses. Have for years."

Years? "Why the devil have I never heard of them? Never met them?"

"Ya never spent much time in the kitchen, lad." Seamus grimaced and shook his head. "To see the Raffertys, you've got to be around where the free food's kept."

"Free?"

"Aye. They're no closer to havin' a coin in their pockets than I am of bein' the bloody king of bloody ol' England." Seamus's lips curled. "They've not a shred of manly pride between 'em, either, and not surprisin' . . . considerin' how little they have to be proud of." Clearly disgusted by his countrymen, Seamus turned and started walking toward the Garter. "Even if Kevin comes to his senses sometime, Maggie won't. She insists on feedin' that worthless lot anytime they're in town. It's a bleedin' wonder they don't just set up camp in the alley behind the Roses." He hunched his shoulders and walked through the connecting arch. He called back over his shoulder, "I'm off. I'll visit with Ike till the air clears."

Intrigued, Cutter stared after him for a few seconds. Then, from the corner of his eye, he noticed the abandoned account books. Obviously Maggie had forgotten everything in her haste to see their visitors.

Thoughtfully Cutter turned his head and looked at the closed kitchen door. As much as he wanted to keep avoiding Maggie's company, he simply had to get a look at these Raffertys.

* * *

"Ah, Maggie, darlin'," the old man said with a sigh, and dug into a plate of beef and potatoes she set down in front of him. "You set the finest table in California, love."

"California?" the grizzled, near-toothless man beside him argued. "The whole damned country, brother. The country!"

"True, true." A third man, no cleaner than the first two, piped up, then lifted his flagon of beer and drained it. "Maggie, darlin'," he said, and held out the glass toward her, one hand clutching his throat. "If you wouldn't mind, lass. I've a terrible thirst on me."

Cutter stepped further into the shadowed doorway and watched Maggie's features split into a grin as she lifted a pitcher of beer and refilled the man's glass. It was no wonder she hadn't heard him come in, he told himself. She was much too busy trying to listen to three men talk at one time, each around a mouthful of food.

A more unsavory-looking trio, Cutter had never seen.

Each had unkempt gray hair, one of them substantially less than the other two. All three were cursed with bulbous, red-veined noses in varying sizes and shapes, and their combined stench—even from a distance—was enough to bring water to a man's eyes.

But no one would have guessed that, to look at Maggie. Cutter shook his head slightly as he watched her.

"There's more where that comes from, Mike," Maggie said as she topped off one man's beer, then patted his hand. "You know that."

"I do an' all, dear heart."

"Did we tell ya—" the first man started to say, then pulled a gristly piece of meat from his mouth. Appalled, he stared at it a moment before laying it delicately on the side of his plate. "Maggie, me love," he whispered in a none-too-quiet voice, "ya should keep a sharp watch on that cook of yours. He's usin' bad beef, don't y'know."

"I'll do that, Pat."

Cutter glanced at the cook, and wasn't surprised to see the man thoughtfully fingering the razorlike edge of a cleaver. Cutter grinned and turned back to Maggie and her admirers.

"As I was sayin' "—the first man reached for another helping of mashed potatoes—"me an' the boys, here, have found the Mother Lode at long last."

"Well, now." Maggie patted the shoulder of the man's tattered coat. "That's grand, Pat."

"Aye, it is, girleen. Once we've dug it out, we'll finally be able to repay you and your lovely da for all your kindnesses."

"Whisht." Maggie brushed his statement aside. "There's nothing owed, Pat. The Raffertys are family here."

Family, Cutter thought with a pang. If things had been different, he too would have been family. Cutter blinked, cursed himself for wandering down painful paths, and focused again on Maggie and the prospectors.

The man in the middle ducked his gray head in a half bow. "That's a lovely thought, Maggie, darlin'. Uh, would ya be havin' any more of that fine cake ya gave us last time?"

Maggie held up one hand and signaled to the

cook. Reluctantly, the man carried a three-layer chocolate cake to the table and set it down amid the litter of a huge meal hurriedly consumed.

"Will that do ya for a while, do you think?" Maggie leaned down close to the man called Mike and laid one arm along his filthy shoulders.

"For now, girleen. For now."

"Well, then," she said, and kissed the weathered cheek of each of them in turn, "I'll just be off and getting busy. If you need anything else, you call me, you hear?"

"We will an' all, love," Mike assured her, and Cutter didn't doubt for a moment that they would.

Maggie finally saw him as she headed for the door. Her pleased grin slowly faded, and he could see that she was thinking fast and furious.

He stepped aside and held the door open for her. When she was through, he followed and let the swinging door fall closed behind them.

"Before you say anything, *partner*," Maggie started, "you should know that the Raffertys have been eating here for years, and I'm not about to stop feeding them now."

So that was why her happy smile had died so abruptly, he realized. She had thought he was going to put up a fight over the free food. And maybe he should have. As a businessman, he knew damned well it didn't make any sense at all to give away what you could sell. Of course, they offered free lunches in the saloon every day. But that was done with the expectation that the men eating would also be ordering, and paying for, something to drink.

From the looks of the Raffertys, he doubted they'd paid for anything in years.

Cutter looked down into her features and noted the defiant tilt of her chin. Clearly, she was ready to do battle over this. Instantly the old daguerreotype he'd just been looking at rushed back to mind. Maggie at five, a black eye to prove her a battler for justice.

Now here was Maggie at twenty-six, so beautiful and still so willing to fight to protect what she considered right. But she wouldn't have to fight him over this, he knew.

Those three old foxes were safe in *this* hen house.

Cutter could no more have thrown them out than he could have left, himself. The Raffertys. They didn't belong, either. And with their tattered clothes and lack of money, they were even further outside than Cutter was. But that didn't matter. Outside was outside.

He knew what it was to belong to nothing and to no one. He knew firsthand how much it meant to have at least one place where you could go and know that the people there would take you in.

He remembered all too clearly the loneliness of those first two years he'd spent away from Seven Oaks. Alone. Broke. Hungry. No one to give a damn if he lived or died. The long days and even longer nights of weary travel with no destination in mind.

But, he reminded himself, along with those dark memories were brighter ones, too. The recollection of the day Kevin Donnelly had found him raced through Cutter's mind.

A tall, too-thin eighteen-year-old, Cutter had

been rooting through the trash on the docks, looking for discarded food—or perhaps a coin or two. Something, *anything*, to help him fill the aching void that his stomach had become.

The short, graying man with the thick Irish accent had clapped him on the shoulder and guided him home. Home to a saloon where a sharp-tongued housekeeper and four little girls waited. And in a matter of minutes, Kevin Donnelly had had Cutter settled at the family table before a plate heaped with more food than the boy had seen in a month.

Wary, cautious, and still bleeding from the internal wounds his family had dealt him just two years before, Cutter had accepted the meal and watched the closeness of the Donnelly clan with envious eyes.

And as they'd slowly drawn him into their tight circle of love, Cutter had gone carefully. He'd wanted to be a part of them, to belong. But he'd lived in fear that they would find out what he really was—that they would discover that he wasn't any good. That he'd been disowned by the only family he'd ever known.

He'd lived in fear that he would be cast out of the warmth a second time.

Over the years, Cutter had accepted their love, but hadn't quite been able to bring himself to depend on it—or return it. He'd learned the hard way that the only person anyone could ever really count on was himself. And he'd learned that love could become hate in an instant, that lives could be shattered with a word ... that love, suddenly snatched away, was the cruelest weapon in the world.

And the fear had never left him.

"Cutter?" Maggie said, and her tone assured him it wasn't the first time she'd spoken. "Are you listening to me a'tall?"

He gave himself a mental shake. "Yeah. Yeah, I'm listening, Maggie."

She folded her arms across her chest, and Cutter noted briefly and with thanks that she was wearing a high-necked white blouse with long sleeves and ruffled cuffs. Even her skirt that day was a floor-length, subdued, coffee brown. In his weakened condition, he didn't know if he could have withstood the temptations of another gown like the one she'd worn two days earlier in the cellar.

"Well, good," she continued. "I want you to know I meant what I said. I'll not be turning the Raffertys away, no matter how much they eat."

"Fine."

"I don't care what you say—" She broke off abruptly and stared at him. "What did you just say?"

"I said fine. Feed them all they can eat."

"You don't know the Raffertys." Her arms fell to her sides, and her entire posture relaxed. "They could eat the wallpaper off the walls if you left them to it long enough."

Cutter shrugged. He almost enjoyed confounding her like this. "We'll get new wallpaper, then."

"What are you up to?"

"Not a damned thing, Maggie."

"Well." A slow smile curved her lips, and Cutter's breath caught. "Thanks, Cutter. I'd expected a fight on this—but thanks."

"You're welcome." Lord it felt good to have her smile at him and mean it.

"Do you mind my asking why?"

"Why what?"

"Why you don't mind the Raffertys' cleaning out the kitchen."

A half-strangled chuckle drifted from his throat. "Does there have to be a reason?"

"Yeah," she said slowly. "I think so."

He shrugged. "Let's say I understand them."

Her brow wrinkled. "You didn't believe any of their nonsense about finding a gold mine and paying us back, did you?" She shook her head firmly. "They've been saying the same thing off and on since I was a girl. And no one's ever seen a glimpse of any gold."

"No." Cutter glanced at the closed kitchen door. From behind it, he could just hear the three men badgering the cook for more food.

A strange, sad smile crossed his features and was gone before Maggie had a chance to identify it. This wasn't what she'd been expecting at all. Strange to think that Cutter still had the ability to surprise her, after all these years.

Then, slowly, realization dawned. The flash of sadness on his face. His saying he understood the Raffertys. Of course.

Maggie felt like a fool. She should have realized earlier that the Raffertys would no doubt remind Cutter of the first day he'd come to the Roses.

"I suppose you do understand them, after all," she said softly.

"Better than I care to think." He shoved one hand through his dark blond hair, then thrust it deep into the pocket of his well-tailored black pants. Legs spread wide, he shifted slightly from foot to foot.

Obviously the memories made him uneasy.

"But it's different for you now, Cutter," she said quietly. His gaze snapped to hers, and Maggie saw the shadows that were a part of him slip fitfully across his blue eyes.

"Is it?" He shook his head slowly. "I don't think so. Not really."

"But look at you." She waved one hand at him, indicating the fine suit of clothes. "Well dressed and well fed. Owner of two saloons. You've done well, Cutter. Can't you see that?"

"Done well?" It sounded as though he was talking more to himself than to her. "I wonder."

Maggie laid one hand on his forearm. For the first time since delivering her threat to drive him out of his mind with want, she was touching him with a gentle concern that had nothing to do with seduction, but was simply the need she felt to reassure him somehow.

"It's not just your business, Cutter," she said softly, "or your fine clothes." She paused and waited for him to look at her again. "It's you. You're not alone anymore, Cutter. You're one of us. You're family."

He winced, and took a step back . . . a single step that Maggie was sure had put him out of her reach.

"Family?" He said the word as if he were speaking a foreign language. "For how long?"

"What kind of question is that?" she asked, almost afraid to hear the answer.

"The only important one."

"How long?"

He nodded.

She shrugged. "However long you want it to be true, I suppose."

"No." Cutter shook his head and gave her another sad, strange smile. "What I *want* has nothing to do with anything."

What were they talking about? she asked herself silently. Aloud she said firmly, "If I say you're family, Cutter—you'll be family forever."

"Nothing is forever, Maggie. Especially family."

"Love is forever." She said it quickly, almost desperately.

Something was going on. Something she didn't know anything about. The play of dappled sunshine across his face seemed to reflect the changeable emotions he was trying to explain to her. It frightened her a bit to watch a shutter drop over his familiar features, closing her out.

"Love?" he repeated gently. "Maggie, love lasts only as long as someone needs it to. No longer."

"Ah, Cutter," she said on a sigh. "For a smart man, you're a bit of a fool at times."

One side of his mouth lifted in a tired smile. And in that halfhearted grin, she recognized the wary, hungry young man he'd been so many years before. The teasing glint was gone from his eyes, and in its place was a haunted, cautious look.

How had she known and loved him for so long and so well and never guessed at this lost, sad side of him? And how had he managed to live with the Donnellys—be a part of them all—and discover nothing about loving?

"You don't know anything about the love I'm

talking about, Cutter." Maggie stepped up close to him and laid the palm of one hand over his heart. The steady, rhythmic pounding beneath her fingers reassured her, and she continued. "Whoever you learned loving from was sorely lacking."

He glanced down at her hand before looking into her eyes again. A mocking smile now touched his eyes, deepening the shadows there. "I suppose you could say that."

"Well, then," Maggie told him gently as she raised up on her toes, "pay attention, darlin'. 'Cause you have a better teacher now. And you'll stay in my class until you learn it right."

Then she kissed him.

Chapter 9

It wasn't a seduction.

The moment her lips touched his, Cutter knew the difference. This wasn't yet another of Maggie's ploys in her not-so-subtle war of temptation.

This was something different. Something more. Something far more dangerous to him.

This was love.

Even a man bent on refusing the emotion could recognize it.

And it scared the hell out of him.

His first instinct was to pull away—keep as much distance between them as possible. Cutter's mind knew that kissing Maggie would only make an already unbearable situation worse. Unfortunately, his body instantly responded to her and refused to listen to his more-rational brain.

Gently, tenderly, she moved her mouth over his. Her right hand reached up and cupped his cheek, and he felt the warmth of her all the way down to the emptiness in his soul. Her breath dusted lightly against his flesh, and each small puff of air was like a benediction, a blessing.

Cutter bit back a groan. Somehow, this tenderness was even more difficult to withstand than her blatantly tempting behavior.

Everything in him cried out to hold her. To clasp her to him and never let go. His hands itched to caress her. His body ached with wanting her. Yet that voice in the back of his mind cried out a warning. To lose himself in her, to accept the warmth she offered, would be to turn his back on the one thing he'd been working toward for years.

Justice.

Summoning the remaining dregs of his will, Cutter grabbed her waist with both hands and set her back from him.

"Maggie," he said when he thought he could speak without betraying how shaken he was, "you've got to stop this."

"Stop what?" Her already dark green eyes took on the shadowed depths of a forest in the night. He watched the rapid rise and fall of her breasts and knew his own breathing wasn't much more steady.

Cutter ran one hand over the back of his neck. "Don't play this game anymore, Maggie."

"I don't know what you're talking about, Cutter."

"Like hell you don't," he snapped, and immediately regretted it. He'd get nowhere with her if he made her mad.

"What's the matter?" she asked. "Am I beginning to bother you?"

"Beginning to?" He laughed—a short, harsh laugh that scraped his throat and didn't hold a trace of humor. "You know damned well what you're doing to me."

She smiled.

"But can't you see that it doesn't change anything?"

"No." Maggie lifted her chin and stared at him defiantly. "I think it changes everything."

"Well, you're wrong." Cutter inhaled sharply, then blew the air out in a rush. "It leaves us right where we were nearly a year ago."

She paled a bit, but her rigid posture didn't slip.

"Yes, I want you." His gaze moved over her, quickly, thoroughly, then snapped back up to look her directly in the eyes. "But wanting isn't loving."

"I know that."

"I don't think so."

"I'm not a starry-eyed little girl, Cutter." She took a half step toward him and stopped again. "I'm twenty-six years old. I grew up in a saloon, for God's sake. I know about men's *wants*. Lord knows I've seen enough men make fools of themselves over women through the years."

He opened his mouth to speak, but she cut him off.

"But I know something of love, too. And I know that when a man looks at a woman the way you look at me . . ." Her voice trailed off.

Cutter's gaze dropped. "I can't give you what you want."

"Can't, or won't?"

He snorted and looked back up at her. She looked proud and confident and so damned beautiful. "Is there a difference?"

"You know there is." Maggie folded her arms over her chest and tilted her head to one side. "For reasons I haven't figured out yet, you've decided that you won't let yourself love me."

Cutter clenched his jaw tight.

"But I will figure it out, Cutter." One foot tapped against the wooden floor. "The only way you can stop me is to sign over your half of the saloon and leave town."

Damn, she had a hard head.

"And if you'll remember," she added, her voice silky, "you left town once already. It didn't help."

"Coming back hasn't helped much either," he pointed out.

"That's your own fault."

She turned away and started walking toward the table where the account books were still scattered. Cutter's gaze locked on the sway of her hips even as he told himself she was doing it deliberately.

"Now," she said with a glance over her shoulder as she took her seat at the table, "if you'll excuse me, I've got to go over the books."

Dismissed.

She'd finished what she had to say and then dismissed him as though he were a schoolboy who'd stepped over the line of good behavior. Cutter glared at the back of her head. He found himself wondering if the partnership was worth all the trouble he was having.

But with his next breath, he assured himself that it was. A new singer was coming. Jake was now performing his Blue Blazer mix nightly, and soon the billiard tables would be arriving from St. Louis. With the money he'd put aside over the years—even minus what he'd had to pay Kevin—added to the profits from the Roses, in another month or so he would have enough money to go back to Georgia. To tie up the loose ends of his life that he'd left dangling so many years before.

He would settle with his family and then brush the dust of memories from his mind and soul. If only it were as easy to rid himself of the knowledge of what he was. A bastard. Maybe then he would have had a chance with Maggie.

"Good morning."

Cutter glanced at the front door and just managed to contain a groan. Mary Frances. Just what he needed, he thought. Yet another Donnelly woman.

"Hello, Frankie."

"Morning Frankie." His voice echoed Maggie's as he started moving toward the stairs.

"Where are you off to, Cutter?"

He didn't even look back as he answered his partner. "To the office." His bootheels clattered on the polished floor as he nearly sprinted up the stairs, entered the office, and closed the door behind him.

"Just what is going on here, Maggie?"

Looking away from the closed office door, Maggie glanced at her sister, then stood up and walked to the bar. She couldn't quite decide whether or not she was pleased that her sister had chosen that moment to make a surprise visit. Oh, her little chat with Cutter hadn't been going anywhere, but the fact that Mary Frances was in the saloon at all heralded trouble. Normally the younger woman avoided the Roses as she would a plague-ridden shack.

"Coffee, Frankie?" she asked.

"No, I don't want any coffee," her sister shot

back. "What I want is to know why in heaven Cutter is living in Da's room."

Digger tossed back the jiggerful of whiskey, then turned his head to stare at the man standing next to him. True, the fellow didn't look like much, but then, he didn't cost much, either.

"So you understand what it is I want, do ya?"

"Sure." The younger man twitched slightly, and his narrow frame seemed to shiver with the movement. "When do I get paid?"

"After the job's done, o'course." Ah, well, Digger told himself, stupid men were easier to order about, anyway.

"Right, then." The rail-thin, dark-haired man nodded. "I'll be back here tonight."

"I'll know if ya did it or not, y'know."

"Yeah, I know."

As the younger man left, Digger followed him with his gaze. Probably a waste of time, but hell. It was fun. And Lord knew, if it caused Cutter a speck of trouble, it was worth it.

"Because I love him."

It made perfect sense to Maggie, though she was willing to admit that it might have come as something of a shock to Mary Frances. But then, she reasoned, if Frankie had looked up from one of her books occasionally, she might have noticed that a whole lot of things were going on around her.

Then again, Maggie thought as she gazed thoughtfully at her sister, maybe she wouldn't have. Frankie had spent most of her twenty-four years determined to avoid noticing life at all.

She even dressed as though she were trying to blend into the background, to be overlooked.

The plain, dove-gray dress she wore was simple and unadorned. It fell listlessly from her hips, and Maggie was sure that Frankie was wearing only one petticoat. The gray gown, which was a bit loose around Frankie's slightly plump waist and bosom, wasn't the least bit flattering. And no doubt that was exactly why Frankie had purchased it. Even her strawberry-blond hair had been tamed into submission and woven into a braid that lay like a reluctant crown around her skull.

Now Frankie stared at Maggie as though she'd lost her mind. "You love Cutter? Since when?"

Maggie poured herself a cup of coffee, then walked to her sister's side. Ushering Frankie to a nearby table, she waited until they were both seated before saying, "Since I was ten years old."

Frankie's jaw dropped. "You're serious."

"Of course."

"Well, then, no wonder Rose came to see me." She folded her hands neatly together on the tabletop. The only sign of her agitation was a high blush staining her cheeks.

"Rose?" At the thought of her interfering housekeeper, Maggie frowned. She'd settle up with *her* later. "What did she say?"

"Oh, only that my older sister had invited Cutter to move into Da's room—"

Maggie smiled.

"—*and* that she was flaunting herself shamelessly in front of the man!"

Frankie's cheeks burned even redder, and

Maggie realized just how worried her younger sister must have been to come to the Four Roses. Mary Frances had never liked the saloon. In fact, except for attending family meetings once a month, Maggie couldn't remember the last time Frankie had come by.

"Are you, Mary Margaret?"

"Am I what?" She gave herself a mental shake and determined to pay attention.

"Flaunting yourself."

"Every chance I get."

A quick intake of breath was the only sign of Frankie's increasing distress. After a long pause, she asked "Why?"

"It's very simple, really," Maggie told her with a shrug. "I'm trying to trap Cutter into admitting that he loves me too."

"Trap?" Frankie shook her head and looked at her sister as if she were a stranger. "You think you can trap a man into love?"

"He already loves me, Frankie. He just hasn't admitted it yet."

"Maybe there's a good reason for that."

"Maybe."

"Don't you have any pride?"

Pride. Why was everyone so blasted concerned with her pride? "Yes, I do, Mary Frances. Too much pride to hide how I feel anymore. Why the hell shouldn't I admit to loving a man?"

"There's no reason to swear at me, Maggie."

"Dammit, Frankie." Maggie shook her index finger at her sister. "Don't go getting all stone cold and stiff on me now."

Frankie's features froze over.

"Would you rather I was ashamed of being in love?"

Her sister reacted to the change of Maggie's tone. Her shoulders relaxed, and the grim set of her chin softened. "No." She looked down at her tightly laced fingers and shook her head gently. "But aren't you afraid?"

"Of what?" Maggie leaned in closer and laid her hand across her sister's.

Frankie glanced up and met Maggie's now-concerned gaze. "What if he doesn't love you, Maggie? What if, after all you're doing ... he doesn't want you?"

Want? A small inward chuckle died quickly. She already knew he wanted her. He'd made no secret of *that*. But what about Frankie's other concern?

A curl of worry spiraled down Maggie's spine, and she swiveled her head slightly to look up at the office door. She was so sure in her own mind that he loved her; the thought that he might never admit it hadn't occurred to her.

Oh, he protested and claimed that he didn't love her. But what he said and what he felt were two different things. She was sure of it. She knew it, deep inside her.

He did love her. He did. The incredible feelings they'd shared ... the times when they'd been together ... that all had to mean *something*.

But what if Frankie was right? she asked herself. What if, despite everything ... he tossed her aside? What if he could never bring himself to admit it? What then?

Maggie swallowed heavily. All those months before, when he'd apologized for making love to her, she'd thought then that no pain could be greater than what she'd felt that night. And then, when he'd left and been gone for months, the loneliness had threatened to kill her.

But now—now that she'd admitted to loving him, now that she'd as good as told him that she was determined to marry him—wouldn't the pain of rejection be unbearable? She had risked it all this time. She'd gambled everything on the belief that he loved her.

Maggie drew in a deep breath. When the stakes were this high, she told herself, she had to play every card in her hand.

Because if he left her again—if he turned his back on her one more time—it would be over.

Even a hardheaded Irishwoman had limits to what she was willing to go through.

This was their last chance, whether Cutter knew it or not.

"Maggie?" Frankie asked. "Are you all right?"

Dragging her gaze away from the office door, Maggie turned to her sister and forced a smile. "Fine, Frankie. I'm fine."

Before she could say anything else, a faraway voice bellowed into the sudden stillness.

"Maggie, darlin'!"

Frankie's eyes widened as she looked toward the closed kitchen door. She stared as if she could see through it to the room beyond. "Who is that?"

Maggie's lips curved in a half smile. "The Raffertys."

Frankie gasped and grabbed her throat. All trace of color left her face. Even her hair looked pale. Her eyes even wider, she whispered hurriedly, "All of them?"

"Of course." Maggie shrugged. "When have you known one to travel without the other two?"

Mary Frances shuddered. "Never."

Obviously, memories of the Raffertys' previous visits were racing through Frankie's mind. Laughter bubbled in Maggie's throat, but she refused to give in to it. Yet.

"Oh, good Lord!" Frankie leaped out of her chair as if her skirts were on fire. "I, uh . . . oh . . . good-bye, Maggie," she said hastily, and started for the front door.

The moment the door slammed behind her, Maggie gave free rein to the laughter choking her. Maybe it was the tension of the morning. Maybe it was the new worries Frankie had managed to instill in her. But whatever the cause, Maggie's chuckles went on and on, shaking her body, until she had to prop her elbows on the table and cup her face in her hands.

It was only then she noticed the tears on her cheeks.

David walked past his father as if he were invisible.

When the old man shouted for him to stop, David didn't break his stride. If possible, he wanted to get out of the stiflingly perfect house and down to the Roses without a fight.

His father's hand on his arm abruptly ended that hope.

"You're not going out this evening."

"I'm a grown man."

"Still living off the largess of your father."

The barb stung, but David could hardly dispute it. In fact, he'd often wondered why he bothered to stay in the cold, empty house. The only reason he'd come up with was that his very presence infuriated his father.

That seemed more than enough.

David yanked his arm free, snatched up his coat and hat from the hall tree, and grasped the brass doorknob.

"I'll shut that place down."

"You can't. Saloons aren't illegal."

"Whorehouses are," the judge pointed out.

"The Roses is not a whorehouse."

"And I'm supposed to take the word of a drunk for that?" The judge's eyes narrowed as he gazed at his only child. "One word from me and the place will be shut down."

"You flatter yourself, Father." David shook his head tiredly. "In fact, perhaps you should stop by some night. You'd be surprised by just how many of your friends frequent the Four Roses." A half smile touched one corner of his mouth. "Who knows? Maybe it'd do you some good."

"As it's done you?" The judge snorted derisively.

"You have no idea how much that place has done for me," David replied quietly.

"I know what it's done *to* you."

"What?" David reared his head back and stared at his sire through already blurry eyes. "Are you referring to the fact that I'm a drunk?"

"What else?"

The old man was livid. Small patches of deep red formed on his cheeks and temples. The pulse point in his throat pounded like a blacksmith's hammer, and the grim, tight lines of his mouth straightened even further.

Every inch of his father's slight body quaked

with outrage and if David hadn't already had a
few drinks, that might have been enough to
keep him from antagonizing the man further. As
it was though, the warm, bourbon glow cours-
ing through his veins insulated him from such
trivial things as caution or tact.

"Ah, *Father*," he breathed, and the older man
took a hasty step back to avoid the rush of
liquor-soaked air directed at him. "You give the
Roses far too much credit. That worthwhile
structure merely provides me with the means to
slake my unquenchable thirst." He leaned forward a bit, staggered, and righted himself again.
"You, dear Father, are entirely responsible for
awakening in me the thirst itself."

Judge Harper's features hardened. The patches
of red darkened, and a vein in his temple began
to throb. But David didn't notice. He had already
stepped outside, and was concentrating completely on navigating the short flight of steps
leading to his waiting carriage.

The crowd was even larger than it had been
the night before.

Cutter leaned against the bar and let his gaze
slide over the jostling throng. Ladies in fine silk
gowns brushed up against weather-beaten prospectors. Cowboys in town on business propped
their dusty boots on the brass footrails, alongside the elegantly polished shoes of well-
dressed gentlemen.

Some of the girls from the Garter wandered in
and out of the crowd, dazzling the lonelier men
with promise-filled smiles. A high-pitched laugh
cut short abruptly caught Cutter's ear, and he
turned toward the sound.

Lilah. His lips quirked. He hadn't seen her in days, and, in truth, hadn't given her a thought. As he watched her now, leaning against the chest of a man old enough to be her grandfather, he could hardly credit the fact that he'd once thought bedding Lilah was the best a man could feel.

She looked up just then, caught his eye, and winked. In spite of himself, Cutter chuckled. Lilah was . . . Lilah. Her one and only concern in life was taking care of herself.

Almost unwillingly, he shifted his gaze to the far corner of the saloon. Even across the huge crowd of people, Cutter's eyes went unerringly to Maggie. So different. So different from Lilah and from the people in the world he'd left behind so long before.

He watched as she smiled at first one, then another, of their customers. She treated everyone alike, he noticed, not for the first time, from the bankers and lawyers to the working cowhands to the panhandling Rafferty brothers. They were all the same to her. And they all received her warmth and humor and friendliness.

As he watched, she leaned down close to one of the men, apparently trying to hear what he was saying. Lamplight made her copper curls dazzling. Her pale yellow gown hugged her figure and set off to perfection her smooth, creamy flesh.

The cowboy she leaned over reached up and drew his fingertips across the pale expanse of her chest. Immediately Cutter straightened and took a half step away from the bar. He watched as she snatched the man's hand, only to have the determined cowboy grab her with his free hand and drag her down on his lap.

Something dark and hot flickered in Cutter's gut. The sights and sounds of the saloon fell away until all he saw was the cowboy . . . and Maggie. A rush of fury swamped him, and Cutter started moving without conscious thought. His jaw clenched tightly, his fingers curled into fists, he was halfway across the room in seconds. His gaze locked on the cowboy, Cutter willed the man to look at him, to feel his rage at seeing another man's hands on Maggie's body.

But the cowboy didn't look away from his captured prize. In fact, he appeared to be well pleased with himself. Laughing up into Maggie's face, the man pulled her even closer, clearly intent on stealing a kiss or two.

Cutter could hardly breathe. Shoving his way through the crowd, he didn't even hear the disgruntled customers shouting at him. All he could see was that cowboy. All he knew was that he wanted nothing more than to feel his fists crash into the younger man's face.

So intent was he on his own plans, Cutter didn't notice Maggie drawing her hand back until he saw her closed fist slam into the cowboy's jaw. The young man's head snapped back from the impact, and Maggie clumsily pushed herself to her feet.

Shaking the soreness out of her right hand, with her left she reached up to the pile of curls on top of her head and pulled out her hatpin.

Grinning, Cutter watched as she waved the long, sharp piece of steel under the cowboy's nose. But even knowing that she had the situation well in hand didn't slow him down.

Though the cowhand had been taught one lesson, Cutter knew he wouldn't be happy until the man had found out what being tossed into the street felt like.

It seemed to take forever to reach his goal, and when he finally did, Cutter had to snatch the cowboy away from Maggie.

"Leave him be, Cutter," she told him with a steely look at the young man, whose vest was clutched in Cutter's fist. "We've come to an understanding, haven't we?"

"Yes, ma'am." The cowboy jerked her a nod, but kept his eyes fixed on Cutter's dangerously narrowed gaze.

"Fine." Cutter tossed Maggie a quick look. "Then I'll just see our customer to the door, shall I?" He didn't wait to see if she was going to argue with him. As soon as he'd finished speaking, Cutter started dragging the protesting cowboy toward the front doors.

Chairs toppled, people scattered, and a sprinkling of laughter followed in their wake. Cutter paid no attention to any of it. Instead he concentrated completely on the man in his grasp.

Once at the doors, Cutter pushed the cowboy through with a shove hearty enough to land him in the street. Quickly, the younger man rolled over onto his back, lying in the dirt to watch the furious gambler approach.

"Mister"—Cutter spoke through gritted teeth, and every word was agony—"you so much as step one foot into the Roses or the Garter again, and so help me God, I'll tear you apart."

"I didn't mean no harm," the cowboy insisted, and scooted back a bit farther out of reach.

Cutter took two quick steps, leaned over the man in the dirt, and snatched his shirt front. Lifting him slightly, he looked him squarely in the eye. "I don't give a good goddamn *what* you meant. You stay away from here—and keep the *hell* away from Maggie Donnelly!"

"Yessir." The cowboy's eyes were wide as saucers.

Cutter glared at him for another moment, then released him abruptly. The man dropped like a stone, slamming into the dirt. Pulling a long, deep breath into his lungs, Cutter told himself that it was over. Finished.

Hell, the cowboy looked scared enough to stay out of San Francisco completely in the future!

He smiled to himself and stepped up onto the boardwalk. As he went back inside the Roses, all he could think about was seeing Maggie. Holding her. Reassuring himself that she was all right.

Cutter was still pushing his way through the crowd when the front window shattered.

He glanced to his left in time to see splintered shards of glass fly into the startled crowd.

Chapter 10

⟨ ⟩

A customer toppled from his chair.
Maggie fell instinctively to her knees beside him.

All around her, people dove for cover, upending tables and chairs and knocking one another aside in their panic. As her gaze flew from one group to the next, Maggie's mind began to churn. What the hell was happening? She hadn't heard any gunshots. And who would want to shoot up her place, anyway?

Another ear-splitting crash sounded out over the noise of the crowd, and the remains of the first window shattered. A rock as big as a man's fist rolled to a stop at Maggie's feet. Wildly she told herself that the rock explained how—now she wanted to know who and why.

For the moment, though, all she could do was stay low and wait until the attack was over.

The room exploded in a frenzied racket as one rock after another was hurled through the wide front windows. Keeping her head down, Maggie watched as the hand-painted roses decorating the saloon windows were obliterated in an instant.

Long, daggerlike shards of glass rained down on the customers, now desperate to escape.

Maggie turned her face away from the windows and looked across the room, hoping for a glimpse of Cutter. She'd seen him reenter the saloon. Heart pounding, breath caught in her chest, she stared openmouthed as her familiar surroundings dissolved into a sea of chaos.

Over the sounds of chair legs scraping against the floor and heavy oak tables being overturned as people sought shelter, Maggie heard several frightened women begin to scream. She bit down hard on her lip to keep from joining them. Men shouted to be heard above the uproar, and the once-well-mannered crowd quickly became a mob.

Maggie, at once terrified and angry, was torn between the desire to jump for cover and the need to fight her way through the crowd to the outside, where she might catch up to whoever was behind this mess.

A sharp, stinging pain in her right arm decided her. She glanced down and saw blood well up from the neatly sliced flesh of her forearm. Instinctively she dropped her hatpin and clapped her left hand over the wound, hoping at least to slow the bleeding. Gritting her teeth, Maggie tried to keep watch on the crowd—and what was left of her windows—from behind the dubious shelter of a slat-backed chair.

Still her gaze continued to search through the mass of people, searching for Cutter. Even though she knew she'd never be able to spot him among the hordes racing aimlessly around the room, she couldn't keep herself from trying.

Someone nearby moaned, and she shifted her gaze to the floor beside her. An elegantly dressed man lay on the floor, a piece of jagged glass imbedded in his shoulder.

Maggie reached for him, wincing at the movement. Gently she laid her right hand on his hair. "Lie still, mister. This'll be over in a minute."

He looked at her out of the corner of his eye and gave her a pain-filled grin. "Happens all the time, huh?"

"Sure thing." Maggie nodded, swallowed heavily, and continued the lie. "Livens up an evening, doesn't it?"

"Yes'm," he said, then closed his eyes.

She didn't know if he was still conscious, but she hoped he wasn't. The glass dagger impaled in his shoulder, no matter how painful, would have to remain where it was until a doctor could see him. Until then, there was nothing she could do except hope that he would be comfortably unconscious. After a moment, she dragged her gaze away from him and stared at her surroundings.

People raced past her in their haste to get out of the building. Maggie propped her chair in front of the fallen man, hoping to protect him from being stomped to death, just as a small man in a dapper black suit tripped. He fell face first to the glass-littered floor in front of her, and the crowd ran right over him.

From her vantage point, Maggie could see him but not reach him. His brown eyes opened, and his gaze locked on her. Helplessly she watched as dozens of people stepped on or kicked the little man in their frenzy. His features screwed up in pain, and short groans shot from his throat, but no one seemed to hear him. Like a herd of cattle spooked by lightning, the members of San Francisco society moved with a driving force that couldn't be stopped. Unthinking, unseeing, they were all swept up in a mindless panic.

The little man didn't stand a chance.

His eyes squeezed shut against the pain, the man tried twice to rise, pushing himself to his hands and knees, but each time, another surge of people knocked him back to the floor.

When someone at last stopped, Maggie's breath caught on a sigh of relief. It took her a moment to recognize the tall, slender man in a torn black suit. But when he reached down, Maggie looked past the straggly blond hair and bloody split lip. She smiled briefly as she watched David Harper brace his long legs against the rush of the crowd and grab the fallen man's shoulders. Gritting his teeth, he gave a powerful yank and plucked the smaller man out of harm's way. Then David tucked his prize tight against his side and started running again.

For the first time in months, Maggie was glad David had been at the saloon. And by the grace of God, he was sober enough to be of help. She turned away to watch the tight knots of people as they swarmed toward the nearest exit. They crowded together in the brand-new archway joining the Roses and the Garter. Shoulder to shoulder, pushing and shoving, rich and poor alike struggled to escape.

But when the next rock splintered through a window, it sounded farther away, and Maggie knew that their attacker had now started in on the Garter.

As one, it seemed, panicked customers from both saloons turned and began to push their way back through the rubble of furniture toward the Roses' front door. Blind panic fed their progress. Driven by their fear, they stampeded across the room, going through what they couldn't push aside or go around. The terrible racket pounded in Maggie's brain as steadily as the rocks still being thrown through the windows.

Something moved above her, and as Maggie glanced up, fear clutched at her. A rock must have struck one of the chandeliers, she thought desperately. The crystal-and-brass light fixture was swinging on its chain in a wide arc, casting oddly-shaped shadows that flew about the room. She mumbled a quick prayer that the groaning chain would hold.

If the chandelier fell, it would only take seconds for spilled lamp oil to ignite under the flames and burn down what was left of the Roses. And when the Four Roses was nothing more than a pile of ashes, it still wouldn't be over. On the Barbary Coast, where most of the buildings were ancient wooden structures, dried out from the sun and salt air, a fire would feed itself until it had consumed everything in sight. From saloons to warehouses to perhaps even the ships at dock in the harbor—everything could be gone by morning.

"Maggie!"

She tore her gaze from the swaying lights

above her and searched frantically for the owner of that voice.

Surprisingly, it took her only a moment to find him. In the sea of people, only one person was fighting his way in her direction. All the others, concerned with their own escape, were blocking his way. Maggie watched as Cutter made his way through the crowd. Like a crazy man, he kept moving, no matter the obstacle. Shoving and pushing, shouting to be heard over the din, he kept coming. His clothes were torn, and there was a slight trail of blood lying along his left cheek.

He'd never looked better.

Maggie leaped to her feet and started moving toward him. He waved one arm at her and shouted, "Stay down, damn you!"

Instead, she glanced to where a wall of windows had once stood. All that remained were a few stubborn shards of glass, jutting up from their frames. The danger was over.

There was nothing left to smash.

The man in the alley behind the Roses listened to the clamoring voices and smiled. He wasn't quite sure what was happening, but whatever it was, it made his plan much easier to carry out.

Crouching low in the shadows, his back to the cold wind blowing in off the ocean, the man struck a match. The flame leaped into life, skittered, and died. Cursing under his breath, the man struck another match and this time cupped his palms around the eager flame until it was steady. Then, carefully, he held the burning match to the corner of a waiting rag.

The rag, soaked in oil, at first smoldered; black smoke rose up, twisting, curling, then disappearing in the wind. Softly, caressingly, the man whispered encouragement to the tiny flames just beginning to creep up the edges of the rag. A satisfied smile curved his narrow lips as the fire grew and began to spread along the line of oil-soaked cloths he had laid out in preparation.

Shaking out the match, he tossed it aside and stood up. He hunched deeper into his coat and stared down at the flames as they swayed and writhed along their path of destruction.

A moment more, he told himself. Only a moment. He only wanted to be sure that the fire was well underway. Then he would be off. He'd go to the Plaza, he told himself. Somewhere where there were plenty of people. People who would be able to swear that he was miles away from the Barbary Coast on the night the whole damned place burned down.

Smiling to himself, he turned and hurried away.

"Damn you, Maggie!" Cutter kept shouting even though he knew she couldn't hear him. If the damned people in his damned way would shut their damned mouths, he thought furiously, he'd be able to make her hear, make her get down and out of danger. Obviously she wouldn't do it on her own.

The whole bloody building was exploding, piece by piece, and there she stood—her bright red hair like a beacon—practically *demanding* that someone shove a piece of glass into her!

He'd never felt so bloody useless in his life. He couldn't reach Maggie ... he couldn't get outside and find the bastard responsible ... and he couldn't make those damn fools around him see that, with their blind panic, they were creating more danger than there was already.

If they would just get down—crawl under the tables, wait it out—no one would get hurt. As it was, he knew from the groans and gasps of pain he heard that no one would be leaving the Roses unmarked that night.

Someone grabbed at him to steady himself and managed to latch on to the black string tie around his neck. Cutter's head snapped back, and he pushed blindly at whoever was holding him. Tugging himself free, he lowered his head and plowed through to the edges of the crowd. Only a few more feet, he told himself. Once clear of the mob, he'd be at her side in a couple of steps. Then, Cutter promised himself, he'd throw her to the goddamn floor and sit on her, if he had to, to keep her down.

She reached up to push her hair out of her eyes, and Cutter saw the blood running down her arm. It fell onto the skirt of her pale yellow gown in great red drops, soaking into the fragile material.

"Dammit, Maggie," he shouted, and knew his words were swallowed by the general pandemonium. "You're already hurt!" How badly? he asked himself. Lord, how badly? "Sit down, damn you!"

If she heard him, she wasn't paying any attention. She took one step toward him, then stopped and glanced back at the man lying behind her. Good, Cutter thought. If she was too stubborn to look out for herself, maybe at least she'd stay put for the injured man's sake.

"Almost through," he muttered, and shoved past the sweating, fat man in his way. He ignored the man's red-cheeked fury and concentrated instead on the small bit of floor that separated him from Maggie.

What made him look, he wasn't sure. Even much later, when he'd had time to think about it, Cutter couldn't figure out just what it was that had caught his attention. But whatever the reason, he turned his head to the left in time to see one last rock come hurtling through what remained of the front windows.

Before he could move, before he could shout another warning, it was too late.

As if aimed at her, the fist-sized rock slammed against the side of Maggie's head.

She stared at him for a heart-stopping moment. Her green eyes widened in shock and pain. She took a stumbling half step toward him, and then her eyelids slid shut. Her body seemed to collapse in on itself. As Maggie slumped bonelessly, he threw himself forward and managed to cradle her head in his arms just before they hit the glass-littered floor together.

Ike took the back door from the Garter. It was quicker. He'd already tried the new arch and found it impassable. And with the patrons of both saloons streaming into the street, he knew the alley was the only way he'd reach the Roses in time to help.

He had a pretty good idea of just who was

behind this mess, and once he'd made sure everybody was all right, he'd go calling on the mean little bastard.

For the moment, though, he was too busy to think about what he'd do to Digger once he got his hands on him.

Long legs flying, Ike rounded the corner of the Garter and sprinted through the dark alley. Familiar, ugly odors assaulted him as he ran— rotting food, cheap whiskey from broken, discarded bottles, and the stench of the unwashed men sleeping in the shadows. He squinted into the darkness, trying to avoid stepping on anyone or anything that might slow him down.

He heard his heart pounding and the ragged sound of his labored breathing. Out in the street, shouts and screams rang out, drowning the usual din from the off-key pianos and tuneless guitars. The alley had never seemed so long to him before. So dark.

But not completely dark. A nagging in the back of his mind made him slide to a stop. He stared into the shadows, blinked, and looked again. No, he wasn't crazy. There *was* a light there. Where there should have been nothing but blackness, a small, flickering light danced and wavered in the wind.

Flickering.

Fire.

Even before the thought had taken root in his mind, Ike was moving once more. He leaped at the long line of oil-soaked rags and stomped his booted foot down on them. Again and again the stubborn flame sprang back into life, and each time Ike put it out. With the toe of his boot, he poked at the rags, dragging them away from one another, then began to kick dirt over the stubborn flames until the last, lingering light was gone.

Breathing hard, Ike stared down at the small pile of rags and, just for a moment, considered the destruction they would have caused.

In his own mind, he was sure Digger was responsible for the rocks. That was the kind of thing Digger enjoyed. Causing other folks trouble. Making life as hard and ugly as he could. Ike had known folks like Digger all his life. Folks with small, mean minds forever plotting little cruelties.

But a fire?

Ike reached up and rubbed the back of his neck. If he hadn't come through the alley, that fire would have had time to take hold, would've burned down the Roses ... probably the Garter ... and who knows how much else of the Coast.

Would Digger have risked that? Risked having his own little rathole of a place burn down just to see to it that a "darky" got taught a lesson?

He shook his head slowly. No. Ike didn't think old Digger would have been willing to part with anything of his own in his fight to get rid of Ike and Cutter. And a fire was just too much for any man to control.

Shifting his gaze from the still-smoldering pile of rags, Ike looked around the alley slowly, carefully. Shadows melded into one another, creating patches of inky darkness— blacker spots where no light fell—where anyone might have been able to hide. A curl of unease crawled up Ike's spine, and for a minute he thought he felt someone watching him. But the feeling passed as soon as he reminded himself that whoever had set that fire was probably long gone.

If the fellow was smart enough to use a slow-burning oil rag as a fuse ... he was smart enough to know to get the hell out of a fire's way.

With a long, last look, Ike turned and went on around the corner to the Four Roses' kitchen door. He'd tell Cutter about this, see what he thought. As for Ike, he was already sure about his own ideas.

It looked to him like Digger wasn't the only problem they had to worry about.

She opened her right eye cautiously. The dim light from a nearby lamp stabbed into her brain, and Maggie moaned just before closing her eye again.

"Oh, no, you don't," a deep, familiar voice said. "You've been asleep long enough. Wake up."

"Don't shout."

Maggie lifted her right hand to her forehead and tried to soothe the hammers beating against her skull. It was no use, though, the pounding went on and on.

"Lie still," the voice demanded.

"Make up your mind."

"What?"

"I *said*"—Maggie opened her right eye again and glared at Cutter—"make up your mind. You want me to wake up, then you want me to lie still."

"Lay still *and* stay awake."

Maggie sighed and resigned herself to the inevitable. She certainly wouldn't be going back to sleep anyway. Her head hurt far too much to allow that.

She opened both eyes and carefully let her vision adjust to the light in the room. The pounding in her head picked up a bit, then settled down into a steady, throbbing rhythm. Glancing toward the foot of her bed, Maggie at last gave Cutter her full attention.

He looked dreadful.

A wicked-looking cut angled down his forehead and stopped just above his right eyebrow. Several knotted, black thread stitches held the gash closed, and she winced, just looking at them.

If there was one thing Maggie Donnelly hated, it was doctors. Always wanting to poke you and prod you and pour disgusting potions down your throat. She looked at the long line of stitches again and would have shaken her head if she had been sure the action wouldn't kill her. Doctors! A seamstress would have done a better job of sewing. At least then the stitches would have been even. By the look of the wound, Cutter would carry a scar as a permanent reminder of ... what? she wondered silently.

How had he gotten hurt? Why was her head fair to splitting?

"Feeling better now?" he asked, his whispered drawl falling like a balm on her pounding head.

"Not really," she admitted, and studied him more closely.

It wasn't only the wound on his forehead that had him looking like some kind of hangdog pirate. One of his jacket lapels was hanging loose, dangling over his shirt front, and his string tie was missing. His formerly pristine white shirt was covered with grime and what looked like dirty brown water marks. But the most surprising stain was a huge footprint. Right in the middle of his chest.

"What in heaven happened to you?" she whispered, then clutched at her dry, raspy throat. She felt as though she'd swallowed a pillowful of feathers, each with a quill firmly attached.

"Heaven had nothing to do with it," Cutter assured her as he moved to her side. He picked up the pitcher from the bedside table and poured a small amount of water into a waiting glass. Then, seating himself on the edge of the bed, he gently lifted her head from the pillow so she could drink from the glass he held to her lips.

The water was cold, and tasted better than anything she could remember. And as soon as she'd eased the hurt in her throat, Maggie told herself, she would ask Cutter why she was in bed—she glanced down—fully clothed.

He pulled the glass away before she was finished, and the look she shot him was the most welcome thing he could have imagined. She was getting back in fighting form.

"The doc says you're not to have a lot of liquid right at first," he said as he set the glass back down on the table.

"Is this the same doctor who can't sew a

straight hem?" she asked, and reached up to run one finger down the row of stitches decorating his forehead.

"The same," he allowed, and captured her hand in his. Holding her hand between both of his, Cutter smiled for the first time in hours. He'd just lived through the longest night of his life, and every bone and muscle in his body was drop-dead tired. Strange that right now, he thought, all he wanted to do was grab Maggie and dance around the room with her.

As long as he lived he would remember those past several hours. He'd been hunched at the foot of her bed, staring at her—willing her to wake up—since the doctor had left her.

Even with the doctor's assurances that Maggie would be all right, Cutter had hardly breathed all night. In the cold, dark silence, he'd called himself every kind of a fool. It was all his fault.

She was lying there injured . . . unconscious . . . because he'd come back to San Francisco. Because he'd bought his way back into her life only months after leaving her.

Because he hadn't been able to stay away.

If he hadn't run into Kevin—if he hadn't allowed his own need for retribution to rule his life—Maggie would be safe and he would be just a memory to her.

Maybe, his brain chided, that was the *real* reason he'd come back. Not for the saloon. Not to satisfy a vow he had made too many years before. But because he couldn't bear the thought of never seeing her again.

No. Cutter shook his head wearily. He was too tired to be trying to think. Too angry to come to any reasonable conclusions. His lips tightened into a grim line. Angry? That was not a strong enough word for the rage that had kindled and built in him during the long night. Cutter was willing to accept the fact that his presence had brought down this trouble on Maggie.

But he knew that the man responsible for the damage belowstairs was the one to blame for her injury. Digger Wicks. It had to be. And as soon as he was convinced that Maggie was fine, Cutter was going to be paying a visit to Digger.

"Is that frown for me?" she asked quietly, and tried to tug her hand from him.

Cutter's grip tightened slightly, and he blinked away his wandering thoughts to smile at her. "Hell, no," he said. No sense having her worry about Digger at that moment. Quickly he came up with a comfortable, teasing answer. "It's aimed at that doctor for ruining my good looks."

She chuckled, moaned softly, and asked "Cutter, what's going on? What happened to you, and why am I lying here with a head bigger than Kevin's the morning after St. Patrick's Day?"

"Don't you remember? The saloon?"

Her eyebrows drew together as she tried to think.

"The rocks?" he prompted.

Maggie closed her eyes on a sigh, then opened them again to stare up at him. "The windows."

"Is everybody all right?"

"Cuts and bruises. We were lucky."

"You don't look so lucky," she pointed out. "Who stepped on you?"

Cutter glanced down at his shirt front and grimaced. "When you and I hit the floor, somebody stepped right on top of me before I had time to roll us out of the way."

She shook her head slightly, then squeezed her eyes shut at the accompanying pain. "I don't remember that."

"It's not surprising. You passed out when the rock hit your head." Before she could ask, he added, "You're all right, though. Got a knot the size of a hen's egg, but you'll do, otherwise." Cutter reached up with one hand and touched his forehead. "Nothing quite so pretty as mine, I'm afraid."

"Oh, I don't know." Maggie smiled. "It makes you look sort of ... dangerous."

His eyebrows lifted, and he winced as the stitches pulled.

"Does it hurt?"

Cutter swallowed a knowing smile. He well remembered how she loathed doctors. "No more than yours, I'll wager."

"Mine?"

He lifted her right hand so she could see the long line of neat black threads stringing along her forearm. Fortunately, the wound hadn't been nearly as bad as it had looked.

"Oh ..." Her gaze flew from her arm to his shirt front and up to his face. "Then the ... spots ... on your shirt are—"

"Blood," he finished from her.

"My blood?" Maggie groaned, and looked again at her stitches.

"Mostly," Cutter allowed, then added, "but not all."

She nodded and pulled her hand from his grip. Slowly she reached over and touched one of the knotted black threads. Her mouth flattened out, and she swallowed heavily.

Cutter saw her expression change but didn't remark on it. He knew what she was thinking. Maggie Donnelly—fighter, fierce opponent, a woman who would leap into danger without thinking about her own safety—simply couldn't bear the idea of a needle piercing her flesh.

She stared blankly at the doctor's handiwork until Cutter commented dryly, "That doctor really ought to try his hand at a quilt sometime. His needlework's as fine as any I've ever seen."

Maggie released a long, sighing breath; then her head tipped to one side and her hand went lax.

Cutter shook his head.

She'd come through a near riot and then fainted at the thought of a needle.

Rose crept down the hall to Maggie's room. After the goings on of the night before, there was no doubt the girl needed all the sleep she could get. From the looks of the saloon, Maggie would be needing all of her strength just to put the place to rights again.

Keeping to the long, narrow carpet that ran the length of the hall, her footsteps were muffled, just as she wanted. No one needed to know she was checking on things. Cutter had been downright stubborn about watching over

Maggie. Though Rose didn't doubt for a minute that he would do a good job, she wouldn't have been able to rest a bit until she'd seen for herself that Maggie was all right.

The door was closed. Rose frowned and glanced over her shoulder at Kevin's room, across the hall. That door stood wide open, and one quick look was all she needed to see that Cutter wasn't there. Turning back to Maggie's door, Rose grasped the brass knob and slowly, carefully, turned it.

As the heavy panel swung soundlessly open, Rose's gaze fell on the two people inside the big room. Maggie lay stretched out on top of the covers. She still wore her ruined yellow gown, and a quilt had been haphazardly tossed over her. Clucking her tongue softly, Rose looked down at the man on the floor.

Seated with his back to the bed, within reach of Maggie, Cutter was slumped forward, his head on his chest. He didn't look in the least bit comfortable, but when a snore erupted from him, Rose decided not to worry about it.

Inhaling sharply, she stared at the two people Kevin Donnelly had maneuvered so nicely. She'd known the man nearly thirty years, and yet even Rose had been surprised when he'd first told her his plan.

It was still hard to credit, she thought, and shook her head at Kevin's boldness. Not many men were foolish enough to think they could arrange for their children to fall in love.

And if he were here right now, Rose would have been pleased to tell him that his little plan was failing. Oh, there were enough hot looks passing between Cutter and Maggie to fry a steak on ... but longing and loving were two different things.

She snorted indelicately. Just try to explain *that* to a man, though!

As Rose turned and headed for her own room at the opposite end of the hall, she found herself worrying. If, by some miracle, Cutter and Maggie were to come to some sort of understanding, she thought, it would only mean trouble for the other three girls.

Kevin Donnelly was not a man to give up without finishing a job he'd set for himself.

Chapter 11

"**T**his is *his* fault!"

Maggie kicked at a broken chair leg and sent it skittering across the littered floor. Even before it landed with a thud up against the wall, she had turned around and started walking toward the bar. Flicking an angry glance up at the shattered bar mirror, she ignored the fact that Jake was trying to talk. "I don't care what you say, Jake. If it weren't for Cutter's coming back here, none of this would have happened."

"You don't know that, boss."

She frowned at him. "Boss, am I?" Hands on her hips, Maggie challenged the big man. "And what do you call *him?*"

Jake shrugged. "Boss."

Fuming, Maggie spun away from her bartender and stared blankly at the destruction around her.

In the harsh afternoon sunlight, the saloon looked even worse than she'd thought it would. Several of the chairs were broken beyond repair. A few of the chandeliers were dotted with smashed crystals, and Maggie's temper still flared when she thought about the brand-new beer-glass pockets she'd had installed under some of the poker tables. Somehow, in the fray the night before, the three-sided cast-iron trays had been knocked off the tables, leaving deep gouges in the wood.

A brisk wind blew in through the wide-open window frames, and Maggie shivered. Wrapping her arms around herself, she turned in a slow circle, willing the mess to disappear as completely as Cutter had.

Her fingers began to tap against her upper arms as she remembered waking up to find her partner gone. Oh, he was quite a partner, she told herself furiously. Cutter was more than willing to take a share in the profits—or order billiard tables—or hire a new singer ... who, she added silently, still hadn't arrived. But when it came to the real, hard work that involved taking care of things ... Cutter was nowhere to be found.

He hadn't bothered to help with the cleanup. He hadn't bothered to tell her where he was going.

Hell, he hadn't even bothered to say good-bye!

And worse yet, no one would tell her where he had gone.

With one hand she reached up and began to rub her right temple. Maggie's head still ached, and she hadn't had a thing to eat since just prior to the ruckus the night before. The grumbling noises from her stomach, though, only fed the flames of her fury.

All right, she admitted, maybe Cutter hadn't had anything directly to do with the damage done to her saloon. But by all that was holy, she thought, nothing like this had happened *before* he'd become a partner—he, with all of his fine ideas!

She shot a quick look at the archway leading to the Garter. There was a brilliant notion! If it were not for him, the whole damn crowd would have left by the Rose's front door and been gone. But no! He had joined the saloons, so all of those panicked people had raced back and forth between the two, like a child playing one parent against the other.

Her head began to throb, and she groaned quietly. Even that was due to him, Maggie told herself. If she hadn't been trying to meet him, that stinking rock never would have hit her in the head!

And, she argued with herself, if she hadn't been born a Donnelly, she might have been working in a library instead of a saloon.

Oh, it was no use. It did no good trying to live your life by "*if-I'da's.*" If I'da done this or if I'da done that . . . you could wander down that road forever, and never reach a destination.

Disgusted, she grabbed the back of the nearest chair, pulled it away from the table, and dropped down onto it.

She couldn't keep thinking about how things might have been. And raging against Cutter wasn't the answer either, as well she knew. The damage was no more his fault than it was Kevin's for building the saloon in the first place!

Maggie frowned, picked up a broken glass from the tabletop, and tossed it onto a nearby pile of rubble. It wasn't the destruction of her place that had made her so furious. That could be fixed—and would be, she promised herself, in a day or two.

No. Something else entirely was bothering her—something Maggie could hardly make herself consider. She'd begun to think that perhaps Cutter would never admit to being in love with her. Blankly she stared out at the street. Lifting her chin into the cold, clean wind as it swept across the empty window frames, she let herself remember the unmistakable expression on his face the night before. Desperate to get to her, to protect her, his emotions were plain to anyone with half an eye. Why wouldn't *he* see it?

And hadn't Rose grudgingly admitted that Cutter had sat at Maggie's bedside all night long? Would a man do that merely for a partner?

"Boss?"

Maggie blinked, pushed her thoughts aside, and half turned to look up at Jake, hovering nearby. "What is it?"

"There's, uh . . ."—the big man jerked his head in the direction of the front door—"somebody here. Askin' for Cutter."

Maggie leaned around Jake and stared at the doorway. Silhouetted in the sunlight at her back, the woman was turning her head this way and that, surveying the shambles of a saloon.

She was dressed in a simple yet elegant gown. Her deep-pink shirtwaist was tucked into a perfectly tailored dark gray skirt. The toes of her black high-heeled boots peeked from beneath the hem, and Maggie could see that one of those shoes was tapping nervously against the floor.

Pushing herself to her feet, Maggie started for the door. As she came nearer, Maggie noted the other woman's clear, pale complexion, the dark slash of highly arched brows, and deep-set brown eyes. Her black hair was piled into a mass of curls on top of her head, and a tiny hat decorated with a completely useless bit of pink netting sat perched atop the curls.

There wasn't the slightest bit of doubt in Maggie's mind as to who the woman was. It seemed only right that she had arrived that day, of all days.

Closing the space between them, Maggie smiled, held out her hand, and asked unnecessarily, "Michelle Fontaine?"

The pretty woman smiled. "Yes." Clasping Maggie's hand in her own, she added, "You must be Maggie Donnelly. Cutter's told me so much about you."

"Don't see why I had to wait for you," Ike grumbled.

"You know damn well why," Cutter snapped, and flicked a quick glance at the big man walking beside him.

"I ain't—" Ike paused, pulled in a deep breath, and started over. "I'm not afraid of the likes of Digger."

"I know that!" Cutter stopped dead on the boardwalk and waited for Ike to turn and face him.

He still wasn't ready to cope with this, Cutter told himself. He needed sleep. He needed food. And, he thought as he lifted one hand to his aching head, a headache powder wouldn't have been completely out of line either.

But there would be time for all of that later. Just then, he knew, the most important thing to do was to face down Digger Wicks. Glancing up at his old friend, Cutter saw what it had cost Ike to wait for his company. But, dammit, now wasn't the time to do anything that might cause even more trouble.

Granted, on the Coast things were run a little more casually than in most other parts of the country. But even there, Ike might have run into one or more fellows who didn't take to the notion of a black man beating up a white man. And judging by the set of Ike's jaw and the tightly leashed strength in his clenched fists, that was just what he had in mind.

Not that Cutter blamed him a bit. Hell, he would have liked nothing better than to thump Digger Wicks so hard, the man would have to look up to see his shoes. Every time he thought about Maggie's injury, a red haze swam in front of Cutter's eyes. If it had not been for a bit of good Irish luck, she might have been killed. And if she were ever hurt again—in any way—Cutter swore he would personally kill Digger Wicks.

For the present, however, he would settle for threatening the man within an inch of his life. Anything else, and Digger would only retaliate in a way that would hurt more people. And at the moment, there was enough for Cutter to think about already.

Taking a deep breath, Cutter said flatly, "I know what you want to do." Ike opened his mouth to speak, but Cutter quickly cut him off. "Hell, I'd like nothing better myself than to feel Digger's jaw under my fist."

"But?"

"*But*," Cutter shot back, "isn't there enough going on, as it is? If we go in there, fists flying,

Digger will only send more of his thugs to the Roses tomorrow night. Or the next."

Ike's features froze. A spark of . . . something flashed in his brown eyes, but Cutter couldn't read it.

"Fine. We'll do it your way for now," Ike finally agreed. "But before we see Digger, there's somethin' else you should know about. Somethin' about last night."

"What?" Instinctively Cutter braced himself. He knew he wasn't going to like what he was about to hear.

In short, clipped sentences, Ike told him about discovering the beginnings of the fire.

"Son of a bitch!"

"Still feel like doin' nothin'?" Ike asked softly, and folded his arms across his massive chest.

Fire. Cutter's too-tired mind conjured up images of what might have happened. The total destruction. The loss of life.

Maggie. Trapped in a burning saloon.

His jaw clenched, he shot his friend a quick, dangerous glance. "Let's go," was all he said before he started walking again. Absently, he heard Ike running to catch up with him.

Just a few short blocks from the lights and noise of the Barbary Coast, a world of misery existed that most men avoided like the pox. Thieves and killers hid in the shadows and eked out a living by preying on those foolish enough to wander the narrow dirt streets.

Cutter's features tightened imperceptibly, and he was glad he'd taken the time to strap on his sleeve gun. Idly he unnecessarily adjusted his right coat sleeve. He knew that the straps and bands holding his two-shot derringer in place were hidden from sight, but it didn't pay to take chances.

Their hurried steps took them down the long, winding boardwalk that came to an abrupt end at the edge of the wharf. Stepping down into the dirt, the two men kept walking.

Ramshackle buildings that looked as though they had been built by drunken blind men leaned against one another to keep from falling down. There were inch-wide gaps between the slats of wood, and each time a fresh gust of wind whistled through the shacks, the weathered wood rattled as if keeping the beat.

The stench of rotting fish was overpowering. It clung to the land, the buildings, like an overdressed dowager's perfume. There was no escaping it, and even the strong ocean wind wasn't enough to clean the air so that it was fit to breathe.

Former sailors, now too old to leave port, sat sprawled in the dirt, staring out at the sea that had stolen their youth. Tipping coffee-brown bottles filled with the cheapest rotgut whiskey they could find, the old men sought oblivion, where for a time they could be young and strong again.

Cutter stepped around them carefully, then continued on, ignoring the whores plying their trade with newly arrived seamen. If it would have done any good, he might have tried to say something, to warn the green young men that the girls who found them so interesting were probably working for Mother Comfort.

He shook his head and went on. They wouldn't have thanked him, and they sure as hell wouldn't have believed him, if Cutter had tried to tell them that they stood a better-than-even chance of waking up with a sore head, on board a boat bound for China. Mother Comfort and the rest of those who ran Shanghai palaces preferred selling their "customers" to ship captains who could promise to keep the men at sea for at least two to three years.

From the corner of his eye, he watched Ike shrug deeper into his well-tailored coat. Cutter felt Ike's uneasiness and knew the big man could sympathize far better than he with the young men walking unknowingly into servitude.

A moment later, though, all thoughts of the foolish young seamen fled as Cutter spotted Digger's place.

At the far end of the dirt road, a small shack sat apart from the others. The weather door stood open, and hanging crookedly from a broken hinge was one of a pair of batwing doors. Cutter glanced up briefly at Ike, then turned his gaze back to the gaping black interior of Digger's bar.

Without a word, the two men walked toward it.

Wryly Maggie watched as her bartender fell all over himself in his eagerness to wait on Michelle Fontaine.

In all the time she'd known him, Maggie had never seen Jake grin as much as he had since the pretty singer had strolled in the front door. Even more astonishing, in the past several minutes, he had served Michelle tea, and at that moment was setting a tray of sandwiches on the table in front of her. Staggering behavior from a man who normally believed that a world-famous mixologist such as he shouldn't be bothered by the tedious act of actually having to serve customers.

Oh, mixing drinks was a talent. But serving could be done by anyone.

The big man set the tray down on the table and stood back, smiling with all the pride of a barn cat bringing a rat to lay at the feet of its owner.

"Thank you, Jack," Michelle told him with a smile.

Maggie lowered her head and bit her lip.

"It's Jake, ma'am," the bartender corrected gently.

"I *am* sorry. Jake."

Jake blushed, and Maggie was so astounded, she simply stared at him. But as long, silent seconds began to pass and he made no move to leave, she was forced to say, "Don't you have to finish cleaning up the bar, Jake?"

The big man didn't move. Moments ticked by.

"Hmm?" He shot a quick glance at Maggie before turning his adoring gaze back to Michelle.

"The bar," Maggie repeated firmly. "Remember?"

"Oh." Jake grinned again, and Maggie simply stared at him. She'd never seen the man like this. "Oh, yeah. Right, boss."

He took a couple of hesitant steps away, then stopped, turned back to Michelle, and promised solemnly, "You need anything, miss . . . anything at all . . . you just call on Jake."

"Thank you, Jake." Michelle smiled at him, and Jake nearly melted. "I'll do that."

Maggie was impressed. Even the woman's speaking voice was fluid, musical. It was no wonder Cutter had hired her. Between the woman's obvious effect on men and a voice that already promised to be special, Michelle Fontaine would bring in more customers than the Four Roses had ever seen.

Suddenly, though, Maggie took a good, slow look at the woman opposite her. If the singer had had such an effect on Jake, what had Cutter's reaction been to her? Had he hired her, not for her talent, but for ... other reasons?

Mentally Maggie compared herself to the elegant creature and knew she came up short. Her hair was too red, her skin too pale, and the few freckles dotting her nose stood out like a glaring imperfection when held up alongside Michelle's creamy skin. And besides all of that, Michelle Fontaine was a singer. Not a saloon hall singer. A singer. Someone who could no doubt fit in anywhere. With anyone.

Maggie Donnelly was a saloon keeper. And that occupation was generally not useful in securing an invitation to the finer places.

"Do you mind if I ask what happened?" Michelle asked, snapping Maggie out of her depressing thoughts.

"What happened?"

"Here." Michelle's arms stretched out, gesturing around the ravaged room.

Maggie laughed shortly. Of course the other woman was wondering about the saloon; she was probably thinking that she no longer had a job.

"There was a ... disturbance," she finally

said, "last night. No one was badly hurt, though, so we were lucky."

"Yes ..." Michelle glanced about the room, then looked back to Maggie.

"Don't worry. I know it doesn't look like it now, but by tomorrow night, everything will be up and working."

"By tomorrow?"

Maggie smiled. "In San Francisco," she said with a shrug, "we're used to digging ourselves out of disaster quickly." Instantly her mind recalled all the times Kevin had told her about rebuilding after the fires that had raged through the city during the early years. No matter how many times the mostly wooden city burned down, the citizens had simply rebuilt it. And each time they had made it bigger—and better.

It wasn't only fire that had devastated San Francisco, either. Maggie remembered a small earthquake or two, herself—not to mention storm surf that pounded against the coast, drowning the unwary, sinking boats, and carrying off buildings constructed too close to shore.

No. Fires, earthquakes, high tides, and mud slides hadn't been enough to slow San Francisco *or* the Donnellys. A few miserable rocks certainly wouldn't stop them.

"You'll see," Maggie told the disbelieving woman. "By tomorrow night this place will look even better than it did before."

Michelle Fontaine stared at Maggie for a long moment. Then, slowly, a smile touched the corner of her mouth. She nodded and said, "Maggie, I think you and I are going to be friends."

Maggie saw the gleam of understanding in the other woman's eyes and told herself that perhaps she and Michelle were more alike than she'd thought.

As she reached for one of the sandwiches, she heard the front door open and turned to look.

David Harper stepped inside and stopped on the threshold.

"Not open today, Harper," Jake told him.

Instantly, memories of the night before raced through Maggie's brain. In vivid detail she recalled how David had risked himself to save the life of the man who had fallen beneath the feet of the crowd. Surely that act alone was worth a free drink.

"It's all right, Jake," Maggie called out.

David's head swiveled around to look at her.

"Give him whatever he wants," she continued. "On the house."

Jake grumbled but reached beneath the bar for David's favorite brand of liquor. But the younger man paid no attention.

Maggie noticed that even when Jake set a glass and a full bottle on the bar top, David didn't even glance in that direction. Instead his gaze was locked on Michelle Fontaine.

Like a man waking up from a long, deep sleep, he started across the floor. His legs moved jerkily, as if he'd forgotten how to use his limbs. His handsome yet somewhat bruised features were frozen into a mask of awestruck wonder. But the shine in his eyes was what staggered Maggie.

David Harper was looking at the Four Roses' new singer as if she'd just stepped down from heaven.

Surprised and more than a little wary, Maggie got to her feet as David neared their table. Hoping to head off what could have proved to be an embarrassing situation, she turned to Michelle and offered, "I'll take you up to your room at the Garter now, so you can freshen . . ."

Maggie's voice faded away, leaving her sentence unfinished. Anything else she might have said died unuttered as she looked into Michelle's face.

The singer looked just as dumbstruck as David.

Dark eyes wide, her lips slightly parted, her breath came in rapid gasps as though she had just seen an apparition. Glancing from one of them to the other, Maggie told herself she might as well have been a fly on the wall, for all the attention either of them was paying her.

She threw a quick glance at Jake, checking to see if he was seeing what she was. The disgusted expression on the bartender's face left her no doubt.

"If it's all right with you, Maggie," David said softly, his gaze still locked on Michelle, "I'll see the lady to her room."

Before she could utter a word, Michelle had slipped her fingers into David's outstretched hand and stood up.

"Michelle Fontaine," she said, her voice breathy, urgent.

"David Harper," he answered, and swept his gaze over her face with a lover's care.

Dumbfounded, Maggie stared at the two people still holding hands, unsure of what to do. She had never seen anything like it. It was as if no one else in the world existed for either of them.

Tenderly David tucked Michelle's arm

through the crook of his elbow and covered her fingers with his right hand. Still staring down into the other woman's deep brown eyes, he asked Maggie, "Where is she staying?"

She hesitated a moment, swallowed heavily, and murmured, "Cutter's room. At the Garter."

He nodded and straightened slightly. Then, without another word. David Harper, tall, handsome, and *sober*, led Michelle through the arch connecting the two saloons.

Maggie stood stock still, staring after them. When they'd gone, the room seemed quieter, somehow, as if some charge of energy had dissipated.

Shaking her head slowly, Maggie half turned toward the other end of the room. Jake looked as stunned as she felt.

"What do you make of *that*?" she asked.

The bartender's jaw snapped shut, and his lips twisted into a disgusted frown. "Never saw anything like it. Who woulda thought? Harper, of all people!"

She knew what he meant. It was strange. First David's heroics of the night before . . . and then this. He'd even refused a free drink! A week earlier, Maggie would have sworn that never would have happened. Humph! she thought. That certainly ought to prove to her that no matter *how* well you knew a body—he could still surprise you.

Jake started slamming things around at the bar. She heard him brush broken glass aside and listened to the sharp, distinctive *tinkle* as the pieces hit the floor.

Before she could say anything, though, Jake started talking, more to himself than to her.

"Wait until Ike gets back from Digger's," he said, and gave a bar towel a vicious shake. "He's not goin' to believe this!"

Maggie smiled; then, a heartbeat later, her smile dissolved. Slowly she repeated to herself what the barman had said. Taking a few quick steps in his direction, she shouted, "Digger's? Is that where Ike and Cutter went?"

Jake's face blanched. Eyes wide, he looked horrified at the realization that he'd just let the cat out of the bag.

His guilty expression was all the proof Maggie needed.

In seconds, she got the rest of the story out of him.

Well, that explained why Cutter hadn't bothered to tell her good-bye before leaving. He knew bloody well that she would never have let him leave without her. The Four Roses was more hers than his, and if he was going to deal with the man who had tried to destroy it, then she had a right to be there as well!

Sparing one last glare for Jake, Maggie marched across the floor, slapped her palm against the front door and, as it crashed open, stepped through it, never breaking her stride.

Maggie Donnelly would *not* be ignored!

Cutter wouldn't have thought it possible, but the inside of Digger's place smelled even worse than the outside.

His gaze slipped about the one-room building as he tried to adjust to the gloom. Even in mid-afternoon, the place was dark. Dank. Except for a few oil lamps spread frugally around the room, the only light came from the small slivers of sunshine stabbing through the gaps between the wood-plank walls.

Slowly, as his vision cleared, Cutter was able to spot a handful of men slumped at a few of the tables. Busy day, he told himself wryly.

"What d'you want?"

Digger's voice brought Cutter around quickly. At his customary corner table, Digger sat hunched over a none-too-clean jigger full of whiskey.

"You know why we're here." Cutter was determined to restrain his impulse to beat the man senseless, but he would be damned if he was going to play guessing games with the miserable old razorback.

"Yep." Digger reached out with the toe of one boot and dragged another chair closer. Deliberately he propped his feet up on the seat of the chair and cocked his head at his two guests. "Reckon I do, at that."

"Who did it for you, Digger?" Cutter asked in a dangerously quiet tone.

"Did what?" The older man laughed, and his chest rattled from the unfamiliar exercise. "Oh ... you must mean all them windows that got broke."

"That's right." From the corner of his eye, Cutter saw Ike take up a position on his right side.

"Yeah." Digger flashed them a quick look from his flat, dead eyes and admitted, "I heard you got quite a breeze whippin' through the Roses about now."

"You listen to me, you miserable little swamp rat." Cutter took a half step toward the old man, and only stopped when he heard the familiar *click* of a gun's hammer being drawn back.

Digger waved a negligent, dirty hand at some faceless body in the far corner. "Leave off," he said. "These boys know better than to try anything in here." He turned his gaze on Ike and sneered. " 'Sides, they can't prove nothin'."

A heartbeat later, Cutter continued. "We all know you did it, Digger. You're just damned lucky nobody got killed."

That wheezing laugh sounded again, and Cutter had to fight the urge to wrap his fingers around the man's thick neck to choke off the noise.

"Yeah. I'm a lucky kinda fella," Digger allowed, then picked up his drink. After he had tossed the contents down his throat, he snorted, waved to his friends, and said, "Looka there, boys. A tame darky dressed up like some kinda *gentleman*, or somethin'."

Ike tensed.

Cutter straightened up and felt the strength of Ike's anger spill from him and pour into his own soul. It burned with a hot, raging flame, and it was all he could do to keep it banked.

Pulling in a deep breath of the foul air, Cutter gritted his teeth, clenched his fists, and said, "You're right. We can't prove you were there, Digger."

A low laugh shot from the man and scraped across Cutter's already raw nerves.

"But if one more thing goes wrong at the Roses—*anything*—we'll be back looking for you."

"Well, you got me real scared, Cutter." A sharp breeze through the wall behind him ruf-

fled Digger's wild gray mane and sent it twisting about his ears.

"What about the other?" Ike muttered thickly,
and Cutter could tell from the sound of his
voice that his friend was using every ounce of
his will to hold himself in check.

"Nobody talked to you—boy."

Cutter snapped. That was simply too much
for anyone to stand. In an instant, he'd leaped
forward, kicked the chair out from under Digger's feet, grabbed the edge of the table, and
flung it aside. With his path clear, he lunged for
the disreputable old thief and caught him by the
collar of his filthy shirt.

Digger's wide, rheumy eyes stared back into
Cutter's with the certain knowledge that he was
a dead man if he made one wrong move.

As if to ram that point home, Cutter flicked
his right wrist, and the derringer slid into his
palm. The ivory grip felt cool and comfortable
in his hand. He smiled slightly and held the barrel up under Digger's chin. Tightly, he said,
"Tell your boy in the corner to throw his gun
down or his boss is gonna be spread all across
this wall with the rest of the trash."

"Boss?" came an uncertain voice from the
shadows.

"Do it!" Digger stammered. "Do it, ya fool!"

Immediately Cutter heard the sound of a pistol hitting the floor. He smiled. "Everybody else,
too," he told the wild-eyed man, and pushed
the barrel a little more tightly against his throat.

"You heard 'em! Do it!"

Three more guns hit the floor. Cutter grinned
and kept his gaze locked on the slippery old
devil. "Good. Now we'll talk about what my

partner, here, had to say." Glancing back over his shoulder, he nodded. "Ike?"

The big black man's features were cold and hard, though Cutter thought he detected just a touch of satisfaction gleaming in his friend's eyes.

"It's about the fire."

"Fire?" Digger croaked. "What fire?"

Cutter's grip tightened. "It's rude to interrupt."

Digger blinked.

"The one somebody set behind the Roses last night," Ike prompted. "You know anything about that, *old man?*"

Again, Cutter's fingers tightened around Digger's throat, and the man squirmed, his eyes widening even further.

"Well?" Cutter asked him. "Answer the man."

Helpless fury blazed in Digger's eyes as he glared, first at Cutter, then at Ike. Giving his head a barely noticeable shake, he managed to whisper, "I didn't set no fire. Are you crazy?"

Cutter's fingers loosened just a bit, and the man sucked in a gulp of air before sputtering, "A fire would burn me out too, y'know. It'd wreck everything!"

He didn't want to believe Digger, but unfortunately the miserable old bastard made sense.

As if reading Cutter's mind, Digger went on. "Why the hell would I want to set fire to the Coast?" He clawed futilely at Cutter's hand. "A fire down here would take off faster'n a cut cat!"

Tossing a quick look at Ike, Cutter saw his friend jerk him a nod. Immediately Cutter released his prisoner. Digger slid down the wall and crumpled into a heap on the floor. Stretching his neck, Digger rubbed his throat, glared up at the two men, and spat at them, "A coupl'a rocks is one thing. Fire's another. If somebody's torchin' your place, Cutter—it ain't me. You best watch your back. You *and* your tame darky."

Cutter flinched, and Ike put a restraining hand on his arm. "Don't bother," he muttered.

After a long moment, Cutter nodded, kept his derringer aimed at Digger's mangy head, and began to back toward the door.

If Digger was telling the truth, they had more trouble on their hands than they'd thought.

Chapter 12

Maggie stepped into the street and immediately jumped back to the safety of the boardwalk. A brewery wagon lumbered past, its huge wheels groaning under the strain of the weight they carried. She frowned and flicked a quick glance at the driver, perched high above her. The man was shaking one fist at her and shouting out curses loud enough to wake the dead ... which was what she would be if she didn't watch her step.

The next time, as she jumped off the boardwalk, Maggie gave a quick look in either direction, then ran across the wide dirt street. Grabbing up handfuls of her skirt, she yanked the hem free of the ground and leaped up onto the opposite walkway. Elbowing her way past the people thronged outside the saloons, she kept moving, her anger urging her on.

"What is happening to everything?" she muttered.

How had her nice, neat, dependable little world fallen apart so quickly? Just three weeks before, her life had been easy, uncomplicated.

Familiar voices called out to her, but she didn't stop. People she'd known all her life were now simply obstacles to pass on the boardwalk.

She listened to the brisk tapping of her heels against the wood planks and concentrated on Cutter.

Why hadn't he told her about going to Digger's? Why had he left her while she was still asleep? How could he pretend to be her partner, when he had no intention of actually sharing anything with her?

She squinted into the late-afternoon sun and noticed a few slate-gray clouds that had begun to roll in off the ocean. Wonderful, she told herself. Now rain was on its way. With the entire front of the saloon open, rain was the worst possible thing that could happen just then.

They'd probably get a hurricane.

Gritting her teeth, she hurried her steps. She turned sideways and slipped between a fleshy whore in a faded red dress and a small man wearing a derby hat and wire-rim spectacles. A fog of perfume drifted up from between the huge woman's pendulous breasts, and Maggie grimaced, eager to get away.

But the little man reached out and snagged her arm. She stopped abruptly and turned to look at him. His eyes were wide, pleading. His narrow chin wobbled unsteadily, as if he couldn't believe what he had gotten himself into. However eager he might have been to change his mind about the whore, Maggie thought, he wasn't going to use her to do it. Slowly her gaze shifted to his hand on her arm, and reluctantly he let her go.

"Hey, Maggie," the big whore said as she snatched the slightly built man by the collar and dragged him to her side. "What'cha doin' out before nightfall?"

Maggie glanced at the big woman and shook her head. She must have been angrier than she'd thought, she told herself. She hadn't even recognized Fat Alice.

"I'm on my way to Digger's, Alice. Looking for Cutter and Ike," she said quickly, ignoring the panicked look in the little man's eyes. If everything the men said about Alice was true, the puny fellow wouldn't regret spending time with her.

Besides, Fat Alice's heart was as big as the rest of her.

"Shoot, honey." Alice grinned, and her heavily rouged cheeks split with wide dimples. Paste rubies twinkled from between the folds of flesh at her neck. "They ain't at Digger's anymore."

"Where are they?"

"Well . . ." Alice plucked the derby from the man's head, and her sausagelike fingers began to thread through his thinning black hair. "Don't rightly know about Cutter," she said, tipping her head back to think. "But Ike . . . he's over at Racquel's place. Seen him there just a minute or two ago." She turned and grinned down into her captive's sweating features. "Just before I found me this little 'un, here." Alice looked up at Maggie and winked. "Ain't he the cutest little thing?"

The runt swallowed heavily, and Maggie watched his Adam's apple bob up and down. She shook her head and hid a smile. He'd survive. And probably, she thought, would come back looking for Alice within a week.

"He's adorable, Alice," Maggie assured her, already heading for Racquel Santiago's little bar at the corner. "Thanks for your help."

"Anytime, honey," the whore answered. Then, in an eager tone, she told the man still plastered against her side, "You come on with Alice, dearie. I'll make you feel ten feet tall."

Maggie walked away, a half smile on her face, despite her rampaging thoughts.

Just inside Racquel's tiny bar, Ike sat at a table, with Racquel herself on his lap.

"Maggie, what are you doin' here?" he asked, and held Racquel down when she would have gotten up.

"Looking for you. And Cutter," Maggie snapped, and nodded a greeting to the dark-haired beauty with him.

"Well, Cutter ain't . . . isn't here," Ike told her simply. "He's down at the dock, near Gianni's boat."

"Why?"

Ike shrugged. "Said he had to get thoughts of Digger out of his head. But mostly, I think, he just wanted to get the stink of that place out of his nose."

Maggie studied the man briefly. He looked calm enough, but the frown lines between his brows were etched deeply into his forehead. He held a glass of beer in his right hand, and his knuckles stood out in pale relief against the darker tones of his skin.

"How's Digger?" she heard herself ask, and braced herself for the answer. Though she didn't give a tinker's damn about the grotesque man's health, she didn't want to think about Cutter's and maybe also Ike's, having killed him. Even on the Coast, murder was generally frowned on.

A grim smile darted across his full lips, then

disappeared. He'd heard the unspoken concern behind her simple question.

"Digger's as good as that no good son of a"—he glanced up at her—"gun ever was." Ike lifted the beer glass and took a long sip of his drink. "How'd you know where we went?"

"Jake," she answered shortly. Then, taking a breath, she told him exactly what she planned on saying to Cutter. "The two of you should've told me about Digger. About the fire."

"Yeah."

He didn't seem surprised that she knew all about it.

"Was it Cutter's idea not to tell me?" Of course it was, her brain shouted, but she waited for Ike's answer nonetheless.

Ike only shrugged. Clearly, he was unwilling to get his partner any more deeply into trouble.

Maggie frowned at him. She'd known Ike long enough to be sure that she wasn't going to be getting any more information out of him. She was wasting time. The man she needed to talk to was Cutter.

Without a word, she turned abruptly and rushed back out of the bar. Behind her, Ike stared at the empty doorway and shook his head.

Cutter stood at the end of the short dock, staring off at the horizon. The wind rushed in off the water, tugging at his hair and the edges of his jacket. Salt spray blew up into his face, and he inhaled deeply, relishing the clean, tangy scent. He only wished the spray and wind could blow through his mind and whisk away all the thoughts that kept clamoring for his attention.

Fire.

Jesus, what next?

Cutter shoved one hand through his already wind-tossed hair and rubbed his scalp viciously. If Ike hadn't stumbled on those smoldering rags . . . it didn't bear thinking about.

Dammit, who was behind that?

He knew damned well it wasn't Digger. Cutter snorted. As much as he would have liked it to be, it wasn't. Digger was vicious, but he wasn't stupid. A fire would have been a disaster for him, too.

A man doesn't put himself out of business just to get rid of competitors.

Cutter pulled in a deep breath and blew it out in a rush. He determinedly closed his mind to thoughts of Digger and instead concentrated his gaze on the far distance. Squinting, he saw that yet another ship was coming in.

He swiveled his head slightly and looked over the already crowded harbor. From skiffs to canoes to fully rigged sailing vessels, there were at least thirty ships already docked in the bay. Their wooden hulls screeched with eerie precision as they pitched with the roll of the waves.

Seamen aboard the crafts shouted to one another as they went about the business of repairs or unloading cargo. And all around Cutter, the harsh, strong odor of fresh fish rose up as the fishermen unloaded their day's catch.

Beneath him, ocean water slapped at the wooden pilings of the dock, while on the pier behind him, wagons creaked and rolled down the embarcadero, carrying away the freight sent to San Francisco from around the world. In the beds of those rickety wagons, Cutter knew, were fine silks from China, fruits from the Hawaiis, and household goods from back east.

All vessels in the world eventually ended up in San Francisco Bay, only to sail off again in search of more adventure.

Adventure.

Hell, Cutter had found more adventure right in the heart of the Coast than he'd ever wanted.

He snorted. If he'd had any sense at all, Cutter told himself, he would have jumped onto the closest ship and sailed off to ... anywhere. Disgusted, he rubbed his jaw with one hand and dismissed the thought immediately.

The oceans simply weren't wide enough.

No matter where he went—Maggie would be there with him.

Cutter slapped his left hand down on a rough wooden piling. The damp, craggy surface bit into his palm, and he welcomed the distraction. Idly he began to pick at the weathered, flaking wood.

A pair of sea gulls swooped low in a wide arc, then dove at Gianni's nearby fishing trawler in a futile quest for food. Gianni's deckhands were used to their tricks, and waved them away easily.

Cutter let his head fall back on his neck, and he squinted into a painfully blue sky. A reluctant smile curved his lips as he watched the birds soar high, then turn into the wind before falling into plunging dives.

Sea gulls.

His gaze shifted, and focused on the seawater lapping against the wooden dock.

What the hell was he doing there? He had expected to live his life in Georgia. Yet here he was, perched on a precarious dock, staring at the Pacific Ocean.

Suddenly tired, he rubbed his eyes with the tips of his fingers, and wasn't even surprised when old memories began to slip through his brain.

Memories of people left behind him long before.

In his mind's eye, he saw his father's stern features. Pale blue eyes topped by bushy white eyebrows, a strong jaw, and a no-nonsense lift to his square chin. Gruff and usually hiding behind a bad temper that was more pretend than real, the elder Cutter was the only person save the Donnellys who'd ever given a damn about him.

Or so he'd thought.

Grimly Cutter forced himself to remember the day the family had gathered in his late father's office to hear the reading of the old man's will. The day Cutter had discovered that his father's "love" hadn't extended beyond lip service. In his memory, Cutter could still hear his father's lawyer speaking.

"And to Cutter, my oldest son," the lawyer read, *with a quick glance at the sad-eyed sixteen-year-old across from him, "I leave my confidence that he will make a name and a place for himself in the world. I have seen to it that he has received a good education and am confident that he will do well wherever he chooses to go."*

Shocked, the young Cutter had sat in stony silence while the lawyer went on to read, "To my younger son, Tyler, I leave the house, Seven Oaks, and all properties and monies pertaining thereto. To my sister Charlotte, I leave . . ."

With a stroke of a pen, his father had told the world that though he had a fondness for his bastard son, even he knew that Cutter wasn't good enough to inherit anything.

The image of that scene faded, but in its place came the memory of his half brother, Tyler, who'd inherited their father's looks—and everything else. Only eleven when their father died, Tyler had been just as eager as the rest of them for Cutter to leave Georgia forever. Though legitimate by birth, by nature Tyler had always been the *real* bastard.

Memories rushed into Cutter's head. Aunt Charlotte's cold, empty, razor-mean eyes swam before him. His father's sister, Charlotte had never forgiven Cutter for existing. She'd never forgiven her cherished brother for taking on the raising of his mistress's child. But mostly she had never been able to forget the woman who had been her brother's mistress.

Charlotte had hated Cutter's mother until the day she died. And when that day came, Charlotte simply transferred her hatred to the living reminder of the woman's existence.

Cutter.

His lips quirked, and a humorless chuckle rumbled through his chest. Odd, he told himself. Charlotte couldn't forget his mother—and he couldn't remember her. Since she'd died when he was only three or so, a few vague recollections were all he had of her.

A soft voice. Long blond hair. And hands, gentle despite the calluses covering their palms.

Cutter shook his head. Not a hell of a lot. He sucked in a gulp of salt air and told himself it

was a pretty miserable thing that a man his age
had more memories of those he hated than of
those he'd loved.

The long walk along the embarcadero had
cooled Maggie's temper a bit. Maybe it was a
good thing she'd seen Ike first. It had given her
the time to let her thoughts settle some. Lord
knew, it would be hard enough to get answers
out of the man, as it was. If they started fighting, she would never find out a damn thing.

Someone shouted to her, and Maggie glanced
over at the nearest boat. Lifting one hand, she
waved to Tony Gianni and his sons as they
lifted their catch of fish from the hold.

She sniffed. From the smell of things, they'd
had a good day.

But thoughts of the Gianni family and fishing
vanished in the next instant. Her gaze locked on
a lone figure at the end of the dock.

Cutter.

Despite her anger—despite her frustration
with the man—her heartbeat staggered slightly,
and a knot of warmth spread inside her.

Leaning against one of the old pilings, he
stood with one foot crossed casually over the
other, hands in his pockets. The wind ruffled his
hair and pulled at his clothes. He was staring
out to sea as if searching for something, yet not
expecting to find it.

Silhouetted against the backdrop of open sky
and wide ocean, Cutter looked . . . lost.

And something deep inside Maggie responded.

As quietly as she could, Maggie walked along
the dock until she was right behind him. If he'd

noticed her, he gave no sign—until she said, "Michelle's arrived."

A moment passed, then he answered simply, "Oh? That's good."

Maggie smiled inwardly. The doubts she'd had earlier about Cutter's interest in his new singer evaporated. Obviously, Michelle concerned him only in terms of business.

"Why am I not surprised to see you here?" Cutter asked quietly after a long moment of silence.

He still hadn't turned toward her, so Maggie talked to the back of his head. "I don't know, Cutter. Maybe it's because you feel guilty."

That got his attention. He glanced at her over his shoulder. "Guilty?"

"Yes. For not telling me where you were going."

Cutter gave her a twisted smile and shook his head.

His blue eyes looked shadowed, tired. The flesh around his new stitches was an angry red, and the way he held himself told Maggie that he needed to lie down and sleep for several hours. But instead of saying any of that, she heard herself say, "You left while I was sleeping."

"I had to."

"To see Digger?"

His eyes narrowed slightly, but he ground out, "Yeah. But who told you?"

"Jake."

Cutter sighed heavily. "Big-mouthed, interfering—"

She cut him off. "You should have told me."

This had nothing to do with Jake, and he knew it. "About Digger—the fire . . ."

"Fire, huh?" He laughed then, but it was a weak, shallow laugh. "Is there anything good old Jake left out?"

Maggie took one step closer and laid a hand on his arm. "I don't know, Cutter. What else is there?"

He looked down at her hand briefly before looking back out to sea again. "Nothing. Maggie. That's all."

Beneath her hand, his forearm was rigid. His muscles felt as though they were made of iron, and she knew her touch was disturbing him. Deliberately she squeezed his arm, and repeated, "You should have told me."

"I would have."

"When?"

Cutter looked at her, started to speak, then shrugged.

"That's what I thought." Maggie's hand fell from his arm. Strange, she told herself, how quickly the banked fires of anger could leap into life.

"Maggie . . ."

"No, Cutter." She looked up into his eyes, silently demanding that he listen to her. "We're partners. If nothing else—we're at least that."

"I know . . ."

"You don't act as though you do," she shot back.

Cutter moved so fast, she gasped in surprise. Turning, he reached out and grabbed her upper arms. Gripping her tightly, his thumbs digging into her flesh, he bent his head until he was looking directly into her startled eyes. "Dammit,

Maggie!" he whispered, his voice harsh and ugly. "I'm not talking about the usual partnership things ... sharing the profits or fighting over Jake's Blue Blazer!"

"No," she countered when her initial surprise had faded a bit. Trying to jerk herself free, Maggie said, "You're talking about the Roses itself. And about somebody trying to burn it down!"

"Wrong again," he snapped.

Cutter straightened up and pulled her tightly against him, so she had to tilt her head back to look into his eyes.

Jesus! he thought. *Why can't she understand this? Why doesn't she see how dangerous this mess is and how much worse it might get before we figure it out?*

She squirmed again, trying to break his hold, but Cutter wasn't about to let her go. Not yet. Instead his gaze moved over her features hungrily, desperately. And that desperation colored his voice when he finished what he'd started to say.

"This isn't about partners worrying over a saloon, dammit!" He lowered his head until his mouth was just a breath away from hers. "This is about you. Your safety."

"What?"

"Dammit, Maggie," Cutter whispered, "don't you see? If Ike hadn't stumbled on that damned fire, you could've been killed!"

"Everybody could have been," she pointed out.

"Damn everybody else," he said, and he didn't even care how callous that sounded. It was the truth. Ever since hearing about the fire, he'd been haunted by images of Maggie, unconscious and trapped in a burning building. "It's you I'm talking about, here."

"I can take care of myself," Maggie said stiffly.

He snorted. "In a card game, maybe."

"Don't treat me as if I'm a child."

"Then don't talk like one."

They stared at each other for what seemed forever. Blue eyes met green, and neither pair held a trace of backup. Seconds passed, and Cutter felt the pounding of her heart against his. The warmth of her stole into him and took his breath away.

As bone weary as he was, his body still hummed with wanting her. Even when she wasn't trying, she pushed him to the edge of his endurance. And just then he was simply too tired, too worn down, to trust himself.

Abruptly he released her. Taking a half step back from her, he turned his head and once again stared out at the distant horizon. "Can't you see that I'm trying to protect you?"

"That's not your job," she said quietly.

"What?" he glanced back at her.

She held herself rigidly. Her features were tight, as if she were fighting her own internal battle for control.

When she spoke again, her voice shook a bit, but steadied as she continued.

"My lover," she started, and let her gaze slip from his, "or husband would have the right to try to protect me. My partner is just that. Business."

"Maggie," he said with a groan.

"Have you changed your mind then, Cutter?"

she asked, and sarcasm dripped in her tone.
"Are you ready to be a husband—a lover?"

Cutter's jaw clenched. His hands curled into
fists at his sides. "I've already told you . . . I
can't."

Maggie froze. Her posture was stiff, unbend-
ing. Her eyes held a cold fire that burned him
even as he felt the chill of her gaze.

"Fine," she said quietly. "Then as my partner,
I'd like to talk to you back at the Roses—about
the fire and what we do next."

Maggie waited for his reaction. A blind man
could have seen that it was killing him to stand
there and not touch her. But he was just hardheaded enough to manage it.

Only a few hours earlier, she had begun to
think that he was finally coming around. When
she'd awakened to find him sitting beside her
bed—when she'd seen the worry, the fear,
etched into his features, Maggie had hoped . . .
Well, she told herself. It didn't matter what
she'd hoped. Apparently, Cutter was as determined as ever to keep her at arm's length, no
matter what the cost.

Why couldn't he see that together—the two of
them—they could handle any problem? Why
did he feel he must continue to shut her out?

Several lifetimes passed before Cutter finally
nodded. "All right," he said, "we'll talk."

Maggie wanted to kick him.

Instead she turned back toward shore. When
he didn't move, she stopped, pushed her wind-
blown hair out of her eyes, and asked impatiently, "You coming?"

His gaze swept over her, and Maggie felt
goose bumps race across her flesh. Even there,

on the dock, in sight of half of San Francisco, he could set fire to her body with a glance.

Slowly, he shook his head, and answered, "Not yet." He shoved his still-fisted hands into his pockets in a lame attempt to hide his torment. "I think," he said, and his voice shook with the emotions he was trying so desperately to hide, "I'll stay here awhile longer." He deliberately adopted a casual pose and leaned one hip against the wooden piling behind him.

She took a step, then stopped. Sighing softly, Maggie admitted to herself that she couldn't leave him like that.

Maybe it was because he looked so . . . beaten. Maybe it was because she was tired too. Hell, maybe it was because they *had* come perilously close to losing everything the night before. All she knew was that she needed to feel his arms around her, even if only for a moment.

Before she could change her mind, Maggie stepped up to Cutter, ignored his surprised expression, and wound her arms about his neck. He didn't need encouraging. With a quiet groan, Cutter's arms closed around her and held her with a gentle strength that threatened to cut off her air.

"I'm sorry," he whispered, then turned his face into the curve of her neck. "I should have told you."

"I'm sorry too," she said, and ran the flat of her hands over his shoulders and back. "I shouldn't have attacked you like a madwoman."

Cutter chuckled and lifted his head to look down at her. With one hand, he stroked the line of her cheek. "We do spend quite a bit of time apologizing to each other, Maggie mine."

"Aye, we do," she said and rubbed her cheek against his palm. "But there's no one I'd rather fight with than you."

He gave her that lopsided grin of his, then planted a quick kiss at the corner of her mouth. "The feeling is entirely mutual, madam."

Maggie smiled at him and realized that she was feeling a good bit better. "So, Cutter," she asked, "shall we go on home now?"

Again Cutter shook his head, and reluctantly released her. "I still think I'll stay for a while. Do some thinking."

"All right, then," she said, and knew she had to accept the fact that further talking would have to wait. At the same time, though, Maggie wanted him to know that she had no intention of letting the whole situation drop. Quietly she added, "But this isn't near over, Cutter."

Chapter 13

Whistling softly, David Harper adjusted the way his black broadcloth tailcoat hung, flicked his fingertips over the black silk lapels, then tugged at the rigid collar of his white dress shirt. Half turning before the full-length mirror in his bedroom, he nodded to his reflection and reminded himself to give the housekeeper a big bonus. She'd done an excellent job of freshening up his evening wear in a remarkably short time.

Then he turned back to face his reflection squarely again and tried for the third time to make a decent bow out of his black silk cravat. He was too long out of practice, certainly. But one would have thought one wouldn't have forgotten how to do such a relatively simple task.

He cursed softly and dropped both ends of the cravat in disgust. He had no choice, he told himself. He needed help.

The wall clock in the hall chimed seven, and he hurriedly stepped to the doorway, stuck his head out, and bellowed, "Mrs. Hallstead!"

From downstairs, he heard her shout in answer and knew she would be coming soon.

Quickly he looked about his room, silently asking himself if he had everything. The large, airy chamber was in complete disarray. Clothes were tossed over chairs and across the brass footrails of the wide bed. The curtains were pulled open, allowing the night air to swirl through the room, sending the lamp flames fluttering.

One corner of his mouth lifted in a half smile. It certainly took more to get him ready for society these days than it ever had before. He reached up and hurriedly smoothed his hands over his coat pockets. Billfold, watch—he reached into the inside breast pocket of his coat and felt for his silver cigar case. Then, tapping one finger against his vest, David reassured himself that his small gold match case was safely tucked away.

Yes. He was ready. Except, he reminded himself, for the tie.

His freshly brushed hat sat on a nearby chair, and he leaned over to pick it up. Running his forearm over the glossy silk brim, he smiled to himself, then flicked one finger against its stiffness.

God, it had been too long since he'd been this excited about anything.

As he stared at the hat, his hands began to shake. David tossed his black high hat onto the knob on the brass footrail, then clenched and unclenched his fingers spasmodically in an attempt to stop the tremors. After a long moment, the shaking stopped as suddenly as it had begun.

Apparently, he thought wryly, it had also been too long since he was stone sober.

And for the first time in months, he'd spent

an entire afternoon without even *thinking* about a drink. Amazing.

"Going somewhere?"

David glanced up as his father stepped into the room. His stomach churned slightly, but he ordered himself to calm down. Nothing was going to ruin that evening.

"Yes, I am," he finally answered, and walked back to the full-length mirror to try his hand at the tie again.

"A bit overdressed for your friends at the Four Roses, aren't you?"

In the mirror, David watched his father's features twist into a disapproving frown. Deliberately, he did his best to ignore it.

Strange how much harder that was to do when sober.

"I'm not going to the Roses tonight," David said, and then corrected himself with an inward smile. "Well, I am. But only briefly. To call for my companion."

"Companion?"

David's hands stilled and dropped to his sides. Drawing one deep breath after another, he forced himself to control the anger beginning to build inside him. "That's what I said."

"Elegant name for a whore," the judge observed acidly.

David spun around to face his father. "She's not a whore."

"Naturally. All ladies of good breeding reside in saloons."

"She just arrived in town today."

"Then she's an exceptionally fast worker, even for one of her kind."

"What's that supposed to mean?" David had

to ask, even though he knew it was a mistake to allow himself to be drawn into another of his father's vicious tauntings.

The judge advanced on him, and David took an instinctive step back. His father noticed and smiled slightly. "You fool. You're the son of a rich man. Of course this bitch is going to attach herself to you! That's how she makes her living."

"You know nothing about her."

"If she's living at the Four Roses, I know all I need to."

Silence stretched out between the two men. As it had for years, the few feet of space separating them seemed as wide as two oceans—and just as impossible to cross.

David stared at his father and tried to look at him objectively, as he would at any other stranger. What he saw was an old man, his features heavily lined, carved by bitterness and dissatisfaction. His eyes looked out on the world through a haze of animosity, and his lips were closed in a rigid line of disapproval. The older man reeked of a life wasted.

Chances not taken.

Words unspoken.

David shuddered slightly as he realized that if he'd gone on as he had been doing, very probably he would have ended his life much as his father had—bitter and alone.

But no more.

His chance was there. And he was going to grab it and hold it close. All he had to do was somehow find the audacity to face up to his father.

Taking a deep breath, he said calmly, "You

know nothing about her, Father. You know nothing about me."

"Hah!" The old man took a step toward his son. "I know that a drunk and a whore are a bad match in anybody's estimation."

"For the last time," David said through gritted teeth, "she's not a whore. And if you'll look closely, Father, you'll notice that I'm not drunk."

The housekeeper bustled into the room and came to an abrupt halt at the sight of the judge. "Oh, I beg your pardon, sir."

"Come in, Mrs. Hallstead." David took the woman's arm. "Father was just leaving, and I need help with this blasted tie."

"Yes, sir," the tall, thin woman muttered, and locked her gaze on the black silk cravat at David's throat.

As her nimble fingers worked on his tie, David glanced at his father. "Thank you for stopping by, Father. Good night."

"Where are you taking this ... person?" the judge snapped.

David flicked a wicked glance at his father, so he could be sure not to miss his reaction. "As a matter of fact, I'm taking her to the Grand Hotel for supper and dancing."

"The Grand?"

"That's right."

"People will see you," the judge said, fuming, as he cast a wary glance at his housekeeper.

"And no doubt," David tossed in, "they'll be green with envy at my good fortune."

"This has to stop, David," the judge said. "I won't allow you to disgrace me this way."

That tone in his father's voice dredged up years of memories. Instinctively David wanted to hide—or, better yet, find a bottle. Then he remembered that Michelle was waiting for him. Something new entered his mind. Something weak and untried—but struggling valiantly to survive.

Courage.

He closed his ears to his father's disparaging tone. He pretended not to hear the censure to which he was so accustomed.

Mrs. Hallstead, finished with her task, stepped back. David glanced into the mirror and forced a grin. "Excellent job, Mrs. Hallstead. Thank you."

She nodded, kept her gaze firmly lowered, and fled the room.

David snatched up his hat, gave himself one last glance in the mirror, then looked at his father. The old man was nearly purple with rage.

He thought about saying something, but decided against it. After all, this sudden burst of boldness might not last. Why tempt the fates that had sent it to him when he most needed it?

The only important thing now was, he was alive for the first time in months—and Michelle was waiting.

Deliberately, he set his hat on his head, shoved his hands in his pockets, and said cheerily, "G'night, Father. Don't wait up."

Then he left the room and took the flight of stairs with a light, skipping step. He nodded at the butler when the man opened the front door; then David walked directly out to the waiting carriage.

He never looked back.

He didn't hear his father, in a fury, smash his fist into the glass face of the hall clock.

In the semidarkness of Kevin's room, Cutter stared up at the painting of Seven Oaks. He didn't even ask himself why he did it. He only knew that whenever he doubted himself or the wisdom in his quest for justice . . . he turned to the painting.

He rubbed his chin thoughtfully. It was so long since he'd been in the house that his memories of the interior were fuzzy, indistinct. He couldn't remember the color of the drapes in the dining room. Was the fireplace in the morning room of brick or stone?

Odd how a man's brain plays tricks on him, he thought. Several years before, he'd have been willing to stake every cent he had *and* his reputation on the belief that he would never forget a damned thing about Seven Oaks. Very strange, Cutter told himself. He remembered the exterior of the building in detail. The style, how it was situated on the rich Georgia soil. Where the gardens were laid out.

Of course you do, his mind yelled at him. Haven't you been staring at this bloody painting for nearly ten years? That brought him up short. If he hadn't commissioned the painting, would he truly have forgotten everything about the big house?

No. He shook his head. Impossible. Hadn't he *tried* to forget, at first? Hadn't he tried to push away the memories of that house and the people in it? Hell, it was only when he'd finally surrendered to the inevitable recollections that his dreams had stopped torturing him.

It was as if he'd been given a sign of some kind. Something had been telling him to go back and face those people—prove them wrong.

"Ah, Christ!" Cutter muttered aloud, and turned away from the painting. In the half light of one oil lamp, he crossed the room and stopped before one of the three big windows on the far wall.

Staring through the shining panes, Cutter told himself that Kevin's room certainly didn't have the view Maggie's did. From the windows, he looked out over the alley and the rest of San Francisco. Lamplight shining from the windows of homes and hotels formed hundreds of spots of light glimmering in the darkness. Cutter smiled and squinted, narrowing his vision until the splashes of light resembled the fireflies he recalled from warm summer nights.

It was foolishness, and yet he headed back down the road of memories.

It wasn't his job to protect her, she'd said. He didn't have the right.

Right? Hell! He didn't have the *right* to anything.

Bastard ... Worthless ... No damn good ... The words, the voices, echoes of ugliness that wouldn't die, rattled through his mind. Over and over they sounded out, just as plainly, just as clearly, as they had so many years before. And, just as he had then, a part of him still believed them.

How the hell could he explain that to Maggie? It would be like trying to explain . . . a tree to someone who had never seen one.

Impossible.

She couldn't understand. She'd been wanted, cherished. Raised in a family that had blossomed and thrived on the love it fostered. Even as a child, she'd been sure of her place in the world. A father, sisters—even Rose had stood behind her. They'd formed a wall of protection and stood between Maggie and betrayal . . . hurt.

How could he explain to her what it was like to be betrayed by the very people who pretended to love you? By the father you believed in? Hell. She'd never had someone turn on her whom she trusted.

Until he'd come along.

Oh, yeah. He'd done a grand job with Maggie. All he'd wanted to do was spare her— and himself—hurt. But what he'd managed to do was give her even more pain.

He would have liked nothing better than to be able to go across that hallway, step into her room, and tell her he loved her. But he couldn't. And if that made him a coward, then he'd just have to find a way to live with it.

Shit. He was a damn fool to walk away from her, and he knew it—logically. In his more rational moments, Cutter knew that Maggie loved him. But somewhere deep inside him, he carried the seeds of doubt. *He'd* said he loved Cutter, too. And in a corner of Cutter's mind, a tiny voice whispered, if he'd been worthy, his father would have loved him. The old man would have left his son something in his will besides good wishes—if the son had deserved it. Right?

It was Cutter's fault that he didn't deserve his love. Wasn't it?

And if he'd somehow ruined *that* love, wouldn't he do the same with Maggie's?

"Dammit," he muttered thickly. "Enough!" Deliberately, he silenced that disturbing voice. It wasn't his fault. They were wrong about him. All of them. His family.

But even as he thought it, Cutter knew that until he proved it—to what was left of his so-called family *and* himself—he couldn't be the man Maggie wanted.

Turning away from the windows, he walked to the bedside table and poured himself a healthy measure of Kevin's good Irish whiskey. Lifting the glass in a silent salute to no one, Cutter raised it to his lips and tipped the amber liquid down his throat.

Fire swept through his veins. He smiled slightly and poured himself another. Too much thinking wasn't good for a man, he told himself. The silence must have been getting to him.

With the saloon closed for repairs, the only noise came from the neighboring taverns in subdued waves. It was hard to believe, Cutter thought, that there were people out there without a thing on their minds beyond the next drink. Or the next card game.

It was even harder to remember a time when he'd been one of them.

A knock at his door startled him, and he turned toward the sound. As if he could see right through the solid oak panel. Cutter knew exactly who was on the other side.

"Come in, Maggie," he called out.

She opened the door and hesitated on the threshold. Back-lit from the hallway, her face was in shadow, and still he thought she was the most beautiful woman he'd ever seen. Just being in the same room with her was enough to make his body hard, ready.

He didn't even question his response to her anymore. It simply *was*—like a blue sky or a cold day in winter.

Jesus, he was in trouble. Cutter took another sip of his drink before speaking, and when he did talk, his voice sounded surly even to him. "What do you want, Maggie?"

"To talk." Her voice was steady, even.

He envied her her control.

"Now's not a good time," he said on a laugh that died halfway from his throat. *Not unless you want to talk in bed.* And *that* image was enough to make him take another, longer sip of whiskey.

"There's never a good time with you, Cutter," Maggie countered, and stepped into the room. "You've been avoiding talking to me all evening."

"Apparently I didn't do a good-enough job."

She stiffened, and he cursed under his breath.

Deliberately Maggie closed the door behind her, and Cutter swallowed heavily. She was wearing a nightgown and robe. And Lord help him, the outer garment was a deep green silk that made her eyes shine. In the soft lamplight, her pale, creamy skin seemed to glow. His fingers tightened around the glass until he thought he might crush it. Through gritted teeth, he said, "Tomorrow, Maggie."

"Now, Cutter."

Maggie watched him as she took a step closer, and then another. His features were drawn tight. His eyes looked cloudy, dark, as if he'd been carrying the weight of the world on his back for far too long.

His black tie lay undone around the collar of his wrinkled white shirt, and his sleeves were rolled up to his elbows. Her gaze shifted from his strong forearms to the V of flesh exposed at his open collar. Suddenly, though, he turned away and walked to the windows. His silent steps told her he was barefoot.

Maybe he was right, she thought, and tried to swallow past the huge knot in her throat. Maybe she should have waited until the next day.

No, she told herself quickly. By the morning he would have thought of some other way to avoid her. If they were to talk, it would be here. And now.

She wouldn't find a better chance to catch him alone, she knew. With the saloon closed, no one was around. Rose was in bed at the far end of the hall. The saloon was a quiet, empty place, save for the two of them.

"I waited for you to come back this afternoon."

He flicked a glance at her. "I know. Sorry."

Maggie moved slowly across the floor toward the window and wished momentarily that she'd taken the time to dress before coming to his room. But when she'd made the decision, she hadn't wanted to waste any time, for fear that she would change her mind. So there she stood, in her nightclothes, alone in the near darkness with the man who'd introduced her to the pleasures a body could feel.

A tingle of excitement curled in the pit of her stomach, and Maggie deliberately ignored it. When she was just a foot or two from his side, she stopped. Her gaze fastened on the tight grip he had on the glass in his hand. A brief smile darted across her lips and disappeared again. It was a small comfort at least, that he was as affected by their closeness as she was.

She inhaled sharply, drawing his Irish-whiskey-scented breath deep inside her. When she finally spoke, even Maggie was surprised by her first question.

"Why did you really leave before I woke up?"

Cutter's head snapped around, and he looked at her through troubled, confused eyes. He let his gaze slide away from hers before saying stiffly, "I already told you. I had to talk to Digger."

"That's not the only reason," she insisted, refusing to let him off the hook that easily.

"Really?" he asked shortly. "What's the other?"

"You were afraid of me."

"Afraid?" Cutter gave her a lopsided grin that never touched his eyes. "Of you?"

"Of how I make you feel." She knew it. She'd felt it the moment she'd awakened to find him gone.

"No, Maggie." He shook his head, finished

his drink and set the glass down on the windowsill. Turning to her, he said *"You're* the one who's afraid of what I feel around you."

"Me?" Now Maggie laughed, but there was real amusement in her chuckle. "You're a bit confused here, Cutter. Maybe it's the drink, eh?"

"I'm not confused," he insisted, and lifted his hand to run one finger down the length of her silk-covered arm. "And I'm not drunk, either."

Maggie shivered slightly but held herself still otherwise. She wouldn't back away and let him know how his touch affected her.

"Aren't I the one who's been saying all along that you love me, Cutter? Aren't I the one who brought the word *love* into this in the first place?" She swallowed: her voice sounded breathy, anxious.

"I'm not talking about love, Maggie." He reached for her again and this time traced lightly around the deep, lace-edged neckline of her robe with his fingertips.

Her body jumped, and he gave her a wicked, satisfied smile.

"I think you dragged love into this because you're afraid that all I feel is lust."

Maggie flushed. She felt the heat rush into her cheeks, and it was all she could do not to raise her hands and cover her face so he wouldn't see it. Lust, he'd said? Oh, aye, there was plenty of that between them, heaven knew.

But it was more than that. Much more. And he knew it as well as she did.

"No, Cutter," Maggie answered in a surprisingly steady tone. "As much as you'd like to think there's nothing more between us than a moment's shared passion"—she reached up and cupped his cheek gently—"we both know different."

His eyes closed, and she felt his jaw clench tightly.

"When we come together, Cutter, it's like nothing else in the world." Maggie smoothed her thumb over his cheekbone. Cutter kept his eyes carefully shut. "In bed and out, darling, we were made for each other." She let her hand fall back to her side, and only then did he open his eyes to look at her again. When he did, she added softly, "And *that's* what you're afraid of."

Chapter 14

"**I**s this all a part of your plan?" Cutter asked, and to his own ears, his voice sounded as tight as the rest of him felt.

"What plan is that, Cutter?"

She smiled at him, then ran the tip of her tongue over her bottom lip. He watched, breathless.

"The plan where you drive me crazy." Oh, and it was working even better than she could have hoped, he thought. His chest heaved with the effort to draw air into his lungs.

"Oh, yes . . ." she said, that slow, delicious smile still in place. "I remember."

Cutter let his gaze slide over her figure, displayed so tantalizingly in the emerald green silk. Unerringly, his gaze stopped at her breasts. Under his hungry look, Maggie's breathing altered, and the rapid rise and fall of her chest drove him further toward madness.

And, his weary brain taunted him, that was exactly what this was. Madness.

Desperately he fought to continue the inane conversation. If he kept talking, maybe he'd quit thinking about . . . He shook his head.

"And this?" he asked, indicating her outfit.

"Was coming to my room wearing nothing but a bit of green silk and lace part of the plan?"

Slowly she shook her head, and her wild red hair shimmied around her shoulders. "No, Cutter. This isn't part of a plan." She shrugged. "This is just me."

Lord help him, he knew she was telling the simple truth. Maggie was the only woman he'd ever met who would have admitted to something so outrageous. And maybe that was a part of why she had such a powerful effect on him. A woman so sure of herself that she had no problem at all about visiting a man's room in her nightwear was a woman worth knowing.

He sucked in a gulp of air, and wasn't surprised when it stuck in his throat. "Lord, Maggie mine, you do make life hard for a man. . . ."

Maggie cocked her head, gave him a half smile, and asked, "How hard?"

Cutter's lips quirked. Trust Maggie to get to the heart of the matter. "As hard as life can get, I suppose."

"Ah." Maggie nodded thoughtfully and took a step closer to him. "Well, you know what they say, Cutter. . . ."

He couldn't take his eyes off the swell of her breasts. "No, what do they say?"

She stopped directly in front of him, reached out, and ran the tip of her finger down the front of his shirt. "When life gets . . . hard, it usually takes two people to solve the problem."

If she so much as said the word *hard* again, his body would shatter. Any harder and he'd be a damned statue. The tip of her finger slipped under the fabric of his shirt, and he felt her touch as if it were a match flame. Without conscious thought, Cutter's hand shot out and skimmed over her waist to cup her breast.

Her head fell back on her neck, and she smiled on a sigh.

"Ah, Cutter, my love, that's grand."

"Maggie mine," he whispered, and leaned toward her, "that's only the beginning."

She looked up into his eyes, and he saw a wicked sparkle in those shimmering green depths. "Then you're saying you still have a *hard* problem, do you?"

His jaw clenched, Cutter shook his head. "You're an evil woman, Maggie Donnelly."

"Aye, and aren't you the lucky one, though?"

The ache in his groin was overpowering. His entire body felt as if he were poised at the edge of a cliff, waiting only for a signal to jump.

His thumb moved gently over the hardened peak of her nipple, and she instinctively arched toward him.

Suddenly, though, she pulled back and half turned toward the door. "Did you hear something?"

Only my own will disintegrating, he thought dismally. Aloud, he managed to croak, "No."

"Strange," Maggie murmured, her brow furrowed, "I was sure I heard glass breaking." She lifted her chin and looked at him. "But that can't be right. We don't have any windows left, do we?"

Glass. Windows. Breaking?

She might as well have been speaking German. Nothing was making sense to his muddled mind. He was far too preoccupied with the way the green silk clung to her—

Cutter turned toward the door and paused. Maggie started to speak, but he held one hand up for silence. That time, *he'd* heard something.

Carefully, he crossed the bedroom floor to the door. He cautiously turned the knob and swung the door open just wide enough for him to slip through. Cutter didn't want to take the chance that the bloody door would pick that night to start squeaking.

He felt her right behind him. At the landing he leaned over the mahogany railing and peered down into the dark, deserted saloon.

"Do you see anything, Cutter?"

Her breath brushed against his cheek when she whispered.

He shook his head and motioned her to silence.

The sound came again, and he strained to hear it. To identify it. Glass, yes. But not a window breaking. After all, as Maggie had pointed out, they had no windows left.

Glancing over his shoulder, Cutter mouthed the words, *Stay here.*

Maggie frowned, clamped her lips together mutinously, and shook her head.

Another silent speech. *Dammit, Maggie.*

Her lips formed the word *no*.

Gritting his teeth, Cutter glared at her, hoping to intimidate her into doing what she was told.

She glared right back.

He knew he couldn't stand there all night and silently argue with her. He would just have to do his best to push her out of the way if they came upon anyone.

This time he simply waved her into place behind him, and fortunately she moved quickly into position.

He was thankful to be barefoot, so he could move fairly soundlessly down the carpeted hall. Crouching low, he inched forward. One of Maggie's hands was locked onto the waistband of his pants; her knuckles were digging into the small of his back.

He stopped suddenly, and Maggie stepped right into him. Cutter staggered, then caught himself. He ought to be locked up, he told himself. Barefoot, chasing down who knew what, with a half-naked woman clutching at him. Thinking about *that* wouldn't help him any. Glancing back down the hall, he desperately tried to avoid looking at Maggie at all. Instead he stared thoughtfully at the open door of his room and considered going back for his gun. Silently he cursed his own rampaging body for having kept him from thinking of a weapon sooner.

Downstairs, more glass broke, and his decision was made. Cutter knew he couldn't afford to waste any more time. He would just have to be even more careful than he'd planned to be. And maybe, he thought, he'd have time to pick up a piece of wood from the rubble of broken furniture that was stout enough to use as a club.

His mind raced with every swear word he'd ever heard. Cutter had never felt more vulnerable in his life. Sneaking downstairs in the dead of night to confront an intruder—perhaps an *armed* intruder—barefoot, with a woman wearing her nightgown! That was *not* a good idea. Strange, he told himself, how things seemed to happen to him around Maggie Donnelly.

From belowstairs came the *tinkle* and crash of more glass being broken. Cutter paused and groaned quietly.

"Where do you think he is?" Maggie whispered, and Cutter jumped.

Hand splayed against his back, he looked over his shoulder at her. She was leaning into his back, her breath warm on his cheek. A glint of excitement shone in her eyes as she looked past him into the darkness below.

"Can you see him?" she whispered close to his ear, and to Cutter it sounded as though she were shouting.

He swiveled his head around and twisted his features into a wild frown. Rolling his eyes, he held his index finger to his lips briefly, then shook his head in exasperation. For God's sake! Couldn't she keep quiet for a few bloody minutes?

His lips moved soundlessly and, he hoped, much too quickly for her to be able to see that he was mouthing every curse that entered his head.

Maggie grimaced, wrinkling her nose at him. Then she shrugged and nodded.

More glass broke, and Cutter turned back to the stairway. Damn you, whoever you are, he thought viciously. By the sound of it, the Roses was certainly losing a lot of—something.

Bent double at the waist, Cutter started slowly down the stairs, with Maggie hot on his heels. Grumbling under his breath, he fought to keep his balance as the skirt of her green silk gown wrapped itself around his ankles.

Keeping low, he was both thankful for and disgusted by the inky blackness of the saloon.

Not only was it easier for him and Maggie to hide; their uninvited guest also profited by the darkness.

Never had the staircase seemed so long. Briefly, he thought of just how many times he'd sprinted up its length in a matter of seconds. Now, taking one step at a time, cautiously measuring each footfall, it was taking an eternity.

And Maggie was so close to him, he could feel her naked form outlined against his back. He had to force himself to keep from thinking about her. A distraction as powerful as Maggie could have gotten them both killed.

Glass broke again just as Cutter and Maggie reached the bottom step. Once more, he turned and motioned to her to stay put. Again she shook her head wildly. He wasn't surprised.

Now that they were downstairs, they could hear the stealthy, muffled movements of the intruder. Whoever it was was moving around behind the long bar. Soft grunts and an occasional whispered curse were the only other sound, save for the now-expected crash of breaking glass.

Cutter paused a long moment, took in a gulp of air, and stepped off the bottom step onto the main floor.

Immediately he gasped and leaped straight back, jerking his right foot high off the floor. His hands wrapped around his foot, Cutter staggered backward, knocking Maggie flat on her back. As she fell, she smacked her head against the newel post and yelped.

From across the room, their startled intruder dropped whatever he was holding, and a much louder crash sounded out. Probably, Cutter thought in disgust, it was the bar mirror. Seconds later, whoever it was ran out of the saloon and through the front door. His hurried footsteps were lost amid the outside noises.

"Dammit, Cutter!" Maggie shouted, and pushed him off of her. "You let him get away!"

When she tried to get past him in what would prove to be a futile attempt to follow the man, Cutter's outstretched arm stopped her.

"Sit down!"

His voice thundered at her, and Maggie sat.

"There's glass all over the damned floor," Cutter grumbled, his hands still clutching his injured foot. "And most of it is in my foot!"

David couldn't stop smiling.

With Michelle in his arms, he felt, for the first time in his life, that everything was as it should be.

Her fingers lay gently in his left palm as he guided her around the dance floor. With her head tilted back, she stared up at him, and in the dark, shining depths of her eyes, David saw the future. A long, happy future.

The music ended, and as the last strains of the violins faded away, he heard someone ask, "David?"

Carefully he tucked Michelle's hand into the crook of his arm before turning to face the man who had spoken.

"Judge Taylor," David said evenly. "How nice to see you." And that wasn't a complete lie. Now that he had Michelle alongside him, talking to one of his father's cronies wasn't near the trial it had always seemed to be.

The tall, distinguished-looking older man raked his gaze over David and was unable to completely hide his surprise. Of course, David could hardly have blamed the man for that. The last time they'd met, the judge had spent twenty minutes lecturing him on the evils of drink. David had been thankful that he was much too drunk to listen.

"Is your father here this evening?" the judge asked, his gaze shifting beyond David to the milling crowd leaving the marble dance floor.

Lord, I hope not, David thought, but said only, "No, sir, he's not."

Judge Taylor hooked his thumbs behind his lapels, rocked back and forth on his heels and let his gaze slide across Michelle's form.

She looked exquisite. Her dark hair done up in curls that fell from the top of her head and just brushed across her shoulders, she wore a full-skirted gown the deep, rich color of a fine red wine. Small diamond earrings were her only concession to jewelry, and even those were overshadowed by her beauty.

Michelle looked as though she'd been born to frequent elegant places like the Grand Hotel.

David stood a bit taller, straighter. He'd never been more proud. He felt like marching to the bandstand and introducing her to the cream of San Francisco society. He wanted them all to see her, to know her. David wanted the world to know he'd found the woman for whom he had waited a lifetime.

Swallowing back the smile created by that mental image, David said simply, "Your Honor, I'd like you to meet my fiancée, Michelle Fontaine."

Michelle tipped her head up and smiled at David before nodding toward the judge.

The man's dumbfounded expression lasted only a moment, but it was long enough for David.

He braced himself for what might come. Knowing his father's friends for what they were—anything was possible. And certainly this would be only a small sampling of what he would receive from his father when *he* learned the news.

"Fiancée? Well, well. Fontaine, eh?" The judge was musing aloud, and he began to rock back and forth more quickly. "Don't believe I've heard the name before."

"I'm not surprised, Judge Taylor," Michelle said, and even her voice was beautiful. "I've only just arrived in your city."

"Really?" Taylor's bushy salt-and-pepper eyebrows lifted almost to his receding hairline. "Then I assume you and young Harper, here, were acquainted before?"

David frowned slightly, but Michelle didn't appear to notice.

"Not at all." She grinned up at her fiancé as if they shared a wonderful secret.

"I'm afraid I don't understand." Judge Taylor obviously had no intention of dropping the subject.

"It's very simple," David said, but the sudden tension in his voice belied his words. "Michelle and I met this afternoon. This evening"—he spared her a smile before looking up at the judge again—"she agreed to become my wife."

"Most unusual," Taylor said, and stroked his chin as if searching for a beard that wasn't there.

"Isn't it, though?" Michelle agreed. "I never

really believed in love at first sight. Until to-day."

"Yes, well . . ." Judge Taylor harrumphed. "Does the judge, your father, know?" he asked David.

"Not yet. But he will as soon as I return home." In fact, David wasn't looking forward to telling his father of his plans. Not that he didn't love Michelle. He'd never been more sure of anything in his life. It was only that the thought of facing down his father was enough to send a chill scuttling through David's blood.

But now that Judge Taylor knew, there was no avoiding facing his father. In fact, David wouldn't have been surprised if the fast-flying information had reached his sire before he returned home.

"I see," Taylor continued, and nodded sagely at a passing acquaintance. He turned to Michelle and looked down at her. "And *your* people?" he asked. His sharp-eyed gaze had become critical, as if he were memorizing everything about her in order to pass on the information later. "What do *they* have to say about this ill-advised undertaking?"

Michelle stiffened under his regard, and David tensed. When he would have spoken, though, her fingers tightened on his arm in a silent signal. Reluctantly, he kept quiet, in deference to her.

"This 'ill-advised undertaking,' as you put it," Michelle began gently, "would have been welcomed by my people once they'd seen how happy David has made me with his offer."

"Would have been?" The judge pounced on

her turn of phrase like a beggar on a loaf of bread.

She dipped her head momentarily, then stared back at him, her chin defiantly lifted. "I say 'would have been,' because my family is dead. I am alone in the world now."

"Not any longer." David patted her hand and received a brilliant smile as reward.

"No. Not any longer," she amended.

The judge cleared his throat and impatiently frowned away a waiter carrying a silver tray laden with filled champagne glasses.

"My sympathies on the loss of your family, of course," he said, without the slightest trace of sincerity. His eyelids halfway closed, he tipped his head back and looked down at Michelle along the length of his nose. "If you have no family in San Francisco, to whom do we owe thanks for your visit?"

David prepared himself for the judge's reaction. Undoubtedly it would be worth remembering. He only hoped Taylor wouldn't make a scene that would embarrass Michelle.

"Actually, I came to your lovely city to accept a position here."

"Ah . . ." The judge breathed heavily, and somehow managed to put a world of censure into that one syllable. "So you—work?"

Her fingers tightened again on David's forearm, and he noticed the rigid set of her shoulders as she met the judge's critical glare head on. David almost smiled.

"Certainly, I work."

"If it doesn't seem impertinent," Judge Taylor shot back, "may I ask where?"

"I am a singer, employed by the Four Roses, here in San Francisco."

David grinned. He watched the judge's features pale, then flood with barely concealed fury. Naturally, Judge Taylor wouldn't have approved of someone from the Barbary Coast actually having the temerity to rub elbows with society. In fact, as David watched, the judge took a hasty step back from the two of them, as if to avoid contagion.

"Four Roses," he said, and his voice shook with his effort to remain calm. "Isn't that a tavern?"

"Actually, no." David felt light-headed as he cheerily corrected the older man. He was actually beginning to enjoy himself. "It's the best damned saloon on the Coast."

The judge audibly gasped for air, and a terrified waiter began to flap a linen napkin in front of the man's face. Taylor's face was beet red, and his mouth opened and closed as if he were a beached fish.

Soft, swirling music rose up as the band once again began to play. Couples started to drift onto the dance floor.

Turning away from the judge, David glanced down at the woman he loved and asked, "Would you care to dance?"

Michelle looked up at him, pride and love shining in her eyes. "I would be delighted!"

"Excuse us, Judge," David said with a grin, then took Michelle in his arms and stepped into the circle of dancing couples.

Dammit, be careful!"

Maggie tightened her grip on Cutter's right

foot. "Stop being such a baby. If you'd only hold still, this would be over in a minute or two."

"Yes," he snapped, "for now! But after having you gouge and poke at my foot, I'll be lucky if I don't end up losing a leg!"

She jabbed his instep with the tweezers, and smiled in satisfaction when his leg jerked.

"Let go," he complained again. "I can take care of this myself, you know."

"Oh, certainly," she replied, and lifted his foot closer to the lamp beside her. "At *least* as well as you took care of the intruder."

"Now, that was hardly my fault."

"Whose was it, then? Mine?" She glanced at him, then looked back at her work. She had already pulled three slivers of glass from the sole of his foot, and there were two more that she could see.

Maggie cringed at the thought of his having to perform that task for her. Even the idea of glass being buried in her foot hurt. So to keep his mind off what she was doing, she had been baiting him for the past fifteen minutes. It was working better than she had hoped.

"Not entirely your fault," he conceded.

"Well, thank you very much."

"But it certainly didn't help much to have you attached to the seat of my pants like a pickpocket at a country fair!"

"Keep your voice down," she warned with a glance at his closed door. "You'll wake Rose. And if she comes in here now, she'll insist on doing this herself."

His eyes widened slightly, and Maggie dipped her head to hide her smile. That threat should keep him quiet for a minute or two. Rose

Ryan, good woman that she was, was not known for having a gentle hand when it came to wounds.

"Fine," he said. "I'll be quieter. But you have to admit that I could have done better without having you hanging onto me."

"Perhaps," she conceded, and set the tips of the tweezers on the jagged edge of a sliver of glass. As she yanked it free of his flesh, she said, "But you also would have done better with a gun and some shoes."

"Ow!" Cutter jerked his leg back, but she refused to let go.

Tightening her grip on his ankle, Maggie leaned to one side, deciding how best to approach the remaining glass shard.

"Shoes and a gun, huh?" he asked, stretching his neck, trying to see what she was planning next. "If you'll remember, neither of us was dressed for pursuit."

Maggie's eyebrows shot up and wiggled. "Well, now, there're pursuits ... and then there're *pursuits!*"

"You're toying with an injured man, here."

"I'm trying," she agreed cheerfully.

"And I doubt most nurses prefer to work in green silk."

"Aren't you fortunate, then?" she mumbled. The tweezer points came together on the glass, and with one quick move, she had the last piece out of his foot.

"There," she sighed. "That's done."

"Thank God," Cutter said sharply. His lack of appreciation clear from his tone, he added, "The next time I need medical help, I believe I'd prefer to wait for the Raffertys to come back to town!"

"Hmph!" Maggie stood up, set the tweezers down on the nearest table, then bent down to retrieve a pan she'd brought in earlier. In the bottom of the tin washbasin, a clear liquid sloshed noisily as she set it down again next to the bed. "That's the thanks I get, is it?"

"You want thanks?" His rumpled hair fell across his forehead, and his eyes were wide as he stared at her. "For poking holes in my foot?"

"Didn't anyone ever teach you any manners at all, Cutter?"

One side of his mouth lifted in a sardonic smile. "I don't believe situations like this have been adequately covered in the etiquette manuals."

"A pity."

"Isn't it?"

He looked down at the sole of his foot and winced as he trailed one fingertip over the swollen, reddened flesh. "It'll probably get infected," he mumbled to no one in particular. Snorting a harsh laugh, he finished lamely, "And I'll die because of broken glass. Now, *there's* an epitaph any man could be proud of!"

"It won't get infected, Cutter." Maggie smiled sweetly at him.

"And how do you know that, Dr. Donnelly?"

Still smiling, she looked him squarely in the eye and assured him, "Because I'm about to see to it."

"What?" He tilted his head and watched her suspiciously.

"It's something Da taught me."

"Kevin?"

Obviously, she thought, mentioning her father's name hadn't done a thing to make him feel better. Inwardly her smile grew to a wide grin. Wisely, though, she kept him from seeing it.

"Aye." She nodded sagely, and reached out for his injured foot. Her hands on his ankle, she pulled him around quickly, not giving him a chance to fight her off. "He believed in cleaning a wound well, you see."

"Oh." Cutter blew out a rush of air, relieved. He glanced down at the basin and asked. "Won't you need more water?"

"No," she said with an innocent smile, and lowered his foot closer to the pan. "This is more than enough."

He shrugged.

"And besides," Maggie added as she shoved his foot down hard in the clear, cold liquid, "this isn't water, Cutter. It's—"

"—kerosene!" he shouted and tried, unsuccessfully, to drag his foot free.

Chapter 15

" '**W**hore?' "

Seamus scratched his head, then glanced at Ike. "Now, why the hell would they paint that on the front of the place, d'ya think?"

Ike shrugged, but kept his gaze on the front wall of the Roses. Apparently, the same fellow who'd ruined all the glassware in the place had also taken the time to leave them a message. The word *whore* had been painted on the front of the saloon sometime during the night, in huge, scrawling letters. Rivulets of red paint, which had run from the bottom of each individual letter, gave the appearance of fresh blood.

Ike shuddered and told himself he was being foolish. At least, he thought, the paint hadn't yet dried, and that would make it a hell of a lot easier to clean up.

He glanced over his shoulder at the people walking by. As usual, folks kept their minds on their own business. Besides, on the Coast, what was a little paint?

"Still," Seamus was saying, "seems pretty stupid to me. The word *whore*, I mean." He tossed a half smile at the man beside him. "Down here, it's more of an advertisement than a insult."

266

"Just get it cleaned up, Seamus."

"Right, Ike."

The guard stepped into the Roses, crunching the remaining bits of glass underfoot as he went.

Ike looked down at the mess and shook his head. Despite Cutter's arguments to the contrary, Ike was sure that all their trouble was because of him. Hell, he was almost used to it. No matter that the damned war was over—some folks would never get used to the idea of a free colored man.

His usually affable features hardened as he turned to look at the street behind him. Thoughtfully he studied the faces of the people who passed him. Familiar faces, most of them. People he worked with. People who stopped in the Garter to talk to him.

Who was it? he wondered. Ike's brow furrowed, and he folded his arms across his massive chest. Which smiling face hid the ugliness behind all this?

Digger?

No. That was too easy. Besides, he told himself with a strangled laugh, he was pretty sure Digger couldn't read or write.

A beer wagon rolled by, its wheels screeching in protest. The driver shouted a hello and waved to Ike as he passed. Ike nodded to him, then tossed a quick glance at the still-dripping red paint. Whoever was behind all this would soon learn that it would take more than paint and some broken windows to chase Ike Thorn out of town.

He hadn't come that far and worked that hard to quit now.

Deliberately, he stepped off the boardwalk, into the middle of the crowd, and walked down the center of the road to the corner restaurant for breakfast.

Maggie heard him limping down the hall and poured him a cup of coffee just as he entered the family dining room.

"Afternoon, Cutter," she said cheerfully. "How's the foot?"

"Wonderful." He plopped himself down into the chair opposite her and winced as he straightened out his leg. Glancing at her, he added, "Nice trick, that kerosene. Why didn't you just set fire to me?"

She smiled sweetly at him and batted her eyelashes for effect. "You were worried about infection. Now you don't have to be concerned."

He mumbled something she didn't quite catch, and Maggie said, "What?"

"Nothing," he snapped, and reached for the bread plate.

"Butter?"

"No, thanks." He gave her a false smile, and asked, "Did you find enough glasses to replace what we lost?"

Maggie sighed and propped her elbows on the tabletop. Cupping her cheeks in her hands, she said, "Not enough, but some. Ike spent the morning talking to some of the other saloon owners, and each one was willing to sell us a couple of dozen glasses." She shook her head slightly. "But we still don't have nearly enough."

Just thinking about the destruction behind the bar made her want to groan. All of the fine crystal, most of the heavy glass beer mugs, and every last one of the jigger glasses had been smashed by their mysterious intruder.

When she and Cutter had first gone downstairs that morning to investigate, Maggie had been surprised that Cutter had only picked up a few pieces of glass in his foot the night before.

From the bottom of the stairway, all along the length of the bar, through the front door, to the boardwalk was a wide path of shattered glass. Whoever had done it had obviously enjoyed his work. He had smashed nearly every piece of glass in the place. The only reason the few remaining pieces had survived was no doubt because she and Cutter had interrupted the man before he'd had a chance to finish.

Maggie bit down on her bottom lip. It was hard to imagine someone being so maliciously destructive. Oh, perhaps it shouldn't have been, considering what had happened to the windows two nights before. But somehow this seemed worse.

Someone had taken the time and energy to deliberately lay down a path of smashed glass ... as if he'd wanted her and Cutter to follow the path of destruction that led to the painted insult on the front wall.

Cutter spoke, and Maggie's thoughts snapped back to the present. "After lunch I'll head over to the Grand and the Occidental hotels. Maybe I can strike up a deal with the bartenders."

"What kind of deal?" She sat up straight and took a sip from her cup of coffee. "They won't want to part with their glassware any more than the Coast owners did."

Cutter shrugged and winked at her. "Maybe

we can trade a few cases of Kevin's Irish whiskey for enough glasses to get us through."

"Da won't like that," she warned.

"Da's not here," he pointed out.

"True." And she added silently, *It would serve the old goat right.* It seemed only fair to give him a little grief, after he'd saddled her with a partner she hadn't wanted. On the other hand, she thought, perhaps her da had done her a greater favor than even *he* knew, by sending Cutter back to her.

As he snatched up a piece of fried chicken from the platter nearby, Cutter waved the drumstick at her. "And while I'm downtown, I'll wire St. Louis and order more crystal."

He looked so pleased with himself, Maggie couldn't help asking quietly, "And will you be walking?"

Cutter frowned, took a big bite of his chicken leg, and glared at her as he chewed.

Lost in the hustle of afternoon foot traffic, a lone man stood in the alley across the street from the Four Roses. He'd been keeping watch for some time. It pleased him to know that the whoremongers and purveyors of alcohol were having to deal with the destruction he had delivered the night before.

He frowned briefly and remembered his fright when the gambler and his lover had nearly stumbled on him in the dark. If it hadn't been for his foresight in leaving broken glass at the bottom of the staircase, they might have caught him.

And that couldn't happen. Not until he had finished what he'd set out to do. Then it

wouldn't matter. His work would be complete—
his objective reached.

The man smiled as he watched one of the
hired help scrub at the sign he had painted. It
would take more than scrubbing to rid themselves of that word. And even if they did manage to cover it up or paint over it, the stain
would remain.

Just because a whore was not publicly named
as such, did that make her any less a whore?

A week later, things were back to normal
around the Four Roses. Actually, better than
normal. Since its reopening, the crowds had
been bigger than ever. It seemed that a lot of
people enjoyed the idea of gambling at what
might be a "dangerous" saloon. Some of the
newer customers even looked disappointed
when nothing out of the ordinary happened.

Maggie, however, was delighted. Though the
last week had been relatively peaceful, she
couldn't rid herself of the notion that their troubles weren't over. She kept waiting for the next
attack. Too often, she found herself staring at
the wall of recently replaced windows as if the
intruder were standing on the boardwalk, looking in. And each time a customer entered the saloon, her gaze darted to the door, and she held
her breath uneasily.

Logically, she knew it was pointless to attempt to keep watch over a place as busy as the
Roses—after all, it wasn't as if she would have
recognized their attacker if she'd seen him. But
something inside her refused to stop.

During the day, she could convince herself
that her feeling of approaching disaster was

simply a reaction to what had already happened. At least she was able to sleep during the off hours, since Cutter had hired an extra man to keep watch. But at night, with the crowd milling about, and the noise and bustle surrounding her, Maggie felt ... vulnerable.

He could have been anyone. He might even have been a she. Maggie shook her head. The situation was impossible. Her nerves were stretched as tightly as a drumskin. Every sound, every laugh, scraped along her spine like fingernails on a blackboard.

And she knew Cutter was in just as sad a shape.

Instinctively she let her gaze slide over the noisy mob, until it came to rest on Cutter. Embroiled in yet another of his almost constant card games, he appeared to be in complete control.

But Maggie knew better. His temper was shorter than normal, and his mouth, usually curved in a wry smile, was now generally held in a grim, straight line. They had hardly spoken to each other during the past few days. And if she were being reasonable, she would have admitted that they both had been far too busy for any kind of conversation.

But she was tired of being reasonable. Since he'd come home, there had been nothing but one crisis after another, and all Maggie really wanted to do was to scream out her frustration.

Hell, even her plan to drive him crazy with lust had been failing of late. Of course, her heart hadn't been in her flirting, either, so she really hadn't been giving it her best. Still, Cutter was so preoccupied, she doubted that he'd have noticed her being tossed over some cowboy's shoulder and carried off into the night.

Her lips twitched at the thought, and briefly she considered arranging something of the sort. Briefly. But if she was right and he *didn't* notice, then she'd have been humiliated—and just then, she couldn't have stood too much more.

Maggie's self-confidence was already suffering. She had never imagined for a moment that he could have held out for so long against her blatant attempts at seduction. It certainly gave a woman pause when her man could ignore her with such apparent ease. And it was no help, either, that her own desire for Cutter was just as strong as ever.

In fact, the one thing that might have helped her live through the past week or so was the one thing that Cutter hadn't been giving her. His arms around her. His voice, quiet and intimate in the darkness. His body covering hers and driving away her fears with the force of his passion—his love.

Why was he being so damned stubborn about that?

Couldn't he see that he loved her? That he needed her?

Maggie's fingers curled over the arms of her chair. Worrying at her bottom lip, she glared at Cutter from across the room and willed him to look at her. But he didn't.

Maybe, she told herself, it was time to stop playing this stupid, childish game and demand that he admit to caring for her. Maybe what was called for here was a good, old-fashioned, clearing-the-air sort of fight.

Perhaps even an ultimatum.

Before she could think better of it, Maggie pushed herself to her feet and started toward him. She'd hardly taken more than a step or two when a commotion at the front door caught her attention.

Immediately she turned to look.

The first thing she noted was the rifle held high in the air. Her heart stopped, staggered, then began to beat again in the next instant, when she caught a glimpse of burnished auburn hair. When the owner of that head of hair shouted, "Maggie, girl! Where are ya?" she grinned, lifted the hem of her skirt, and pushed her way through the crowd to the door.

"What the hell?" Cutter laid his poker hand face down on the table and looked over his shoulder. Who was shouting for Maggie? He couldn't see a damned thing, so he stood up and craned his neck to peer over the heads of the people who filled the room.

He couldn't see Maggie, and that worried him. Cutter would rather have had her where he could keep a watchful eye on her. That whole business of the faceless attacker wasn't over, he knew. And the thought of Maggie and the intruder's coming face to face had kept Cutter lying awake every night.

She was just the kind of woman who would go rushing out to meet danger head on and never give her own safety a moment's thought. Well, Cutter had been thinking of little else all week.

Oh, he'd gone through the motions of getting the Roses up and running again. And during the crowded, busy nights, he had kept his mind occupied by playing one poker game after another. But the long hours he'd spent in his room had been torturous.

Cutter was plagued by distorted visions of what might have happened if Maggie had been alone the night the intruder had smashed up the place. His imagination created new scenes— terrifying scenes—where Maggie was hurt and alone, and he couldn't find her.

Couldn't get to her in time.

Just remembering those visions sent Cutter's heart into a rapid, hammering beat. And now someone was there, shouting for her. *Who?* He stepped to one side and squinted, trying desperately to see past the blue fog of cigar smoke and the elaborate hats worn by most of his customers. Then he saw it . . . a man's arm stretched up high over the crowd, and in the tightly clenched fist, a rifle.

Mouth dry, palms damp, Cutter moved, then stopped just as abruptly. An incredibly fat woman in purple satin stepped in front of him, and he was trapped. He tried to get around her, but it was as if she had sensed what his next move would be and shifted her bulk to prevent it. The violet ostrich feather in her hair swung, first one way, then the other, with her jerky movements, and each time, the soft whip slapped Cutter across the face. Several of the feather's long, delicate strands flew up his nose and swished across his eyes. Cutter jerked his head back, but it was too late.

He sneezed violently, the fat woman turned to glare at him, and Cutter sneezed again.

"Really!" Her tone was high-pitched and frosty. "Cover your face, young man!"

"I beg your pardon," Cutter said with a grunt as she ground the heel of her shoe into his foot. Wincing, he tried to keep his gaze on the still-upraised rifle across the room, and told the woman stiffly, "I need to pass through here, please."

She puffed out her sizable chest to amazing proportions and sniffed, "I'm not stopping you, am I?"

Just the thought of trying to squeeze past that intimidating bosom would have been enough to quell a lesser man. Then Cutter heard that loud male voice again. This time, it came as a wild, jubilant howl.

He jerked his head up in time to catch a glimpse of Maggie elbowing her way through the crowd. She was smiling! As she neared her objective, the man with the rifle tossed his gun to Jake, over the heads of the startled people surrounding him. The bartender caught the weapon with a flourish and grinned as Maggie launched herself into the other man's open arms.

Stupefied, Cutter gaped at the scene across the room. The crowd seemed to part magically, giving him an open view of a tall man in buckskins with a wild red mane and a full auburn beard lifting Maggie off her feet and swinging her high in the air.

Buckskin then grinned up at her like a lovesick puppy, and Maggie, much to Cutter's disgust . . . grinned back. Then, as everyone in San Francisco watched, Buckskin let Maggie slide down the length of his body, until her feet hit the floor. He still didn't release her, and Maggie looked as though she had no intention of breaking away.

The man's big hands held onto Maggie's waist with a too-familiar ease, and Cutter's gaze locked on the sight. Something inside him flared up and began to burn with a heat that seemed to sear his soul. His breath caught around the hard knot in his chest. His eyes burned with the strength of his unblinking stare—but he couldn't look away. Buckskin bent down and slanted a long, deep kiss across Maggie's mouth, and the cheering crowd roared its approval. It was all Cutter could do to keep from shouting them down with his *own* roar.

A roar of outrage.

Anger.

Jealousy.

Jealousy?

The word flashed in front of his eyes like a warning beacon from a lighthouse. But it was too late. Maybe it always had been too late for him, and he'd just been too stubborn to see it.

"Relax, Cutter," a deep, familiar voice said from close by.

"Huh?" he turned, saw Seamus, and turned back again, unable to stop watching the *happy* little scene unfolding at the front of the saloon.

"I said, relax, man," Seamus repeated, and stepped closer to his boss. "He'll do her no harm. Not him."

That was certainly a matter of opinion, Cutter thought, but he said only, "Who is he?"

"Rancher. Does some trappin', too, I hear." Seamus shrugged and followed Cutter's gaze to the two people now talking and laughing together like old friends.

"A rancher ..." Cutter was still focused on the couple across the room from him. "Trapper? What's he doing here?"

"Him and his family have a place in ... Wyomin', I think. But he comes through 'Frisco two or three times a year," Seamus told him. "Always comes by to see Maggie, too."

"What's his name?" Cutter ground out, even though it didn't matter. He didn't care what Buckskin's name was, as long as he went back to Wyoming. Quickly.

"Benteen," Seamus answered. "Jericho Benteen." Then, on a laugh, he added, "Just you be glad he's come alone this time. Once, he brought his brothers along ... took us nearly three days to clean the place up after the Donnybrook they threw in here."

But Cutter wasn't listening anymore.

He didn't want to know anything about the rancher.

He didn't care about the man's family.

As he watched Jericho Benteen laying his hands on Maggie, the truth reared up and punched Cutter in the face.

He couldn't bear the thought of any other man touching her.

Maggie laughed delightedly at something the rancher said, and Cutter's jaw clenched tightly. He heard his heartbeat thundering in his ears and felt his blood racing through his veins, feeding the flames of a jealousy that only seemed to burn more brightly as the minutes passed.

Even as he started across the room, brushing past the big-bosomed woman without a thought, Cutter's head reeled from the impact of several hard truths.

By all that was holy, she'd been right from the start.

It was useless to fight it any longer.

Whether or not it was good for either of them . . .

Whether or not there was a future for the two of them—Cutter loved Mary Margaret Donnelly.

And the only man who would be holding her that night . . . was him.

Chapter 16

grabbed his leg, holding very tightly, as Maggie

"**Y**ou get prettier every time I see ya!"

Maggie smiled up into Jericho Benteen's shining green eyes and told him, "Ah, now, you're just partial to redheads."

His auburn eyebrows wiggled as he gave her a wink and said, "Anybody with a lick o' sense is partial to redheads, girl!"

She reached up and gave a long strand of his reddish-brown hair a playful yank. "What're you doing in town this time, Jericho?"

"Ah." He finally released his grip on her waist and leaned one elbow on the bar top. "Just wanted to wander around a bit before I leave."

"Leave?" Maggie's brow furrowed. "Leave for where?"

Before he could answer, Jake handed Jericho his rifle and asked, "What'll it be?"

The big man paused and tilted his head back to stare up at the ceiling. He rubbed his bearded jaw for a long moment, then finally turned to the waiting bartender. "Surprise me, Jake."

The other man gave him a wicked grin and rubbed his palms together expectantly. Without another word, he moved off down the bar and grabbed his dog-eared copy of *How to Mix Drinks, or the Bon Vivant's Companion.*

Jericho chuckled. "He's takin' this serious, ain't he?"

"Always does," Maggie agreed. "Now tell me where you're off to."

The tall, handsome man leaned down until he was looking her straight in the eye. "England," he said, and then laughed at her dumbfounded expression.

For one brief moment, Maggie looked him up and down, considered his wild hair, full beard, and the buckskins that covered him from neck to toe. Then her gaze swept over the rifle that he held as if it were an extension of his body.

If he was telling the truth, England would never be the same.

"For the love of heaven," she said, astonishment in her tone, "why would you be going there?"

Jericho cradled his rifle in the crook of his arm. "Well, this friend of Micah's wife—her pa's havin' some trouble back to the old country, and he's laid up, so he asked one of us boys to go."

"Micah's *married?*"

"Oh, hell, yes!" Jericho shook his shaggy head again and smiled to himself. "And that woman leads him a dance, I can tell you!"

"Well," Maggie said, glad for the chance to take her mind off Cutter and the problems at the Roses, "then tell me! I want to hear *all* of it."

Jericho opened his mouth, then shut it again just as quickly. He was staring at someone just beyond her shoulder. Suddenly Maggie was sure who it was.

"Who's your friend?" Cutter asked as he stepped up behind her.

Maggie half turned to look up at him. He was positively glaring at Jericho. His features were cold, stiff, as if they'd been carved of marble. Glancing back at Jericho, Maggie saw that the big, redheaded rancher wasn't in the least put out by Cutter's fighting attitude. In fact, judging by the half smile on his face, Jericho Benteen looked as if he were enjoying himself.

But then, she remembered suddenly, there was nothing the Benteens liked better than a good fight. Instantly, images of the destruction he and two of his brothers had caused to the Roses a couple of years before flashed through her mind. She dismissed the visions as abruptly as they had appeared, and told herself that she had better get a good, strong grip on the situation. They simply couldn't afford to shut the place down again for a few days.

"Cutter," she started, "this is Jericho Benteen. Jericho, Cutter."

"Cutter what?" Jericho asked pleasantly.

"Just Cutter," the other man snapped.

"Only one name?" he asked, the reddish eyebrows lifting. "Don't hardly seem right, does it, Maggie?" he asked, his gaze still fixed on the other man.

"One's all a man needs," Cutter informed him tightly, "if it's the right one."

"Yeah? The right what?" Jericho prodded. "The right name? Or the right man?"

Maggie's gaze shot back and forth between the two men. She couldn't understand what they were saying and not saying to each other. And just then, she didn't care. All she could think about was keeping them apart long enough for Cutter to cool down.

By all the saints, she asked herself with another quick look at him, what was wrong with the man? For days, he'd hardly talked to her, and as soon as she started enjoying herself, he marched over like the Angel Gabriel, with his sword drawn.

Even as that thought raced through her mind, the answer struck her. A warm, delicious heat coursed through her body, and Maggie had to fight the urge to scream in triumph.

Ah, jealousy was a lovely thing.

Her lips curved in a self-satisfied smile that she had to dip her head to hide, and her heartbeat quickened. Joy bubbled in her chest and spread throughout her body like hot whiskey on a cold night. Every inch of her was suddenly, inescapably on fire. Her knees shook, her hands were trembling, and what she wanted more than anything in the world was to turn around and kiss Cutter until he couldn't breathe.

But she didn't.

That would have been too easy for him.

Besides, she thought, the best way to make his sudden jealousy work for her was to feed it.

"Here ya go, Jericho." Jake spoke up, interrupting the two men. Carefully the bartender set a tall, thin crystal glass on the shining wood bar and stepped back. Like a proud father, he stared at his concoction for another moment before lifting his gaze to Jericho.

The redheaded man frowned at the mixed drink, then glanced at the bartender. "All right. What is it?"

Jake puffed out his substantial chest and announced, "That's a *pousse-café*."

Shocked, Jericho's mouth fell open briefly. His face—what wasn't hidden by his beard—flushed a deep pink. He looked pointedly from Jake to Maggie and back again, a frown twisting his lips. "Ya ought not to say such things in front of Maggie, Jake. Didn't your ma teach ya nothin'?"

Cutter snorted.

Jake shook his head tiredly. "It ain't dirty, Jericho. It's French. Means . . . after coffee."

"Hell, I ain't had no coffee!"

"You don't *have* to drink coffee first; it's just what they call the bloody drink!" Obviously, the bartender's creative sensibilities were being sorely tried.

"Well." Jericho shifted his feet uneasily, still unsure about the sound of those words. "If that's what they mean, then they ought to damn well *say* that."

Cutter muffled the chuckle that shot from his throat.

Maggie swiveled her head and glared at him.

"Shoot, Jericho," Jake insisted, "forget the dang name and try it, will ya?"

"I don't know," the man said, and bent to study the drink in front of him. "It's almost too durn pretty to drink."

Jake beamed at his carefully layered mixture.

"What's in it?" Jericho asked.

The bartender reached out and pointed to each of the four separate colors in turn, saying, "On the bottom is the red Curaçao, then there's yellow Chartreuse, and then green vanilla, and on top is the brandy." Jake beamed proudly. "If you'd like, I can set fire to the brandy for ya. Looks real pretty."

Jericho looked appalled. "Maybe so," he allowed, and ran one hand over his full, bushy beard, "but I don't believe I want to hold a fire up this close to my face."

"Ya blow it out before you drink it." Jake shook his head as if disappointed in his most adventurous customer.

"I should smile, I would!"

"Maybe the 'gentleman' would prefer a simple beer, Jake," Cutter said quietly.

Maggie heard the challenge in his statement and hoped for one brief moment that Jericho hadn't. It was a foolish hope, and, like all such things, died quickly.

Jericho shot Cutter a fast look, then reached out, grabbed the drink, and downed the beautiful concoction in one long gulp. He slammed the empty glass down on the bar, blinked his watery eyes, and gasped "Damn, that was good, Jake."

Jake nodded, gratified, and walked away to tend to his other customers.

"Maggie," Cutter said, his voice hard and determined. "I need to speak to you—up in the office."

"Not now," she answered, and though she didn't look at him, she could feel his tension.

"It's important," Cutter added, and his tone made it clear that he wasn't going to brook an argument.

"It'll have to wait, Cutter." Maggie risked a quick glance at him, and was pleased to see that the stamp of jealousy was still etched on his features. His blue eyes looked a stormy gray, and his jaw was clenched so tightly, it was a wonder he hadn't broken any teeth. Turning back to Jericho, she laid a hand on his forearm and told Cutter, "Jericho's asked me to have supper with him, and we're just going to leave now. Isn't that right?"

The moment seemed to last an eternity. If Jericho didn't understand what she was trying to do, this could be very embarrassing.

But she shouldn't have worried. Jericho Benteen looked down at her and winked, bless his heart. "That's right, darlin'," he said, and dropped his left arm around her shoulders. His fingers moved over her arm familiarly; then he pulled her up close to his side. "And I already waited long enough for ya. We best get goin'."

"Maggie . . ." Cutter held himself so stiffly, he looked to be standing at full attention.

Jericho shifted his rifle into a more comfortable position, then said pointedly, "I'll have her back right early, Papa. Don't you worry."

For a moment, Maggie thought Jericho had taken things a bit too far. But despite the anger she read in Cutter's eyes, he didn't make another move to stop her.

"We'll talk when I get back," she offered quietly. "All right?"

Long, tense seconds crawled by. The muscle in his jaw began to twitch. One small part of Maggie's mind began to protest. She shouldn't be doing this to the man she loved, for heaven's sake. *Look at him!* she thought. He seemed miserable.

And a small voice in the back of her mind whispered, *Good.* She'd waited long enough for Cutter to come to his senses. If a push was what he needed, then by God, she would arrange that push.

Finally, Cutter jerked her a nod. Then, with his gaze locked on Jericho's proprietary grip on her, Cutter added, "I'll be waiting."

"You do that, son." Jericho laughed and turned Maggie toward the door.

As they moved through the crowd, Maggie concentrated on Jericho's arm draped over her bare shoulders. She resisted the impulse to turn and look at Cutter, telling herself that it might only serve to weaken her resolve.

But just before she and Jericho stepped out into the night, Maggie chanced a quick look behind her.

He hadn't moved. Cutter still stood ramrod straight at the bar, watching her. Customers moved around him as if he weren't there, and Maggie noticed that even in that crowded, noisy, overheated room, Cutter was completely alone.

Cutter's gaze shot to the wall clock again. The hands seemed to be standing still. Yet even as he thought it, he knew that it wasn't so. Maggie and Jericho had been gone for three hours—it just *felt* like three hundred!

Three hours! Nobody took three hours to eat supper. What else were they doing? Where were they?

"Shit!" He pushed himself away from Maggie's desk and began to pace the confines of the office for the umpteenth time. He knew exactly how many steps it would take him to cross the floor to the door.

Twenty-two.

Then twenty-two back again.

He'd crossed that bit of space over and over. If he'd been walking in a straight line, he probably would have reached Denver by then.

He passed the desk and went on to the wide windows. With one hand, he drew the heavy draperies aside and stared out at the night, but with the lamps lit behind him, all he could see was his own reflection staring back at him.

He'd raked his fingers through his hair so many times, it stood out from his head in a wild halo. His tie was loosened and hung down on either side of his unbuttoned collar. He'd long since tossed his coat aside and rolled his shirt sleeves up to the elbows.

Cutter snorted at his reflection. He looked just like what he was: a man at the end of his tether.

Abruptly he let go of the drapes and once again began to pace.

Who the hell was this Jericho Benteen? And how much did he mean to Maggie?

Over and over, his mind re-created the image of the buckskin-clad man lifting Maggie high into the air, then kissing the breath out of her. And time after time, Cutter forced himself to recall that Maggie had answered the man's kiss with unbridled eagerness.

What the hell was going on?

For weeks she'd been teasing, tempting, and tormenting him—trying to get him, Cutter, to admit that he loved her. Then some wild-haired mountain man had come into the saloon and she'd forgotten Cutter's existence?

He shoved his fingers through his hair and squeezed his head between his palms, trying ineffectually to silence the voices in his mind.

What good was it doing? he asked himself. Thinking and rethinking all of that hadn't answered any of his questions.

It had only created more.

In the past few days, he and Maggie had hardly spoken to each other—there'd been so much to do before reopening the Roses. But that wasn't all of it, he knew.

Cutter had simply used that excuse to keep his distance.

That night on the stairs had made him realize a lot of things, not the least of which was his feelings for Maggie.

Jesus! he thought, letting his head fall back. He couldn't remember ever having been that scared. Oh, not for his own worthless hide, Lord knew he'd been in tougher situations than *that*. After all, what was a glass-breaking sneak thief, compared to an angry loser in a card game, armed with a .44?

No, his fear that night on the stairs had been something different. Something deeper.

He straightened up and stared at the closed office door in front of him. But instead of the white-painted panel, he saw the visions that had haunted him for the past few days.

Visions of the way that night might have turned out.

Images of Maggie, shot. Lying on the floor of the Roses, bits of broken glass scattered around her, shining like diamonds. Her green eyes forever closed, and the dark stain of blood spreading as it soaked into the fine emerald silk of her nightgown. In his mind's eye, Cutter saw himself lift her limp body from the floor and clutch it to him. Her head fell back, and her glorious hair spilled over his arms. He kissed her, then called her name.

He told her he loved her.

But it was too late.

He was too late.

Cutter shook his head abruptly to clear the terrible dream image. He turned away from the door, and his gaze shot unerringly to the sofa. Instantly his brain conjured up the memories of the one night he and Maggie had spent together, nearly a year before. On that very sofa, in a mindless blur of passion, they had come together and created a fire that was still smoldering in each of them.

His body tightened, and each breath he drew was more painful than the last. He remembered it all—every moment, every touch. And most especially, he remembered the look on her face when he told her he couldn't love her.

He blinked repeatedly until the old images faded away, leaving him alone again in the office.

Soft lamplight brushed away the shadows in the corners, yet Cutter still felt them. Shadows of everything that had happened in his life to bring him to this point. Shadows of broken promises and shattered trust. Shadows of love denied.

He snorted a half laugh at his latest predicament. After all they'd been through, it seemed only natural, somehow, that it would have come to this. The night he was finally able to admit to loving her, Maggie was out having supper with another man.

A quick glance at the clock told him only another ten minutes had passed. Hmph! At that rate, he told himself, it would take a week or more just to reach morning.

But no matter how long it took, he would be there. In the office. Waiting. And when she returned, he thought, he wouldn't waste any more precious time talking. He would grab her in his arms, carry her to bed, and make wild, sweet love to her—exactly as he'd wanted to all those long, lonely months.

He didn't care that she'd gone off with Benteen, leaving him behind. It was probably the best thing she could have done, he thought reasonably. The past, interminably long, three hours had given him time to think, to realize just what it was that she meant to him. To convince himself that no matter what tasks still lay ahead for him, Maggie was a part of him.

Cutter began to pace again. His hurried steps as he crossed and recrossed the wooden floor echoed in the emptiness. With one hand, he reached up and rubbed his jaw, then the back of his neck. His head ached and pounded with each beat of his heart. Every nerve in his body was alert, strained to the breaking point.

Yes, he told himself firmly as he again checked the clock, only to find that the minute hand had hardly budged, she'd done the right thing, leaving him behind like that. In fact, whether he knew it or not, Jericho Benteen had done them a favor. Maybe the next day he would even buy the rancher a drink. A friendly gesture to—

His thoughts came to an abrupt halt, and he spun around to face the door. He hadn't imagined it. Under his watchful gaze, the doorknob slowly turned. As the heavy door swung open,

Cutter tried to remember all of his fine intentions. Don't waste a moment. Tell her you love her, he reminded himself. Grab her.

Hold her.

Kiss her.

Love her.

Then Maggie stepped into the room, and her brilliant green eyes locked with his. Even Cutter didn't recognize his voice when he shouted, "Where the *hell* have you been?"

Maggie blinked, then closed the door behind her. She gave Cutter a smile that she hoped didn't look as shaky as she felt, and said, "Don't you remember, Cutter? Jericho and I went to supper."

His features flooded with color, and Maggie took a brief moment to study his appearance. Apparently the last three hours had been every bit as long for him as they had for her.

Not that she hadn't enjoyed Jericho's company, of course. A sweet, kind man with a wonderful sense of humor, Jericho was as lively a companion as any woman could ask for.

But he wasn't Cutter.

Lord, she thought, life would have been so much simpler if she'd only fallen in love with someone like Jericho. He wouldn't have minded in the least marrying a woman like her and giving her all the babies she could ever want.

But life wasn't simple. And she didn't love Jericho, no matter how much she should have.

She loved Cutter. Now Maggie could only hope that he was finally realizing that he loved her, as well . . . because she was fast losing what little patience she'd been blessed with.

"Of course I remember," Cutter snapped. "Haven't I been sitting here in this damned office for the last three hours, waiting for you to get back?"

"Three hours?" she asked, and casually strolled to the sofa. Seating herself, she took her time arranging her skirts before asking, "Were we really gone that long? I had no idea."

Actually, she'd asked Jericho the time nearly every ten minutes, until the poor man had simply handed over his pocket watch to her.

Cutter ran his fingers through his hair again, and Maggie hid a smile. By the looks of him, he'd been doing it quite a bit that night.

Slowly he drew in a long, deep breath, and blew it out again in a rush of emotion that sent the air in the room to crackling.

"Fine," he ground out. "You didn't notice the time. But don't try to tell me you were eating supper that whole time. *Nobody* eats that much!"

She forced a laugh. "Of course not, Cutter. After supper, we took a long walk along the embarcadero." Maggie glanced at him, then quickly looked away. One look had told her all she needed to know. He looked awful. His features drawn and grim, his eyes shadowed, he held himself as if awaiting another blow.

She gave it to him.

"It was *so* romantic, what with the ocean breeze and all the stars." Maggie shook her head and smiled as if in fond memory. "Jericho was . . . *well* . . ."

Cutter didn't need to know that Jericho and she had spent their time on the embarcadero throwing stones into the ocean in an impromptu contest.

"Jericho was what?"

"Oh." She shrugged. "Nothing." Jumping to her feet, Maggie went on, "You know, Cutter, I'm a bit tired. If it's all the same to you, why don't we talk in the morning?"

"I don't think so."

"I don't see why not," she ventured, and took a step toward the door.

He took two quick steps toward her and grabbed her upper arm in a firm yet gentle grip.

Maggie's insides began to flip and spin. Expectancy filled the air in the closed room, and she suddenly found it hard to draw a breath. She heard Cutter's ragged breathing, and knew they were both feeling the same whirlwind emotions.

But that wasn't enough, not this time. She wouldn't be drawn into another tumult of passion, only to be set aside the minute reality crashed down on them. This time she needed to hear him say what he felt. She needed to know that he wanted more from her than a moment's release.

"You gave him three hours, Maggie," he said, and the husky timbre of his voice danced along her spine, making her tremble. "Surely you can give me a few more minutes."

It took every ounce of her will, but Maggie forced herself to say, "You've waited this long, Cutter. What's one more night?"

"I've waited a hell of a lot longer than three hours, Maggie."

"What?" She glanced up at him and was caught by the raw need shining in his eyes.

"I've waited a lifetime for you, Maggie." His

hand cupped her cheek tenderly. "I was just too stupid to know it until tonight."

Close, she thought. So very, very close. And yet, it wasn't enough. She kept her gaze locked with his, searching the blue depths of his eyes for the one truth she most needed to see. Anxiously Maggie whispered, "What do you know, Cutter?"

He inhaled sharply, and one corner of his mouth lifted slightly. "I love you."

Chapter 17

"Did you hear me?"

Maggie blinked, stared at him, and slowly released the pent-up breath in her chest. Her heartbeat quickened, until she felt the resulting thuds against her rib cage. Swarms of butterflies burst into life in the pit of her stomach.

She knew he was waiting for an answer. She saw the confusion—the worry—on his features. But for some reason, now, when she needed it the most, she couldn't find her voice.

"Christ, Maggie!" His voice was harsh, rough with desire and frustration. "I said, I love you!"

A slow grin spread across her face. She swallowed past the lump in her throat and answered, "Aye. I heard ya."

"Well," he retorted, "don't you have *anything* to say?"

"One thing."

"What's that?" Wary, he watched her through hooded eyes.

Maggie leaned into him and threw her arms around his neck. Threading her fingers through his disheveled hair, she drew his head down to hers. Just before she kissed him, she said, "What took you so bloody long?"

The soft smile on Cutter's lips dissolved under her mouth's caress. His arms went around her waist and drew her up tightly against him. His hands moved over her back and behind like a drowning man clutching at a lifesaver.

Maggie parted her lips for him and gasped when his tongue slid inside her mouth. The dizzying warmth of him spread through her, making her knees weak and her head light. After dreaming of this moment for months, the reality of it was almost too much for her.

He lifted one hand, cupped the back of her head, and kissed her with the hunger of a man long denied. His tongue dipped in and out of her mouth in an erotic dance of promises to come. She met him eagerly, touch for touch, caress for caress, until she had to pull back from him to drag air into her straining lungs. When she tipped her head back, Cutter's mouth slid to her throat. His lips moved over the sensitive flesh of her neck, and his teeth nibbled at the raging pulse point at the base of her throat.

Maggie clutched at his shoulders as though she would fall off the edge of the world if she let him go. She felt the tension in him, felt the tightly reined hunger and the need.

His right hand slipped to her behind and dragged her pelvis up against him. She gasped again at the hard, tight feel of his body along hers. A delicious, damp warmth started at her center and spread throughout her body in a heartbeat. Like a flash flood in summer, heat raced through her bloodstream, sweeping away rational thought, leaving her shaken.

When his hand slid up her back and began to tug at the hooks of her gown, a soft moan rose up in the back of her throat. One by one, the hooks fell free, and Maggie felt the cool air whisper against her fevered skin.

Her only thought was to be closer to him, to feel his flesh against hers ... to lose herself in the warmth of his body. Slowly she began to edge her way toward the sofa, but Cutter stopped her.

He straightened up and drew a long, ragged breath. His fingers smoothed a fallen lock of fiery hair off her forehead, then drew a long, caressing path down the line of her jaw. "Not this time, Maggie," he said softly. "This time we do things right."

Then he slanted his mouth across hers for a heart-stopping moment. All too quickly, he stepped back from her and spun her about. She heard him struggle for air at the same time that she felt his fingers doing up the hooks at the back of her gown.

Light-headed from the tumultuous emotions crashing through her, Maggie stood silent under his ministrations. But each brush of his knuckles against her bare back sent tremors rocketing through her. It required an effort to breathe; thinking was impossible. She wrapped her arms about her middle and allowed him to turn her around to face him.

Maggie's gaze locked with his, and in his eyes, she saw everything she'd ever dreamed of seeing. Instinctively she reached for him, but Cutter grabbed her hands. His lips curved into a lopsided grin, and he shook his head slowly.

"If you so much as breathe on me again, Maggie," he said, "we'll end up here on the floor." He swallowed heavily. "Go on to my room. I'll be right behind you."

He was right. She knew it. For this night, she wanted more than a quick tumble on a too-short sofa. But then his words registered, and she shook her head.

"No?" He sounded dumbstruck.

"Not your room," she said quickly, remembering that Cutter was staying in Kevin's bedroom. Maggie knew she would never have been able to lie with a man on her father's own bed! Instead she told him, "Come to my room, Cutter."

He nodded, and while she still had the strength, she left him and stepped into the hall. Her steps were shaky, and she looked neither left nor right, concentrating instead on putting one foot in front of the other.

From belowstairs a wall of noise and smoke and perfume rushed at her, but it couldn't penetrate the glow she felt burning inside her. Nothing else mattered—not the saloon, her father, her sisters . . . not even their nameless attacker. Nothing was more important than this time with Cutter. She'd waited too long for that moment to allow anything to interfere with it.

The familiar, dimly lit hall had never seemed so long before. It seemed to take forever to reach the quiet of her own room. As she stepped inside, she noted absently that Rose had already been there. Maggie's bed was turned down, the flowered quilt folded back invitingly. Only one lamp was lit against the darkness, and Maggie smiled at the shadowy, intimate room.

Cutter slipped inside and quickly closed the door, then turned the key in the lock.

Without another word, he solemnly drew her into the circle of his arms.

Maggie sighed and gave herself up to the heat engulfing her. When his lips trailed over her throat, she concentrated on the incredible sensation of his warm breath against her flesh. When his fingers once again moved to unhook her gown, Maggie's only thought was for him to hurry. She needed to feel him. She needed to press her breasts against his chest and feel their hearts beating as one.

The same urgency gripped him, and in seconds he had finished with the long row of hooks down the back of her gown. Maggie stood absolutely still as he reached for the long copper pins securing her hair. One by one he pulled them free, then smiled as he held her steel hatpin out in front of her.

"I don't think you'll be needing this tonight," he said softly, and leaned over to set her weapon down on a nearby table.

Maggie shook her head and felt the heavy weight of her hair tumble down her back. She gave him a sidelong glance and remarked teasingly, "A woman should always have a weapon handy, Cutter."

"Ah, but you do, Maggie, love," he whispered, and bent to plant a small kiss at her temple.

She sighed, closed her eyes, and asked, "What weapon is that, then?"

"Yourself, Maggie Donnelly," Cutter told her, and dipped his head to claim her lips in several short, breathless kisses. "Your magnificent self, Maggie."

Placing his hands on her shoulders, Cutter smoothed his palms along the length of her arms. The sapphire-blue silk slid along her flesh like a soft breeze, until it fell free of her body and lay in a discarded heap at her feet. His gaze swept over the woman standing before him, and she nearly took his breath away.

Only one of the lamps in the room was burning and its wick was turned low. In the soft, dim light from that solitary lamp, Maggie looked beautiful.

Her high, full breasts were hidden only by the shamelessly thin camisole she wore, and her small waist was held in the grips of a boned corset. Beneath her full petticoat, he knew she wore lace-edged white pantaloons, and suddenly he felt an overpowering need to see her without the layers of clothing separating her from him.

Slowly he reached for her corset strings. When he tugged them loose, Maggie did the rest. Her gaze locked on him, her fingers moved over the lacings with calm, deliberate movements. A small eternity passed before she'd finished her enticing act and tossed the confining garment aside.

Cutter's hands moved over her waist and rib cage. She sighed, and he wasn't sure whether it was because of his touch or the relief of being rid of the damned corset. Then, as he moved his palms up to cup her breasts, he found her nipples hard, erect. His thumbs circled the sensitive flesh, and she swayed on her feet.

He caught her easily up in his arms, walked to the bed, and with one hand tossed the coverlet to the foot of the mattress. Tenderly he laid her down on the fresh, cool, sweet-smelling sheets. When she reached up for him, Cutter didn't bother to remove the fine lawn camisole, but bent his head to her breasts and stroked his tongue across first one rigid nipple, then the other. And as he lavished attention on her breasts, the fabric became damp and clung to the outlines of her flesh.

Maggie twisted beneath him. Her back arched, and her hands moved up and down his shoulders and arms.

"Holy Mother, Cutter," she breathed, and her voice shook. "Don't toy with me now, man."

"Ah, Maggie, my love, we have all night." He shifted slightly and brushed her lips with his. "What's your hurry?"

Her eyes opened, and she looked up at him with frank and open hunger. "It's been too long, Cutter. I need to feel you against me."

He inhaled sharply. Every nerve in his body leaped to attention. Each breath he drew seemed as if it would be his last. He couldn't get enough air into his lungs, and was damned if he cared. Cutter looked into Maggie's green eyes and lost all sense of everything but her.

How had he ever stayed away so long?

How would he ever be able to leave her?

Her fingers moved to the buttons of his shirt,

and Cutter stopped thinking entirely. Maggie tugged at the ivory buttons impatiently, her teeth worrying her bottom lip as she concentrated. When she spoke, her voice was a whisper, but it struck straight to his soul with the accuracy of a well-aimed arrow.

"I need to feel your warmth under my hands," she said. At last the first few buttons fell open, and she slid her palms over his chest.

Cutter's breath caught. Her fingertips caressed his flat nipples, and he barely managed to stifle the groan building in his throat. But she wasn't finished. Twining her fingers through the dusting of golden hair on his chest, she told him, "I need to feel you inside me, Cutter. Deep inside me."

"Jesus, Maggie," he breathed as he yanked his shirtfront open and heard the remaining buttons skitter across the wood floor. "What you do to me . . ."

When his chest was bare to her touch, he lifted her gently and tugged at the pink ribbons of her camisole until he could pull the garment from her. Naked, her creamy flesh calling to him, Cutter lowered his head and took one of her nipples into his mouth.

Maggie's body jumped at the first contact of his tongue against her flesh. But immediately she gave a satisfied groan and arched her back, silently demanding more. And he heard her. Cutter began to suckle her breast, and Maggie thought she would die.

Wild, delicious spearheads of delight lanced through her body and settled in the core of her. The damp tingling between her thighs became an almost unbearable ache. She lifted her hips instinctively, seeking the release she knew Cutter could give her.

His mouth worked at her breast with delicate deliberation. His tongue stroked her nipple, and as he gently sucked at her flesh, Maggie's fingers slid through his hair, holding him to her. She wanted him never to stop. She never wanted those feelings to end.

All the long, lonely months without him faded into memory. The pain and frustration of the past few weeks—working with him and not being able to touch him—dissolved under the onslaught of pleasure he was showing her. Nothing mattered.

Nothing outside that room mattered a damn.

And then he moved. Maggie moaned in disappointment, but her sigh ended abruptly as Cutter simply shifted and turned his attention to her other breast. Once again her body began that long climb toward the fireworks only Cutter could unleash.

Maggie's eyes opened wide, and she pushed her head back further into the feather pillow beneath her. Her fingers grazed over his broad back, and she dragged her nails lightly across his flesh.

His hands slipped to her waist and fumbled with the drawstring of her petticoat. Instinctively Maggie reached to help him. With both of them straining to be rid of the last few pieces of clothing separating them, it was only seconds before Maggie's petticoat and pantaloons were drifting to the floor.

Cutter pushed himself off the bed then, and left her side only long enough to yank off his boots and pants. She watched him undress in the dim light, and when he was naked, he came back to her. He stretched out alongside her and ran his palm over her flat belly. Once more she arched her back, moving into his touch. When his left hand slipped around her waist and he turned her to face him, Maggie moved in close. She melted against him, pressing her body along the length of his.

Flesh against flesh, heat against heat, they fit together as if made for each other. His thunderous heartbeat was an echo of hers, and Maggie clutched him, holding him to her as tightly as she could. Cutter's hand inched down her thigh, and when his slow, stroking motions moved to the inside of her leg, she opened herself to his touch.

Then his fingertips caressed her damp warmth, and Maggie moaned softly. She twisted slightly, swiveling her hips against his hand, and again he heard her silent demands.

Slowly his fingers slipped inside her body and Maggie held perfectly still. She wanted to savor this moment, this feeling. She wanted to be able to recall the feel of him inside her. Then his thumb stroked the sensitive bud of flesh at the heart of her opening, and her already taut body jerked in response.

It was too much, too quickly. She felt as if she couldn't stand it. And even as she told herself that she would die if he didn't stop, her hips arched and twisted against his hand. With her every movement, the pleasure increased, and her breath was coming in short gasps. Her goal was close, so close. Her body tightened as his

fingers continued to move in and out of her
with a steadily increasing rhythm.

Briefly she opened her eyes and looked up
into his. She held his gaze as she reached for his
hardened flesh and encircled him with her fingers. He groaned, squeezed his eyes shut, and
whispered "Jesus, Maggie!"

She'd hardly heard him groan before he rolled
her over onto her back and levered himself over
her. He knelt between her spread thighs,
scooped her bottom up in the palms of his
hands, and lifted her hips slightly from the mattress.

In one swift, hard thrust, he entered her, and
Maggie gasped. But this was no time for quiet,
leisurely loving. This was a moment for which
they'd both hungered for months. As one, they
moved in an ancient dance, their labored breathing the only sound in the room.

When the tightly coiled spring deep inside
her suddenly snapped, sending tremors of delight shuddering through her, Maggie held onto
Cutter as if it meant her life. And as his body
was claimed by the same overpowering sensa-
tions, she held him even more tightly and whispered her love.

"Would you hate living in New York?" David
asked the woman cuddled close to him.

"No." Michelle tilted her head back to look
up at him. "I can sing anywhere. But what
about you? Your home is here."

The soft cadence of her voice was almost
lost in the steady rush of ocean water against
the wooden pilings beneath the pier. Muted
light from an oil lamp spilled through a port-

hole of the ship moored on their right. That small corner of the docks was nearly deserted. The denizens of the Coast were either already drunk or putting forth their best efforts at becoming so.

During his months of frequenting the Roses saloon, David had gone often to the piers at dockside and was now generally accepted as belonging on the Coast. He shuddered to think of what might happen to a well-heeled visitor to the docks that late at night, but was sure in his own mind that he and Michelle were safe.

David pulled her even closer to him and wrapped both arms around her. He stared blankly out at the dark ocean and let the rhythmic slap of the water reach into his soul and calm him. He concentrated on the steady, even sounds. The whispered rush of the waves as they hit the breakwater. The creaking of the boats tied up at dock. The regular, even breathing of the woman in his arms.

As she laid her head on his shoulder and snuggled against him, he thought about what she'd said.

His home? No. He hadn't had a home in years. Oh, David told himself, he had much more than so many of the poor souls wandering the docks, trying to scavenge a life for themselves ... but so much less than he'd always wanted. He had a place where he hung his clothes. A warm, dry bed to sleep in every night. Plenty to eat. But those things had nothing more to do with a home than a child's drawing did with the works of the Italian masters.

Actually, until he'd met Michelle, David had

given up hopes of *ever* having the kind of home he'd secretly longed for. He drew in a long, deep breath of salt-tinged air and closed his eyes.

The vision in his mind was so clear, it was as if the little house were already a reality. A small place, with a warm fire, soft, inviting furniture, and bright, colorful rugs on the wood floors, cheerful paintings hung on the walls, and the windowpanes gleaming in the sunshine. There would be books and plenty of time to read. Laughter and children clamoring for his attention. And there would be a woman. A wife. The *one* woman in the world he would love forever.

Instinctively his arms tightened around Michelle. Opening his eyes, he stared out at the ocean once more. Now that the dream was within his reach, he wasn't going to allow his father—or his own cowardice—to destroy it.

He only hoped to God he was strong enough to face the man down long enough to claim his dream.

That thought worried him. David had spent so many years doing what was expected of him—he'd even become a lawyer because his father had commanded it. Hell, the only spark of rebellion he'd shown in his entire life had been his recent descent into the liquid oblivion of a whiskey bottle.

Michelle lifted her hand and gently stroked his cheek. David's eyes squeezed shut briefly. It had been a miracle, finding her. He knew that. And he also knew it would be foolhardy to ask for another miracle from whatever gods had so blessed him.

But he had to.

He opened his eyes again and studied the splashes of phosphorescence shining on the dark water. The damp of the wooden piling he leaned against had soaked into his jacket, and he shivered.

David *needed* another miracle. Something to give him the courage he would need to turn his back on the man who'd ruled his life with an iron fist. Something to replace the false courage he'd lost when he'd stopped drinking.

Something to make him worthy of Michelle.

Languidly Maggie stretched, and sighed contentedly. A small smile curved her lips as she rolled to her side and curled up against Cutter's warmth. Her right palm on his chest, she rested her chin on her hand as the fingertips of her left hand trailed lazily across his flesh.

His breathing slowly became more steady, and Maggie kept her gaze locked on his familiar features, waiting for him to open his eyes and look at her. She wanted to see the love in his eyes. She wanted to luxuriate in the knowledge that he'd finally realized that they belonged together.

Eyes still closed, Cutter reached for her. His left hand smoothed over her shoulders and back, and Maggie sighed. This was how it should have been. As it had been meant to be, she told herself. The two of them, together.

Instantly she recalled the first night they'd come together. She smiled, remembering the rush of passion and the tangle of arms and legs as they'd tried to find a comfortable position on the office settee. Maggie shook her head slightly and let the images slip away. Though she would always have a soft spot in her heart for that incredibly short sofa, there was a lot to be said for a bed.

"Ah, Cutter," she whispered. "We've wasted too much time. We could've been together this whole past year, darlin'." She reached up and touched his cheek gently, then smoothed back his hair. "Was it really so almighty hard to admit to loving me?"

His arm around her tightened slightly; then he released her.

Maggie frowned, but moved with him as he propped himself up against the headboard.

Finally he opened his eyes and looked at her. Maggie stared into the familiar blue depths and felt the first stirrings of foreboding.

"Maggie," he started, his voice heavy with regret.

She cut him off abruptly. "Oh, no, you don't, Cutter." Reaching behind her, she dragged the sheet up from the foot of the bed and held it in front of her. "I'll not let ya start backin' out of this now. . . ."

He shook his head, pushed both hands through his hair, and told her, "I'm not trying to back out of anything. Will you just listen to me for a minute?"

"That depends," she countered quickly, "on what you're wantin' to say." Maggie scooted around on the bed until she was kneeling, facing him, the white sheet clutched tightly against her. "If you're thinkin' about tryin' to say that you don't love me after all, then *no!* I won't listen."

"That's not what I—"

"But if you're plannin' on doin' the sensible thing and askin' me to marry ya, then, fine." She waved one hand at him. "Go ahead and talk."

"Goddammit," he snapped. "Will you let me get two words out before you start telling me what it is I'm supposed to be thinking?"

"That depends too," she said, and her throat almost closed as she added, "are those two words goin' to be good-bye?"

Chapter 18

⟨~⟩

"**G**ood-bye?"

"Aye." Maggie nodded abruptly. "I know you know the word. I've heard it from you before—on a night much like this one."

"That wasn't good-bye," Cutter argued.

"What, then?"

What, then, indeed? he asked himself, and frowned at the realization that she was absolutely right. He'd done this to her once before, and Maggie wasn't the forgiving kind. If he wasn't careful, he just might find himself looking down the barrel of a loaded pistol before the night was over.

Jesus! It was a chore and a half keeping his thoughts straight around her. Of course, looking at her then, half naked, her hair in a wild red tangle, he was lucky he could think at all. Cutter reached up and rubbed the back of his neck. Maybe he shouldn't even try, he told himself. Maybe he should silence the voice in the back of his mind and simply lose himself in the glory of loving her—holding her.

But even as that thought flitted through his mind, Cutter realized it wouldn't solve anything. Sooner or later, he and Maggie would have to deal with the one thing preventing him from being the man she wanted.

The one thing he was having such a damnable time saying.

"Cutter?"

His gaze snapped to hers.

"It's not the lovin' you object to, is it? It's the idea of marryin' me."

His jaw dropped. He shouldn't have been so stunned, he thought. What the hell else would she have been likely to think, given the way he'd been acting? Christ, he'd really made a mess of things.

"It's got nothing to do with you, Maggie," he started, but she cut him off.

"How can it not?"

"Not the way you're thinking of it."

She pushed her hair back out of her face and glared at him. Cutter could almost see the wheels turning in her head, and he knew that he wouldn't have long before she started in again.

He had to say something.

Quickly.

If he'd had any sense at all, he would have tried to calm her down before talking to her. Cutter looked directly at her and saw that the soft, emerald-green color of her eyes had darkened until they were as dark and dangerous as a stormy sea. No, he told himself dismally, there would be no calming her.

And there was no way to avoid saying what he had to.

He sucked in a gulp of air and made a futile grab for a corner of the sheet. She snapped it out of his reach.

"Well?" Maggie demanded, and then crossed her arms indignantly over her chest. "If it's not me, then we're gettin' married. Right?"

"It's not that simple, Maggie." But even as he said it, Cutter knew that wasn't enough of an explanation.

"There's nothin' simpler, man. Either ya love me . . . or ya lied to me."

"I wasn't lying."

"Then say it again."

"I love you." Odd, he told himself, how easy it was to say those three small words once that first, terrifying time was over. "I *do* love you, Maggie."

She tilted her head and narrowed her gaze as she frowned at him. "That should make me happy, Cutter. Except that I have a feelin' there's a *but* comin'."

He made another grab for the sheet, but when she wouldn't let him have it, Cutter swung his legs off the bed and crossed the room to where his pants lay crumpled on the floor.

"What're ya doin'?"

He glanced back at her and was struck again by just how beautiful she was. Kneeling in the center of the rumpled mattress, she held that sheet to her chest as if it were a knight's shield. Her hair fell like waves of fire all around her shoulders, and her mouth was still bruised from his kisses.

Dammit, didn't she know that if he could have, he'd have jumped right back into that bed with her and never gotten out? But he couldn't. At least, not yet.

Deliberately, he looked away from her and pulled his pants on.

"You're goin' to leave without tellin' me what's wrong?"

Her voice trembled, but when he glanced at her, he saw that she was holding herself rigidly, determined not to show him how upset she was.

"No," Cutter said, and walked back to the edge of the bed. He grabbed one of the spindle-rail footposts and squeezed. "Nobody's leaving till we have this settled between us. But if we're gonna talk, Maggie, I at least want my pants on." Silently he considered how Maggie might react to what he was going to tell her. He decided quickly that it would be a wise move to protect his privates as best he could. A voice in the back of his mind added that, should she simply throw him down the saloon's center staircase, at least he would not have to greet his customers stark naked.

Maggie just stared at him thoughtfully for a long moment before she nodded. Tugging the rest of the bed sheet free, she wrapped it around her, plopped into a sitting position, and looked up at him. "Fine. Now that we're both 'decent,' what's goin' on, Cutter?"

"It's a long story, Maggie."

"I've got all night."

He snorted a laugh. It figured that Maggie wouldn't be willing to give an inch.

"All right," he said, then she cut him off.

"Wait." Holding one hand up to him, Maggie asked, "First, tell me the truth, Cutter . . . do you really love me?"

He'd never seen that look of doubt on her features before, and he hoped he'd never see it again. Knowing that *he* had brought his proud, strong Maggie Donnelly to such a turn was almost more than he could stand.

Cutter let go of the spindle post and reached for her. Gently his fingers trailed down the line of her jaw, then tipped her chin up. He bent down and brushed one soft, lingering kiss against her lips, then straightened.

"Yes, Maggie. I really love you."

She blinked the moisture from her eyes and impatiently shoved her hair back from her forehead for the umpteenth time.

Hands at his hips, Cutter stared down at her for a long time, trying to think of the easiest way to tell her what he had to. Then an idea hit him. Holding out his right hand, he said, "Come with me."

She took his hand, scooted off the edge of the bed, and followed him across the room, her feet tangling in the sheet. Cutter paused at the door, opened it, and poked his head into the hallway.

"All right," he said over his shoulder. "No one's out there; come on." He took two steps, and then Maggie slammed into him, her feet hopelessly caught in the flapping sheet. Quickly he scooped her up, carried her across the hall and into his room, then kicked the door shut behind him. He set her down on the edge of his bed and walked across the room to the cold hearth.

"What's this about, Cutter?"

"This," he said, and pointed up at the painting hanging over the mantel.

"Your family's house?" Maggie shook her head. "I don't get your point. What's the house got to do with us?"

"Not the house, Maggie." Cutter turned to

stare up at the painting, as he had so many times over the years. He barely winced as the familiar twinge of pain slashed at him.

Long moments passed, and the only sound was the muted roar of the bedlam belowstairs. He kept his gaze fixed on the familiar facade of Seven Oaks as if the words he needed so desperately would suddenly appear.

But how did he admit to the woman he loved that the family she spoke of was nothing more than a collection of people who'd joined together briefly for a common cause—getting rid of Cutter?

It was a hard thing to own up to—the cold, simple fact that you were unwanted. No good. He shuddered as the memory of his father's final slap from beyond the grave rocked through him. Jesus! His own father.

"I think I understand now, Cutter," Maggie said, and pushed herself to her feet.

"Huh?" He half turned from the painting and looked at her as she walked up to him. She moved like a queen. Even that ridiculous sheet and the way it flapped and swayed about her legs looked ... elegant, somehow.

"I said, I understand." Maggie lifted her chin and shook her hair back over her shoulders. With her right hand, she gripped the edges of the sheet together, hoping that he wouldn't see the trembling of her fingers.

She should have known, Maggie thought. Hadn't that damned painting, and all it represented, always been a part of him? She'd never said it before, but she'd never cared for the look of that bloody house. An awful pile of rock and stone. But one look at it was enough to tell anyone that Cutter came from a fine family. A *wealthy* family. Probably had as much in common with Irish saloonkeepers as beggars had with the Grand Hotel.

"Understand what, Maggie?" Cutter's eyebrows drew together, and the flesh around his stitches puckered. "I haven't told you anything yet."

"There's no need," she shot back, and blessed whatever god had given her the strength to keep her voice from shaking. "It'd be plain to a blind man."

"What would be plain?" He turned his back on the painting and took a single step closer to her. "What in hell are you talking about?"

Maggie took a step back, staying just out of his reach. She'd already let him touch her far too intimately. One more touch of his hand, and she just might dissolve right there in front of him.

"Your fine, grand house, there," she said tauntingly, and waved one hand at the painting. "It's a sure bet that no one in that house would be welcomin' the likes of *me* into the family."

He looked as though she'd hit him in the head with a club. But she wasn't fooled. Maggie sniffed and went on.

"What is it, Cutter? Am I not good enough for ya? Is that it?"

"Oh, for God's sake!"

"Leave the good Lord outta this, Cutter!" Maggie snapped. "This is between you and me."

"You think I'm ashamed of you?"

"There's no need to shout it out like that!" she shot back as the banked fires of her anger began to flare into life. "Besides, what else am I to think?" She lifted her chin slightly and glared at him. "The thought of marryin' me turns ya to stone, and to explain yourself, ya bring me in here and dangle your bleedin' mansion in front of my nose!"

"Mary Margaret Donnelly, if you'll just shut your pretty mouth for five goddamned minutes," Cutter ground out from between gritted teeth, "I'll tell you everything."

"Fine."

His eyebrows drew together, and he looked at her warily. But he needn't have been concerned. Maggie had decided to keep quiet. She didn't trust herself not to screech at him if she spoke again.

After a long moment, Cutter started talking.

"That *mansion*, as you call it, would count itself lucky if you ever stepped foot in it."

Despite her best intentions, she opened her mouth to argue, but he stared her into silence.

"The only problem is," he went on, "they'd never let you in."

"Hmph!"

"Not because of *you*, Maggie." He shoved his hands into his pockets and let his gaze slide away from her before he added, "Because of *me*."

"What?"

He snorted a half laugh, and the derisive sound tore at her.

"Hell, Maggie. I'm not the pampered son of a wealthy family." Cutter swung his head around to look at her. "I'm the bastard son of an old man and a young woman too poor and too lonely to say no to him."

He took a long, shuddering breath. Now that it was finally said, Cutter realized that it hadn't been as difficult to talk to her about that as he'd always imagined it would be. In fact, he thought, it felt surprisingly good to have it out in the open. Curiously enough, even the tight knot of shame and hurt that had lodged in his chest for years seemed a bit smaller ... looser.

The growing silence in the room finally penetrated his mind, and Cutter looked at her.

Amazing, he told himself as he stared at her. She was actually speechless. And her surprise couldn't have been more evident if he'd told her that he was the rightful king of England. Dammit, he felt as if he were standing naked in the middle of the street. Was she just going to stare at him all night? Didn't she have something—anything—to say?

He couldn't stand the silence any longer, and rushed to fill it himself.

"When my mother died—"

"How old were you?" she asked quickly.

"Huh? Oh ... three, I think." He shook his head and went on. "Anyway, my father brought me to his house." He nodded at the painting. "*That* house. A couple years later, he got married, and then had a legitimate son—"

"You have a brother?"

"Half."

"A brother."

"Don't make more of it than there is," he warned. "Tyler and I are nothing like you and your sisters."

"Tell me the rest of it," she prodded, and kept her gaze locked on him.

Cutter tried not to look into her eyes. He

didn't even care if that made him a coward. He just didn't want to watch sympathy or shame creep into the green eyes he knew so well.

"Tyler's mother died not long after he was born. Our father raised us—he and his sister, actually."

"An aunt as well?"

He dismissed that woman with a snort. "Yeah. Charlotte. She could've given Digger lessons in meanness." Cutter shook his head slowly and told her the rest. Old pain rose up in him as he said quietly, "After my father's funeral, the family—Charlotte, Tyler, a couple of my cousins, and I—gathered in the old man's study to hear the will read."

Cutter ran his fingers through his hair, gave another quick glance at the painting, and then shifted his gaze until he was staring blankly at the far wall, lost in memory.

"Most of that afternoon is still pretty hazy to me, really. But I'll never forget the look on Charlotte's face when the lawyer read my father's instructions concerning me."

He swallowed heavily, sucked in a gulp of air, and rushed on. "My whole life, that man had *loved* me. Taught me, whipped my butt when I needed it—treated me just like he did Tyler. But in the end, when he had to decide how to divide his property ... he left everything to Tyler."

"Cutter."

"There's more. To everyone—his sister, my cousins—he left something. To me he left only his contempt."

"Cutter."

"Let me finish," he said quickly, and held up

one hand. "It wasn't the money, Maggie. I didn't give a good goddamn about his money—never had. It was the fact that he'd told the whole blasted world that his bastard son wasn't good enough to inherit. His bastard was just that, a bastard. Not worthy of being a true Cutter. Not worthy of anything."

He snorted a mocking laugh, rubbed his eyes tiredly, and said, "Charlotte didn't waste a bloody minute. She handed me twenty dollars, a bag with some of my clothes in it, and showed me the door."

"And that's when you came to San Francisco?"

"Eventually, yes."

"And what's all this got to do with you and me?"

"What?" He spun around and stared at her, astonished.

"I asked—"

"I heard you," Cutter shot back. He just couldn't believe it, that was all. How could she even have asked that question?

"Then answer me."

"Everything." He waved one hand at the painting behind him. "That house . . . those people . . . Jesus, Maggie! I'm a bastard! My own *father* didn't want me!"

"So?"

"*So?*" Anger swept through him, hot and unreasonable. He'd waited and worried about telling her what had been the overriding shame of his life, and when he finally had, she brushed it aside as if it meant nothing? "How the hell can I marry you? You have a family, people who care. I'm *nothing! No one!*" He slapped the flat of his hand against the painting, and it rattled in its frame. "Ask them! They'll tell you that a bastard has no business calling *anything* his own."

"For the love of God, Cutter." Maggie took a step toward him. "You would let a passel of fools tell you who you are and what you're worth?" Eyes wide and glinting furiously, she continued, "Does my love mean so little, then? Does what we have together count for nothin'?"

"It's everything, Maggie." Cutter felt the truth of that simple statement echo in his brain. "But I can't offer you a future until I've settled with my past."

"Settled with it?" Maggie tightened her grip on the sheet she still held wrapped around her. "And how're you goin' to do that?"

He glanced up at the flat, painted surface of Seven Oaks and felt a small thrill of satisfaction. "I've been saving my money for years, and I've got almost enough."

"Enough for what?"

Cutter answered her, but she might as well not have been in the room. His voice was hushed, dreamy, as he finally spoke his plan aloud. "To go back to Georgia. To buy that damned house."

"You don't even know if it's for sale."

He chuckled. "Everything is for sale—at the right price."

"Say you do buy it. Then what?" she coaxed. "Throw *them* out?"

"I don't know. Maybe." His gaze stayed fixed on the painting. "Maybe it'll be enough just to show them that I'm as good as they are."

Maggie grabbed his arm and forced him to turn to face her. "You're better than they are,

Cutter. Would you have thrown a boy out on the streets to survive on his own?"

"No." His voice was hard, and the shadows in his blue eyes were dark, filled with an old, old pain.

"Then what do they matter?" Her fingers dug into his forearm, hoping for a reaction from him. He seemed so far away from her that Maggie was afraid that if she didn't reach him then, she never would.

It was as if the man she had just lain with didn't exist. And this man, this tormented Cutter, was someone she didn't even know. How could he have thought that it would make a tinker's damn worth of difference to her what side of the blanket he was born on? She was only glad that he'd been born at all!

How could he let those people—she refused to call them his family—ruin their future together?

"You *still* don't understand, Maggie," Cutter finally answered her. Looking down into her eyes, he added, "*You've* never had your home and your family snatched from you. *You've* never stood alone under an onslaught of curses and taunts. *You've* never been thrown away!"

"Oh, yes, I have," she said, an accusation in her voice.

He had the grace to look ashamed, before he said in a quieter tone, "Until I face them—prove to them they were wrong—I'll always be the bastard son. The throwaway."

"God almighty, Cutter," she breathed, willing him to hear her. "They've already stolen your past . . . now you're handing them your future."

"No." He shook his head and stepped back

from her. "You don't understand. How can you?"

"I understand love. And I understand meanness and spite." Maggie threw a quick glance at the painting she was quickly coming to loathe. "Maybe those people are gone from there now. How do you even know if the damned place survived the war?"

"I don't. Not for sure." He shook his head. "But it did. I feel it."

"Everything you're feeling now belongs to that sixteen-year-old boy!" Her voice was rising, her temper exploding, but Maggie didn't care anymore. The thought that he was willing to put her aside in favor of settling a long-dead debt was infuriating.

At the same time, she believed she could understand the depth of the pain he must still have felt when the memories surfaced. Thoughts of her own father filled her heart and mind, and Maggie tried to imagine what it would be like to have Kevin turn his back on her.

Still, despite Cutter's memories, despite everything, she knew he loved her. Somehow she had to make him see that the best way for him to take revenge on those who'd hurt him so desperately was to love and be loved, to live a full and happy life.

"I know what it must have done to you—your father doing what he did. But, Cutter, to have your future, you must stop holdin' the past so closely."

Cutter rubbed his head with one hand. "I don't know if I can."

"Let the past stay in the past, Cutter. You've

left that lost, lonely boy far behind you." She reached for him, but at the last moment let her hand drop to her side. "The man you've become is so much more important. You've built a life for yourself. You have friends. You have *me*."

"Don't you think I know all that?"

"Then why are you fighting it so?"

"How do I let go of the one thing that's kept me going for years?" He shook his head, and a half laugh choked in his throat. "The only reason I've done as well as I have is because of *them. Him*."

Maggie's temper shriveled into a small, cold knot of disappointment in her chest. He couldn't see that what he'd accomplished would have been his, no matter what. He was willing to credit even his successes to his father. Cutter didn't realize that it was his own character, his own nature, that had made him what he was.

And if he couldn't see himself, how the devil was she going to make him see her?

"You're a fool, Cutter." She muttered it under her breath, but he heard her.

"I knew you wouldn't understand this, Maggie. But I had to tell you." A tiny, sad smile touched his lips as he added gently, "Soon I'll have enough money to go back to Georgia."

"You're leavin', then?"

"Not forever."

"For how long?"

"Just long enough." He laid his hands on her bare shoulders, and Maggie felt the heat of him shoot through her body like the last bolt of lightning from a dying storm. She almost didn't hear him add, "Then I'll come back and we'll get married."

Astonished, Maggie stared at him. "Just like that?"

"Huh?"

"I said, once you've gone south to show off and preen before folks who shouldn't matter a damn to ya, *then* you'll come back to me?"

He frowned at her and let his hands drop to his sides.

"Well, don't bother, Cutter."

"You don't mean that."

"I bloody well do," she snapped, and turned her back on him. Before she could talk herself out of it, Maggie had marched across the floor to the door. Looking back at him over her shoulder, she added, "If my love isn't enough now, it won't be enough then, either. There'll always be somethin' else for you to prove, Cutter."

"Maggie—"

"No." She jerked him a nod. "You go—back to Georgia. Back to those who treated you like dirt. And when you're through playin' lord of the manor, find yourself somewhere else to go. But don't come back here."

"Goddammit, Maggie," he shouted suddenly, and Maggie heard the desperation in his voice. "I've been planning this for years. You can't expect me just to turn away from it!"

"I don't expect anything from you anymore, Cutter. Do what you will."

"Maggie," he said as she pulled the bedroom door open, "I will be back. I'm a partner in the Roses, remember?"

She stopped dead in her tracks. A partner. How could she have forgotten that, even for an instant? Well, something would have to be done about it. And soon. She wouldn't be able to live out her years in any kind of peace with him in the same city ... let alone in the same saloon.

"I mean it, Maggie," Cutter said, his voice quieter now, more calm. "Nothing between us has to change."

"Ah, Cutter," she said, and glanced at him briefly. "*Everything* between us will change."

Chapter 19

B y the end of the week, no one at the Roses
was smiling. Employees and customers
alike had felt the sharp side of Maggie's tongue,
and Cutter was the one being blamed.

No one was sure exactly what had happened
between them, but since Maggie froze up like a
mountain lake in winter every time Cutter
showed his face, most folks figured she had
good reason. And those same folks felt compelled to tell Cutter he'd better do something
damn quick, before Maggie did something
they'd *all* regret.

Frowning slightly, Cutter told himself it
would have been a sight easier to drag a fishing
boat out to sea with a tow rope between his
teeth than to talk to Maggie. She'd made it perfectly clear that she wanted nothing more to do
with him.

He could hardly credit the fact that the
woman who'd come wildly, passionately alive
in his arms a few nights before was the same
woman who now looked through him as if he
were a pane of glass. Oh, he didn't blame her
for being mad ... but she could at least have
talked to him.

He leaned back against the curved, slat-back

chair and lifted a glass of wine from the table. As he sipped the blood-red liquid, Cutter looked over the rim of the glass at the crowd around him. Hell, he told himself, even the mad crush of people in the Roses seemed more subdued, more restrained. It was as if Maggie's mood had descended on all of them, making the Four Roses a very unenjoyable place to be.

Cutter frowned, took another sip of wine, then set his glass back down. Jake was surly, Seamus wasn't talking at all, Ike continually offered unwanted advice, and even Frankie had stopped by only that morning to tell Cutter that he should stop upsetting her sister.

Hell, he'd have loved to stop upsetting her . . . but he didn't know how. Every time he tried to talk to her, she smiled politely, looked right through him, and nodded mechanically every couple of seconds. She wasn't listening, and wasn't even bothering to *pretend* very well. But then, he didn't have to talk to her to upset her. Since that last night together, his very presence had been enough to make her freeze over and start barking at anyone who came near. Cutter would have thought—no, hoped—that she would be over her anger by then and have realized that going to Georgia was something he *had* to do.

But of course, he told himself grimly, Maggie Donnelly would never have done anything that reasonable.

His fingertips drummed on the tabletop as his gaze slid over the faces in the crowd. Some familiar, some strange, none of them meant a damn thing. In fact, the whole blasted saloon could have slid into the ocean, and Cutter wouldn't have cared. Unless, of course, Maggie was in it.

Along with his problems with Maggie, there remained the still-unsolved question of just who was behind the attacks on the Roses. Nothing more had happened, but that wasn't very reassuring. Actually, the quiet had had just the opposite effect on everyone.

It was as if they were waiting for the other shoe to drop. They all knew it was coming—they just didn't know when.

Even if he'd had the money, he couldn't very well have left when there was still a threat of danger. Cutter grumbled and reached for the wineglass again. Because of Maggie and the unrelieved tension of waiting to be attacked, he couldn't keep his mind on a card game long enough to make any more money, either. His entire life was being stalled, and there wasn't a damn thing he could do about it.

"You up to hearin' some news or are ya likely to bite my head off?"

Cutter looked up at Ike, grimaced, and took another swallow of wine. He hadn't even seen his friend approaching the table. Oh, he was a *fine* one to be keeping watch for trouble. "What news?" he finally asked, in a tone that said he really wasn't all that interested, but anything was better than nothing. "Maggie hire somebody to kill me?"

"Don't know. Maybe." The big man shrugged as if it were a reasonable question. "Wouldn't blame her none, myself . . ."

"Ike—"

"But"—Ike cut his friend off—"this ain't about Maggie."

"Then what is it?"

"Thought you'd like to hear somethin' Racquel just came and told me."

Interested in spite of himself, Cutter did wonder what had caused Ike's lady friend to leave her place of business at such a busy hour.

"Digger's dead."

"Huh?" Cutter simply stared at the bigger man. That was not what he'd been expecting.

"Yeah." Ike nodded thoughtfully. "I always thought I'd be real happy to see the old bastard in his grave. Funny, isn't it? I'm not." He rubbed one hand along his jawline. "I might even miss him."

"Hmph. Yeah, like you'd miss the ache of a bad tooth once it's gone. What happened to him?"

"Happened just like we always figured it would. Seems one of his boys finally got tired of takin' orders from him. Shot him once. Right where he should'a had a heart."

Digger dead. Cutter glanced up at Ike again and knew the man's thoughtful expression reflected his own. Digger's being killed had been only a matter of time, Cutter knew. But somehow, knowing the filthy old man was gone wasn't the comfort it should have been. Ridiculously enough, he knew just how Ike felt. In an odd way, Cutter, too, felt he would miss the old snake. After all, when your enemy is dead . . . whom do you hate?

Besides, Digger's death was yet another change in a week when everything had been turned upside down. Christ! Wasn't it time they had a little peace?

"Ya want me to tell Maggie?"

"No," Cutter answered, and immediately began to search for her face in the crowd of people. "I will."

"She's over at the Garter," Ike told him. "Michelle wanted to see her about something."

Cutter nodded and pushed himself to his feet like a tired old man. Once he was standing, he met Ike's worried frown, and snapped, "What?"

"Nothin'." The other man shrugged again. "Ain't—isn't any of my business what you two do—"

"Thank you," Cutter answered, and started to walk past him.

"—but," Ike rushed on, and Cutter stopped dead, waiting for the inevitable advice, "sure is stupid, seein' two folks buttin' heads, when they should be talkin'." Ike's tone was wheedling.

Cutter inhaled sharply. He was getting almighty tired of all this well-meant interfering—especially since he was beginning to think people were right. During the past few days, he'd even noticed that his long-planned triumphant trip to Georgia didn't hold the same appeal it once had.

In fact, ever since he and Maggie had gone head to head over his past, old memories had ceased to plague him as they once had. The pain he'd lived with and nurtured for so many years had slowly begun to shrink, until now it was hardly more than a bothersome ache. And the trip to Georgia, once a cherished, fond desire, was now only something to be finished so his life could go on.

But he was going.

Soon.

He wanted the past settled and his future begun.

"I am sorry, Maggie," Michelle said, and grabbed the other woman's hand in hers. "I know my leaving will cause you trouble."

"Nonsense." Maggie gave her a forced smile. "Don't worry about that at all. We'll find another singer."

Michelle squeezed her hand tightly, then let it go. "Thank you, Maggie." Snatching up a red silk gown from the pile of clothing on her bed, Michelle began to fold it carefully before packing it in the waiting trunk. "I can't believe I'm actually getting married!" she said, her tone hushed, excited.

Maggie choked back a flash of jealousy. She refused to become the kind of woman who couldn't be happy for someone else because of her own unhappiness. Of course, standing in Cutter's old room at the Garter wasn't making the situation any easier, although there certainly wasn't much left in the room to remind her of him. Michelle's clothes and hats were strewn about the room by a woman obviously more interested in haste than neatness. The rich floral scent of expensive perfume hung in the air, and Maggie noted the overturned crystal bottle on Cutter's dresser. Idly she uprighted the perfume bottle and replaced the heavy carved stopper.

"I know it sounds ... unusual," Michelle

said softly, "running off to New York and marrying a man I've known only a couple of weeks . . ."

Maggie shook her head and pushed all thoughts of Cutter aside. There'd be plenty of time for that later. Instead she forced a cheerful note to her voice. "You're talking to a woman who grew up in a saloon, Michelle. There's not much that strikes me as unusual."

The other woman laughed and picked up another gown to fold. Instinctively Maggie moved to help her. "I think it's wonderful, and I'm happy for both of you. As a matter of fact, I've never seen David Harper look better than he has these last two weeks. You're good for him."

"We're good for each other," Michelle assured her. Her smile slipped a bit, and her brows drew together in a worried frown. "But from what David's told me, his father wasn't at all pleased with the news of our marriage."

Maggie could have well imagined. If the judge had been against David's hanging about a saloon, what must he have said to the notion of his son's marrying a saloon-hall singer?

"What his father thinks isn't important. It's what you and David feel that counts."

Too bad, she told herself, that she couldn't make Cutter see that. She'd waited. Those past few days had been real torture, waiting for him to come to his senses and see that she was right, that he didn't need to go back to a place that had never wanted him . . . that all he really needed was her.

Stubborn fool.

Her fingers tightened around the cool,

smooth silk, until she was afraid she'd dam-
aged the fabric. With a start, she dropped the
dress to the bed, smiled at Michelle, and said,
"I'll go have one of the boys bring up your
other trunk."

"Thanks," Michelle mumbled, but her
thoughts were obviously miles away.

And why shouldn't they have been? Maggie
asked herself. This woman was marrying the
man she loved and moving off to New York for
a fresh start in life. As she left the singer's bedroom, Maggie felt that flash of jealous envy stab
at her again.

She went downstairs, silently telling herself
that she was as big a fool as Cutter—pinning
her dreams on a man who couldn't see the future for the past.

After telling the Garter's barman to have one
of his boys carry the empty trunk up to Cutter's
room, Maggie turned to go back to help
Michelle. At the very least, she thought, the task
of packing would keep her busy enough to
avoid seeing Cutter for a while longer.

"Maggie!"

As if conjured by her thought, she saw Cutter
pushing his way through the crowds, toward
her. Maggie ground her teeth together and wondered briefly if she had enough time to bolt up
the stairs before he reached her. Again, though,
it was as if he'd read her mind. He redoubled
his efforts, and reached her side before she
could retreat.

"What do you want, Cutter?"

"To talk."

"There's nothing more to say." She lifted the

hem of her yellow satin gown and half turned from him.

Cutter caught her upper arm in a firm grip and brought her back around to face him.

Maggie's gaze dropped to his imprisoning hand and stared at it until he released her and let his hand drop to his side. Only then did she look up into his shadowed blue eyes. She should have felt some sort of satisfaction in the fact that he looked so bloody miserable, she thought.

But, strangely, she didn't.

Instead his misery fired her smoldering anger. If he hadn't been so blasted hardheaded, none of this would have been necessary. Neither one of them had to be unhappy. They loved each other. Unfortunately, love simply wasn't enough for Cutter.

That last thought served to stiffen her spine and added a cold edge to her voice as she spoke. "Say whatever it is and be quick about it. I have things to do."

His jaw clenched, and a muscle in his cheek twitched. As he opened his mouth to speak, though, another voice intruded.

"Maggie!" David almost shouted as he hurried up to her. "Where's Michelle?"

"Upstairs," she said, and didn't take her gaze off Cutter. If she had, she might have noticed the high spots of color in David's cheeks, or the sheen of worry in his eyes. Without another word, David left them and raced for the stairs.

"He's in a hurry," Cutter remarked, his gaze still locked on Maggie.

"He's a man in love," she retorted. "He and

Michelle are getting married. They're leaving for New York tonight on the late train."

Cutter drew in a deep breath, but didn't say anything. So Maggie made one more jab. "Apparently, David doesn't believe the past is important—neither his *nor* Michelle's. All *he's* interested in is their future. Together."

Cutter's lips twisted in a frown, and his eyes narrowed a bit. His chest seemed to swell with the deep breath he drew into his lungs, and Maggie waited, almost hoping for another fight.

Instead the man in front of her simply nodded. "I'm glad for them."

"Me too. Now, I've got to go back and help Michelle pack."

"Digger's dead."

Maggie stopped and glanced up at him. *That* was what he'd wanted to tell her. "How?"

"Shot. By one of his own men."

"That's that, then." But even as she said that, she knew it wasn't enough. A man's death— even Digger's—should have meant more. To someone.

"What do you mean?" he asked.

She lifted her shoulders in a small shrug. "Only that now there shouldn't be any more problems around here."

"Didn't we already decide that Digger wasn't behind all of the attacks?"

"Who else, then?"

"I don't know," he admitted, and shook his head. "But Digger? No. It doesn't feel right."

Nothing felt right, she told herself. Not anymore. Aloud, though, she only said, "Right or not, I'm betting the trouble will stop now. So you can leave for Georgia whenever you're ready."

"Not yet."

"Why the hell not?"

He snorted a strangled laugh at her outrage. "I don't have enough money yet, Maggie."

Money. Money and misery. That was all he was interested in, after all. She gathered up a fistful of her skirt and turned toward the stairs. Over her shoulder, she asked him, "Just how much money do you need to prove what a big, important man you are, Cutter? How much is enough to impress that lot you carry around your neck?"

He took one swift step toward her, closing the small space separating them. Angrily he whispered, "Why can't you see that I only want to go and settle my past?"

"You don't want to settle it, Cutter." She shook her head, unworried by his anger. "You want to *glory* in it."

"Goddammit," he muttered as she began to climb the stairs. He curled his fingers around the cherry-wood bannister's newel post and squeezed. Cutter watched her go and felt an almost overpowering urge to pick her up, toss her over his shoulder, and walk out into the night. He would keep going until he'd found a place far away from everyone in their lives, and he would keep her there until they'd reached some sort of understanding.

But he couldn't do that. Hell, he couldn't do anything until their mysterious troublemaker was found. Then, he thought with a determined half smile, then he would *demand* Maggie's attention. Hah! One corner of his mouth lifted into a wider smile at the thought of demanding *anything* from Maggie.

He wouldn't have put it past her to simply up and leave San Francisco the moment he was gone. Why, knowing her, by the time he'd returned from Georgia, she could have gone anywhere in the world! Cutter frowned. He might have to spend the rest of his life following her from country to country, always just a step or two behind her.

As those thoughts took root, Cutter frowned and stared up at the top of the stairs. Maggie was gone.

Maggie knocked once on Michelle's door, then stepped inside. Ordinarily, she wouldn't have dreamed of intruding on the couple, but she knew that if she didn't, she'd have to turn around and face Cutter again. And at that moment, it was the last thing she wanted to do.

David and Michelle, standing side by side, both turned to look at her when she entered. Their expressions mirrored each other's. But neither of them looked as Maggie would have expected. Instead, they both looked . . . scared.

"I'm sorry," Maggie started to say.

"Come in, come in," another voice, from the far corner of the room invited her. "This is perfect. I couldn't have hoped for better."

"Get out, Maggie," David ordered through gritted teeth.

"Nonsense, David," said the still-hidden man. "It's only right that *she* be here as well."

Maggie hesitated. She shouldn't have. She

should have left the room instantly. But that other voice had caught her off guard.

Taking advantage of her hesitation, the man in the corner stepped out of the shadows and waved a menacing-looking pistol at her. "Come inside," he said calmly, "and close the door behind you."

"Judge Harper?" she whispered. "What are you doing?"

"Something that should have been done long ago," he said in a calm, even tone that belied the madness in his eyes.

The balcony doors were standing wide open, and the heavy drapes billowed up from the ocean breeze sweeping through the room. Maggie shivered, but it had nothing to do with the cold wind caressing her.

Judge Harper took a chair that had been set directly before the empty hearth. Seating himself, he waved the barrel of his gun at Maggie again and said, "Come along, Miss Donnelly. Stand there"—he pointed with the gun—"just next to the jezebel who stabbed her claws into my weakling son."

David tensed, and as she crossed in front of him, Maggie could feel the tightly coiled tension in him. He was ready to leap at the old man. And if he did, someone was going to die.

Michelle's face was unnaturally pale. She stood stock still beside David, her hand clutching his, her gaze riveted on the wild-looking old man sitting in judgment on her.

"This is all your fault, Miss Donnelly," the judge said, his tone carrying mild disapproval.

"My fault?" Maggie choked out the words. In truth, she didn't know what to say. The wrong thing might push the judge over the narrow precipice he was straddling and turn Cutter's old room at the Garter into a bloodbath.

"Of course." Judge Harper shook his head, and wisps of gray hair waved in the breeze like swaying snakes. "If you had only paid heed to my warnings and closed down your house of evil, I would not have been forced now to do what I must."

"It was you?" she whispered, before she could stop herself. Not Digger. Not any of the people they would normally have suspected. A judge. A respectable man. A pillar of society. "*You* smashed the glasses? *You* started the fire?"

"Of course." The judge stretched his neck and ran one finger of his free hand around the collar of his shirt. Then, smoothing his hair a bit, he went on. "A father must do what he thinks best in order to protect his child." His gaze hardened as he looked to David. "Even a *thankless* child with no moral fiber and a whiskey bottle where his backbone should be."

"Father." David's voice was strained, hushed. And when he spoke, Michelle clutched at him all the more tightly. "Father, let Maggie and Michelle go," he pleaded. "This is between you and me, isn't it?"

"No!" The judge frowned and pushed himself to his feet. His finely tailored black suit was rumpled, as though he'd worn it for days. "You still don't understand, do you?"

Maggie held her breath and kept her eyes on the gun in Judge Harper's unsteady hand. The muzzle of that pistol looked as wide as the opening of a cave. At any minute, she fully expected to see a blast of flame explode from the barrel as the first bullet left the chamber.

And until that happened, no one would be coming upstairs. No one would guess that anything was wrong. There would be no help coming, she realized with a start. They were on their own as they faced down a man intent on killing them.

Judge Harper shook his head again and looked at his son. "I could never harm you, David," he said slowly. "You're my *son*."

"Father, please," David interrupted.

"No!" His father shouted the word, and both Maggie and Michelle jumped in response. "Don't beg! For God's sake, man! Get some gumption!" For the first time, the judge's expression took on a look of bitter distaste as he stared at the younger man. "I examined you the moment after you were born, you know. I saw with my own eyes that you were indeed a male child." He shook his head and frowned. "Hard to credit that now, though."

"Mr. Harper." Michelle's voice cut into the old man's tirade.

"Ah!" he crowed. "The harlot speaks!"

Michelle winced, and Maggie saw David tense even further. Desperately she prayed for some sort of distraction—before it was too late.

"I love your son," Michelle was saying, and, even terrified, her voice carried the lilting cadence of her singing voice. "And he loves me. We only want to be married—"

"*Married!*" Judge Harper thundered, and took one step toward the pretty woman standing alongside his son. "That will *never* happen, I assure you! What would people think? What would they say?" He rubbed the barrel of the pistol along his cheek and began to mutter under his breath. "I would be ruined. A laughingstock. Could never hold my head up in this town again. No." His head tossed from side to side. "No, no, not that. Not married. Never. Not if I have anything to say about it."

He was nearing the edge—Maggie felt it. The old man's mind had slipped so far away that he might never reclaim it, she realized. She took a half step forward, but David lifted one hand toward her, successfully halting her. Glancing at him, she saw that he was still as terrified as the rest of them. But she saw something else, too: a steely determination.

She only hoped it was enough.

A knock on the door sounded out just before the panel swung wide open. Cutter stopped dead on the threshold, his gaze fixed on the gun pointed at him.

At any other time, the expression of stunned disbelief on Cutter's face would have left Maggie dissolved in helpless laughter. Now, though, Maggie felt the wild rush of hysteria sweep through her. Laughter and tears lodged in her throat, and she gulped heavily to choke the emotions back, knowing that if she gave in to them, she might not be able to stop.

She glanced quickly from the judge to Cutter and back again. Any hopes they might have had of grabbing the gun from Judge Harper while he was distracted by Cutter died almost immediately. The old man was mad, but he wasn't stupid. In seconds he had the pistol pointed at the three people in front of him again.

Maggie's gaze slid helplessly to Cutter. She watched in admiration as he straightened up, smiled devilishly, and asked, "Is this a private party?"

"Not at all," the judge answered, barely sparing a glance at the man in the doorway. "It's only right that you should be here as well."

"A kind invitation, thank you." Cutter sauntered into the tense situation as though he were attending a garden party. "Is there a special occasion being marked by this gathering?"

Judge Harper snorted. "A whoremonger trying to speak like a gentleman. I admire your spirit, sir."

"Again," Cutter drawled with a half bow, "my thanks."

"Stand near the others," the judge snapped, clearly no longer amused by the gambler's nonchalance.

"Of course." Cutter slowly moved to join the three people crowded together. As he approached them, though, he said conversationally, "Maggie, my love, why don't you go down and get us all some refreshments? I'm sure the judge is feeling a bit thirsty after his exertions." His gaze cut to the still-open balcony doors. "It couldn't have been easy—a man of his age making that climb."

Maggie took a half step, but the judge stopped her.

"No one is leaving until I've done what I came to do." He waved the gun barrel at

Michelle. "You. Jezebel. Step forward and let's have this finished."

It wasn't Michelle, but David, who moved. He took one step and placed himself directly in front of the woman he loved.

"Move, David," his father ordered.

"No."

Judge Harper pulled the hammer back and aimed the pistol. "Haven't you been listening? I have to do this. For your sake. Not mine."

"For my sake, leave her alone."

"Never."

"Then you'll have to shoot me, too, Father."

"I don't want to do that."

"Then don't, Judge," Cutter whispered. "Just put the gun down and we'll all go downstairs together."

"Ha! The whoremonger speaks like the snake in Eden. Just do this and all will be well. Just eat the apple, Eve." The judge shook his head vehemently and glared at Michelle. "It started there. The temptations. The sins. All with woman. All with Eve. And now . . . *her!*"

Cutter stole a quick look at Maggie and wondered frantically if he would be able to reach her in time, should the judge start shooting. He poised himself to jump and waited his chance.

David took a step toward his father. "It's over, Father. There are too many people here now—too many who know. You can't get away with this. Let it go." With each sentence, he took another small step, until the distance between him and his father was no more than an arm's reach. "Michelle and I are leaving San Francisco. No one need ever know. Your reputation is safe."

"Leaving?" the old man breathed, and his eyes shone with confusion.

"Yes," David went on, and Cutter could only hope the young man knew what he was doing. "We're going to New York. I'll practice law there, as you've always wanted me to do."

"New York?"

David's fingers cautiously curled around the barrel of the gun. "Yes, we'll be married when we reach the city, so no one here will know anything about it."

"*Married?*" His voice stronger now, the judge's features were screwed up in a mixture of shame and rage. "To *her?*"

The old man struggled to pull the gun from his son's grip, but David refused to let go. Cutter stepped forward, and David shouted at him, "No, stay out of this!"

Maggie grabbed Michelle and dragged her to the floor on the other side of the bed. Peeking over the top of the mattress, Maggie watched as the silent, awful struggle went on between father and son. His madness had given the judge a terrible strength, and Maggie saw that David's grip on the gun barrel was loosening. From the corner of her eye, she watched Cutter move in on the two men just as an ear-splitting explosion rattled through the room.

When her eyes opened again, Maggie saw David staring at his father in open disbelief. Then, slowly, the young man dropped to the floor.

"You old fool!" Cutter barked at the white-faced judge just before he grabbed the pistol and pushed the older man into a chair. Tucking the gun into his waistband, Cutter then bent down to examine David's wound.

Michelle shoved past Maggie and was by her lover's side in an instant, cradling his head in her lap. Her tears fell onto his forehead like a soft rain, and her quiet sobs were the only sound in the now too-quiet room.

Maggie leaned over Cutter's shoulder and asked, "Is it bad?"

"He's been shot," Cutter snapped back. "It's not good." A moment later, he sighed, looked back at her, and added, "He took it high in the shoulder. He should be fine."

A clatter of running footsteps sounded in the hall, and Ike came through the open doorway. "What the hell . . ."

"Get the sheriff," Cutter said shortly, "and a doctor."

"But who did—" Ike started. At least a dozen men stood behind him, shifting their positions and trying to peek around the big man.

Cutter frowned, stood up, and pulled Maggie into the circle of his arms. Jerking his head at the old man in the corner, he said, "The judge."

"Son of a bitch," Ike said on a rush of breath.

"Exactly." Cutter held Maggie even more tightly, until he was reassured by the steady beating of her heart against his. "Now, get going, Ike. And close that door behind you."

Ike turned, shouted at the nosy crowd, and pulled the door firmly shut as he left.

Glancing down at the wounded man, Cutter released Maggie reluctantly, pulled a handkerchief from his coat pocket, and bent down again to stop David's bleeding.

"My father?" the man asked as Cutter tucked the folded piece of cloth under the bloodstained shirt and began to press down.

"He's all right," Cutter muttered, and couldn't keep the disappointment out of his voice. If justice had been served, it would have been the old bastard himself lying there, staining the rug. "Crazy as a loon, but all right."

David nodded, folded his fingers around Michelle's hand, and closed his eyes. "He's a man with an obsession," he said softly, "and this is what it's brought us to."

"Be still, David," Michelle whispered, and smoothed her fingers across his forehead.

"Don't worry," he answered softly. "We'll get to New York. Nothing will stop us now."

In seconds the door opened again, and a dark-haired man in evening dress entered the room, followed closely by Ike. "Mr. Shore said someone was injured here?"

Cutter stood up.

The man moved in closer, took one look at David, and said quickly, "I'm a doctor. If you'll help me get him on the bed, we'll take care of this mess right away."

Quietly Ike walked across the room, pulled the judge to his feet, and took him out into the hall.

Once David was in good hands, Cutter drew Maggie to the balcony and held her tightly again. For the moment, there was no animosity between them. Their disagreements and hurts were forgotten in the rush of gratitude they felt at being alive.

But as they stood together in the moonlight,

Cutter kept repeating to himself what David had muttered a few moments before.

. . . a man with an obsession. And this is what it's brought us to.

An obsession.

Wasn't Cutter's own determination to rid himself of painful memories an obsession as well?

And what might his obsession end up costing him? And Maggie?

Chapter 20

"**Y**ou can't mean this!"

Maggie met Cutter's astonished gaze and lifted her chin defiantly. "Yes, I do."

"You're as crazy as the judge!"

"Not crazy," she corrected. "Determined. I'm not going to go on living like this, Cutter."

"Like what?" He leaned down and planted both palms on the edge of her desk. "For God's sake, things are finally beginning to calm down around here! The judge is on his way to a nice, safe place where he can play with dolls all day long ... Digger's dead ... hell, even David won't be in the hospital more than a week, the doctor says. Then he and Michelle will be off for New York!" He pushed away from the desk suddenly and shoved both hands in his pockets. "For the first time in weeks, we won't have to worry about *anything*."

"Just about your leaving."

His features froze, and he gave her a slow nod. "That's what this is about, then. My trip to Georgia."

"Of course." Maggie stiffened her spine. "Now that everything else is settled, you'll be leaving, and I'm not staying here to watch you go."

351

"I told you it won't be for a while yet."

"I know," she said quickly. "You don't have enough money yet. Well, my plan will take care of that."

"This isn't a plan, Maggie!" he countered. "It's insanity."

"Not at all." She'd been thinking about it since she'd left Cutter on the balcony the night before. After that first instinctive rush to hold him, she'd realized that nothing between them had changed. He would still be leaving her.

So she'd left him first, and locked herself in her bedroom. And during the long, lonely hours that followed, she had come up with the only solution that made any sense. Now all she had to do was make him see it.

"It's the answer to both our problems, Cutter."

"I don't *have* a problem, Maggie."

She wasn't about to discuss it all again, so she said only, "You do now."

"Dammit," he argued, "what about your father? What would he have to say to this plan of yours?"

"Doesn't matter," Maggie snapped, although she didn't care to think about Kevin's reaction when he heard about this. "He's not here, and if truth be told, this is all his doing, anyway."

"You've made up your mind, haven't you?"

"Indeed I have, Cutter. I'll not live like this—waiting for you to leave, thinking about what might have been."

Cutter groaned silently. It didn't matter how many times he assured her that he would be back. She didn't believe him.

But this—to cut cards for the full ownership of the Roses? It was nuts.

"It makes perfect sense," she was saying, and once again laid out her plan. "We cut cards for the place. High card takes it all."

Cutter watched her and knew what this was costing her. She loved the Roses every bit as much as her father ever had. She'd made it the place it currently was. It was a part of her.

And she was willing to lose it to rid herself of him.

"If I win," she continued, "I'll give you the rest of the money you need to leave, and you go back to Georgia immediately. Then you can go wherever you please . . . so long as it's not here."

"Maggie . . ."

"If *you* win"—she swallowed heavily, and he heard her voice break as she said—"the Roses is yours, and I'll leave. Either way, you'll have the money you need to get out and I'll be free of living with the sight of you."

"Jesus, Maggie, it doesn't have to be like this."

"Then you agree?"

What else *could* he do? It was killing him to see her so miserable. He met her gaze and slowly nodded. He would have agreed to anything that would help her. And if this was what she needed just then, so be it. But no matter what she thought, it wasn't over between them. He'd be back. And he'd find a way to convince her to marry him. It didn't really matter which of them owned the Roses. Once they were married, it would belong to both of them. That was as it was meant to be—the two of them. Together.

"Good, then." She stepped out from behind the desk, crossed the room, and opened the office door. Glancing back at him, she said, "let's get on with it, shall we?"

"Where do you plan on doing this?"

"Downstairs." She forced a smile that never touched her eyes. "In front of plenty of witnesses, so there'll be no question about anything later."

"Fine." Anything, he thought. Anything at all to end this. Besides, the sooner it was done, the sooner they could put it all behind them.

He followed her down the long staircase and tried not to notice the sway of her hips ... the way her red-gold hair lay against her back ... the regal way she carried herself to what might become a crushing loss. To look at her, no one would have guessed that she was about to risk the life she loved on the turn of a card.

They walked through the small crowd of early customers to a corner table that was set up and waiting for them.

In the center of the table lay a single deck of cards, its seal unbroken. Maggie picked it up, slit the paper seal with her thumbnail, and tipped the cards into her palm. She offered them to Cutter. "Do you want to shuffle them?"

He shook his head. "I trust you."

Her lips curved slightly. "Fine." Expertly she riffled the cards until they'd been thoroughly shuffled, then set them face down on the table.

"Fan them," Cutter said quietly, and was reminded of the first time they'd done it. It had turned out in his favor that time. Now he wasn't sure what he was hoping for, because, in fact, no matter which way this bet went, Cutter knew he would lose.

Maggie smoothed the cards into a wide arc, each card touching the other. Several of their customers wandered up to the table, curiosity plain on their faces.

"What's goin' on, Maggie, girl?" Seamus asked from behind her, and she half turned to give him a weak smile.

While everyone listened, Maggie quickly explained the stakes of their bet. Cutter felt everyone's gaze shift to him, but he kept his eyes on Maggie. Despite her bravado, he knew what this was costing her, and he found himself suddenly wishing he hadn't agreed to the bet at all.

Seamus stepped up closer to Maggie and muttered something only she could hear. As Cutter watched, Maggie shook her head firmly, clamped her lips tightly together, and looked up at him.

"Well, Cutter, will you go first, or will I?"

He felt the stares of the people around them and gave her a half bow. "After you."

"Right, then," she said, and pulled in a deep breath. Slowly she reached out, fingered the cards delicately, then picked one, sliding it face down toward her.

She stared at the back of the card for a long moment, as if she could see through it to the pips on the other side. Finally she raised her gaze to his. "Your turn," she whispered.

Cutter nodded and lifted one hand. Seamus's voice stopped him.

"Pull your sleeve back, Cutter."

Cutter froze. Looking at the burly Irishman,

he said quietly, "You know I don't cheat, Seamus."

"So I do," the other man acknowledged. "But this is important. It'd be best if you pulled the sleeve of your coat back—just so's nobody has any doubts about it."

Cutter glanced at Maggie. One look into her eyes assured him that *she*, at least, hadn't considered the possibility that he would cheat. That was some consolation, he supposed.

Irritably Cutter grabbed the fabric of his right coat sleeve with his left hand and tugged it back, proving to everyone that he wasn't wearing a gambler's sleeve rig. He couldn't really blame Seamus for checking. There were any number of professional gamblers who wouldn't have thought twice about slipping an ace into a sleeve rig to win a bet that big.

Silently he shrugged his jacket back into place. Without a word, Cutter simply reached over, selected a card, and tossed it, face up, onto the table.

Nine of clubs.

A wild release of pent-up breath shuddered out from the surrounding crowd. With his card fairly low, Maggie had a better-than-even chance of beating him.

She bit down on her bottom lip and took a deep breath before flipping her own card over.

Someone gasped.

Five of diamonds.

Maggie looked up at Cutter, and pain stabbed at him from the depths of her eyes. He reached for her, but she stepped back and shook her head.

"Maggie," he said softly. "This doesn't have to mean anything."

"A bet's a bet, Cutter," she said thickly. "I'll stay in a hotel tonight and be gone in the morning."

"Gone?" he asked, fighting back a sense of panic. "Gone where?"

A long moment passed as she thought about it. Finally she said, "To the ranch, I think. For a while."

The knot inside Cutter's chest relaxed. The Donnelly ranch was only a few hours outside of town. She wasn't going far. *Yet.*

She turned around then and headed for the front door. She wasn't even going to go upstairs for her things. A cold, hollow feeling crawled through Cutter as he realized just how desperate she was to be away from him. Lord, how had he managed to hurt her so badly, when all he'd ever wanted to do was love her?

"This'll not set well with himself—Kevin," Seamus told Cutter in a voice thick with emotion.

"To hell with Kevin," Cutter muttered. Maggie's father didn't concern him at the moment. Maggie did. "Go with her, Seamus. See that she gets safely to a good hotel."

"I will and all," the husky Irishman said. "And maybe I won't be back either."

Cutter grimaced, turned, and walked back up the stairs to the office. *His* office now. Alone.

Three days later, Maggie was close to losing her mind completely. The quiet at the ranch was enough to suffocate a person. Strange that she'd never noticed it before, she thought. In the past, when she'd come out for a long weekend away from the city, she'd always enjoyed the slower pace, the peaceful surroundings, the trees and the animals.

But before, she'd always known it was temporary. This time, it was permanent.

Maggie tipped her head back and stared up at the branches of the giant cottonwood above her. Permanent. She watched the leaves dance in the wind and heard the papery rustle as they brushed against one another. From somewhere close by, a bird began to sing, and in the distance, she could hear cattle lowing. Permanent. On the other side of the ranch, water in the creek bed tumbled over the rocks and added its soothing tone to the peaceful, calm setting.

Maggie gritted her teeth. If she had to stay there another week, she would end up talking to herself and sharing a room with Judge Harper.

At that thought, she leaped up from the bench at the base of the cottonwood and began to pace the ranch yard. Even as bored as she was, she didn't want to go in the house. Since Frankie, Al, and Rose had arrived to comfort her, she'd hardly been able to take a step without one of them intruding. Between the three of them and Terry Ann, Maggie's nerves were almost shot.

They meant well, she knew. But, dammit, she didn't want to talk about Cutter. She didn't want to think about him. Wasn't it bad enough that she dreamed of him every night? Wasn't it enough that any time she closed her eyes, she saw his face?

Turning slightly, she stared off into the distance in the direction of San Francisco. What was happening there? Was he well? Was business good? Did anyone miss her?

She stopped short and stared up at the deep-blue sky overhead. Maybe what she needed was a complete change. Not just the ranch, but a different city entirely. Maybe a different state, or another country.

Maggie ignored the ache of loneliness that welled up in her at the thought of leaving everything familiar. It would be hard, true. But would it be any harder than living this close to Cutter and not being able to be with him?

She nodded to herself and started walking toward the house. With her decision made, there was no point in dawdling about.

It had been three days, and Cutter was close to losing his mind completely. The noise of the saloon never stopped. There was a constant roar of conversation, and even in the office, with the door closed, he couldn't escape the sounds. Strange that it had never bothered him before. A crowded saloon had always felt . . . comforting, welcoming. He'd loved the excitement, the fact that no day was like the one before. But then, before, Maggie had been there. And when she was around, he really hadn't noticed anything else.

Jesus, he missed her. He missed talking to her, arguing with her. Holding her. Kissing her.

Cursing under his breath, he jumped up from behind his desk and stomped over to the closest window. Throwing back the drapes, he stared out at the miserable weather and told himself that even nature was punishing him. He'd never *seen* rain and wind like that in the spring. And it was cold. Deep-down, bone-chilling cold.

He glanced over his shoulder at the fireplace across the room. Absently he looked at the hungry flames as they devoured the cedar logs on the grate. If Maggie were there, he told himself, they could have been together, in front of that fire, with a nice, cold bottle of champagne to keep them warm.

But Maggie wasn't there, a voice in the back of his mind taunted. She was gone—driven away by the very obsession that had kept him from drawing her close.

Obsession.

There was that word again.

Cutter grumbled under his breath, dropped the drapes back into place, and walked across the room to the private door. He needed to be outside. He suddenly needed to feel the cold, the wind, the rain. He needed to *feel*.

Pulling the door open, he raced up the narrow flight of stairs to the roof door and pushed it wide. Stepping out into the storm, his clothes were immediately drenched by the pounding rain, and the cold sea wind drove the damp deep into his bones. He shuddered, but didn't retreat. Instead he stalked across the roof to the low wall edging the building. Leaning his palms on the rough, wet stone, he stared up at the rolling black clouds and let the needlelike drops of rain pelt against his flesh.

Again and again, the voice in his head whispered, "Obsession." Since the night he'd watched Judge Harper shoot his only child, Cutter had been haunted by that word, haunted by the realization of what an obsession had cost the judge.

His child.

His career.

His sanity.

Cutter shivered from a chill that shook his soul. Wasn't his own obsession costing him as much?

True, he now had the money to take the revenge he'd planned for so long. He frowned suddenly. He'd had the money for three days. But he hadn't left yet.

Why?

Cutter shook his head, and his sodden hair slapped about his face.

He had the money, but Maggie was gone.

Maggie.

Strange, he thought. Since she'd left, he'd been more alone than he'd ever been in his life. Not even the feeling he'd known that terrible day when he was thrown out into the world at sixteen could equal the emptiness that had surrounded him for the past three days.

His fingers tightened on the old, weatherworn stone, and his jaw clenched. He stared out in the direction of the Donnelly ranch and wondered what she was doing. Wondered if she was still there.

Cutter's breath caught. Shit. She might have left the state by then, for all he knew. No one would tell him anything about her. Rose had left only hours after Maggie, and when he'd stopped by the Four Roses Hotel the day before, to talk to Frankie, he'd discovered that she, too, had left for the ranch.

The Donnelly girls were coming together to support Maggie and keep him, Cutter, out.

God, he needed to see her again ... hold her again.

He pushed away from the wall, shoved his hair back from his face, and blinked rainwater from his eyes.

How could a man be as stupid as he was and still continue to breathe? he wondered. It was all so simple. So plain.

Maggie was right.

She'd been right all along.

Turning, he raced across the roof, back down the stairs, and into the office. He didn't stop, but went straight to the fireplace and the painting now hanging over the mantel.

Reaching up, Cutter took down the old painting of Seven Oaks and stared at it for a long, silent moment. Then, slowly, a smile creased his face. Bending down, he carefully laid the painting across the burning cedar logs.

In minutes, a curl of black smoke lifted from the center of the painting. Then, in a puff, tiny flames licked a hole in the middle of the canvas and began to eat away at the familiar scene. As the white columns and gracious oaks disappeared into the fire, so too did the pain he'd carried for far too long. Cutter's smile blossomed into a grin, and he suddenly felt years younger.

Not even needing to watch the painting be completely devoured, Cutter left the office for his bedroom at a run. He had to get changed. Hell, he had a lot of things to do, and very little time.

He didn't need Georgia and the people who'd already shown him he wasn't wanted. All he needed was Maggie. His family was *there*, in California.

And he hoped he wasn't too late to claim it.

"Don't see why *you've* got to go anywhere," Al complained again, and Maggie bit down on her lip to keep from repeating the argument they'd already had twice.

"For once," Frankie said, her voice even and calm, "I believe Al is right. There's no reason for you to leave. If you don't want to stay at the ranch, come back to town with me."

Maggie shook her head and folded another dress into the trunk on the floor beside her. The Four Roses Hotel was much too close to the Coast ... and Cutter.

"Shoot, Maggie." Teresa Ann plopped herself down on the mattress and knocked over a stack of Maggie's underthings. As she righted them, she said, "You haven't even been here a week. Don't go yet."

Maggie smiled at her youngest sister. It would have been nice to spend some time with Teresa. But there was no sense in hanging around. Her mind was made up, and she was going to go. First to New York ... then maybe to Europe.

"You three get out of here and leave your sister be," Rose ordered in a no-nonsense tone that got everyone moving. "We've lots to do before our train leaves in the morning."

Maggie rolled her eyes but didn't say a word. Once she'd announced her decision, Rose had adamantly insisted that she accompany her. Knowing it was useless to fight the older woman, Maggie had agreed. And if she were to be honest, Maggie would also have had to admit that she was glad for the company.

If only Rose would stop talking about Cutter.

As if on cue, the older woman started in.

"Europe," she said with a sniff, grabbing one of Maggie's dresses to fold it. "Why you'd want to see that old, dirty country is beyond me. Didn't we all endure steerage just to be shut of the place?"

"Rose . . ."

"If you ask me," the woman went on, hardly drawing a breath, "a trip to Europe should be something you do for your wedding."

Maggie inhaled sharply and stared at her housekeeper. Rose wouldn't look at her. She just kept talking.

"Of course, ya can't very well be having a wedding trip if you're running away from the groom, now, can ya?"

"Cutter and I weren't engaged, Rose."

"Not yet, to be sure." She nodded, and a lock of gray-streaked hair fell over her eyes. "But ya hardly gave the boy-o time, did ya?"

Maggie shook her head. It was hopeless. Sometime during the past few weeks, Rose had appointed herself Cutter's champion, and obviously nothing was going to sway her now. Although Maggie fought down a sad smile, she had to wonder what Rose would have said if she'd known that Cutter and Maggie had "anticipated" a wedding.

Hmph! The woman probably would have been at the Roses immediately, with a shotgun in Cutter's back, demanding that he do the right thing. Maggie swallowed. That was exactly why no one would find out from her what had gone on between her and Cutter. She would have no man in marriage who'd had to be dragged kicking and screaming to the altar.

"Maggie?" Al poked her head in the room. Clearly annoyed, she grimaced and added, "you'd better come out here."

Frowning, Maggie dropped the dress she'd been folding and followed her sister to the front of the house. The door was standing open, and Al walked through it to stand on the porch beside Frankie and Teresa.

Curious now, despite the curl of worry beginning to uncoil in her belly, Maggie stepped out onto the porch and stopped short when she saw Cutter.

He was still astride his horse, his hat pulled low over his eyes, and his black broadcloth suit covered with a fine layer of trail dust. Clearly, he'd been riding like a madman. His horse's breath was labored, and the poor beast looked as if it wanted to fall down in the shade somewhere.

A sudden movement from behind Cutter caught her eye, and Maggie leaned to one side. Seated on the horse's rump, directly behind Cutter, was a small, rabbity-looking man with wire-rimmed glasses, a bowler hat pulled down to his ears, and a nervous tic in one cheek. As she watched, the little man shifted position and winced. Obviously, riding on the rump of a horse for any length of time wasn't very comfortable.

Maggie shook her head and looked back at the man smiling at her. "What are you doing here, Cutter?"

"I've come to bring you home, Maggie."

Al shifted on the porch and moved to stand protectively beside her older sister. Cutter frowned.

"I am home, Cutter."

"Ah, Maggie," he said, dragging his gaze from Al. "You know that's not so. The Roses is your home. Always has been."

"I don't own the Roses anymore," she said, and was surprised that the words could still bring a sharp stab of pain.

"I'm not talking about owning. I'm talking about belonging."

She shook her head, refusing to listen.

"Maggie," Cutter said, and his voice dropped to a hush. "I've come to ask you to marry me."

Teresa gasped.

From inside the house, Maggie heard Rose say, "Saints be praised."

Maggie frowned. The proposal had surprised her, but there was still much he had to explain. "What about Georgia?"

"What about it?" he repeated, and grinned at her. The little man behind him tugged at Cutter's jacket, and Cutter half turned. "Be still now, mister."

The little man grunted.

"I thought you were going back to your family," she pointed out.

"I already have," he countered, and stared deeply into her eyes. *"You're* my family, Maggie." Cutter nodded at her sisters too. "All of you Donnellys are my family."

"Hmph!" Al snorted.

Cutter laughed. "Even you, Al."

"Why should I believe you, Cutter?" Maggie fought down the rush of hope flaring to life in her breast. She couldn't go quickly yet. Though he was saying everything she'd longed to hear, she felt she couldn't risk her heart without getting more assurances. Maggie simply couldn't have gone through losing him again.

"I burned the painting," he said softly.

Maggie blinked. Maybe he did mean it. If he'd let go of that painting, maybe he *was* willing to let go of all it represented, as well.

"I'll make you a deal," he suddenly said, and Maggie's gaze snapped to his. There was a gleam in his blue eyes, and she watched him warily.

"What kind of a deal?"

"We'll cut cards for it," he offered with a shrug. "If I win, we get married and run the Roses together."

"And if *I* win?" she asked.

"If you win, I'll sign the Roses back over to you and leave your life forever." He paused, leaned forward a bit, and added, "If that's what you want."

"I don't know . . ."

"We'll even use your cards," he offered gamely, "just so you don't have to worry about a marked deck."

Cutting cards. Gambling. Taking a chance. That was who she was, Maggie told herself. And maybe it was the perfect way to decide. After all, if he was willing to risk losing her forever, maybe their future deserved to rest on the turn of a card.

"Deal," she said.

Cutter grinned and reached around behind him. Offering his arm to the little man, Cutter swung the stranger to the ground. The short, bespectacled fellow immediately began to rub his backside and flex his knees.

"Who *is* that?" Al snapped.

Cutter winked at her. "A friend."

They trooped into the house and walked straight through to the dining room. As everyone grouped around the table, Maggie reached into a drawer and pulled out a deck of cards. This was no fresh, new deck. The seal had long since been broken.

Keeping her gaze locked with Cutter's, Maggie shuffled the cards, then spread them out on the tabletop. Quickly she reached out and plucked one card from the deck. As before, she kept it face down.

Cutter swallowed heavily, gritted his teeth, and picked a card. Staring at her, he turned his over.

Ace of spades.

Al cursed.

Frankie heaved a long sigh.

Teresa clapped.

Rose muttered a short prayer.

Maggie shoved her card back into the deck, sight unseen.

"Aren't you going to look?" he asked.

"What's the point?" She shrugged. "I can't very well beat an ace, can I?"

"You might have tied," Al told her.

Maggie ignored her sister's comment and stared up into Cutter's eyes. "I won't marry you only because of this, Cutter. Not just because of a bet."

"Then marry me because you might be pregnant."

Her eyes nearly popped out of her head. Heat

flushed her cheeks, and she could only gape at him silently.

"Holy Mother of God!" Rose dropped into the nearest chair and crossed herself.

"You son of a bitch!" Al snarled at him.

"Oh, Maggie," Teresa sighed, "how romantic!"

"Oh, dear," Frankie murmured.

The little man in the corner clucked his tongue disapprovingly.

"Damn you, Cutter . . ." Maggie flushed with embarrassment. He hadn't had to tell the whole world their private business.

"I *will* be damned if you don't marry me, Maggie," he said. "Damned to a lonely, empty life."

"I beg your pardon, but I think—" The rabbity man's voice matched the rest of him—reed thin and squeaky.

"I paid you fifty dollars already," Cutter reminded him sternly. "Now, shut up and sit there."

"Well!" The stranger's thin lips pursed, and he seated himself gingerly on the edge of a chair.

"Who *is* he?" Maggie asked.

"Never mind him," Cutter told her. "This is about us. Maggie." He ignored everyone else in the room. Dropping both hands onto her shoulders, he pulled her close against him. "You were right. Nothing is more important than us—what we have. And if you give me half a chance, I'll spend the rest of my life making you glad you did."

She looked up into the blue eyes that had haunted her dreams for years. And for the first time, she saw that there were no shadows lingering in their depths. For the first time, she saw only love in Cutter's eyes.

Wasn't all loving taking a risk? she asked herself. And wasn't a *chance* at happiness better than nothing at all?

A slow, sweet smile curved her lips as she reached up to stroke his cheek. "I'll take that bet," she whispered, and didn't stop smiling until his lips came down on hers.

"That'll be enough o' *that!*" Rose interrupted. "No more lovin' till after a proper weddin'," she ordered. "That shouldn't take more'n a month or so to arrange."

"Oh." Cutter grinned and glanced at Rose. "It'll take far less time than that," he assured her. "All right, mister, get busy and earn your fifty dollars."

Everyone turned to stare at the little man as he rose from the chair in the corner of the room. Carefully the rabbit pulled the bowler off his head, reached into his coat pocket, pulled out a book and opened it, then squeaked. "Dearly beloved ..."

Maggie laughed, threw her arms around Cutter's neck, and squeezed him.

In seconds the little minister was asking, "Do you—" He stopped, glanced at Cutter, and said, "I'll need your full Christian name for the legalities, you know."

Everyone in the room turned to look at him. Even Maggie couldn't contain the curious glint in her eyes. No one had ever heard Cutter's full name. It was a better-kept secret on the Coast than the whereabouts of Mother Comfort's Shanghai ships.

Cutter frowned slightly, first at the minister and then at each of the women in turn. Finally, looking only at Maggie, he said stiffly, "I expect this to remain a *family* secret."

She nodded, a smile already blossoming on her face.

Cutter stiffened, looked at the man in front of him, and said slowly, "My full name is . . . Beauregard Thorndyke Cutter."

Al snorted, but everyone else managed to swallow their laughter.

Cutter grimaced painfully.

Maggie shook her head. "I don't know about this, now, Cutter. A name like that's a *dreadful* burden to have to live with."

He reached for her and closed his arms around her waist.

Still smiling, Maggie said, "Don't know if I can get used to a husband by the name of *Beauregard*."

Squeezing a little harder, Cutter pressed her body against his and dipped his head low. "You'll manage," he ground out, and brushed his lips across hers in a silent promise.

Maggie gasped, wound her arms about his neck, and nodded. "Aye. I believe I will," she whispered.

And the little rabbit man nearly shouted, "I now pronounce you man and wife!"

Hours later, alone in the darkness of her bedroom at the ranch, Cutter and Maggie lay entwined in each other's arms, wrapped in the soft glow of loving and being loved.

Cutter sent up a silent prayer of thanksgiving

that he'd come to his senses in time to claim Maggie as his own.

"Cutter?" she murmured softly.

"Hm?"

"Were you really willing to risk losing me on the turn of a card?" Maggie asked.

Cutter groaned silently. Hell, no, he hadn't been willing to risk that. But how would she take it if she knew the truth? She might be angry, but she couldn't very well leave anymore, he reassured himself. They were legally married, and the union had been consummated twice that night already.

He had nothing to lose by telling the truth.

"There's something you should know," he said, and wrapped his arms tightly around her.

"What?"

"Well . . ."

Maggie pulled her head back and looked up at him. In the dim, moonlit room, Cutter could barely make out her features, but he knew those green eyes of hers were fastened warily on him.

He shook his head. He hated like hell to admit it—but she had to know. "I cheated."

"What?" She put one hand on his cheek and forced him to look at her. Slowly her features became more distinct in the shadows.

"I cheated." Cutter shrugged. "I wore a sleeve rig loaded with an ace. I just couldn't take the chance that you'd win and send me packing."

"Ah, Cutter," she crooned, "we really *were* made for each other."

"What do you mean?"

She shrugged. "I cheated too."

Cutter grinned, then kissed her, long and hard. After a moment, though, something occurred to him. He pulled back a bit and asked, "Maggie? How did you cheat? Were you going for a low card? Or a high one?"

She didn't answer him, just smoothed her palm over his abdomen, dragging the tips of her nails gently across his skin.

"Maggie?" He stifled the groan threatening to choke him. Had she wanted to marry him? Or had she wanted him out of her life?

Her lips closed over his flat nipple, and Cutter sucked in a gulp of air through gritted teeth. Desire, hot and demanding, pulsed in him. He took a moment to steady his breathing, then asked, "Are you going to tell me or not?"

In answer, her tongue slid across his sensitive flesh, and she moved to straddle his hips. As she leaned down toward him, Cutter ran his hands over her body and muttered, "You're not going to tell me, are you?"

She shook her head and briefly tasted his lips before sitting up straight over his middle. As she lifted herself up on her knees to take his hardened body inside her, Cutter groaned. "Ah, who the hell cares?"

"I love you, Cutter."

Epilogue

Four Golden Roses, one month later ...

Mary Frances walked slowly into the dining room, heedless of the fact that she was an hour late for the family meeting. She'd had a church-ladies' meeting that morning, and it had run late. There'd been no real reason to hurry, anyway, she'd told herself.

In the month since Cutter and Maggie had gotten married, everything had been running so smoothly, there hardly seemed a need for a family meeting that month.

Then she noticed that everyone seated around the dining table was looking at her. All three of her sisters, Rose Ryan, and even Cutter, were staring at her helplessly, as if they knew she needed help but realized there wasn't a thing they could do.

Well, really, she'd never known them to be so upset before, just because she was late.

"Where have you been, Frankie?" Maggie asked.

"At St. Timothy's."

"That's appropriate—I hope she lit a candle," Al muttered, and shut up quickly when Cutter glared at her.

"What's going on?" Frankie asked of no one in particular. A decided chill was beginning to

374

sweep through her body, and she desperately needed someone to tell her not to worry.

"Da's been at it again," Maggie said, and stood up, her fingers wrapped tightly around a slip of yellow paper.

"Father?" Frankie echoed, and in her heart, a frantic voice was shouting, *No!*

Lifting her right hand, Maggie held the paper out to Frankie and said, "Now *you're* the one with a new partner."

Frankie fainted.

Avon Romances—
the best in exceptional authors
and unforgettable novels!

Avon Romantic Treasures

Unforgettable, enthralling love stories,
sparkling with passion and adventure
from Romance's bestselling authors

CAPTIVES OF THE NIGHT *by Loretta Chase*
76648-5/$4.99 US/$5.99 Can

CHEYENNE'S SHADOW *by Deborah Camp*
76739-2/$4.99 US/$5.99 Can

FORTUNE'S BRIDE *by Judith E. French*
76866-6/$4.99 US/$5.99 Can

GABRIEL'S BRIDE *by Samantha James*
77547-6/$4.99 US/$5.99 Can

COMANCHE FLAME *by Genell Dellin*
77524-7/ $4.99 US/ $5.99 Can

WITH ONE LOOK *by Jennifer Horsman*
77596-4/ $4.99 US/ $5.99 Can

LORD OF THUNDER *by Emma Merritt*
77290-6/ $4.99 US/ $5.99 Can

RUNAWAY BRIDE *by Deborah Gordon*
77758-4/$4.99 US/$5.99 Can